Snowflakes

R.J. Devlin

A CIP catalogue record for this book is available from the British Library.

ISBN   978 1 8384962 0 3

Registered with the UK Copyright Service, registration number 284740521

Printed and bound by Imprint Digital, Unit 1, Seychelles Farm, Upton Pyne, Exeter, Devon EX5 5HY.

This book is dedicated to the members of Avon Gorge Earth First! and Bristol Housing Action Movement, who lived it.

Acknowledgements

Thanks to all the musicians who sang with us, inspired us and kept us sane through it all, particularly the artists who kindly gave permission for their lyrics to be quoted in 'Snowflakes.'

'No One's Slave, No One's Master' Theo Simon. Lyrics reproduced with author's permission.

'One Way' The Levellers. Reproduced courtesy of Universal Music Publishing.

'Mountain Song' Lyrics modified by permission. Original lyrics by Holly Near, Hereford Music.

Snowflakes

Prologue

Warriors of the Rainbow

The Life You Save

Snowflakes

Retrospective.

What you've got to remember is that well, Martha was my friend but she really was a drip. She was scared of everything. She used to jump if I said a swear word. I mean we were the ones getting the word of the Lord shoved down our throats every Sunday, but she acted like she had her own personal demon prodding her with a pitchfork every time she heard the word 'bugger!' And she didn't even know what it meant. Well neither did I, but you know. We were kids.

Anyway we were over the woods one late afternoon in August and I wanted to show her my treehouse. And she wouldn't climb the tree. Not even one foot off the ground. I mean yeah, you're scared, but my brothers would have mocked me into the Stone Age if I'd let them see it so I *had* to climb that massive ash tree at the top of Boston's field. And I had to jump off the shed roof, and walk across the river on the ice when they dared me. My life would have been mud with them if I hadn't. You have to find your balls. Even if you haven't got any. Even if you're a girl.

But Martha. What could you do with her? I mean she was pretty bright. And she could be really funny, not always on purpose. But when danger threatened she'd run a mile in the opposite direction. She was always this pale frightened face, hung with straight mousy hair. And I mean, she was my friend but she *was* a mouse. Squeak. Pass the cheese. Perhaps that's why she didn't like cats.
Mind you, when we were young she used to like cats. She was always coming round to stroke all our lot. When we were both about nine. Before all the racket and the moving and all that.
We had seven cats then, well thirteen when we had the kittens. That was the day Martha first came.
I was in my secret den at the bottom of the garden. My brothers hadn't found it yet. They didn't play in the garden much anymore, they were off roaming the fields. And all the massive overgrown bushes down there at the end of the garden made a good den.

A weeping willow, long unpruned, towered above the lesser shrubs matted into its trailing branches – guelder rose, forsythia, flowering currant. There were no thorns, just flowers, so you could push your way in if you knew where the secret gap was. Once inside no one could see you, and the light filtering through willow sprays was enough to green the mossy dell underneath.

I had a hiding place in the disused rabbit hole at the base of the trunk. I kept my tin in there, with my writing book and sweets. The wind rustled the leaves as the willow wept silently. It was peaceful.

I was there one afternoon writing with a couple of the cats lying next to me, one draped over my leg, when I heard rustling footsteps. Instantly alert, I sat up sharply. The cats shot into hiding and I whisked behind the willow's trunk. Someone was crying. I peered out through the spyhole in the forsythia.

It was the new girl. The thin, pale one who never said anything. She'd fitted herself into a gap in the ragged hawthorn hedge that divided the two gardens near the bottom and was sobbing in a quiet, hopeless way. Her face was streaked and grubby where she'd rubbed at it.

'What's the matter?' my bush said eventually.

She jumped, literally jumped, like a startled kitten. Her actual feet left the ground.

'Who's there?' The words were gasped out in her surprise.

'Me.'

She looked wildly about.

'I'm in here.' I pushed the branches aside and her eyes found my face among the leaves.

'What are you crying for?' I asked, straight to the point. She looked quickly away. I waited, puzzled. Then she spoke in a low, slightly hoarse voice.

'My...' She tried again. 'My mum went mad on me.' She ended in a sob, and threatened more waterworks.

I didn't want to get drowned, so I said:

'My mum's always doing that. Take no notice.'

She looked at me curiously, tears drying. Her flowered dress was droopy and she wore NHS specs, bandaged at the hinge with insulating tape.

Well, she was a bit drippy, even without all the crying. But you know, she was my age, or a bit younger. Someone to play with. So I asked the question that was to change both our lives.
'D'you want a wine gum?'
After that, Martha was always round. We made her her own secret entrance through the forsythia. She'd be there more often than not that summer.
'Can I come in and play?' she'd ask. 'Are the cats here?'

She wasn't allowed pets. Or to get dirty. Or tear her clothes. Or answer back. Jeez, her house must have been like church. Quiet though. I could do with a bit of that. Mart wouldn't have lasted five minutes in our house with all those lads wrecking the place. I used to go down to the willow to get some peace. Bang, crash, shout, yell. It was like London Zoo in our house. Four brothers rampaging through the lounge like gibbons. Mum shouting all day long.
'Put that down! Pick that up!'
Make your mind up, love.
She was the squawking parrot to their gibbous whoops. But we were all right til the gorilla roared.
I wasn't bothered. I had my den and my books and the cats and the tin with the exercise book and my sweets.
And now Martha.

Like I said, she was a drip. After that first day I never caught her crying though. Sometimes her eyes were red, but. That's normal for kids anyway.
I didn't cry, me. Sometimes my eyes would water and I'd hug one of the cats and soak her fur. But that was just, cleansing. My eyes probably had dust in them. Funny, the cats would never squirm away those days. One or other of them would lie warm and heavy on my knee until I was quiet. Once the grey one licked my face. For the salt.

Martha was all right though, apart from being a bit soppy. I don't mind a bit of soppy actually. Makes a change from brothers running round ramming cowboy pistols in your back or snatching your stuff out of your hands.

Martha didn't shout or push me over. We never had a fight. It was really relaxing on those days under the willow. Martha knew a lot of stuff, she was always reading too. But not proper books like Arthur Ransome and Diana Wynne Jones and Clive King and Ian Serailleur. She did like Watership Down, though, because it was more accurate, she said.

See, Martha always wanted to know how everything worked. She read boring books about cells and molecules and stuff under the microscope. She knew the name of every plant in the village. So did I, but in English. I knew them as themselves, flowers, scents, shapes, the way they grew, their nature. I knew them like they were people. A lot less hassle than people of course.

Martha knew them differently. I couldn't always understand what she was on about.

She was rubbish at art though. And she would never write a story, though when she did get to talking her face would light up with the animation that dissolved the blank mask she wore when other people were around.

'Why don't you ever write anything?' I asked her again and again.

'Dunno how. I'm rubbish at writing. You can do it. You're better at it than me.'

She always said that, pushing her glasses up her nose, curtaining her lank hair over her eyes, withdrawing even from me.

So one day, long after we fell out, I tried.

❄

'Go home then. See if I care.'
Bridget was angry. Martha never wanted to do anything good. It was always 'my mum'll go mad' this, and 'my dad'll kill me' that. So how come she was still alive?

Martha stood at the foot of the great yew tree, trying hard not to cry.
'Bridge...' she began.
'Are you coming up or what?' Bridget's voice carried faintly down.
The treehouse was hidden deep, veiled by dark swags of canopy.
'You can go home after. You won't be late.'
'I-I can't.'
'Why not?'
'I-I can't get up.'
'What? Up here? God, what a baby. I'm coming down. Get out the
way.'

She crawled out of the door, swung round easily and let herself
down, stepping from branch to branch, hugging the trunk, long legs
stretching tiptoes to the next branch. Peels of reddish bark floated
down as she worked out along the lowest branch and dropped the
last five feet.
'Here. Let me give you a leg up. Get hold of this branch and get
your foot in that fork there and sort of swing.'
'Where?'
'There, you div. In that little crook down there.'
'Can't reach.' Martha moaned, standing there passively. Bridget
thought she'd never seen her look more drippy.
But Martha was shorter, she supposed. A bit younger. She made a
step with her interlaced hands.
'Here you go.' Bridget looked around suddenly. 'Hurry up.
Someone's coming.'
'So what?' said Martha, swinging her body uneasily back and forth.
'So it's a bloody secret isn't it? I don't want anyone else up here
spoiling it.' She tensed. The rustling was getting louder. She could
hear footsteps thudding now. Big, stupid footsteps, sounded like.
Worst kind.
'Come on! Now!'
They looked at each other.
'I can't.' said Martha.
'You've got to. Don't go all mousy on me. Hurry up!' Bridget
wondered if she could get up the tree and shove Mart into a bush
quick enough to hide them both in time.

'I can't.' she repeated.
'Why?' demanded Bridget.
'I – I'm..'
'..I'm scared of heights.' Martha mumbled.
That tore it. Martha had known it would and Bridget heard it rip.
Martha was scared of everything. She was useless. Some friend, thought Bridget bitterly. She won't do anything with me, and now someone's gonna find the best den I've ever had and wreck it.
'Bridge? Are we still best friends?' Martha stood there plaintively.
Bridget, boiling with rage, scrambled frantically back up the trunk with no breath to spare for a reply.
'Get out! Get lost!' she hissed when Martha showed no sign of moving.

Martha looked round hastily and hurried to squeeze behind the brambles on the other side of the clearing. From there she could crawl through the tunnel in the long grass and get into Boston's field. She brushed away the bits of bark that Bridget's ascent had spat into her face, climbed the fence, cat-quiet, and slipped away. There were a dozen ways home from here.
The footsteps thudded on up the track, hesitating at the clearing, looking at the scuffed ground.
Halted at the foot of the tree where scraps of bark were still pattering to the forest floor. Looked up for a moment. A grumble of words might have been heard if Martha had still been near enough to hear them. The figure turned away and carried on down the path, back to the village.
Long after dusk, Bridget sat on in the ancient yew, until the church clock's first notes of ten o'clock found her descending slowly to walk home alone.

Like I say, I liked Mart, I really did. But so often I saw the way she'd freeze, white-faced, as if just waiting for some predator to pounce and finish her off. She used to make me angry sometimes, but I couldn't help feeling sorry for her. It was only a matter of time before some hawk thudded into the earth and snatched her away. I used to think.

❄

Since the blizzard came though, there's been time to think again. Time to remember, with the snowflakes swirling and dancing against the blackness outside the window, the wind howling in the chimney and the stove crackling like distant fireworks. As I become more absorbed in my work, the piece of newspaper that started the fire lies forgotten on the sofa next to me. The cat sprawls drowsing by the fire, twitching slightly at the crack and piff of damp firewood. It's peaceful.

❄

1. Telephone Tree

'Go home. You can't do any good.'
Martha's mother was well into one of her famous demotivational speeches.
'You're not going to change anything.'

The pips went and Martha made way for the next caller. It was a forty-five minute wait for the lone phone box next to the camp, the queue stamping its feet on the freezing petrol station forecourt, early January dark sparkling frosty around them.
Martha pulled on her two pairs of woolly gloves, adjusting the second pair so that they covered the holes in the first, dragged her two woolly hats back down over her ears and headed back to camp. She climbed the frozen wooden fence and moon-walked over ice-hard digger ruts to the fireplace. The kettle was on. More new visitors had arrived. The Tango Hotel was popular this winter.

When Martha got off the train at Newbury Station back in August and found her way to the office she found herself in the middle of a scene like the Antarctic Survey crossed with the London Stock Exchange on Black Wednesday. Corridors were strewn with bundles of climbing ropes and tarps, jerry cans and boxes of food were stacked everywhere that wasn't covered in trays and trays of paperwork. Phones were ringing, people were everywhere, doing everything. Martha stood, flinching whenever anyone came near, waiting for some coherent instructions to come out of the chaos.

'Yes, we've got a load of new arrivals, where can we send them? Rickety Bridge? no, come in, Oscar Charlie. Oscar Charlie, do you have room for..fourteen, fifteen more, over?...Yeah, we can let you have three more boxes of food and another battery. All right...all right, see what they can do and send them on to wherever you think. Climbing rope? God, you can ask me for anything but that. We'll see what we've got. Ok Oscar Charlie, Tango Bravo over and out.' Now that Friends of the Earth had decided that Earth First! weren't too disreputable after all they had willingly turned their office into campaign headquarters. Martha wasn't at home around filing cabinets, the only other road protests she'd been on were home made affairs run from battered caravans and the sort of function rooms that were free to any group that would sink a few pints in an empty pub on a weekday. As she looked around the scene she spotted the latest flyer pinned to the corkboard on the wall among the news clippings. Phrases caught her eye as she swung back and forth uneasily, waiting to be noticed.

'the new bypass is scheduled to cut through nine miles of woodland destroying three Sites of Special Scientific Interest and an AONB....the site of the English Civil War's Battles of Newbury in 1643 and 1644...permanent loss to archaeology...destruction of wildlife...water voles...the setting for Kenneth Grahame's Wind in the Willows...*Brian Mawhinney's spokesman said...childhood asthma...insufficient evidence. Bulldozing ancient woodland...concerns about water quality in the Kennet...All donations and enquiries to Third Battle of Newbury.'*

Someone was holding out a box and a hank of gaudily striped rope for her to carry. She hastily shrugged her rucksack onto her back, grabbed the gear and was hustled with four others into a muddy car which headed out into the woods.

They were dropped off unceremoniously and found themselves in a woodland clearing. In the middle stood a large white marquee, alive with activity. She moved towards it slowly, edged inside and stood awkwardly, glancing about.

The usual clutter of boxes, bundles of climbing gear and battered army jerrycans was all around. She dumped her burdens with relief. Two muddy, ragged figures, one with blond dreadlocks, one with long wild dark hair, slept on a mound of blankets, arms wrapped around each other. Martha watched them with a mixture of embarrassment and envy, until a brisk older man with a grey ponytail and skinny legs in faded jeans came up to her.

'Hi, what's your name? Just got here?'

'Er, yes.' said Martha. 'My name's Martha. I've just come up from er, Bristol.'

'On the train.' she added, flushing as she realised that once again she sounded like a twelve year old.

'I'm Martin, glad to have you. This is Office Camp. Are you a newbie or have you done any direct action before?'

'I, er, did some training at Leytonstone and went on an action with them. I've done a bit in other places too, um, at Solsbury Hill and Wells...' Martha trailed off nervously.

'Sounds like you're ready to roll. Good. Got any climbing experience?'

Martha was reminded vividly of a day when she stood at the foot of an old yew tree. She gulped.

'I've never done any climbing...er, not yet anyway.' she stuttered.

'Plenty of ground support you can do, though. Have you got a mobile phone?'

She shook her head dumbly.

'Never mind. There aren't that many on the protest although we try to make sure each camp has at least one. It's good you've had a bit of experience. You'll be able to teach the rest. Great, great. Ok, wait here a bit and we'll send you along to a camp, whichever needs a few bodies. We're not expecting work to begin yet so you could have a chance to get some climbing lessons in. But it could kick off at any time.'

'A – all right.' agreed Martha.

❉

Seriously, what did he think Mart was going to teach anyone? Teach them what? How to dither and stammer? I know I'm being mean. But you didn't see her every time a cow looked at her up the fields. Oh God, the cat's sitting on my papers again. Everyone's a critic.

❉

Climbing lessons, Martha thought despairingly. Add fear of heights to the list of things she was scared of. The long, long list.

She drifted outside and watched the throng passing by. Tall, short, long-haired, crop-headed. Blonde, brown, grey. Rainbow jumpers and camouflage jackets. Multiple earrings and runestone necklaces on leather thongs. A few brand-new designer waterproofs paired with green wellies and tweed caps. Filthy unravelling jumpers over mud-caked jeans and black wellies with splits in. Knitted hats in all colours. Tattered khaki fatigues everywhere, and huge army boots squelching along the miry tracks.

A girl with long hair tied up in a scarf wandered up.

'Hiya, have you just got here? Dunno what to do? Me neither.'

'Yeah, I'm waiting to get a lift to one of the camps. Er, I'm Martha. Ha-have you done a lot of actions?' she asked timidly.

'Oh yeah, just got back from storming Parliament for the second phase of the revolution.'

Martha flinched, instinctively turning her face from the grinning girl with the tie-dyed headscarf. Was she having a go?

'I was joking, I'm a raw recruit. Shitting myself actually. My friend at sixth form college has been knocking about here for six months. We live in Newbury so the road's going through our back yard. We're doing 'A' level biology, dunno why though, there won't be any living things left by the time this lot have finished. Have you done any actions?'

'Um, a few. M11 and Solsbury Hill, er, and the Wells Relief Road campaign.'

'Wow, what was it like? Were you scared?'

'I thought I would be, but after the non-violent direct action training at Leytonstone I thought well, they've been doing it for months, I couldn't not help them. They told me that it'd help even to just be there with banners and not risk getting arrested or battered. When I got to the first action I just thought - I'm going to do it - and went over the fence with them.' was what Martha wanted to say.

'Um, it was all right.' was what she did say.

'You're brave.'

Martha looked down and away.

'Who did you go with?'

'Oh, I was on my own.' She felt ashamed.

'No way! I said to Melody, Mels if you want me up those trees you're coming with me to hold my hand every inch of the way. She's over there, getting some tea. Do you want some?'

'Yeah!'

'Come on then. Oh, I forgot, I'm Sarah.'

Mel walked up with a mushroom box full of paper cups of tea and handed them round.

They had just taken a swig when Martin hurried up.

'Are you ready? We've got a lift for you going to the north end of the route, Martha was it, and you two can stay here and catch the next NVDA session. Mel, you could help run it couldn't you?'

'What do you want me to do? I've never done training.'

'Just the legal briefing and passive resistance basics.'

'Er, Ok.' Mel agreed, 'but it's gonna be the blind leading the blind.'

'Martha, before you vanish, are you on the phone tree?' Martin asked.

'Er, no, but I know someone who is.' Martha answered.

'What's that?' asked Sarah.

Martin turned to her. 'Oh, you should really get your name down. Phone tree. We call two people, then they call two more and so on 'til everyone's got the message. When the evictions start we'll need to mobilise quickly and it saves people having to make dozens of calls when the aruga goes up. Plus it means that no-one's got more than a couple of other activists' numbers in case the police get hold of them. Ok, the van's here, hop in Mart.'

Martha rushed her tea, spilling the last of it, and followed promptly, wishing her new friends were coming too.

As they bumped out of the clearing and back onto the main road she thought about the day at Solsbury Hill back in March. The way they'd rushed over and through the security fences and stumbled onto the rutted desolation of the site at Bailbrook Lane, dodging security guards to climb up onto a huge crane. Wedging themselves into nooks and crannies in the machinery, they clung there for hours while the security guards milled about trying to catch people, until they reached stalemate and stood about at a loss. After the pale sun went down security clocked off – all except the one who'd already ditched his yellow jacket and white helmet and climbed up to join the protest amid cheers and whoops. Five o'clock finally arrived and the protestors climbed down, stiff and cold, trudged down the hill and headed in a body to Larkhall chip shop.

But the night before that, sitting round the fire up on Solsbury Hill, the city of Bath laid out like a huge roulette wheel, Martha had felt a stirring. The land seemed vast, the valley ancient, the future a mystery. The fire crackled, jam jars of red wine were passed around and the singing began. In a rosy haze, Martha felt her stiff defences melt and flow, the warmth of the fire and the people blending into one. She felt a smile on her face and joined in the singing. She never sang in front of other people. But this was different.

'No one's slave
I am no one's master...
On my grave
They will write this after I am gone.'

Over and over the words repeated themselves in her head as the boom of the djembe echoed through the weeks that followed.

❄

I dunno about this beginning. Martha never really told me how she got involved in the first place. I remember her telling me what a phone tree was, but how she got from the foot of my treehouse to the foot of the Newbury Oaks, I've got no idea. After we bumped into each other again, she only told me bits and scraps of what she'd been up to. She was always so ablaze with activist zeal there was no room for anything else. Funny, even when Martha's different, she's still exactly the same. Oh well, time to throw another log on the fire. Damn. There's no wine gums left.

❄

The battered blue van pulled up and everyone got out and started unloading.

'Where's this?' someone asked.

'Snelsmore Common.' the driver replied. He was a six footer or more, big with dark scruffy hair. 'I've brought some more rope and karabiners.'

'Here, we can pay you back out of the kitty – or, come to think of it, for that much you'll have to ask at the Office Camp.' said a man whose tendrils of brown hair were decorated with coloured beads. He turned the ropes over, inspecting them carefully. He wore a climbing harness with bunches of karabiners clipped to it like metal lace.

'You're all right. Count it as my contribution.' The tall man straightened up and headed towards the driver's side of the van.

'Mark always has loads of money, and a van. He's probably an undercover cop.' joked one of the older men helping unload the van.

'You can put that in the kitchen bender.' the braided climber told Martha, seeing her standing uncertainly with a box of food. She followed him into the camp. The kitchen was built of pallets and trestle tables with a tarp battened firmly over all, lashed to hazel poles that curved up from the pallet flooring. Cans, bottles and bags of rice and lentils spilled everywhere. What a waste. There were dirty plates and cups crowding on the table top, and empty red Rizla packets with rectangular bits torn neatly out of the cardboard scattered around. Crumbs everywhere. Martha searched in vain for somewhere to put her box and automatically began shuffling things around, making order out of chaos. At last, something she could do right. She'd just achieved a clean work space and tidy shelves, and sorted a load of recycling, when Alex, the climber with the beaded dreads, came in.

'Oh, good one, we needed that. Tea's on, come and get some.'

Martha tried to finish her task, unable to stop while there was so much as a grain of rice out of place, but it was getting too dark to see what she was doing. Alex popped his head round the door.

'Still working? It doesn't have to be perfect. It's a palace compared to how it was half an hour ago. Come on, you've worked really hard. Come and join us.'

Martha went out reluctantly and faced the camp full of strangers. The usual circle of dirty faces was around the fire. Alex sat down on his rucksack and started rolling a spliff. Dirty cups were scattered round his feet. Martha looked at the others. A woman of about twenty in a jacket woven in faded Peruvian designs was chopping onions. Her grubby, singed cardigan sleeves draggled over her hands as she worked. Two men looking identical in muddy combat fatigues were building up the fire. An older man with a scrubby beard and a red face lay at length on a dirty blanket. He had a bomb-shaped bottle of cider at his side and was arguing loudly with Alex.

'I tell you what we should do, we shou' get everybody together, march down the Town Hall. Take these tree branches with us. Fill the Town Hall with trees...it's tree magic, if we use the magic the magic can use us...I tell you, I'm a Pisces, I'm a fishy character. My element's water,' he said slugging down hard on his cider, 'My element's water. I'm, I'm in my element in water. We shou' get a boat, we should, we should go down the river...'

Alex broke into Harry's ramblings. 'Hey, does anyone need a climbing lesson next time I've got a spare minute?'
Sheila pushed back her trailing sleeves again and said 'Oh, here's your chance, Martha isn't it?' She glanced across the fire. Martha dropped her eyes hastily.
'You up for it Mart?' Alex asked.
She hesitated. 'All right.' she said.

Dusk was falling. Even the blackbird had stopped whistling at the edge of the clearing. The stew was a long way from finished. Martha used her torch to find ingredients in the kitchen bender, but saved the battery and carried on chopping and stirring by firelight and a couple of candle lanterns.
'Should have asked Mark for more candles.' said Alex.

'Yeah, you should have.' grumbled Sheila, who was stirring a paste of flour by the light of one guttering tealight. 'Who's got the cleanest hands? Someone needs to make dumplings. Martha, yours look Ok. Here you go.'

Martha took the bowl and started kneading dumplings by feel.

Hope my hands are clean, she thought, *well they will be after this anyway.* She grinned in the dark and thought of telling the others the joke, but self consciousness gripped her stomach, as usual. Keep your head down, keep your head down, she reminded herself. No sense in opening yourself up to ridicule if it falls flat.

'Mmm, God that's better.' Alex sunk his first spoonful of stew. 'Tastes all right but it's a pity I can't see what I'm eating.'

'We couldn't see what we were cooking so it's just as well.' said Sheila.

'But the first bite is with the eye.' said Harry, interrupting his cider to send down some stew. He hadn't moved from his blanket in hours.

'Well, we didn't get it.' Sheila's eyes were laughing in the firelight. 'We've got flapjacks to follow so leave some room.'

'Oh cool, Flapjack Fran's been back.' Martha could only hear the crunch of eating, the glugging of cider bottles.

'Yeah, she's great. I need a bath so I'll give her a hand with the next lot.'

'You might want to rephrase that, Sheila.'

'You know what I mean, Al. It'd be so great to be in a real bathroom, pink soap, fluffy towels, water on tap. *Hot* water on tap.' Sheila passed her bowl back to Alex to dump next to the kitchen bender. 'No bloody dogs on site are there? We don't want the bowls licking out.'

'When did you last have a bath?' Alex asked one of the other silhouettes round the fire.

'Must have been two weeks, no, three.' replied a dark shape, his hair bristling in the firelight. He clicked a cheap lighter that lit his face with a warm glow for a second as he sucked fiercely on a roll-up.

'Well, that's not so long.' said Alex cheerfully.

'For men. Us women like to be clean.' Sheila turned to Martha. 'I find that if you change the underneath layers of clothes often and wash everything you can whenever you can, you stay quite clean. My outer layers are grim but I'm clean underneath.' She pushed back her fraying cardigan sleeves, used too many times to lift hot pans out of the blaze.

Her outer layers were grim all right, like a greened and muddied carapace, thought Martha. But she smelled only of woodsmoke and leafmould. Harry stank of stale cider, tobacco and old biscuits. Martha tried not to make it obvious that she was staying upwind. Talk meandered on.
'Do you think Flapjack Fran has pink soap?'
'Dunno. I've always pictured her house as having everything home made. Like, oatmeal soap.'
'That's just for the flapjacks. You can't make soap out of oatmeal.'
'You can. It's really good for your skin.'
'Bloody hippies. Don't believe you.'
'Well it's true. It's good for eczema.'
Night slowly soothed the voices to silence, cool air washing the day's anxieties away.

After the bubbling of the pot the crew sat quietly late, late at night listening to the bubbling of the nightjars, a sound Martha had never heard before. No moon rose to brighten the dark night, but later owls called incessantly in the wood.
'Tu-whoo. Whoo-oo.'
'Kee-wick.'
Female tawny answering male, thought Martha sleepily, as she crawled into the communal bender and fell into deep sleep under hazel boughs. Night creatures stirred and rustled around the sleeping camp. The murmur of wind in the branches lulled them into calm, deep rest.

❄

'Is that it? The dialogue's a bit – bald – isn't it, Bridge?' said Simon.
'You cats are all the same. Species-ist remarks about my lack of fur.' I said grumpily.

'You're spending too much time with no-one to talk to but animals, Bridge. Having fur is not the norm.' he said.

'It is round here.'

Crunching through frosted snow, Simon and I walked down to where the Severn carried its load of dead branches, whole trees and speeding ducks down to the sea. The snow was still up to our knees as we approached the salt-marshy beach. Dark edged, it was fringed by bobbing Canada geese that barely gave us a glance. I tried not to scan the beach too eagerly but it was like the January sales – pallets, scaffolding planks, stovewood, fence posts, bread baskets – I could build a house with what washed up there on a high tide with a good easterly.

We swept the huge sitting log free of snow and sat watching the winter morning quietly. Simon pulled the pages from his pocket and continued reading.

'I can't believe you wrote this much in a week. How long were you snowed up for?'

'Four days.'

Drifts like angels' wings closed the lane to cars, leaving a small gap to squeak through with snow up to the knees. I saw a snipe in the lane. Birds were fluttering about, too weak to fly. Tiff brought in bird after starved skinny bird. I rescued them, put them in the bath with some cheese and oatmeal, released them out of the window once they'd had a peck and a warm. The farmer's wife down the lane opened a bird cafeteria and had a throng of redwings and fieldfares on her lawn around the feeding station.

A robin hopped around feebly under the cattle grid looking for worms. The ever-roaming sheepdog Pip reached a nose towards it, but it ignored her wearily. She could have been a tyrannosaurus for all it cared.

Three days before, I had just got the new wood supply stacked and covered before the first flakes of the blizzard began to spiral down, turning Tiff into an instant snow leopard.

Back home, I looked nervously around my snow-lightened room. There was plenty of wood, there was the Rayburn for hot water if the electricity went off or the gas bottle for the cooker ran out. There was food, a load of last summer's harvest in the freezer. There was Tiff for company. I was going to be cut off from the world, but it would be Ok. It never stopped Mart, after all.

I'd be all right.

❄

'So – what do you think?'

Simon folded the sheets up and stuffed them into his pocket.

'Umm. Can the victimhood.'

'What do you mean?'

'I mean – is this meant to be some kind of misery memoir?' he asked.

'I hate that expression.' I objected.

'It is, then.'

'It bloody isn't. Martha wasn't a victim...well, she was at first but then, I dunno, she changed. Anyway, if this was a misery memoir there'd be a picture of feet on the front cover.' I said.

'Feet?'

'And a lollipop. You know, every book about a miserable childhood, come to think of it every book about childhood published in the last fifteen years has a photo of some kid's feet on the front cover.'

'Oh yeah, like the kid on the stairs with his head in his hands.' said Simon, catching on.

'Yeah, prevent child cruelty, move to a bungalow.'

Feet. Mine were trudging back up the muddy, rocky road to home. Simon waded thawing puddles in huge army boots with breadbag boot liners. He reached into his jacket and pulled out a brown envelope, extracted the marmalade sandwich inside and walked on munching thoughtfully.

'You're turning into Charlie Chaplin, or Paddington or someone.' I said.

'Didn't Paddington keep his marmalade sandwiches under his hat?' Simon asked.

'If you want to be picky about it.'

'Well, you look like Stig of the Dump. How can you still walk?' He looked at me, slipping and slithering along clutching an eight foot strip of decking, two bread baskets and a bucket with no handle.

'Bound to come in handy.'

'Wombling along collecting junk.' He splashed carelessly through the slush, spraying my trousers with mud.

'Coming from the guy who spent the '90s head down in a skip.' I countered, dropping the bucket to brush hopelessly at my knees.

'Anyway your book doesn't have a cover yet.' We reached the hard ground beyond the puddles and clumped on towards the old farmhouse. The short day was nearly over.

❄

2. Tango Hotel.

Underground, overground.
The Womble tribe evolved at Newbury. Their warpaint was one large 'W' done on their faces in mud, and when they got nicked and were asked in court if they had anything to say, they sang the Wombling Song.

At first it was an anarchist's picnic, a camping trip with extra mud, stirring pots over the fire, watching bats, crawling into the guest bender at night with two sleeping bags and two hats as autumn drifted into winter. Days were spent cooking, gathering firewood, repairing paths, endlessly talking tactics. At night, firelight flickered on the restless hands of people who used anything to stave off the anxiety as the evictions got nearer. Knotting embroidery silks into bracelets until the whole camp was festooned with them. Carving scraps of green ash. Laughing, arguing, smoking, spitting into the fire. Occasionally the whole group would fall silent, staring into the flames, faces still as the quiet dark.
Some of them had been in the Newbury woods for over two years, building treehouses and stringing walkways and nets between giant oaks. The biggest treehouse was the Mothership. It glowed like a giant Chinese lantern at night. The tallest was in a one hundred and twenty foot pine at Reddings Copse. Camps mushroomed all along the route. Skyward, Gotan, Rickety Bridge, The Chase, Tot Hill. The campaign kept in touch by CB radio, each camp with its own callsign based on the NATO phonetic alphabet, developed to help communication in the heat of battle. Romeo Bravo, Tango Charlie. Tango Hotel.

Then the day finally arrived. After rumours, false alarms and every delaying tactic to the tiniest snail had been used up, the diggers were coming. And so were hundreds of yellow-clad security guards.
Martha had heard about the company, and none of it good. They were drafted in to the Solsbury Hill protest too. Half of them had records for GBH and that was before they started on the road

protestors, when one of them threw Kerry over a wall and broke her arm.

She stood in a freezing field at Tot Hill, a ditch, a bank and a hedge between the protestors and the woodland where heavy machinery was advancing. A ditch, a bank, a hedge. And a hundred security guards, planks in a yellow fence. The protestors began to rush the phalanx, spreading out in a line that mirrored theirs. Suddenly a terrified screaming started. The word went down the line that a girl had slipped and fractured her kneecap. She was being carried out and they hadn't even reached the line yet.

Martha stood cold and afraid, waiting for the security team to live up to their bad name and beat everybody senseless, like Solsbury, like the Beanfield. Sarah's white face showed beside her and gave her a sick grin. They somehow went from frozen to running, running, charging the line. Martha was never sure how. She was so scared her whole head was ringing. Ringing and ringing. Scrambling up the bank, through the hedge, through the thick yellow line. It was duck and dodge, running rings round security guards who to her bemused relief didn't seem keen to come to grips just yet. They were past, surrounding the bulldozer, like herding dinosaurs. Quickly they bundled on the frozen ground in front of its blade. The work ground to a halt. The short afternoon ended.

Several great trees had already been smashed apart. Pits yawned where roots had been ripped up. As darkness fell, one of the women lit candles on the wreckage, candles for the dead, twisted limbs and splintered trunks and the golden candlelight warming, soothing the scene of destruction. Martha walked among the dead on that first battlefield, and something woke up inside her, a deep instinct.
She realised how inured they had all become to the slow killing of the planet, to see it as normal, inevitable. The anger and despair she had always felt when she saw land being scraped bare for some development from a bus window was a faint reflection of this sudden, violent realisation that the killing of the very land that supports us, the systematic extermination of every living thing, is really happening.

It's really happening.

They usually perform the executions in private.

She never forgot the early dark, the mute grief of the candles dotted around the clearing lighting the scene of the crime, the splintered wood sharp against the sky.

❄

Simon fidgeted, sighed theatrically, rearranged his long arms and legs in the red velvet armchair by the hearthside.
'What?' I looked up from my scribbling.

Sigh.
'This is really depressing.'
'Well I'm telling it like it was. What Mart told me.' I pointed out, tossing my notebook aside on the sofa. Tiff strolled over and sat on it instantly.
'Where's the hope?' Simon objected. He sat up and fiddled with the damp socks that hung steaming over the fire on the pot-hook.
'I'm coming to that.' Seraphic calm was always a good way to wind Simon up when he was in this mood.
'Bloody hippies, always miserable. Always on the way to their own funerals.'
'I'm just facing reality. You have to face it before you can change it. Martha was good at that, I suppose.' Tiff skittered off as I got up to put more wood on the fire. Clank, thud.
'Yeah, that touch of clinical depression does help it along. Look, this book is going to have to get more cheerful if you want any more lit crit. Get with the comic relief.' Simon ordered, picking up the old cardboard ringbinder again.
'Patience.' I smoothed my imaginary feathery wings and beamed at him for just long enough to try him. He scowled and sat back in his seat.

'Ow! Your cat just stuck its claws in my ass!'
'Oh yes, you're sitting in her chair. She's very territorial.'

31

'She has her own chair?'

'Well once she's coated it with fur I don't want to sit there any more so she wins by default.'

'It's like a wildlife park in here. Things scrabbling in the chimney, spiders the size of Yorkshire terriers.' Simon said, brushing furiously at the layer of fur on his ragged black fisherman's sweater.

'It was one jackdaw. One little one. It was the only one that made it past the baffle plate and into the stove.'

'Yeah, I know. I went to light it and it was looking at me with pale blue eyes and a massive beak like the Devil.' he said.

'You think you've got problems, I've seen The Owl Service.' I said.

'What's that about?'

'Well, there were things scrabbling in the attic. Scrabble scrabble scritch scritch. Really creepy.'

'And what happened?'

'I dunno. I was too scared to watch the rest. We had pigeons in our attic when I was a kid.'

Simon mumbled something that ended with '...still got pigeons in your attic.'

'I heard that.'

❄

Pigeons flocked on the paving stones outside Coventry Cathedral. Waddling along, choking themselves on chips, limping along filthy pavements. Dirty, diseased, flying rats.

Martha sat in the science library at Coventry Polytechnic on the other side of the road, reading about the greenhouse effect. In twenty-five years time, the effects will be so obvious that even the general public will be forced to realise that it's happening – and late, late in the day will start yelling about it, she thought.

'This article's useless.' remarked her neighbour in the next carrel. 'It's not as good as the New Scientist one.'

You useless article, Martha admonished silently. She gazed out of the window again.

People flocked on the pavements, waddling along, choking themselves on chips, limping along on filthy pavements. Dirty, diseased, flying - apes.

She saw everything in those days. The grey polluted air. The dirty grey pavement. The grey sky above grey concrete buildings.

And she thought. How can people live like this?

And she thought. I can't live like this. She was like Heidi in Frankfurt, pining for the trees.

Studying biology was amazing, a magic world. She ate and consumed and devoured the knowledge. How life works. Nerve transmission. Stomata. Codworms. Leaf miners. Palisade layers. Proteinaceous icebergs in a sea of lipid.

The finals approached and Martha fell off the edge of a cliff. Her room. Her income. Her occupation. She looked at the shrinking calendar. Realised that in three weeks time it was all going to stop.

What next? Oh yes, I'm supposed to get a job.

Dream on.

❄

That first evening after the diggers arrived was quiet, grim at first. The group of protestors who'd ended up at Tot Hill quickly formed into a camp to protect the remaining trees, and had already got some rough shelters up and a fire lit before the line at the petrol station phone formed. By this time there were five sitting logs around the fire, all occupied. Calls home had relaxed and soothed most of the crew, and the release from tension showed.

When she got back from the garage Martha shivered up to stand over the fire for a few minutes before sitting down, squashed on the cold ground against someone's boots.

'You must have a cold bum sat there.' one of the older women said, and passed her a cushion to sit on.

'Thanks. I'm all right. I've got er, loads of clothes on.' said Martha. More like a ten-year-old, she thought bitterly. When would she be able to speak to people in words of more than one syllable? When would she start sounding like an adult?

'I've go' so many layers on. I've got that many pairs o'trousers and leggings and knickers on I cannae find my own fanny when I want a pee.' said Morag reflectively.

'Mor-ag...have you no decorum?' Pete grinned, boots set well astride, his muddy rucksack next to him on the log across the firepit from Martha.

'I used to have one but a' left it in ma boyfriend's car.' Everybody laughed except Martha, who looked away and hoped that no-one noticed. She hoped like hell that she wasn't blushing, or if she was they'd think it was the fire heating up her face. Not that she could feel much heat from down here.

'Right, now Morag's finished telling us about her fan-tod, let's get on to tomorrow.'

Pete stood up and stretched before carrying on. The karabiners hanging from his harness clanked as he sat down, carefully hitching up his cowtails to stop them trailing in the mud.

'I don't want to think about it.' said Sarah sadly. 'Today was terrible.'

'Yeah.' said Mel soberly. 'I can't believe they're really doing it.'

'I reckon it's going to be Penwood tomorrow. We've got to be ready.' continued Pete. 'They'll be sending in roving chainsaw gangs so we've got to get up those trees...everyone who can climb...'

'Peter,' interrupted Morag. 'Shift y' tat, let people sit up there. Martha must be perishing.'

Martha was mortified. Social embarrassment was so, so much worse than being cold any day of the week.

'Er, thanks.' she said, and moved onto the log with relief. The warmth of the fire bathed her, releasing her stiff muscles.

'You can't be shy,' Morag advised. 'Get these blokes to shift theirselves, and don't let them leave a'the washing up to you either.'

'Give me a break.' said Pete. 'I'm on tripod duty at five o'clock. Hey, did you hear the new security guard joke? How many protestors does it take to put up a tripod? We don't know, we never get up early enough!'

The laugh went round the circle. The tripods were a stroke of genius for places where there were no trees to occupy. You simply fastened three long scaffolding poles together at the top. Suspended yourself under the apex with a climbing harness and – bingo! Instant tree, take it anywhere. Blockading the security compound at the crack of dawn was a brilliant ploy. They were corked-up in there until they could get someone with insurance for work above ground to remove them.

Martha smiled too, but most of her mind was occupied with the fear of tomorrow and the shambles she was sure to make of her first attempt at tree occupation. She'd only had one climbing lesson back at Snelsmore Common. What if she couldn't get up? What if she couldn't get down? What if she fell? What if she got stuck too low down and they pulled her out and cut her tree down? Bruised, battered. Arrested. Shamed.

What if. What if. What if. Her stomach churned in time to the words.

Someone nudged her and offered her a swig of cider. In desperation she took the bottle in both hands and aimed a generous slug down her throat. Instantly the world looked fuzzier, kinder, and felt warmer. She wiped the spillings off her chin and grinned back at the lanky, long haired protestor who'd handed her the bottle. His brown eyes were bright in the firelight. Sarah was sitting on his other side. The crew suddenly looked a lot less scary.

'Look at her chug it down!' he said admiringly. Martha glanced at him sharply, but his face was devoid of spite. She laughed.

'Pass us it here.' Perry took the bottle back and downed about a litre in one, emerging puffing as if he'd swum a length underwater.

'Aah!' He looked happy. Martha felt happy. Sarah looked a little sour. Martha wondered why.

'Where's all the musicians tonight?' he asked once he surfaced, face flushed.

'Don't know, Per.' answered Will, looking up from the CB radio he was trying to get working. 'They must have all ended up at another camp.'

'We could do with some music.' said Perry. 'When I saw that five hundred year old beech tree go down my heart went right down in my boots.' He looked down at his damp feet and draggled laces.

'I know. And the hawthorn hedge. It's survived three hundred years, to be scraped away to make room for a bloody service station.' Will said.

'You're joking.' said Sarah.

'That's what's going to be here. A fucking service station.' said Perry angrily.

They looked around. At the low barrel-top of tarp they'd thrown up over some hazel poles and floored with bubble wrap. At the handful of small tents dotted about the churned mud of the scarred field and the bit of green plastic sheeting someone had already hung round the pit latrine. Frost sparkled on the ground and ice shone in digger ruts.

'We've already got all the facilities we need right here.' said Mel fiercely. 'Food, bit of warmth, somewhere to sleep..'

'Drink.' said Perry, picking up the bottle again.

'Yeah, drink.' agreed Mel, taking it out of his hand before he could empty it in absentminded despair.

'A few bushes to pee behind.' reminded Morag.

'Once you've found your fanny.'

'Aye.'

'Why are they doing this?' cried Sarah.

'To take a few minutes off the journey time through Newbury.' said Mel bitterly.

'No' really.' said Morag. 'That's just what they tell the locals. So they'll want it. All the research shows that building new roads just mak's more traffic. Makes sense, if you make more space for cars to be in, traffic is gonnae increase to fill it. I mean, if you move out o' a bedsit into a flat, do you live in one room or do you spread out and get mair stuff to fill the space?' She poked the fire with a stick. The wood was frozen, and spat as it thawed and dried out.

'I'd fill all the rooms, and the attic, and end up living in the shed.' remarked Will wryly. 'It's all the electronics, they just grow and multiply.' He put away the repaired radio and tucked all the trailing wires back into his plastic storage box before snapping the lid shut against the damp.

'Well, a' that will happen is that in ten years time there'll be just as much traffic goin' through Newbury. It's all local traffic anyway. A bypass won't even make a dent. The real reason they want it is for the infill. It's a goldmine to them.' Morag went on.

'How do you mean?' asked Sarah.

'First you get ribbon development along the new road, then the developers ge' a foothold filling in the gaps. The minute the turf's broken they're on it like flies on shit.' said Morag angrily. Pete nodded agreement, jingling faintly.

'Yes, and there's this pan-European motorway as well.' joined in Will. 'They're building it by stealth. Bit by bit across Europe. Here, have a bit of superhighway, oops I mean new bypass, honest.'

'Should we be working at European level then?' 'No, it's pointless bothering with big politics, they've got it completely taped up. They just want to waste our energies sitting arguing in meetings to keep us off the streets.'

'And out of the woods.' The fire crackled, smoke swung round the compass and stung their eyes. Morag stirred the pot that was balanced on a bit of grillpan set across two logs that were slowly beginning to smoke in their turn.

'What about the Road Traffic Reduction Bill?' 'Yeah, if we at least had the legislation...'

'Well, it'll come to violence in the end. I jus' wanna kill the fuckers when I see what they're doing.' This from a skinny boy with black hair who had been watching the back and forth without speaking, his eyes wide in his thin face.

'No!' Everyone stopped talking and looked at Martha in surprise. She was pretty sure that it was the cider talking, but she carried on.

'Never go down that road. It's what they want. They can deal with riots and stuff, what they can't deal with is passive resistance. There's only so long the papers can be full of pictures of security guards dragging kids along the ground. They don't like to be seen on the news roughing up defenceless women and teenagers and kids.

They - they prefer to do it where no one can see them.' There was a short silence before anyone answered.

'She's right, we can't let ourselves rise to it.' Pete said kindly to Little Johnny, the youngest recruit who had been silent up til his outburst. 'It's really hard - when they're mashing people up around you.' He glanced across at Martha as if to check her reaction.
'And when they come to chop down my treehouse – my only home.' said Will mournfully. He twiddled the penny whistle that hung round his neck.

'But it's not enough to avoid aggro, avoid violence. We can't even let ourselves start hating.' Martha went on. 'We have to, I dunno, rise above it. If we don't, then we end up like them. Putting people in fear – even people like Sheriff Blandy and bloody Brian Mawhinney – it's just - wrong. It's – it's *fucked* up.' Martha poked the fire angrily, wondering where all the words were coming from. She had said more in the last two minutes than in the last two weeks.
'No one should have to live in fear, not even them. It never goes away. Fear – fear sucks.'
A dozen pairs of tired, smoky eyes glittered in the firelight as they looked at her, startled.

'It's Gandhism.' said Pete.
'It's bloody impossible, is what it is.' sobbed Sarah.
'I know.' comforted Perry.
'Aye, we all know.' said Morag quietly.

The fire was burning low. Sarah got up to put more logs on.
'Better let it die down a bit, then I'll bank it for the night.' Pete advised her. 'With a bit of luck there'll be some embers for tomorrow then.'
'Better get our heads down eh?' said Morag. People began to get up and stretch, and move towards the rough bender that they'd rigged that afternoon.
'Who's going to take first watch?' asked Will.
'I'll do it.' said Martha.
'Ok. Wake me up in a couple of hours and I'll take over.' he said.

He came over to Martha, peered closely at her.

'You spoke. You gave a speech!' he said, smiling.

'I know.' Martha said shyly.

'We were beginning to think you didn't have a voice.' Martha raised her head in surprise and met his eyes. She found herself smiling back.

'Night.'

'Night.'

The fire glowed, purring under its clods of earth. It got colder. There were no nightbirds tonight, no stirring life. The land was still shocked. It lay in an icy silence.

Martha pulled her sleeves up over her hands, wrapped her sleeping bag around her and watched the occasional lorry lumber past on the A34. She didn't know what she was thinking. She turned away from the road. Looked up at the sky and saw the stars come out one by one.

❄

3. Skyward.

This was a list of just some of the things that Martha was afraid of:

Speaking
Heights
Confined spaces
Crowds
Loud noises
Disobeying authority

Number one on the list was still strong but Number Two promised to knock it off the top spot any moment now.
She looked down at her harness. Alex hadn't forgotten his promise to teach her to climb in the weeks before the diggers moved in. Martha wanted to curse Sheila's helpfulness, but still…

'Right. You've got your harness on correctly. Check your buckles are doubled back. Here's your karabiner. Clip it on, that's right, tighten it up and loosen it half a turn. You don't want it jamming on you.'
Martha clipped, twiddled and turned obediently, her head swimming with instructions.
'Now. Your prussik loops. Take this piece of cord, join the ends with a barrel knot – it's like a triple fisherman's knot. Stretch the loop out, see how the knots lock together? You won't get that undone again in a hurry. Ok, same for the other loop.'
Alex showed her how to attach the prussik loop to the fall of climbing rope with prussik knots. The autumn wind tugged at her hair and she stuffed it back under her woolly cap impatiently. *You don't want to get your hair caught in your figure-eight* Alex had warned her. She shuddered.

'Right. Now you clip your karabiner to the top one. Slide it up. That's good. Now the other loop's for your foot. And up you go – bottom loop first, step your way up, then top loop. And you're away.'
He stepped back, crunching on the dead leaves of the forest floor.

Martha slid the bottom loop up a fraction and straightened her leg to lift herself. Slid the top loop up and began to inch her way up. Slide. Inch. Slide. Inch. Her knee creaked with effort, sweat stood on her forehead.

And her lower foot finally left the ground.

She swung wild, panicky. Her face burned with embarrassment as much as with exertion. But Alex was over the other side of the clearing helping someone else.

Martha was glad. She didn't want an audience. This was between her and the rope. Between her and gravity.

Slide, inch. Slide, inch. God, it was hard work. Slide. Stop. She felt her height above ground. Looked down at her lower foot. Six feet up and swaying with the wind.

'Yep, that's far enough.' she thought wryly. Looked up. Christ, the treehouse was right up in the canopy! The tiny patchwork wooden hut with the tar-paper roof wavered a little as the wind caught the huge branches of the oak. The wind was stronger up there. Up there, where she was going because Alex had told her it was perfectly safe and she could do it. She pulled herself up another ten feet, her stomach quivering as she got higher. At thirty feet she stopped. A crow cawed twice, strangely close, and was answered. There was a sudden clap of pigeon wings.

Martha felt sick. She glanced upward again. Some part of her that wasn't preoccupied with the deadly drop beneath her noted the beauty of the branching patterns stark against the sky. The whole tree, huge as it was, swayed as one, and she rode on the swaying. Martha looked back down at her hands on the brightly-striped rope. She could see the strain in the weave, the tightening pull on the knots. There was nothing to stop it breaking, to stop the knot undoing itself...but a tiny part of her was enjoying the ride, as the tree swayed back and forth...

'Come on, Mart! You look like you've frozen. Don't worry, it happens to all of us at first. You just have to hang in there until it passes. Nothing's going to happen, just wait 'til you're calm and carry on.'

Martha tried to take in Alex's advice but she had begun to feel cold and detached. She could hear a dim screaming in her head. The bullying, battering voice that always started up in moments of stress. She hung there, head swimming, overwhelmed by panic. Black clouds blotted out her vision like ink in water, blinding her to everything but fear. She was going to fall. She was going to get hurt. She was going to die. And it would be all her own fault. Stupid, stupid, useless, useless...she deserved it! She deserved to get hurt! The universe was getting ready to deal the final blow that would wipe her out of existence. And worse than the thought of the smashing pain was the sick shame in her stomach. Because she couldn't do anything, and everyone was laughing at her.

'You're useless. You're useless. Get out of my way.'

Her mother slammed her way angrily around the kitchen. Bang. The breadboard went down. Slam. Cupboard door. The rap rap rap of aggressive strides across the floor. Martha flinched as her mother loomed nearer.

Clack. The jamjar. Crash. The cutlery drawer.

'What did I do to deserve you?' she demanded. The words sounded final, as if a sentence had been passed.

'What a waste! Crumbs everywhere. Look at the mess you've made of this loaf. We're not made of money. How many times do I have to tell you?'

She wiped and swept furiously. Turned and strode suddenly across to where Martha cowered. Martha dodged sideways, but too late to avoid the stinging crack on the side of her face.

'Get out of my sight!'

The angry muttering continued as Martha fled, still clutching a jam doorstep. She dodged the furniture in the lounge and slipped quickly out of the back door to safety. Hidden among the bushes at the end of the long wild garden she inspected her sandwich. A slightly stale, crooked hunk of white bread with jam dripping off it. Her stomach heaved at the sight. She threw the bread into the nettles. Her mother would never find it there.

Her heart was jumping in her chest, her head dizzy from the blow. Her eyes were shining with the tears she painfully held unshed.

Stop bawling or I'll give you something to cry about.

Slowly the gentle breeze cooled her stinging face. The soft, rose-scented air soothed her agitation. She wiped her eyes with the backs of her hand, leaving her face grubby. Sobbed once, gulped it down, let out her breath in a rush. Looked up at a flurried sound. A blackbird, glossy feathers, crocus coloured beak. He perched briefly on a branch of her bush. She kept absolutely still, entranced. He let out a whistle through a beakful of worms, was off into the tattered hawthorn hedge to feed his family.

Martha's face softened, muscles relaxed. She didn't know it, but she was smiling.

❄

'You can do it! Come on, Mart, you're nearly there. Anyway I need the figure-eight after you to get down, so you'll have to!'

It was Sheila, leaning out of the treehouse. Her voice was oddly close, conversational. She didn't need to shout. Perhaps the top wasn't so far away after all. Martha gripped her bottom prussik knot and slid it up, swinging shakily as she hung from the harness alone. Slid up the top knot. Hauled herself up another foot.

Trembling.

Everyone was laughing at her. No, they weren't. Everyone believed she could do it...Just another activist, learning to climb. Just like all the others who'd learned this, to get up in the trees. To save the trees. She was doing it, just like everyone else. They were scared too. Just like her.

Inch another step. Hands shaking. One more. One more. Stomach hollowed. Wanted to cry. She was going to die. No, she wasn't. The knots would hold, the rope would hold. She couldn't do anything. She just had to hold on until she was calm. She knew what to do. Just a case of doing it. Slide, inch. Slide, inch.

And again, and again...she hit a rhythm. Carried on. Wanted to sing.

'Inchworm, inchworm

Measuring the marigolds...'

Martha rubbed unshed tears away with her woolly-gloved hand. She didn't know it, but she was smiling.

Inch. Worm

Inch. Worm

Inch. Worm

As she crawled over the threshold of the treehouse, eighty feet above the forest floor, she could hear Will playing his penny whistle in the treetops.

Whistling like a blackbird.

※

Martha remembered her climbing lessons, back in autumn. Pete quickly checked her harness for her.

'Ready? Checked your buckles?' he said.

'Yes.' she answered, grinning back up at him. prussik loops in her pocket, big ones, to loop around the smaller trees of Penwood. Roving chainsaw gangs were turning up at random along the route, hell bent on clearing the trees. Thousands of them. All condemned to die. The sentence had been passed.

They'd been up since 5am. Shivering out of the communal bender, stirring vegan porridge over the fire in the freezing dark morning. Listening to bursts of static over the CB. Filling their pockets with granola bars. Bust cards were handed round. Perry sat pretending to read his.

'Get out of jail free card. You may use this card, keep it or sell it to another player. Will, do you want to buy my get out of jail free card?'

'Silly boy. Make sure you hang onto it, especially for the solicitor's number.' Pete advised Sarah. 'Remember. You don't have to say anything if you're arrested. Just name and address and No Comment. And make sure they let you ring our solicitor.'

They packed into the back of a jeep covered in green tarp. Martha checked her pockets again. It was impossible to see where they were going. They rumbled along, then turned off and bump bump bumped over what felt like a field. Jumping out onto frozen grass, she was running to keep up as the crew headed along a footpath and into the woods.

They were in time. They could hear the sound of chainsaws in the distance but the yellow-clad army in their white helmets were not in sight, the white helmets for security that popped up everywhere like dragonseed, like mushrooms.

Kept in the dark and fed bullshit.

White for security. Orange helmets for chainsaw operators.

Each of them ran to find a climbable tree.   Sarah scrambled into a twiggy, low hawthorn. Martha found a young oak.

Ok, here we go. Loops. Round the tree. Knot's upside down. Try again with trembling, feverish fingers. Clip on. Up you go. Martha slid her loops up the tree, hauling herself up. At thirty feet she found a branch big enough to sit on, scrambled awkwardly up and astride it, found places for her feet. She was up!

She looked around the misty wood, dressed in winter greys and browns. People were still scrambling up trees, some didn't make it and were trapped behind the yellow line as the security guards ran up and cordoned off the area she and her friends were occupying. Some had managed to lock onto each other, around the base of a tree. Others crowded and pushed up against the yellow cordon.   Martha was alone.   The nearest other protestor was twenty feet away up another tree.

The day wore on. Shouts, screams. She watched the women around the tree-trunk being dragged away, their lock-ons cut with bolt croppers after a long struggle. Their boots kicked up clots of wet leaves as they struggled to get a purchase. As the security guards dragged them along the ground their numb feet snagged on roots, stiff ankles twisted painfully round.   Sometimes they dropped someone in a puddle for fun. Lying in cold mud, a girl shrieked as the guard grabbed her arm again in an iron grip. She gasped. 'You don't have to break my arm! Wait, just give me a minute!'

Dozens of saplings in the stretch of woodland had protestors hanging off them, arms outstretched holding onto rope walkways, the figures almost lost in the mist. They looked like the crucifixion scene from 'Life of Brian.' Martha obviously wasn't the only one who thought so. Someone began to shout the famous lines and others joined in, laughing.

Martha unstiffened enough to let out a giggle, and joined in as they started singing 'Always Look on the Bright Side of Life' and trying to whistle with frozen lips. The glade was full of laughter for a few minutes. But the chainsaws soon drowned it out. Whining, screaming, as another and another tree went down. They went through a stretch of three hundred year old oaks as if they were cutting grass. Trees fell, fell, fell, the operators as unconcerned as if they were mowing a lawn.

Martha dozed in her tree. The relentless whining and zip zip of the chainsaws battered at her senses hour after hour. The crashing of the trees became the crashing of household objects as her father smashed up the house again in one of his rages. Crash. Terror. Crash. Destruction. Crash. Hatred.

'I'll kill you! I'll break your neck!' he roared at Martha's mother, so loud that the sound vibrated in Martha's eardrums. Distorted. Smashing plates, cups, anything he could get his hands on up against the wall. 'You useless article!'

He grabbed her mother, shaking her and shaking her by the collar of her dress. Food trickled down the wallpaper. Pieces of broken china were scattered among Martha's felt tips on the floor.

'You'll kill her!' Martha woke with a start.

Crash. Scream.

'Look out!' A tree went down inches away from a protestor in a tree.

'You nearly hit her!' The tree thudded, bounced on the forest floor.

'What about Health and Safety!' bellowed a man's voice. 'You're gonna kill someone! Where's the Sheriff? Why isn't he watching this?' The police stood around unperturbed, arms folded, watching safety regulations being chopped up into as many pieces as the trees. The hired detective agency in their smart green helmets snapped photo after photo of the protestors.

'Make sure you get my best side!' 'I hope you aren't planning anything dirty with these photos!' Yells drifted down out of the trees, from the ragged, half-frozen bundles that were people, lodged in the crooks of the trees.

A shriek. Four security guards were pulling on another ring of protestors locked onto each other in a complex arrangement around a tree trunk.

'You're strangling me! I've got the D-lock round my neck!' a girl cried.

'They could have broken her neck.' someone said angrily as Mel was finally carried away by two security guards.

Martha caught her breath, wishing she could help. But if she got down from the tree she'd be arrested and the tree would be dead in seconds. Zip, zip.

It got colder. And colder. All the granola bars were gone. She shivered. Someone threw her a bar of chocolate and she could have cried when her cold hands missed the catch. They threw another. She caught it. Triumph! She fielded an orange, and felt better.

Dusk drew down at last. The gangs switched off their hell machines and went home. Martha slowly slid down from the tree, awkwardly dropping the last four feet, too numb to climb down.

Her ears rang for hours with the sound of chainsaws. They went home to their burner-less bender with the bubble wrap floor.

The camp was full of people milling about. Martha went to gather wood from the pile, but dropped it as the reaction hit her. She was glad it was dark as she sat sobbing in the woodpile. Perry found her. He wrapped an arm around her. 'We all feel like that.' he soothed. All over the camp people were crying, just standing there with tears running down their faces, wiping them off angrily as they struggled to get the frozen wood to burn, to get a hot meal on. Crying and swearing and getting on with it.

'At least we're here. We're trying.' Perry said defiantly. 'They can't make us stop caring. Right?'

'Right.' Martha stood up, picked up her armful of wood with a shaky smile and went to feed the fire, and chop vegetables, and cheer up Sarah who was looking blank and shocked. They hadn't heard from Mel yet. Probably being kept overnight.

They felt better with some Donga slop inside them, though Martha wondered why it always had to have so much cabbage in it. But at least it was hot.

'I'm definitely having some music after that, if I have to make it myself.' said Perry. 'We've still got no musicians. Ah well, let's see what we can do.' He picked up a catering-size coffee can and started drumming with more determination than skill. Martha grabbed a couple of sticks and beat them together in a counter-rhythm. Sarah was chanting, no words, just 'Hey-yah, hey lah – hey-yaah.'

Thunkety thunk, thunkety thunk.

Click. Click. Click. Click.

A box of peas joined in as maracas. Some clapped their hands. Their feet beat on the ground. The homemade band took off, became music. They were swept away. Dancing, shouting, chanting, jumping. Warm, alive, together.

❋

'Oh God, it was just like that.' said Kerry. She passed back the manuscript, stretched and lay back in the back of her van, nearly squashing the elderly black and white cat who merely blinked and rolled over, paws in the air.

'Do you think I captured it?' I asked. 'I only had Martha's accounts to go on, and her stories and that.'

'God, yes. Too well. I can't read it. The trashing was so fucking horrible.' Kerry said.

'The evictions sounded worse.' I said.

'Don't remind me. Remember those bastards who used to live in the flat upstairs when I lived at Albert Park, the way they used to play that Peter Gabriel song all the time?' said Kerry. She shifted, the van bouncing a little.

'Solsbury Hill?'

'Yeah. I swear the little fuckers were doing it on purpose to torment me. When they weren't stamping about over our heads and chucking rubbish into our garden. And at Newbury, in the evening we'd be listening to the CB and suddenly there'd be these chainsaw recordings just whining through the camp. It was the lorry drivers on their CBs.'

'That's horrible. What did they do that for?'

'Oh, they hated us cos they all wanted the bypass.' Kerry's anger dragged her vertical again.

'What sick bastards.' Even I was shocked. I looked away. Through the window two blue tits were bobbing about the bushes, oblivious to our presence.

I went on. 'Mart wanted to do more. But..'

48

'She was making herself ill. She went on too long as it was.' said Kerry with decision.

'But she wanted to help.' For a minute I sounded as plaintive as Martha ever did.

'She did loads. She never realised how much she was doing. I was the same – I went mad if I did campaigning and I went mad if I didn't. I couldn't – I couldn't stand the cruelty.'

'There's kind of a mad theme going on there.' I poured out another slug.

'Yeah. Pass the cider.' Kerry took advantage of her upright position to reach out and take the jug from me.

We stretched at our ease among the cushions, pale spring sunshine filtering through the dusty windows. Kerry had been off studying ecology and was passing through on her way to a badger vaccination training scheme before she went back to her nature reserve to work.

'I saw your badgers on Facebook.' I said.

'Yeah. Camp Badger.' Kerry removed a soft toy one from behind her back, looked at it and tossed it onto the rear shelf.

'I'm no good at direct action. I spend all my time growing food.'

'You're better off. Everyday stuff, that's what matters the most. Changing the way we live. Green and Black choc hash fudge cake and that. Give us that salad bowl over here.'

'But it's just piecemeal. I hate big politics but it's the only way anything seems to really change.' I passed the bowl and the plate of bread and butter.

'Yeah. And that really is a dirty business. Forget road protestor socks, politicians are all mingin'.'

'I know.'

'Your spring onions are good.' Kerry took another one and crunched it.

'I know.'

'Can I see your polytunnel?'

'Go on, then.'

❄

No matter how much Martha did, it didn't feel like enough. Up at 5am. The new bender had a burner in it by now, but it was full to bursting so she was sleeping in a tent wrapped in two sleeping bags. She got into bed wearing two hats, a scarf, two pairs of trousers, two shirts, two jumpers, two coats. She slept fitfully. One night she woke thirsty and wandered around the camp looking for something to drink. There was a bottle of milk by the fire. She picked it up. It thunked sadly. Frozen solid. It was minus thirteen Celsius outside. She found some wine, drank it, went back to her sleeping bags. And to think that people used to complain about antifreeze in the wine. Bloody good idea, she thought, muzzily half-frozen.

Food appeared by magic. Local people brought a steady stream of offerings. A local woman of eighty made them some scones and sent them with her love, as she couldn't join in the actions herself, she said.

A message of support came from a delegation of Shoshone who were visiting Britain. At Skyward Camp a World War Two veteran handed his medals to one of the tree dwellers. He said. 'I got these fighting for my country. Now you're fighting for our country so you should have them.'

A journalist walked up to their fire one day and gave them a bag of food. 'One of the police gave me this.' he said. 'He asked me to bring it as he couldn't let himself be identified.'

Everybody loved them. Everybody was on their side.

But they were still losing.

Nothing Martha did could stop the trees from falling, could stop the screaming, the terror, the injustice.

'I'll kill you. I'll break your neck. I'll kill you. I'll kill you.'

Zip. Dead tree. Zip. Dead tree.

'Get out of my sight. You're useless. You're useless.'

Nothing Martha did was any good. She kept her head down, she kept on trying, but she failed the land, day after day. She couldn't stop the destruction.

'What did I do to deserve you?'

✳

Martha lay in bed in the dark, heavy-eyed. She tried to go over the afternoon's disaster in her mind, but her small store of nervous energy was used up. Heart jumping, nerves twitching the muscles in her arms and legs as she crept away through the undergrowth with Bridget's 'Get out! Get lost!' ringing in her ears. She'd slipped silently through the overgrown field margin, head barely topping the grass. Padded quietly along one of the lesser-used woodland paths until she reached the ragged hawthorn hedge that guarded her from home. She squeezed through the barricade straight back into the battlefield.
But it was all battlefield now.

'Look at the state of you! Look at your face!'
This was a thing Martha could not do.
'Get up those stairs!'
Crack.
Sped on her way, she got up those stairs, hid in her bed until the smarting died down from red-hot outrage to shamed, resentful glow, and as the late dusk fell, she dropped heavily into an exhausted sleep.
She didn't hear the distant shouting, the banging, the sudden, brief shrieking out in the street, or the moment the ambulance arrived.
In the warm, heavy summer darkness, Martha slept.

✳

4. Ice.

Until you open the shoebox, you don't know whether the cat is alive or dead.

I could tell that the cat was alive. The twitching tail that stuck out of the cupboard door was a dead giveaway. It didn't shine much light on quantum uncertainty, but it did mean that there was a cat prone to chewing things burrowing through my old diaries, letters and photographs.

'Out!' I ordered sternly. Tiff's stern took no notice, her tail still waving interestedly as she sniffed and rummaged.

'Begone!' I grabbed her and eased her gently out, tucking her under my chin for a consolatory cuddle.

'What have you unearthed, puss?'

Until you open the shoebox, you don't know what you'll find.

I opened the shoebox.

It was a big one, that had contained expensive winter boots. Not mine, need I say. Several developers' envelopes of photos spilled out. Prontaprint. Fujifilm. Boots the Chemist. A slide of letters and motley scraps of paper followed. I squatted ankle-deep in white drifts of paper.

At the bottom of the box snowflakes glittered. An old exercise book, covered in silvery paper from some ancient Christmas. The foil snowflakes still shone a little through the years of scuffing and wear. Patches were torn off here and there. It was so familiar.

My old poetry book. Birmingham. Juvenilia. Memorabilia. You name it, it was all here.

This should be a laugh.

The kitchen was damp and chilly. I headed back to the lounge, popped a cheese sandwich on top of the stove and opened the book while waiting for my cheese toastie. Icicles still hung from the trees, but the blue snowlight reflected through the farm windows gave plenty of light for reading the stained, poorly typed pages.

Hmm, drivel, drivel, ooh quite good drawing of my own hand there. No way! I never used to fancy him, what was I thinking. Drunk, drunk, depressed circa 1991, oh, what's this?

'I remember when I was a child
a still-warm step against skinny legs
as I sat on a Sunday evening listening
to the summer evening music. Like
swallows swifting piping, slicing
through the close air...'

I sat back, my toastie forgotten. I wasn't laughing. Nor was I seeing the pale winter walls around me.
The swallows always rode the air inhaling clouds of midges every evening. The sky was full of them, wheeling against the clouds. The house martins were there too, shorter, stockier, black and white. Not as fast fliers, but making their swooping flights from eaves to infinity and back with almost as much elegance. Swifts too, screaming past. Dozens of them. Richard Adams always reckoned that they said 'News! News!' but to me they just said 'Scree-scree' as they hurtled past. There were house martins' nests on half the houses in the village. They were very keen on the house of a boy named Martin, to our delight. Mud hammocks clinging to the angle of the eaves were – normal. Practically part of the architecture.

Then the midges. And the flies. Whole afternoons were devoted to the happy hunting of juicy bluebottles round the kitchen with a rolled-up newspaper. Seven at one blow. Splat! There was a plague of ladybirds during the heatwave summer when me and the boys ran screaming around the garden squirting homemade water pistols made of Fairy Liquid bottles and spent the whole summer, felt like, in our bathing suits. We used to compete over the ladybirds – ten-spot beat seven-spot, but anything was better than the lowly two-spot. And the yellow twenty-two spotters were rarer, and worth turning out the whole gang for a general viewing.

Thunderbugs. Don't know them? They plagued us too, not itchy or problematic, but just – there. Everywhere. Tiny minus-signs of flies clustering on every white surface, then every light surface, then every surface. On our clothes. In our hair. On Martha's lopsided glasses, magnified, to her annoyance. On the page of a book, adding unnecessary punctuation. They specialised in getting inside screens - Joe's Texas LED calculator or the futuristic digital clock my mum got as a free gift from the catalogue. And of course, the TV. Every white area of the picture had flamin' thunderbugs crawling all over it. David Dimblebly's head. The walls of the Tardis. We blew them off, we brushed them off as gently as possible. In the end we just got used to them. Except when they crept into the corners of our eyes.

Wasps were everywhere as soon as you stripped the paper off a Zoom lolly. They orbited every school bin in the playground. They lived in jam jars and marauded picnickers like Tom Sawyer and his Outlaws. The car windscreen would be splattered with insect corpses after a long journey, tiny spiders lived in the wing mirrors to catch them. Moths mobbed in to circle the lightbulb if you left the curtains open on a summer night when the windows were open. Huge brown and grey things flapping round and round like bats, tiny silver and white or delicately-waved green ones, skipping weakly along and hiding in plain sight on the cream anaglypta-and-emulsion walls. And the butterflies?
I read on.

'...the chattering sweep and back
of starlings round the sky,
like tea leaves swirling out from a drain.
And the high distant roar of big pines standing
around the pocket-silent churchyard.'

Watching the starlings was why I sat there on the low wall outside the front door. They swooped and ebbed round the sky in their dozens, hundreds, thousands, pouring their strange shapes round the sky, never colliding in their eccentric formation flying until they abruptly swirled down the drain to roost. The aerial show was just part of summer evenings, like the chirping of crickets, the smell of cut grass, the shouts of kids playing and the screaming of late swifts.

Me and the boys would sit at the top of our den tree, the wizened elder up the field, until late in the evening. 'Down the river' and 'Up the field' were part of the official geography of the village, though not found on any map. *'Listen for the church clock and get yourselves home on time'* we were told. Of course we took it to the wire. It was still daylight after all. The notes of the church bell dropped one by one into the pocket of silence created around the church by the tall pines that stood there, towering over the yews that marked it as an ancient site of worship. The church itself was six hundred years old and its spire was supposed to be the tallest in - the county? The country? We were never sure. All I knew was, you could near break your neck craning to see the top from the ground in front of the door. There was a weathercock on top. You could always see which way the wind was blowing, with the buttresses flying aloft.

'I remember the village when I was a child, I didn't know the rainpouring
neonflashing oil puddled and clangorous streets of Birmingham
then, but my nightlife was wildly exciting, running
small and hunted, playing 'kick the can'
crawling quietly through bushes, cat-delicate,
grass sticking to my knees as I sunk in the mossy underfelt
in a back garden Serengeti, big and lion-dangerous, waiting.
Hiding against walls, hands brick-dusted and printed with ocean waves'.

I remember the buddleia bush as being very tall, though perhaps I was just very small. There were caves beneath it formed among the snowberry bushes, overgrown roses and leafy forsythia. Here the grass was mossy and soft towards the bare knee, and you could look out unseen through the leggy branches. I learnt stealth by watching the cats. But in daytime you'd be distracted by the butterflies. The butterflies!
Small tortoiseshell, common as sparrows, not exciting. Peacocks though, plenty of them, six or more at a time, but impressive. Cabbage white, boring, but worth a look – might be an orange tip. Red admiral later in the year. Painted lady – sometimes you'd do a

55

double-take to see that it wasn't a tortoiseshell after all. But flocks of them of whatever type covered the bush all summer, all the time, like living flowers.

The violet ground beetle we knew as a black beetle that crept under our sleeping bags when we camped in the garden in summer. They used to run busily through the grass, under and over, inside the tent at the edges of the ill-fitting sheet of tarp covered with an old blanket that we slept on. We tried hard not to roll on them and squash them but they always made you jump when you turned up the bed. It was a poor night when you didn't find at least three. The advent of the built-in groundsheet was a turning-point in camping technology. No more sharing your bed with earwigs and black beetles.

The tent was an old one that my brother Sean got in a swap for his old bike at school. It had wooden poles that fitted together and ancient green canvas that rotted over the years until the ridge had splits all along. Tapes tied in bows to close the front flaps, once you'd learned not to peg it down before checking for closure. We never had enough pegs. I remember using rocks and old flatirons to hold the sides down. Lying there at night you could watch the stars come out one by one.

'I'd leave the ended day, drawn in to the bright crowding fug
of home and bacon sandwiches,
closing the front door, with an odd lonely pang, on the terrifying
simple bigness of night, milky cool and mercury blue.
The back door latched shut to keep out our dark hedgehog-rustling
garden,
but for the front a Yale, which closed weightily,
clicked with finality, locking out the huge owlcalling night.'

The almost out-of-range even for a kid squeaking of shrews could be heard as we trudged up the drive to the house. Hedgehogs rustled along lanes of shrubs, grunting away. Tawny owls called, and answered their mates. Bats flittered around the blue-white streetlight.

Oh, it was so beautiful. We knew that, of course, but in another sense, we didn't. Because for us, it was – normal.

※

My cheese toastie was sizzling on the stove. I picked it up with the oven gloves, blew off the ash and ate it absently, thinking about the village. In a winter like this we'd have a bird table up and finches, tits and sparrows queueing up to fight over the food.

'Look, it's a bullfinch!' my aunt would call. On a rare winter visit she enrolled me, Mick and Sean in the Young Ornithologists Club and we got a cool metal club badge of a hovering kestrel. There were always kestrels hovering over the fields, sometimes over town too. There were four bullfinches, two pairs, by the time my brothers and I had run to the window and fought for a space, like squabbling sparrows. Then greenfinches, two, four, six, eight of them, blue tits, great tits, longtails and coal tits, flocks of them descending on the table to be swept away by a fat woodpigeon that spilled over the edges. Plenty of starlings. Huge brawling mobs of them, striding around bowlegged scaring off the other birds, iridescent green and purple – or were they just a freckled black?

Blackbirds, robins of course, always there as they are now. A wren might appear, tiny as a thought, so quick that you think you'd imagined it. Flit, and gone. So many birds. They appeared the minute there was a glimpse of bacon fat, strung up like Christmas decorations for birds.

You'd see lapwings on the school bus. Not on the bus, of course, but out of the windows, in the shepherd's pie fields, as we called the rough brown and white plough of last year's stubble, now that they weren't burning it off any more. A flock would cover a whole large field and you could watch it all along the lane as you passed by.

When it was this cold, you might see a brambling, or the redwings would come through.

It would seem like a long time until spring and frogspawn season, or later, newt-pestering season when we'd spend whole days watching and hunting newts in the pond up the field. Dozens of them, smooth newts and Great Crested, like tiny crocodiles. We'd end up with a jam jar full, then carefully pour them back in before we went home with our net curtain or nylon tight-and-coathanger nets. 'Put it back where you found it and don't be cruel to animals, they're not toys.' we'd been taught.

'Always shut the gate after you and don't go picking the flowers, leave them to grow.   No, you can't carve your name on the bark, you'll damage the tree.   Put your litter in your pocket and bring it home.' You'd think all our mum's rules would have put us off. But it just made the land sacred and more precious to us. We were proud of our stewardship. It was our village after all. We knew every inch of it, every tree, every flower, every nettlebed, every slippery slope.

'Take nothing but photographs, leave nothing but footprints.'

Pity someone didn't teach Brian Mawhinney that.   He carved his name across the whole of the Newbury countryside.

I put the book aside. The writing had come to a standstill today. I felt icebound as well as snowbound.

❄

Blinking in unaccustomed daylight after the blizzard, I tested the boundaries of my snowy prison. Snow drifting over the hedge bank had closed the lane ahead of me. No going further that way. A deep carpet lay over the rutted track to the river in the opposite direction.

After three days, signs of thaw were beginning to show. Trees dripped. The sheet of trodden snow on the steps was beginning to give way to dark damp stone.   My footprints to the woodpile were deepening as the snow slowly melted.   Wandering the snowbound farm, activity still and blanketed, summer life and movement seemed remote and unlikely. I returned indoors to a still blank page.

I picked up the old book, sprinkled with its resilient snowflakes, and leafed through a few more pages. Our den under the elder tree, yes. Remember that. There was another one, nearer home. I used to hide there from stormy weather. It was a large cave formed by hawthorns arching over a slight dip in the ground. Bramble walls surrounded it apart from the low entrance under the thin hawthorn branch we'd picked the thorns off. Low branches running across the floor seeking a way out to sunlight formed seats, and nooks between tree roots were a good place for making...

Dandelion Pie. Of course. It was the Womble Den.
'Why do I always have to be Madame Cholet?'
'Cus she's the girl. Stupid.'
My brothers, the three that were still at home now that Joe was married and gone, got the more active roles. The biggest and strongest was Tomsk. The bright bespectacled one was Wellington. And the smallest, with the clamouring stomach of a baby bird, was Orinoco of course. But all stupid, boring Madame Cholet got to do was stay in the burrow and make dandelion pie. Mind you, Orinoco soon got hungry and started nagging to be taken home once the sweets ran out, Tomsk would invariably end the adventure by punching Wellington and knocking off his glasses as the crux of his argument, and Madame Cholet would soon abandon her culinary duties to climb one of the roof-trees to get away from all their nonsense.

There was one day of unity, though. A day of rage tearing through our house. Screams and shouts and threats rending the air. Slam. Smash. Thump. Run. There were so many days like that. But this day was the day when each of us in our flight, swerving the furniture in the overcrowded lounge, leaping down the steps and along the garden path like panic-stricken rabbits, squeezing through the hawthorn hedge and dashing through our patent nettlebed maze, arrived at the same burrow independently. The Womble Den.
For the first time, we found ourselves hesitantly talking about it. Whose fault was it? Had we done something to deserve it? Was it right, the way our dad carried on? And what could we do about it?
I don't remember much about that day - I know it was long before the time of the final bust-up - but I think we arrived at a game plan together.
To try not to get into trouble. Not to get other people into trouble. Not to grass each other up, no matter what the threat. We went away, not a team, but beginning to grasp the idea of strength in numbers. Working together against the common threat. All of us secretly knowing that Tomsk was a big fat liar because it was him that

doodled on the wall in the first place and blamed it on Wellington. Again.

We came away realising a few things. It wasn't our fault. We didn't deserve it. Also, that Tomsk was a jerk but he was bigger than us so it wasn't good politics to say so until after he left, when the rest of us swore a bigger and better oath without him.

❄

The book was shedding pages as I leafed. I picked them up carefully and fitted them back in. The poetry meandered into teenage years, got drunk, meandered out again and explored early twenties, intense, philosophical, seeking, absorbed. And stoned.

'A candle blazes up like glory
in this empty golden room
at night, all winesoaked...'

Move over, Omar Khayyam!
Oh, this is interesting.

'Reach for the bag that
I've filled with my own magic.
Watch the smooth and clicking stones fall...'

Must have been going through a pretty bloody pretentious stage. Wonder what brought that on. I blame Tolkien myself. But I spent a lot of time reading the runes back then. Obsessively questioning my subconscious about what it wanted and how things might pan out if it got its own way. I even made them a special bag, sewed unevenly out of a piece of silk Paisley pyjama leg fished from a charity shop rag bag and dyed grey to go with the violet ribbon that tied it up. I kept that bag for years...

Was it possible? That my time-capsule of a cupboard. Might contain...oh, my.

Just a three stone spread will do. First stone -

Isa. Standstill. Time of Ice.

Tell me something I don't know. Didn't know they did the weather forecast as well.

I played with the smooth clicking stones a while longer, then reached for my pen. The thaw was beginning. Words were flowing again.

❄

5. Falling.

'Quercus robur, *the English oak, has been a national emblem of strength and survival for centuries. The ecology of the oak bears this tradition out, since it supports a greater diversity of flora and fauna than any other native tree. There are 2300 species associated with the oak, including beetles, flies, wasps, epiphytic lichens, bracket fungi, birds and mammals. 326 are species-specific to UK native oaks.'*

Martha put down her pen and stretched her aching hand. The biological sciences library was quiet, a busy silence hung over the carrels this close to an essay deadline. She picked up the article again and resumed reading, scribbling rough notes as she went. She stared out of the window at the cathedral ruins from time to time, watching the way the jackdaws fluttered between the smaller spires and settled, squabbling, on the tower. A few splashes of colour showed among the ruins as people wandered, gazing around.

'The oak grows rapidly during its youth, during which time it is smooth-skinned. In the slower-growing and senescent stages this is overlaid by a deeply fissured, rugged bark. The acorn crop feeds a large variety of birds and mammals including mice, badgers, deer, squirrels, pheasant and jay. The oak fruits prolifically, but of the thousands of green acorns that fall to the forest floor below, very few will survive to germinate.'

✻

Martha stood on the forest floor looking up into the canopy of the few giant oaks that still clung on. Four or five members of the camp were still aloft. Alex was quickly freeclimbing to the highest branches of his tree. He was fifty, now sixty feet up. Someone else was peering from the doorway of a treehouse set between two broad branches about halfway up. In his knee-length green woollen tunic and russet leggings, he looked like a kid playing outlaws. Long dark hair straggled out of his scruffy ponytail and hung about the dirty face and stubbly chin that showed through the gaps in the hazel weave. A penny whistle still dangled from a string round his neck. He looked out of the door, his breath clouding on the air. It was Will. Two girls were standing on the walkway forty feet up between their tree and the next. Martha noticed how soft and young their faces were under the grime and spirals of woad. God, those two can't be more than sixteen. Lithe-limbed and arboreal, like Gilman's Herland women, they bounced as a bailiff grabbed the walkway. The girls hung on. Still they hung on. They can't fall. They're not going to fall. They bobbed up and down with a fragile grip on the overhead line and their lifelines clipped on to save them.

Sarah was hugging a high branch as a climber approached and started snatching at her legs. The bailiff reached out and began pulling at her as she kicked out desperately. He dragged her down through the boughs as her hands slipped from their grip, her jacket pulled up and her body scraped against the branches. Her shriek was drowned out by the screaming of chainsaws as she clung on anywhere she could. She's going to fall. Oh God! the bailiffs are crazy.

'She's not clipped on! Stop! You'll have her off!' Voices from the crowd shouted angrily as they watched from behind the cordon.

The climber dragged her to the trunk, clipped her onto a line and the others began lowering her to the ground. As she landed her legs crumpled underneath her. Two policemen dragged her to her feet and shoved her towards the waiting van.

Near the foot of the tree, security guards were dragging and piling the protestors' belongings. The benders that had sheltered them for months were a wreck of yanked-up hazel poles and smashed pallets. A few colourful remnants were all that was left of the shelters they'd nestled into - pink blankets, some old purple-patterned curtains and a torn and faded Indian throw in red and yellow lay soaking up filthy water from muddy, oily puddles. Comics, books, clothes and tools were heaped up like rubbish.

Pots and pans, smashed crockery. A guitar with a broken neck and stoved-in body. A sleeping bag trodden into the mud. Dreamcatchers and beads hanging snapped and unravelled from a bender pole. An orange rubber Tango-man doll, idol of a vanquished tribe. Rucksacks and burners and coats and boots and notebooks and homemade birthday cards and letters with love, all piled high.

Martha longed to save something, anything. She had pushed forward as far as possible before the thick yellow line pushed back harder. The Tot Hill crew had done their best to help, running, blocking, veering off as beefy yellowjackets lumbered towards them on a bruising collision course. They had got in the way and underfoot as much as they could, trying to stop the bailiffs from reaching the trunks. At least as long as they couldn't get a cherrypicker in here the oakwood still stood strong, defiant.
Lesser trees had fallen to the chainsaw gangs. All around the remaining defended space was a desolation of churned-up mud, great ruts of digger tracks, sawn stumps of half a dozen species, trunks lying dead, pits yawning where roots had been torn out of the ground they'd held fast to for centuries.

'The open canopy associated with oakwood facilitates the growth of spring and dappled-shade spp. such as Hyacinthoides non-scripta, Primula vulgaris, Anemone nemorosa *and* Digitalis purpurea. *A carpet of spring bluebells provide a vital nectar source for bees in spring and early summer. Woodland flora is therefore bound up with the presence of oak.'*

Among the ruins of the wood a few splashes of colour showed on the torn, compacted earth. Scraps of bunting, a pink hair bead, a split orange hard hat, discarded water bottles where the security guards had been standing, their blue and white labels depicting an idyllic mountain scene.
The security guards were piling brash against the trunks now. Pouring petrol, a gush of fumes. A plume of choking smoke. They couldn't...They wouldn't!
But there was nothing they wouldn't. Deep in the woods, even the ragged remnants dotted around the battle-scarred landscape, the gloves came off, the destroyers revelled in the freedom to be as violent and cruel as they had it in them to be. The ripped-back skin of the earth was no more than a chance to rub salt in the wound.

Clouds of choking smoke billowed over the clearing. Mushroomed-headed security guards retreated, coughing. Protesters, further away, were able to pull scarves up over their mouths and noses but quite a few of the guards had to be treated for smoke inhalation. The smoke rose to the coughing tree dwellers but dissipated before it could seriously harm them. The yellowjackets were worse affected. The attempt to smoke the tree defenders out like wasps had failed. Another standoff.

'In winter, hundreds of birds may find roosts in a single hollow, packed together for warmth. Bats also use the oak for roosting, finding an abundance of insect life among the hundreds of species supported by every phase of the oak's life - from youth to white rot through red rot to the wood compost filling beetle-larvae galleries in aged tree-hollows. Emerging at night, several species of bat find both shelter and food under the eaves of the oakwood.'

As darkness fell, the remaining crew abseiled wearily down like tiny woodland spiders, the beams of their headlamps bobbing. Ground support waited with food and hot drinks, with hugs and warm words, with mute relief.

❄

'Where's Alex?'
'They got him about two o'clock.' Sniff, cough.
'Any trees left on your camp?' 'A couple. Just a couple left.' 'Oh. Oh my God.'
Sarah limped up. Bump. Scuffle. Thud.
'Yo! Sarah!' She was enveloped in hugs by three or four people at once.
'Did they hurt you?' 'Nothing much, they took me into hospital because of the abrasions. My shoulder was sort of sprained and I'm wrecked with bruises but I'm Ok. Alex was there.' 'What happened to him?' 'Busted wrist I think.' 'Oh God, where is he?' 'Dunno yet.'

'Is there room for Sarah in your treehouse Will?' 'M' treehouse's gone. Prob'ly arrest me for vagrancy tomorrow...' Cough, clank.

'Heh. They'll throw us all in the jug for that.'
'You sound cold. You're freezing! Here, get under the blanket. Give Will a massive hug, someone, get him warmed up...' 'Wa-hay!' 'Didn't know you cared...' Shuffle, creak. 'Just heard. Alex got major bail conditions – he can't come within a mile of the perimeter...' 'Bollocks!'
'Jugged! We're all getting jugged!...' 'You're getting plastered...gimme the bottle.'

'Ah, the bastards cut my harness. Fuck, someone give me a rollie. Cheers. Now, someone give me a drink.' Rustle, click-scratch.
'Eh, eh, don't cry, don't let the bastards get you down...you were brilliant today.' 'I couldn't...I couldn't stop them cutting my tree down...' 'Shh..shh..have a drink..here, you have my last bit of chocolate...'
Brzzz...wheeeeoueee...crackle..fzzt...*Tango Charlie, do you copy, over?*... 'What's gonna happen tomorrow? Who's going to be next?'
'...*Romeo Bravo, this is Tango Bravo, do you copy? Tango Charlie, come in Tango Charlie...over.*'

❄

Weeks had gone by. Camp after camp had fallen to the bailiffs, the chainsaws, the bulldozers. Gotan, Kennet, Tree Pixie, The Chase, Manic Sha. Tot Hill.
Granny Ash was a matriarch among ash trees, venerable, ivy-clad. Once again the desperate cat and mouse game to try to keep the cherrypickers away. Once again the afternoon standing helplessly, beaten back by the yellow line, the certainty of instant arrest for aggravated trespass if you crossed the line, the despair of watching the destruction if you didn't. The protestors' ranks were being thinned as fast as the trees. So many had been bailed-off site - handed the Newbury sausage, the bail condition that excluded them from crossing the boundary of a one-mile exclusion zone around the nine-mile route. Plenty in the throng broke bail conditions, risking a guaranteed prison sentence if spotted. Hundreds had been arrested. The bailiffs battered the face of the last man out with their fists as he was hauled down, hanging onto the outside of the cherry picker as

they kicked his shins raw. The police took him off, dripping blood, without a backward glance at the men who'd assaulted him.

Hundreds still swarmed the route, blocking, dodging, scrambling onto machinery, linking arms around barely-controlled panicking police horses, climbing onto the bonnets of police vans. Shouting, singing, pleading, praying, snapping photos and recording video in an attempt to protect the tree defenders in their final stand.
Martha watched, desperate to save somebody, anybody, as the professional climbers turned bailiff rose up in the cherrypicker. Forty feet, fifty feet, still rising, past the safe-operation height limit, its mechanical arm reaching up, up. Climbers chased tree defenders around the branches, a girl freeclimbed higher and higher in desperation until she was grabbed and shoved headfirst into the cherrypicker platform, screaming in terror, sixty feet up.

Day followed day. A man was dragged by a wrist and dangled over a fifty foot drop. Walkways were cut under people, nets slashed with knives on poles, a woman lowered thirty-five feet suspended by her ankle. Bruised, battered, terrified, the tree defenders were coming down to earth, one by one. As branches were chopped away some people were left with nothing to hang onto but the cherrypicker platform itself, lowered with a tree defender clinging desperately to the outside like someone's warped idea of a deus ex machina.
There was going to be no miraculous intervention, unless you counted the fact that so far no one had been killed, to the disappointment of the drama-hungry press. The desperate burrows dug around the trees to stop cherry pickers from rumbling over the fragile earth had been quickly cleared, with too few defenders remaining to occupy them. The last rabbit had been flushed out.

'The immense biomass of a single oak tree is effectively doubled when it is remembered that the root system is just as extensive and complex and has an associated biodiversity as great as that of the aerial parts. The biggest of Britain's mature oaks constitute the largest single organisms in the UK. Yet the oak tree is at once a single organism and an entire ecosystem in its own right. Its strength and resilience was most recently commemorated on the

67

1992 pound coin obverse as one of Britain's most enduring national symbols. Both underground and overground, the oak is part of the national consciousness as well as a unique contributer to the wealth of Britain's wildlife heritage.'

There wasn't going to be a miracle, a fairy-tale ending. The land was fucked, the trees were on the ground, the protestors were exhausted, grief-stricken and traumatised. The remnants of muddy W's daubed onto faces were obscured by bloodied scratches, eroded by time and tears.
Underground, overground. The battle for the trees was over.
There was nothing left to do but pick up the pieces.

❄

6. Drifting.

'Shove all your bits and pieces in the back. Are you in? We're off in a minute.'
'Er, yeah.'

Martha was the last to haul herself up, stepping among ropes, boots and rucksacks. The floor was thick with mud. She dumped her bag and sat on a heap of dirty blankets. Out of the window the smoking ruins of the camp were no longer discernible. The small green scrubby field with their tents and benders and gently-smoking firepit had been turned into a lumpy expanse of digger-rutted mud surrounded by tall sections of Heras fencing, dimly visible through the mist. Clouds of diesel smoke mingled with the fog, blackening the air. Uprooted hedges and small trees were scraped together in a great heap. There were some bender poles among the roots and branches. Martha looked away quickly, dropping her gaze to the muddy floor to avoid catching Sarah's eye.

There was a huge bootprint printed on the end of her cotton sleeping bag, a black brand across the pink and blue flowered print. Under the seats crushed cardboard boxes and black dustbin bags had been hastily stowed. They stank in the warm fug of packed bodies. Pete let the clutch out and they pulled jerkily out of the layby. The windows were beginning to mist over already.

Pete turned his head towards them as he approached the motorway, his beard an unkempt hedge against the light through the windscreen. He rubbed the back of his hand across his dirty face tiredly.
'Right, anyone want to get out before Bristol?'
Somebody coughed. Will shifted his seat on a mountain of climbing gear, clanking like a dungeon inmate in shackles.
'If you let me out at the services before Bath I can get my girlfriend to pick me up.'

He had a girlfriend. Of course he did.

'Ok. What about Bristol?' said Pete.

'Can you drop me near the city farm in St Werburghs?' A girl Martha didn't know looked up from under a woven hat, red and yellow tassled earflaps hanging untied, a tangle of honey blonde hair over her shoulders.

'I'm for Montpelier.' Perry yawned and stretched out his skinny legs in dirty, holed black jeans under combat cutoffs. He clicked his empty Clipper lighter idly as he looked out at the motorway embankment sweeping past.

'I'm sure I can get a train to Redland if you drop me near St Andrews Road.' said a deep, cultivated woman's voice from the front of the van. Martha couldn't see who it was.

'Um, how about Prospect Road?'

'Where's that, Martha?'

'Just by City Road, in St Pauls.'

There was a fractional pause. Pete rubbed his nose and glanced back at her a second before returning his eyes to the road.

'You'll have to give me directions. Don't know that part of town very well. Tell you what, it'll be two forty-five once we get in and I'm at Picton Street for three for a meeting. I'll have to park the van up with all my stuff in it before I head, so what say I drop you off there?' said Pete.

'Uh – Ok.' said Martha, heart sinking at the thought of the long walk home with her heavy rucksack.

'So, you're in Montpelier?' she asked Perry hopefully. *We're neighbours!*

'Yeah, for a few days, anyway. I've a mate with a bit of land over Shepton Mallet. I want to catch up with him and then we'll chill for a bit in my caravan.' He tucked his Clipper back into the ornate copper wire holder that hung from a string round his neck.

'Oh.' Martha thought of her empty, cold bedsit. The thought was chilly. For a second she'd let herself believe in Sarah and Perry coming round for coffee, joining her on demos, reading the Earth First! Action Update together…

'Pete! Got any baccy left?' Perry shouted forward.

'Yeah, in my jacket. Help yourself.' Pete answered.

70

Martha retreated further into her dirty coat, and wrapped the homemade blanket that topped it more tightly round herself.

'Bet the kids'll be glad to see ye, Pete?' asked Morag.
'God, yes, it's been weeks. Need to spend some quality time with the family after that. As they'll no doubt remind me.'
'Aye, it'll be a relief to get home. My other half's probably done nae work around the house for a month. He's going tae meet me at the station in Cardiff though to help hump ma tat home, bless him. I've got so much to do before term starts.' said Morag.
'Oh, what course are you on? asked Sarah eagerly from where she sat leaning against Perry. 'I'm starting at Cardiff this autumn. Ecology.' She hugged Perry in excitement.
'Aye, great, we'll hae to get together. I'm no' a student. I'm starting as a technician in the biology department.'
'Oh wow, I'll be able to see you there then! And Mel's on about coming to Bristol once she's got a job down here. She'll only be half an hour away on the train then.'
'Tell her to try Earthwise Food Coop. Alex's been working for them for two years, on and off. If she speaks to him about a temp job over the summer then she might get a chance to get her foot in the door. That's how he got started.' said Pete. 'I'd come with, but I have to get back down to Carmarthen tomorrow.
'Yeah, great, I'll tell her, cheers Pete.'

Martha looked out of the window. Motorway lamps swooped and flicked past. The grey metal barrier poured endlessly past her eyes, and with the dull roar of the engine dreared her mood. Should she ask Alex about a job at Earthwise too? But there'd be phones to answer. Strangers to talk to. Nearly two years of unemployment to explain away. She remembered her last job interview. Eyes on the carpet, low mumble as she listed her meagre work experience. 'Sorry didn't catch that...Could you repeat that...' then the hmm, hmm as he gave up trying to understand her speech. She felt the familiar sinking of her heart as she saw his face glaze over and the way he began nodding and smiling to cover up his incomprehension. Then the usual brisk dismissal. She could almost mouth it along with them by now. 'Thank you so much for coming in, we haven't got anything that would be a fit for you right now but good luck with your future endeavours.'

Earthwise would never want her. Would anyone?

'Whatever happened to Becca?' asked Morag.

'Oh, she's still on that internship with FoE.' said Pete. 'She's going for it.

'Yeah, she's hardcore. Never stops.' agreed Morag.

The van jolted on with its muddied, weary cargo.

Martha dozed, head still ringing with shouts and screams and crashes. The crew smelled – of woodsmoke, diesel oil, dirty socks, Old Holborn, garlic, stale sweat, cider fumes. But it would all wash away.

She roused from her motorway trance when they pulled in to drop Will off. Martha stared through the back window as they drew away from his dwindling figure, sitting on his rucksack outside a Little Chef.

She realised that she didn't even know his last name.

❄

'Mart - love – do you want to share a taxi back to yours? I'm gonnae catch the train from Temple Meads and we'll go right past your door.' Morag broke into her daze as they turned off the M32.

'Um – that'd be good – but I can't afford it. I'm all right walking.'

'Aye, I know a' about you and your 'I'm all right.' ' Morag answered, smiling. 'Don't worry, we've two earning in ma house, you're fine.'

'Oh, that'd be great, thanks.' Martha's heart warmed, touched by more than the offer of a lift.

The light spring drizzle that heralded their return to Bristol turned into a blattering rain just as they jumped into the cab. Martha lay back in the awesome luxury of the purring, warm car.

'I could get used to this – not much chance of that though!' she said to Morag.

'Aye, it sounds like you've no' been getting the breaks, love.'

'It feels weird going back to normal life. Dunno what I'll do with myself. Everyone's doing something impressive with their lives – except me.'

'It'll come. In time. These others – they're the lucky ones. People like Harry and Wee Johnny, they won't be rolling up to new jobs and degree courses.'

'Where did Little Johnny come from? I never really got to know him.'

'He used to hang out in the pub in Newbury where Harry and the other soaks went when they could afford it. He was underage of course but he used to go there to get away from his stepdad. Better smashed than bashed, y'know. Poor wean's only fifteen.'

'Fifteen!'

'Aye. Harry was that age when he started drinking. History repeating itself.'

'Poor Johnny. Where - where d'you think he'll go now?'

'Alex took him aside. Think he'll go on down to Fairmile. I don't know, it's no place for a kid with problems but it's the only home some of them have, and at least he'll be getting a good influence. But the last thing he needs is something else to be angry about.'

'Security guards bashing him instead! At least there's someone to stick up for him this time.' said Martha angrily. 'Makes a change from what usually – er, what probably happened most of the time'

'That's right, love. In the end, wi' this protesting, the life you save has to be your own, that's what they say. People forget the Earth's not just about trees. It's about us.'

'My house is just there. I have to go. G-goodbye. Um, you were always nice to me...thanks.' Martha stuttered out.

'That's a' right. You take care of yourself and remember – you're just as important as the trees!'

Martha grinned as she swung her bag out of the back seat. Morag's wild sandy curls swirled as she turned to face front, the taxi pulled away, and she was gone.

Martha stood watching the car disappear in the traffic, then turned and lugged her rucksack up the stone steps of the tall shabby townhouse, rummaging for her key, unused for months. She slithered in over a stack of junk mail and unlocked the scarred wooden door that was hers. Dumped her rucksack. Sat down abruptly on the single bed, feeling the odd, upholstered sense of being indoors. The luxury of a level, tussock-free floor, a solid roof, a chair. The cheap mattress felt like floating in clouds as she lay down, pictures flickering in her head.

She fell asleep right there, boots still on, euphoria and fright and grief and relief and excitement all whirling in her head.

❄

Rap. Rap. The sheriff's men were hammering on the treehouse door. A rattle. They were breaking in. The bar should hold them. All those bolts too. Let me sleep.
'Martha. Mart.' Jolted awake. How do they know my name? They must have read it in my file. They knew to come when I was asleep...Operation Snapshot've got my photo...on the bonnet of that police van...mustn't fall off...
'Mart. Martha!'

She woke. Someone was rattling at the door.
'Are you there? Martha!'
She got up groggily and went to open the door.
It was Simon, that funny kid from upstairs. Broke again. He grinned at her, his big eyes bright under his spiky black hair.
'Hey...you're back! How was the end of the world?'
'Hi Simon. Come in. You can put the kettle on.'
Martha was never tongue-tied with Simon. You couldn't get a word in edgeways anyway.
'Have you got any coffee?' he asked, bounding Tiggerlike into the room on thick, grubby darned socks.
'Is that what you woke me up for?'
'No! Well, yes. That, and can you lend me a tenner.' he said, reaching for a couple of dusty mugs.
'Not in there! Wash them!'
'Oh, come on! You've been living up a tree with soap dodgers for the last six months.'
'I don't care. Clean cups.' Martha ordered.

'It's dirty! It's dirty!' A tiny smudge of egg was left on the edge of the plate that Martha had just handed to her mother. She had worked so hard for the last hour making the dinner, but her mother was still screaming. 'You're disgusting! Why can't you do the simplest task?'
'Shut up.'
'Say what?'
'Sorry. I didn't mean you.' Martha apologised.

Simon hurried over to the washbasin to swill the mugs, tripping over Martha's muddy rucksack on the way. He carefully emptied the kettle into the miniscule sink and refilled it with fresh by emptying mugs of water into it. The ancient plastic kettlejug groaned to the boil, steaming up the already dampish room. There was no milk, and the coffee had hardened at the bottom of the jar. Simon expertly prised out a couple of lumps and dissolved them in the mugs with a bit of prodding.
'Here.' They sat in the afternoon gloom, the hot coffee tasting magic.
'So, what happened? I saw you on the news.'
'Did you?'

Martha was startled. Insulated from the outside world for two months, locked into their own private struggle, she'd forgotten that the world was watching.
'Yeah. You were standing on a rope walk up a tree looking well-moody. I felt sorry for the bailiffs.'
'You should've seen what they did! They nearly killed Kerry! They chopped down a tree with her still in it!'
Months of strain spilled over. Martha's anger shocked both of them. To her utter fury, tears were rising.
'Hey...hey. I was joking. You were on page two of the Telegraph as well. I was reading it over this bloke's shoulder on the bus. I was well proud.' Simon looked up at her from his cross-legged position on the floor with a hint of concern. His ragged blue sweater hung in unravelled frills from his wrists as he lifted his mug in both hands.

75

'Yeah...sorry. I...it was really bad. They didn't care what they did, they pulled people out of the trees whatever, however. It's a miracle no one was killed. And the f-*fucking* press were there like vultures waiting for one of us to fall.'

'Sounds like them. Remember all the crap they wrote at Solsbury Hill. Kerry hated them.'

'I didn't know you knew Kerry.'

'Everybody knows Kerry. You can't miss her.'

'Where did you meet her?'

'When we were squatting on Sussex Place. We were there when they brought in the new Criminal Justice Act and made us crap ourselves. God, that's two years ago now.' He took a deep draught from his mug. 'Aah! Haven't had a coffee for three days. Glad you're back!'

Martha grinned back.

'Glad to be of service.' she said shyly.

They sat quietly savouring their coffee. She saw Simon glance unobtrusively around the room, taking in the psilocybin postcard sent from a friend in Glastonbury, the home made dreamcatchers twirling in the draught from the leaky sash window, a faded paisley throw from St Nicks market tacked to the back wall, a drawing of a treehouse done by Kerry, smoke rising from the mushroom-topped flue.

'So, you're one of us, then?' Simon asked, looking up at the Solsbury Hill Mass Trespass poster next to a smaller one with a red No Entry sign on it that said CJA-Free Zone.

'One of who?' asked Martha.

'Nutters. Weirdos. Troublemakers.'

'Don't forget mental cases.' Martha added, watching Simon's reaction uneasily.

'And dolie scum, of course.' Simon grinned back.

'Dolie scum! Get a job!' Martha chanted mechanically, her thin face twitching into a smile.

'Gizza job then! I can do that! Gizza job, you tossers!'

Giggles broke from Martha, sounding more like sobbing than laughter.

' 'What you all need is a good slap and a wash!' ' he went on, plummily. 'You know, they're all such bastards I can't even remember which one of them said that...' Simon's words choked off in laughter.

'He sounds like my bloody parents!' Martha's voice was at full volume for once.

Simon stopped laughing for a moment.

'Not yours too?' he asked softly, looking away from her at the worn carpet.

There was a silence.

'Yeah.'

'They're arseholes, aren't they?'

'Yeah.'

Simon shifted to the narrow bed and held out an arm to Martha. She hesitated, then relaxed sleepily into his shoulder, and they leaned back uncomfortably against the wall.

'I swear they always put these shitty beds in bedsits to stop the underclass from breeding.'

'Yeah, hard to procreate when you keep falling out of bed.' Martha agreed nervously. She still wasn't at home with the language, but it seemed the right etiquette to add:

'Wankers.'

'There is that option, yes.'

'That's not what I meant, Simon, and you know it.' she said severely, trying not to laugh.

'That Yosser Hughes was a tosser too, wasn't he? Making us all look like sad victims. Bollocks to that.'

'And what did all the nice clean Haircut 100 fans say?'

'Let's jump the Tube!'

Worn out from laughing, they sat in companionable silence. The only sound was the whistling of a blackbird in the overgrown garden outside.

'Martha? Can I ask you something really important?'

'Mmm?' she replied into his shoulder, barely conscious.

'Got any biscuits?'

The sound of their giggling was the last thing Martha heard that afternoon as she drifted back into sleep.

❄

'What's in here? What's in there?'

'Honestly Simon, you have the attention span of a – a gnat.'

'Well, I'm hungry. Got any rice? What's in the fridge? Oh – gross.'

'Hold on. Oh...gross.' The smell hit Martha and she too stood back.

'How long's it been there?' Simon regarded the mess from a distance.

'Uh...five weeks at least.'

'Dare we approach it?'

'Get the rubber gloves and heave it out.'

'Why me?' complained Simon, leaning in for another careful sniff.

'Cos I'm lending you a tenner.' Martha passed him the Marigolds from the side of the sink.

'Huh. Knew it'd be something like that.'

Simon approached the fridge cautiously, yellow gloves on, teatowel wrapped round his face like the Lone Ranger.

'Eurgh...oh my God it's stuck...'

'Don't be such a baby.'

'Stand by with the compost bucket, Mart.'

'We are go with compost bucket.'

'Here!' Splutch. Pale-green fungal spores puffed delicately up from the rotten tomato.

'Should have saved that one for Wally Woodgrove.'

'Our esteemed Member? Kerry already did him over.'

'She never!'

'Yeah. Egged him into the Stone Age. He made the elementary mistake of coming to gloat over his victims in St Pauls.'

'Wish I'd seen that.'

'You didn't want to smell it, believe me, Mart.'

'Grim.'

'I heard she kicked him in the esteemed member too.'

'No way! Don't they send you to the Tower or something for that? How did we get him for an MP anyway? Since when does anyone in St Pauls vote Tory?' said Martha.

'Aha, I hear you say, but we done got gerrymandered, didn't we?' Simon pulled off the gloves and threw them aside.

'Huh?'

'Yeah, they tweaked the boundaries so's we've got all the rich people from Redland, Bishopston and St Andrews in here with us as well as Lawrence Hill and Easton.'

'Which is getting gentrified faster than you can say chocolate-coated latte.' Martha frowned, remembering the girl with the too-clean woven hat in the back of Pete's van.

'Exactly. Rich old people vote, poor young ones don't.' Simon continued to open and shut the cupboard doors, searching every shelf hopefully but mostly finding crumbs and empty breadbags.

'Because we're all dodging the poll tax and the bloody Newbury sausage?' Martha stuck the lid back on the compost bin, trying not to think about the black, decomposed slime within.

'What is this sausage? Have you got any sausages?'

'Oh, it was what they called it when they bailed someone off the whole of the bypass route. Because the site was shaped like a sausage.'

'Ah, that's why Mott McDonalds were quoted in Construction News, saying 'It's all gone sausage-shaped.' '

'Were they?'

'You'd believe anything. But yeah, they reckoned the Newbury bypass would never get built. They thought you were going to win. So *have* you got any sausages?'

Martha didn't know what to say.

'Well, they were wrong, because we lost, and everything's dead, and we failed.'

'Hold up! You need food! Well, I need food, and you need beer and about two weeks sleep. What have you got?' They looked at the meagre haul on the kitchen counter.

What Martha had was: half a bag of rice, a tin of tomatoes and some vinegar.

'How much money have you got?' Simon asked diffidently.

'Dunno. Haven't looked since I got some cider two weeks ago. The campaign was feeding us. Spent a lot on train fares back and forth though. And I gave some to um, Will for a load of candles and rechargeable headlamp batteries.'

'Cool. So, so what've you got left?'

'Er...uh, loads. There's £30 in my wallet. Here's your tenner.'

'Thanks.' Simon folded it into his jeans pocket with a sigh.

'Ok, so a tenner on the electric and a tenner left for food til next Monday. We're there! Uh, what day is it today?' Martha hadn't looked at a clock for weeks, let alone a calendar.

'Tuesday. Let's roll, I'm starving.'

His gaunt cheekbones made Martha realise that he wasn't exaggerating that much.

They grabbed a couple of shopping bags and set off for the shops, scuffling through the mound of post that no one had picked up that week.

'Enough mail.'

'It's all junk.' Martha kicked a heap aside impatiently.

'This one's for you. Brown envelope.'

Martha's stomach clenched.

'DSS?'

'Er, nope, British Gas.'

'Almost as bad.'

Martha ripped it open and scanned the figures.

'You know that tenner I lent you?'

'Yeah, you don't want it back do you?'

'Oh – no, but when can you pay me back?' Martha hated to ask.

'Uh...Friday, when I get my Giro.'

'Great. Can you lend me a tenner on Friday as well?'

'Sure.'

'Cool, I'll manage then.'

Martha struggled with the sagging front door and they set off down the road. The rain had eased to a drizzle, pale sunlight glinting through.

'The pavement smells like wet dog.' she said in disgust. She'd forgotten the everyday stinks of the city.

'I know. At least the rain's washed some of the piss away.' Simon wrinkled his nose.

'Are we going to the dust shop then, Simon?'

'Have to. The ripoff minimarket is too far. And it's a rip-off.'

'Do you think some of those cans in the dust shop are antiques?'

'Yeah, they probably got them from Scott's expedition. Waste not, want not.'

'I hate the way you have to wipe the dust off to see the price.' Martha said.

'Which is always mysteriously high considering the can's from 1987.' Simon agreed.

❋

They settled back onto the bed with platefuls of curried elderly vegetables and cans of bitter.

'Who's Will?'

'Huh?' Martha was busy keeping curry out of her lap in the absence of a tray.

'You mentioned a Will. You said Um. You only say Um when you're nervous. Was he cute? Would I have liked him?'

'I'm nervous all the time. Um. He was just this bloke on the protest who lived up a tree.'

'You said Um again. You fancied him!' Simon cracked open his beercan and drank deeply with a sigh.

'He has a girlfriend.' Martha said automatically.

'Tough beans. That rules me out twice over. You did like him then?' Simon set down his can on the battered cabinet that served as a bedside table.

Martha was silent, considering.

'Was he nice?' Simon dropped the teasing note and looked at her with genuine curiousity.

'Yeah. He was nice to me. He didn't laugh at me for being scared of stuff. Yes, he was nice.'

'He must have been. You don't seem to like anyone much.'

Martha was shocked.

'I do – I do like people.'

81

'You can't love anyone if you're scared of everybody. You're too on the defensive all the time.'

'Well, you have to be! People are arseholes! You said it yourself!'

'Hang on. Here's your beer. Eat your dinner. I didn't mean you. I meant anyone. Me. Or anyone.'

Martha subsided, and took a swig of her can of Boddy's. Special offer, probably out of date.

'I opened it over the sink for you special cos it was dented.'

' 'Ank you.'

'You're welcome.' Simon began to eat, giving Martha chance to regain her composure.

Martha surfaced from the beer and the first forkful of dinner.

'Thanks Simon. I-I'm not really scared of you.'

'That may be the nicest thing anyone's ever said to me.'

'Sorry. You're nice too.'

'Not many other people think so.' Simon clinked his can against hers. 'Here's to us.'

'Dolie scum.'

'Weirdos.'

'And mental cases.'

They finished the beer, and sometime during the evening Martha had a giddy memory of staggering up the road in the rain to get more, Simon laughing and stumbling at her side.

❊

Morning. Pale, liverish daylight filtering through the ragged curtain illuminated the woodlouse who wandered across the boards and thin rug. Heading steadfastly toward the hallway where he'd find ample rotting wood to feast on, he was checked from time to time by the scattered wreckyard of the floor. He skirted a chilly huddle of empty beercans, pattered over a jumper full of holes that smelt of campfires, round books and comics, ashtrays made of stale bread and jamjars. He strolled past bookshelves made from bricks and planks, as if passing office blocks. Overspill piles of books were up to twelve stories high. *Stig of the Dump, Pride and Prejudice, The Bell Jar. Biological Sciences, Small is Beautiful, Silent Spring. Birds of*

Britain and Europe, The Secret Garden, The Glass Bead Game.
Cannery Row, Wyrd Sisters, An Anthropologist on Mars.
The Lost World. Z for Zachariah.
Trundling under the instep of a huge workboot, next to its partner -
the old woman who lived in a shoe gone semi-detached - he headed
under the door to dark, mouldy freedom.

Martha woke, surfaced, opened an eye, saw the bright yellow cover
of a Big Bang comic and hastily shut her eyes against the
psychedelic patterns. She felt luxuriously relaxed. Not quite ready
for Russell's weird and colourful world though.
She sat up, dislodging a lump of quilt which slithered to the floor.
She slipped out onto the bare boards, pulled on her jumper and
padded to the kitchen, pushing her feet into a pair of worn but
sparkly flipflops from the Sweet Mart. The kitchen floor was
freezing, as usual. She flip-flopped about, making coffee and
shuffling and stacking away last night's plates. She'd induced Simon
to help clear up in a burst of beer-fuelled energy last night. He'd
been incredulous, but had helped with a drunken will. The
housework equivalent of beer-legs. The sides were soon wiped
down, the tattered teatowel hung with geometric neatness. She found
an inexplicable tin of expensive biscuits on the counter and
remembered – Simon had found them sitting on a wall yesterday
evening and they were completely dry.
'Pretty good fruit of the wall tonight!' Simon had shouted over the
sound of a passing bus.
The crazed pink wall tiles fresh from a 1950s girls school toilet gave
on to mouldy walls that defied all cleaning efforts though. The black
and white lino tiles underfoot were cracked and peeling, and slug
trails crisscrossed the floor. Maybe they'll graze the mould, Martha
thought hopefully.

April sunshine found its way gradually into the dark little room. The
purity of spring sunlight arrested Martha, as it lit up the bunch of
flowers Simon had pinched from passing gardens last night and
poked into a jamjar of water on the windowsill. Light pouring
through the petals transformed them into the miniature architecture
of a cathedral, a temple, the Taj Mahal. She glanced out of the

83

window.   April skies, washed a clean blue after the rain.   Pink campion sprouted from the cracks in the shady back yard, raindrops glistening on leaftips.

A cathedral, a temple, the Taj Mahal.   Martha padded back to her room with her coffee.

The hall was hung with beige patterned wallpaper, bulging and peeling, brown waterstains over the front door, plaster fragments scattered over the cracked quarry tiles.   The doorframes showed signs of ancient violence, scarred and split.   Next door's looked like it had been kicked in at some time and patched with a different coloured bit of painted wood.

Old posters covered the rest of the shabby walls.   The Cure. Siouxsie and the Banshees.   Iggy, clutching a mike in both hands, the long-lost venue torn away at the ragged foot of the poster.

Martha's walls were covered with a creased collection of pictures of trees and birds cut from old magazines, as well as last year's protest flyers.   She looked at her favourite oak tree photo for a minute before padding back to bed and snuggling under her quilt, comforted by home.

Her thoughts drifted back over last night's conversation.

'What you need...what you need, girl, is a party.'   Simon had declared, around his third can.

Martha looked around.   She was drunk, well fed, spring had taken the winter chill off her room and the mould patch under the window had shrunk to its summer extent, like Arctic sea-ice.   Simon had brought her some discarded comics, and she was warmly wrapped in the knitted blanket that Morag had retrieved from the rubble of Tot Hill and engulfed her in, ready for the journey in Pete's broken-heatered van.   And she had company. Real, live, wonderful human company, a rarity in her lonely bedsit.   As far as Martha was concerned, this *was* a party.

'Proper fun. No more worrying about the state of the world.' he insisted.

'Don't know anyone who's having one.' Martha mumbled.   It would be more accurate to say, she didn't know anyone full stop.

'No obstacle. Something'll turn up.' Simon sighed with happiness as he cracked open another can and took that first frosty sip.

Martha thought about that. When she'd been new and alone in the village, Bridget had turned up. After she'd lost Bridget, there was still school, books, animals, trees.

No. For a few years nothing had turned up. She'd had to seal herself up in a tightly closed self-protective world of her own, armoured against the shouting, the smashing, the mocking, the scorn and contempt. She'd survived by constant watchfulness over every word and action. It was usually safest to do and say nothing, at home anyway, and at school she felt as if she had so much to hide, so much to keep in, that it wasn't safe to speak. She felt constantly self-conscious, painfully aware that she didn't match up. Afraid that if anyone got too near they'd find out what her mother already knew. She was useless, useless. And no one would ever want her.

But slowly, slowly, something had turned up.

Getting out of the village school where the teachers tapped their foreheads at her and the other kids laughed, after they'd given up trying to goad her with insults into speaking. The great good luck of landing in a school where the teachers were a bit younger and more progressive than most where she flourished, mute as ever but eloquent on paper at least. The surprised delight of her teachers spurred her on. She'd never experienced approval before, or seen what it could do for a person.

They didn't think she was useless, but. Sometimes Martha wondered if they were just patronising her because she was so silently shabby and unresponsive that any sign of life had to be encouraged. Until her exam results came and she realised that there might just be a future for her after all. A levels followed, then entrance to university and the long struggle to graduation.

Then the cliff-edge.

Martha took another swig but her can was empty. She cracked open the last one and looked meaningfully at Simon.

'Oh God, we're screwed. We'll have to do another beer run.' he said, laughing. 'We'll be buggered for money over the weekend. What the fuck.'

They found a wet fiver on the pavement by the bus stop. Something always turns up.

❋

'Kerry's here.'

Simon stuck his head round the open door.

'What?'

'Kerry. With a massive black eye. And a cabbage. And a kitten.'

'Wow.'

'Yeah. She doesn't do anything by halves, does she?'

Martha jumped up, trailing her knitted blanket.

'Come on up.' She followed Simon up to his room, hovered nervously on the threshold.

'Come in, then.'

She entered, looking around curiously. She'd never seen Simon's room before. And she couldn't really see it now for the mess. A huge desk covered with disembowelled computers and battered textbooks, the house's entire collection of coffee mugs herding around the keyboard. Pages of computer code were pinned untidily on the wall above the desk. Clothes and boots, books and plates mulched the floor. She picked her way through fastidiously and sat on the edge of a chair that was mostly a mound of clothes and computer mags.

'Here.' Simon handed her the cabbage.

'What's this, my new pet?' She held the cabbage, sniffed the fresh dewy smell of it. There was a fat green caterpillar between the leaves. She picked it out and dropped it out of the window into a bush. She'd forgotten what a fresh vegetable smelled like.

'How'd you get the shiner?' Simon asked Kerry.

Kerry sat on the bed grinning, pouring the black and white kitten from hand to hand. She was fresh faced, her hair flung back in

86

waves. Her eye had reached the greenish-yellow stage. She let the kitten go and stretched her legs in pink-flowered leggings from under a fringed skirt.

'Not the Met, incredibly. No, nature done this to me. I got punched by a tree.'

'What did the tree look like after?'

Kerry laughed. 'We were cutting bender poles down the valley and I bent this one back to get at the bottom with my bow saw, and I just leaned a bit too far and lost it and it smacked me one.'

'I expect its bark was worse than its bite.'

'So funny. Such a funny man. What you been up to in town then?'

'Oh, me and Michael coated – yes, coated the DSS with NO JSA stickers. They might have trouble getting the doors open Monday.'

'Cool! Still going, then?'

'Yeah, the Claimant's Union's gone a bit boring, it's all advice sessions and picketing the Jobcentres that're trialling benefit sanctions. But there's still work for an honest fly poster.'

Kerry frowned. 'They are such tossers. One minute they're saying fuck off and die poor person, next minute we're responsible for the end of Western civilization.'

'I know. I spent the last two years in a squat getting my dinner out of skips, but kept on studying for my access course and they still say I'm not trying hard enough.'

'You got a computer, then?' Kerry glanced at the desk.

'Yeah, I was a squeegee merchant for a bit.' Simon looked proud.

'Whoah! You criminal!'

'Yeah, I kept saving up all the 50ps until I got the computer second hand at St Nicks. I got the books out of a skip down the back of the library. They're out of date but they got me started. Once I can get hold of a modem I can get up to date off the internet.'

'Wows! You're gonna surf the net? Have you been on it yet?'

'A bit. Rich mates let me have a go sometimes.'

'Since when have you got rich mates?' Kerry asked.

'Since you and Mart took up road protesting. Ow! Your cat got my toes!'

'Oh, yeah, a lot of them did go to private school I guess.' Kerry caught the kitten, and cradled it on her lap, its eyelids drooping as it fell quickly into sleep, tiny paws outstretched.

'There - there was this bloke at Newbury who went to Winchester.' Martha ventured. She looked away from the kitten, frowning.

'Was that the one you were in love with Mart?'

'No! I mean - shut up Simon, I wasn't. It was Pete, that brought us back to Bristol. His dad's loaded.'

'Oh yeah, I know Pete. Some of them are loaded. I never met rich people before. There was this Tory councillor at Snelsmore Common for a bit. She was well-against the bypass and she just came and joined in. It was weird.' Kerry yawned and rubbed her face, wincing. 'Got any tea?'

'Yeah!'

'Put the kettle on Simon.' Kerry said.

'Hey! Why is it always me?'

'Cos we're knackered from saving the world and building benders and stuff.'

'Ok, Ok. Hey, we scored a load of free biscuits last night. I'll bring them up.' He bounced off down the stairs.

'So, how's it going?' Kerry turned to Martha.

'Oh, all right.' she mumbled shyly now that Simon was gone and the attention was on her.

'Miss the trees?' Kerry asked.

'Yeah! I miss being outside. I miss the - the blackbirds singing every morning above the treehouse.' Martha hugged the cabbage and looked away, out of the window.

'Fucking, fucking government. Ministry for Transport? More like Ministry for tree-killing. Can't believe it's all gone. Oh God, I don't want to think about it. What you gonna do now?'

'Dunno. Can't get a job. Tried for nearly two years. They called me into the Jobcentre for a bloody Restart interview. I took my folder with all my rejection letters and dumped it on their desk. I dropped it in front of them with this massive thump and they just looked at me.'

'How many you got?' Kerry glanced over at her as she scuffed her foot in the litter of Simon's floor.

'Must be – um - over the time – about three hundred. Not counting the ones that didn't answer. Most of them didn't answer.'
'Bastards. But you've got all those qualifications, haven't you?'
'Yeah. But graduate unemployment is five per cent higher than the rest. So I spent three years in college making myself less employable. They forget to tell you you'll be competing with all the rich kids.' Martha scowled at the wall, seeing the paper peeling at the corner.

'Oh. Yeah. Daddy gives them a job in his business over the summer then gets one of his mates that he was in the sandpit with to give them an internship.'
'Yeah, well, maybe I'm just no good.'
'I've seen your CV. Straight A's all the way. Science degree. Keyboard skills, voluntary work, all that stuff you did with the nature trust in the holidays. Impressive.' Kerry said.
'But no work experience. No confidence. No eye contact. Bloody panic attacks. Can't talk.' Martha said angrily.
'Bugger. Aren't they supposed to not discriminate anymore about stuff like that? Equal Opportunity Employers and all that? I thought they had a guaranteed interview scheme? I remember that from when I did a bit of voluntary work for CAB last year while I was waiting for Newbury to kick off.'

'Yes, in theory. But they were the ones who never wrote back, even.'
'Are the Job Centre any good for getting you some help?'
'You've got to be kidding, you go down and ask, and and they label you a *disabled claimant,* which is an exercise in humiliation anyway, and they send you on these courses where they teach you to write a CV and spell your own name.'
'I thought they always spelt your name wrong?' Kerry said.
'Yeah! They just assume that if you can't get a job it's because you've got no brains or education. If you're unemployed and qualified it just doesn't compute. They just stare past you because people like that don't exist. Maybe they think I'm just lazy, or lying about my qualifications.'
'But when you had that temp job in that factory didn't you have to lie about having a degree?'

89

'Yes, if they find out you've got any qualifications they won't take you on. I was desperate for some money that year. I was that close to getting the gas cut off and I needed boots. I'm no good at lying. I wasn't brought up that way. Took me ages to learn how to do it.'

'That's shit.' Kerry frowned. 'Bloody glad I never went to university now. What's the point? It's a waste of time.'
'Job-hunting's a waste of time.'
'Yeah. It's all a load of crap.' Kerry kicked the leg of Simon's desk.
'I just wish someone had taught me how to lie and cheat when I was a kid. They never told me how important it was going to be.' Martha said.
'Too right! I've had it with them. I'm going self-sufficient. Fuck 'em.' Kerry's expression brightened.
'Wow. I wish I could. I - used to live in the country. Grew up in a little village.' Martha said.
'Did you? Me too. Better than this dump. Where was it?'
Martha's face closed.
'Oh, off in the Midlands. Place no one's heard of.'

Kerry looked as if she was going to ask more, then changed the subject.
'After they chopped down that tree I was up, I went all weird for a bit. I was like shaky and crying all the time. And there were these hippies from Wales and they were heading up to Brynhelyn – that's up a massive hill in the Black Mountains – to blockade this opencasting shit. Reclaim the Valleys, where Selar Farm used to be. All that's left now is this massive hole, but there's still a camp up there and they're just getting in the way as much as they can. Anyway, they asked if I wanted to come and chill out with them for a bit. So I said all right, and I've been up there for a few weeks. Building a bender and getting attacked by trees. It's a laugh. You should come up.' Kerry recrossed her legs and looked at the neatly-sewn patches on her knees with satisfaction.
Martha thought of getting out of the city with longing. But would they really want her there?

'What – what are the people like?'

90

'Like? They're like hippies. All hippies are the same. They're Ok. They go on about leylines and smoke too much dope. But they're all right. They gave me Twinkle.' Kerry looked down at the kitten. 'Bloody stupid name, but it had sort of stuck by the time I got her. She's a cool cat. Made her first kill the other day. It was only a moth though!'
Martha looked at the kitten curled on Kerry's lap. It woke, yawned showing tiny teeth and a pink tongue, then sat up, paws tucked under, and looked at Martha with wide mustard-coloured eyes.

'Here. Have a go with the kitten. I'm going for a pee.' Kerry stood up, dumping the cat into Martha's hands. She took it reluctantly, held it awkwardly, avoiding contact. Twinkle wriggled away and jumped onto her knee, purring and treadling, sniffing her hands.
Martha looked at her. Hands encircled her tiny body. Lifted her up to her face. Sniffed the milky, clean scent of brand-new fur. Closed her eyes and held her tight, warm, soft, her tiny motor purring.

'She likes you then. Here's your tea.' Kerry was back, carrying cups and a plate of biscuits on a large flat book. 'Blue Peter Annual 1975. Came in handy.'
'I used to have that one.' Martha said. 'I used to know this girl who had loads of kittens. We were always reading together, and there were cats everywhere.'
'Oh yeah? Was that in your village? What was her name?' Kerry sat down and grabbed a handful of biscuits.
'Bridget.'

✳

7. Phantoms

Kerry shrugged her rucksack onto her back.

'Got your sleeping bag? Got your kitten?' Simon fussed around like a mother cat.
'Right here. She's had some valerian and skullcap. She'll be off her face for most of the journey.' The ball of black and white fur rose and fell gently in the inexpertly-woven wicker cat basket. There was a leafbud or two still sticking out here and there.
'You're experimenting on animals now?'
'Relax. I got them from Pete. He's a vet. Just got back to his practice.'
'Blimey. No wonder he was so good at looking after all you furry woodland animals.' Simon grinned as he peered out of the porch in the grey light of the afternoon.
'I'm off. Got to get the coach. No time to lose. See you.' Kerry stepped down to the path.

'Er, see you.' said Martha. 'Er...'
'What?'
'Er, er, did you mean it about coming up?' Martha hovered anxiously in the chilly hallway.
'Of course. Come anytime. Ask at the post office in Ystradgynlais and they'll point you to the camp. Or call my mobile.' Kerry flashed it proudly. 'Posh or what?'
'You got a Nokia? You'll be getting a briefcase next.' Simon hopped down the cold steps in his odd socks to give Kerry a hug and kiss.
'Bye! Take care! Don't take too many drugs!' he said.
'Bye! Bye Twinkle!' Martha grinned suddenly, waved shyly as Kerry headed off down the road carrying her home on her back like a snail.
'It's going to feel a bit flat now she's gone.' she said to Simon.
'Cheer up. You've still got the cabbage.'

Martha turned back into the house, even more thoughtful than usual.

'Did you hear what Kerry said just before she left?' Simon asked as they went back to the kitchen.

'No, I was getting the cat into the basket. What?' Martha said.

'Reclaim the Streets street party. Brum. Two weeks time. She said she'll be there. If we can get to Michael Wood services her and her mates will give us a lift. Party time! Told you, didn't I?'

'Birmingham?' Martha stopped.

'Yeah. Didn't you say you came from round there?'

'Yes.' Martha said unwillingly.

'Oh, yeah, home sucks, I know. Never mind, I doubt your mum'll be there!'

Martha scowled.

'I was joking!'

She avoided him for the rest of the evening. Later, when he knocked, she pretended to be asleep. She heard him sigh, hover outside for a few minutes in obvious uncertainty, then trudge back upstairs. She lay awake all night regretfully, feeling guilty.

❄

'You're awake. You were spark out when I knocked last night.'

'Oh – um – yeah. I was tired.' Martha said evasively.

'Tired of me and my big mouth?'

'No.'

'Liar.'

Martha turned a carefully blank face to Simon. He was avoiding her eyes as he buttered toast.

She tensed all over, waiting for the next move.

'You didn't answer this morning either, when I knew you were awake, I could see your lamp. You didn't speak to me when I came down. You don't want to go to Birmingham, do you?' he asked. He walked over to the table with his plate of toast and sat down.

Martha looked floorwards and away.

'No. I don't.' she said finally.

'Well, I do.' Simon stared at his plate moodily.

'Fine. You can go. I'm not stopping you.'

'If I say you need a party, you need a party.' He tried to jolly her along.

'Maybe *you* need a party.' she retaliated sulkily.

'Maybe I do. Maybe I need a lot of things. And maybe the world's not all about you.' Simon said flatly, unsmiling.

Martha froze. That's what you get for trusting people, she thought. Another kick in the teeth.

'I-I didn't think it was. No one has to do anything for me.' she retorted.

'Of course they don't. Of course they can see your fucked up life and not want to change it around for you. They want to see the pain you're in every day over the breakfast table.'

Martha was stricken.

'Yeah. That's the look I'm talking about.'

Martha couldn't understand why Simon was so angry all of a sudden. How did they get from parties to this in one jump? She tightened her lips and firmly screwed any tears back.

'You don't need to do anything for me. You don't have to put up with me. I'll keep away from you if that's what you want.' she said.

'Of course that's not what I want. You're just about the only friend I have.' he said angrily, shoving his plate into the clutter on the table. A piece of toast jumped off.

Martha stared.

'Yeah, you heard. And I've got a hangover. And I've run out of money. Don't worry, I can still give you that tenner back and lend you the gas money. I kept it back.'

'You don't have to do that for me.' Martha said.

'Don't I? If the gas goes off we're both screwed next winter. My meter's been off for weeks. If you don't pay your bill they'll put you on a prepayment meter as well then we can both freeze at the same time.' Simon still had a black look on his face.

'I didn't know.' Martha mumbled.

'You didn't know because you weren't here. You were off playing gypsies.'

'I was trying to save something. Anything.'

'Try saving yourself. Or me.'

94

Martha looked at his gaunt face and ragged jumper. At the way the strain in his dark-ringed eyes showed now that he wasn't smiling and the light of laughter had gone out.

'I – I'll try. To save you.'

He looked at her and tried to joke.

'Thanks. I thought I was going to have to stick leaves on my head before you'd notice that I was alive.'

'I'm sorry. The other protesters – they're not thinking of themselves. All they talk about is saving the earth.'

'Well, we're part of the earth, or haven't they noticed that? That lot don't need to think of themselves. They've got Rich Mummy and Daddy to do it for them.'

'They're not all rich!' Martha protested. She tried to tell him. About Johnny. About Sheila, who hadn't spoken to her mum in five years and had lived on bender sites since she was seventeen. About Harry, whose liver was just about gone.

'Sheila sounds cool.' was all he said.

'She was.' Martha said. She was sitting at the table too now, her chin propped on her hand.

'All right..all right, they're not all rich. But we aren't either.'

'I've still got a tenner left.' Martha said.

'Drinks are on you then.' Simon grinned. 'Sorry.' He sighed. 'Sorry. I didn't mean to have a go at you. But..I thought...I thought you'd never come back, you'd just bugger off with the hippies like Kerry did. Or get yourself killed.'

'Like she nearly did.'

'Fuck, yes. I kept seeing bits on Undercurrents videos and in the papers. I was just waiting for the headlines. I was scared shitless.'

'I didn't know. We felt like the rest of the world wasn't there. Anyway, I'm still alive. And I could do with some fun after that lot.' Martha admitted.

'Come to RTS.' Simon had a beseeching look on his face now, like a hungry cat.

'Ok.'

Martha sighed, remembering her vow never to go back, getting ready to break it because of the look on Simon's face. Life without Simon's simple happiness would be like life without sunshine. She sighed and chewed on a knuckle, remembering Catweazle blowing frantically on his thumb to aid one of his spells that didn't work.

'What are you doing?' Simon asked.

'Uh, polishing up my hitching thumb. Brum or bust.' she answered after a minute's thought.

'You reckon?'

She rubbed her thumb on her jumper and held it out to convince him.

'How else are we going to get to Michael Wood?'

'All right! I thought we'd have to go on some grim coach company's dungeon on wheels. We are going to *party!*'

The sun came out from behind the cloud and beamed.

'Strictly speaking, you mean an oubliette on wheels.'

'Stop being pedantic Mart, we're making important plans here.'

'How long since you've had a chance to party?'

'A long...a long time. Long.'

'Been broke?' Martha asked.

'Broke. Broke, broke, broke.' he answered absently.   He turned back to his cold, hard toast. 'This is horrible.'

'I'll do you an omelette.' Martha offered.

'Cheers! What are we going to do with the cabbage?' he asked.

'Oh, yeah. Bubble and squeak then.'

'Bring it on! Squeak away!' Simon's eyes lit up.

'You're back, then?'

'On form!' He jumped up and danced across the kitchen floor, hurling his cold toast into the compost bucket.

It was like living with a grouchy cat. One minute surly, scratching and clawing, next minute frisking across the floor in deerlike bounds, springing on and off furniture with hurrahs, then flopping out exhaustedly to do it all again in two hours time. Martha watched as Simon pranced and sang, then dropped himself into the battered armchair next to the moribund radiator and stretched out his legs, eyes closing.

'Do you want this grub?' she asked half an hour later, standing at the crusty gas stove scraping at a frying pan full of potatoes.

'Mmm. Wake me up when it's ready.' he answered drowsily.

Typical cat, Martha thought. Only wakes up for meals. She grinned as she chopped slices off the cabbage and dropped them into the frying pan. Fresh, green spring cabbage. No withered outer leaves. No mould developing on the stem. She bunged in a couple of undersized chillis that she'd grown on the windowsill last year and remembered that there was a straggly herb patch at the back of the yard. She slipped into her Baghdad-bazaar flipflops and shuffled out to get some. The pan sizzled, giving out lovely smells. Simon stirred in his sleep, and his eyes sprang open as Martha handed him a bowlful of hot savoury breakfast.

'This is the business.' He engulfed the bowl and came back for more. 'I'm going to let you cook again!'
'Ooh, thanks.' said Martha. She wanted to be sarcastic but didn't have the heart.
'I got those herbs out of the yard. Shall we plant some stuff out there this year? We could grow a bit of food.' she said.
'Out there? It's a bit dank.' he said doubtfully.
'I could make some pots. It'd be Ok.'
'I don't do gardening. I can go skipping when Michael comes back with his car though.'
'Who's Michael?'
'Oh, he's this guy I used to squat with. He's the station-master.'
'Oh, I see.' said Martha, who didn't.
'He's been across the water, like, to see his dad. You'll meet him when he comes back.'
'Oh, Ok. Shall we take him to RTS?'
'I shouldn't. Drinks like a fish. Solitary type really.'
'Doesn't the rail company have a problem with that? Which station does he work at?' Martha said.
'You'll see.' Simon grinned.
'Want to help with the washing up?'
Groan. Sigh.
'Go on then.'

❊

There was a twittering outside the window. Martha opened her eyes to a pale dawn. The furniture still looked grainy in the dimness. Twitter, twitter, twit-twit. She recognised that sound. She jumped out of bed and looked out of the window.

Swallows. Twittering, swooping above the yard. Three of them. One swallow doesn't make a summer. Three of them do. One perched unsteadily on the washing line for a moment, then off. The garden wouldn't make a nesting site for them. They needed wide open insect filled skies, pools to swoop over, big old houses to find crannies to nest in. They were just passing through on the way to Eastville Park, only to be seen high up and far off on summer evenings, wheeling round the sky.

But still, they were here. A scatter of sparrows tumbled about in the snowberry bushes, a robin pecked about under the hedgeline. A blackbird whistled up the sun, high in the scrawny ash tree that staggered out of the ragged hawthorn hedge at the back of the garden. Martha watched him, dreaming. If she shut her eyes she could pretend it was the country. A bus rumbled past on City Road, followed by the sound of a bin lorry hitting the loose manhole cover in the street out front with a boneshaking thump. Roaring engines, a smoke alarm peeping shrilly from someone's kitchen. Shit, the toast's burning! Simon must be up.

He was. It was Martha's turn to loll in the armchair watching him scrape toast, apply butter and Marmite and hand a slice to her.

'Mmn thanks. I'm still asleep.'

'Don't blame me, blame Kerry. She was the one who said eight o'clock.'

'Do you reckon we'll make it?'

'Yeah. If we start from the end of Mina Road. It wouldn't work if Mina wasn't a rat run. You'd think that people would use Ashley Road to get onto the M32 but enough people come down Mina Road to get on the motorway, and we shall catch them.'

'Ok.' Martha munched her toast with one hand and had a last minute check through her rucksack with the other.

Simon was rummaging in the recycling. He pulled out a piece of old cardboard box from the box that only got emptied when someone could be bothered to tie it to the back of a bike and pedal it down to the recycling skips at Tesco's.

'Here, you can make us a sign.' he said, passing her a magic marker out of the drawer that was full of candles and screwdrivers. 'Just M5 will do.'

Martha drew the huge M and 5 and her pen squeaked around colouring them in peacefully. It was like doing a colouring book. These broad markers were better than the thin ones she'd had as a kid, she remembered. She carefully replaced the cap to stop the pen from drying up.

'Put your things away! Don't let me trip over them! If I find one item on that floor you'll be for it!'

Martha still tidied neurotically but life at camps and bedsits was slowly teaching her some tolerance for a bit of mess. No longer did she tense up and start to spiral into panic if there were dirty pots all over the kitchen, or dismantled bikes or bundles of washing on the floor. Nevertheless she put the pen tidily into its drawer and checked and rechecked that the cap was on.

'Look at this pen! Where's the top? Don't expect me to buy more once you've ruined them. Kids, kids, bloody kids, nothing but mess and waste and noise, what did I do to deserve you?'

What indeed, she thought, pushing the memory violently away. And today I'll be back in the Midlands. Within twenty miles of her. No, within twenty miles of the dark, poisoned spot on the map where she used to be. The spot which pushed her thoughts away like a magnetic monopole whenever she accidentally thought of it. A sore, a sore that she didn't know how to heal. She finished her toast broodily, answered vaguely when Simon spoke.

'Right, let's do one then.' he said, pulling on his enormous work boots and tying the knotted-together laces hastily. 'Come on.'

They swung up rucksacks, grabbed the sign and left the shabby kitchen, clicking out the dim, dusty bulb as they went. The sun was barely up and the sky a washed-out pink. They trotted quickly along City Road, rucksacks bouncing, beginning to be filled with excitement. Martha gave a little skip now and again to keep up. She remembered doing the same on adventures with Bridget, who had longer legs and strode as fast as her brothers.

Bridget. What was she thinking about all that for.

Streetlights blinked off as they passed. Dogs howled in distant yards. A police siren rose wailing somewhere not far away. The roads were quiet.

Too quiet. They stood at the exit of Mina Road holding up their bit of cardboard hopefully. No one was passing by.

'Are you sure this is going to work?' Martha asked.

'Course.'

'But there's no one out yet. I told you half past five's too early.'

'It'll be Ok.' Simon assured her. She stood shivering, doubting, watching the sun rise ruddy-gold and majestic over Easton, flushing the few tree trunks, gilding their sparse spring foliage, gleaming off odd bits of chrome on the barricade of old fridges around the derelict house near the junction.

Cars began to flow with the sunrise, as if warmed and drawn out of their night roosts. Soon Martha and Simon were coughing and having trouble hearing each other.

'Turn this way. Look at them!'

'What?'

'Look at the traffic!'

Martha looked up unwillingly and tried to look cheerful and bright and only temporarily poor, shying away from eye contact with the drivers.

'You shouldn't have worn that coat.' Simon looked at her critically.

'What's wrong with it?'

'What's wrong with it? It makes you look like a tramp who sleeps in haystacks and steals chickens.'

Martha pushed her hands into the pockets of her worn, shiny Barbour.

'It's really warm. And it doesn't leak.' she said defensively. She surreptitiously flicked away a twig that she found.

'Yeah, and how many poached rabbits have you got in that pocket?'

'It's my egg sandwiches.'

'Poached egg?'

'Boiled, you prat!'

'Ooh, I'm cut to the heart! Give me that sign!'

Simon held it up, smiled winningly, which in Martha's opinion served to make him look yet more like a crazy man in his long black coat with the tattered hem. He stuck out a thumb just to clarify the situation. A red car drew up.

'Wow! I am the business! Come on!'

They hurried forward, the driver wound down the window.

'Going far?'

'Michael Wood services.'

'I'm on the way to Gloucester. I can drop you there.'

'Cool, thanks!'

They jumped in, Martha headed for the back, leaving Simon to talk to the driver.

❅

An hour later they stood under the porch at Michael Wood services, smelling the overpriced, grey service station coffee that they couldn't afford.

'God, I could murder a coffee.' sighed Simon's caffeine addiction.

'So let's have one.'

'Duh! We could eat for a week on what it costs for a cup of coffee and a bun in there.'

'That's why we're going to make our own.' Martha assured him. 'Come on.'

She pushed into the bushes to the side of the lorry park.

'Where are you going?' Simon demanded.

She didn't answer, but started picking up twigs. She pulled what looked like a large catering size bean tin out of her rucksack. A camp kettle. A jar of coffee.

'Here, fill the kettle up.'

Simon took the kettle dubiously.

'What are you doing?'

'Making you a coffee. Go and fill the kettle up.'

Simon gave up and scampered back over the car park heading for the toilets, where water, at least, was free. When he came panting back

101

Martha had laid a neat fire within the base of the bean tin thing and had it blazing. Smoke twirled out of the central chimney. It was a pocket stove. Simon balanced the kettle carefully on top. It was whistling in a couple of minutes.

'Wow, good one!' he said, as Martha stirred hot water into a cup and handed him his coffee. "What do you call that?"
'It's a rocket stove. They designed them for poor countries. They don't use much wood and they heat up really quickly. You just take a pair of tin snips to some bean tins.'
'Cool. You really are a crusty.'
'I'll take that as a compliment.' Martha swigged her own coffee as they sat comfortably on a low grassy mound. A passing driver stared at them curiously as his car crawled past.
'Kerry should be here soon.'
'Yeah, if she's not late. If she hasn't forgotten us.'
'It'll be Ok. I went down the phone box and called her on her mobile last night.'
'God, that must have cost a fortune.' Simon said.
'I know, but we had to make sure. We only said hello and just confirmed eight o'clock.'
'They're good, those phones. Wish I could afford one.'
'Not going to happen anytime soon. Kerry bought hers when she had all those cleaning jobs in Cotham. But she was squatting so she didn't have to pay rent. She saved up quite a bit then.' A huge lorry rumbled up, dust and diesel fumes blowing their way. The wheel arch was higher than Simon's head.

They packed up hastily, emptied the dregs of the kettle into the bushes and wandered out into the open again.
'What colour's their van?' Simon asked.
'Dunno.'
'Could it be blue with pink flowers?'
'Doubt it. They all stopped painting their vans funny colours to put the police off the scent after the Beanfield.' Martha scanned the car park anxiously.
'Could it be white with rust spots and Kerry leaning out of the window?'

'Yeah!'

They ran over. Kerry was shouting.
'Hiya! Hiya! We nearly took off on the Severn Bridge. Windy as hell. Thought we were going swimming.'
Kerry was laughing, rosy faced.
'I've got to have a pee. Jump in the back, be back in a minute. Been waiting ages.' She galloped off towards the service station. Rowan, the driver, smiled at them but remained silent.
They climbed aboard and found seats among the bedrolls and rucksacks. Several demi-johns of home made cider clinked among them. They nestled down and ate egg sandwiches, and Martha soon nodded off among the boots and bags.

She awoke to find them on the outskirts of Birmingham, going up the endless Bristol Road, past the University with its clock tower and the faint scent of chocolate that surrounded Bournville, past countless shabby townhouses like the one they lived in. Row of houses, corner shop, hairdressers, pub, then repeat.
Edgbaston Cricket Ground. Cannon Hill Park. A froth of young tree foliage and a sparkle of water. Then terraces blocked the view again.

'We're nearly there. There, next right turn – Moseley. Park up anywhere you can.' Kerry told Rowan.
They jumped out into warm spring sunshine that gleamed on a street of red brick houses and poplars just coming into leaf.
'Which way is it?'
'Hang on Simon, let's just get our tat out. Here. You can carry the cider.' Kerry was pulling out bags from the side door of the van.
'Oh, yeah, Ok, heave the flagon out and give it me.' Simon put it in the army satchel he'd just pulled out of his rucksack pocket and slung it over his shoulder, looking like a pirate come ashore.

Martha left her rucksack, grabbed her shoulder bag and jumped out excitedly.
'Where are we meeting?' she asked Kerry.

'Just outside the Fighting Cocks on the Triangle. The first lot are gonna surge onto the road from there. There's a load more lurking down the side roads as well with the sound system.'

Martha looked around. There was nothing familiar about this part of town. She was glad. Rowan grabbed his bag and another demi-john and locked up. They strode quickly down the road to the junction, talking and laughing. Their voices rang out along the quiet tree-lined streets.

'How's the camp?' she asked Kerry.

'It's Ok. We put up another treehouse. It's a bit ropy. Ash keeps going on about starting a smallholding.'

'Can you?'

'Not there. It's all cash crop. It's really dark under those larches. The cash crop's useful for teepee poles though. We just go in with a bowsaw and bag a few small ones. Just thinnings.' Kerry said.

'So where could they go to start a bit of farm?' Martha said.

'Ash keeps talking about this farmer he knows further down the valley. He helps him with the sheep sometimes. They get really skittish when Emrys's rounding them up whenever one of those Phantom jets comes swooping down the valley breaking the sound barrier. There's an old stone quarry down there. One of Ash's mates is going over next week to see if he can build a hut up there. Emrys won't mind he reckons.'

'A stone hut?' Martha asked.

'No, just wood and junk and stuff. But there's room for a lot of garden up in the fields, and Emrys might let them use a bit.' Kerry said.

'Wow, that'd be good. I wish I could do something like that. I want to grow some stuff in the yard this year but there's not much room and there's a lot of concrete.'

'Raised beds.' Kerry said. 'We do them on the mountain, the soil's so thin you have to build it up.'

'Yeah, that's what I thought. Get some skip wood and knock some up.' said Martha.

'Get Simon to help.' Kerry looked ahead as she strode along, her eyes scanning for a first glimpse of the protest.

'He says he doesn't do gardening.' Martha said doubtfully.

'He's a lazy bugger. Bet he does eating.' Kerry laughed. 'Simon! Give us a swig of cider!'

Simon came back and they decanted some cider into a handful of smaller bottles with difficulty.

'Here you go. Refuel when you need to. The Brynhelyn crew did a load of cider last year. This guy in the village built a cider press'.

'Where did they get the apples?' Martha asked. She couldn't imagine apple trees growing on a mountain.

'Just people round about the valleys with trees in their gardens, most of them had more than they knew what to do with. We took them some cider after.'

'Is this them?' Martha pointed to a brightly-coloured crowd ahead.

'Yeah, here we are! Oh wow, it's Sarah and Mel! Come on!'

They ran down the last stretch of the road, and hurried to be absorbed into the crowd on the Triangle. More people were coming out of the Fighting Cocks, a large run-down pub on the high street. They joined the group and were quickly absorbed into the throng, panting and looking at each other with bright, nervous grins.

'Hi everybody, can everyone hear?' Mel held a megaphone and stood on a flower tub to be heard.

'Right. You all know why we're here.' she thundered, then stopped, fiddled with the megaphone and started again at a lower volume. 'Because we're sick of choking on fumes. Having nowhere safe for kids to play. Having most of the public space in cities given over to cars. Being scared to cross the road. Communities divided by urban motorways. And piss-poor public transport.' She stopped to draw a breath, teetering on the flower box. 'So, just for one day we're gonna see what a city that's not ruled by cars looks like. We're going to reclaim the streets!'

Cheers.

'This government loves cars and hates people so much that they're not content with the bloody carnage we already get everyday. They've got the biggest roadbuilding scheme since the Romans going on, and some of us have been fighting it!'

Louder cheers and whoops.

'You all know what they did at Newbury, at Stanworth Valley, at Solsbury Hill, at Twyford Down, and what they're continuing to do all over the country! Yes. Build more bloody roads to generate more traffic to make more money for the car lobby to get filthy rich and move into their lovely chocolate box villages in the Cotswolds, leaving the rest of us to choke on their shit and see our communities ruined. So today's our day to reclaim a bit of what's ours. Are you with me?'

'Yeah!!' The cheering rose to a deafening roar.

'So let's go! The sound system is coming...let's do it!' Mel hopped off the box, and the megaphone dropped to her side. She and the others around her moved slowly into the middle of the road. The rest of the crowd followed, spreading out across the road.

They waited for the lights to turn red, then surged as one, like a huge bus made of people, into the centre of the junction. Some sat down straight away, some milled nervously on the outskirts, waving placards, weaving streamers in and out of lamp posts and boxes to mark out a party space. Martha could hear a Levellers song in the distance. The sound got closer, she could feel the bass, her feet started dancing, everyone cheered as the sound system hove into view. She heard gasps and laughter as the pedal-powered road train, made of several bikes knocked together with big yellow and green flowers surrounding the speakers trundled into view.

'We're running down the heartless concrete streets, chasing our ideas – Run!'

Martha was lost in a dancing, jumping, laughing, singing crowd. Motorists sat bewildered at the traffic lights which continued to flick red, amber, green, but nothing was moving. Police sirens sounded in the distance. The party cheered them on, people were unfolding tables and setting out food and stalls full of Earth First! leaflets.

'More cider! More cider! This is a cider-powered sound system!'

Simon was up on the lead bike, pedalling away, sweat dripping off his brow. Martha refilled his bottle and poured a bit down him.

'Cheers!'

'How long are you going to keep it up?' Martha said, grinning at his jerking, ungainly long arms and legs.
'All night baby!'

After ten more minutes he fell off the saddle, laughing, and Kerry took over.

The police had arrived, and were trying to herd people to the side of the road.

'Clear the road please. You've had your say, you've made your protest, now we need to keep the traffic moving. Over to this side, please.'

The party took as much notice of them as if they had been bluebottles. Probably less. A small group was being pushed towards the pavement. Martha nudged Sarah and they ran over to help.

'Quick, sit down! Ok now all link arms and bundle on the ground.'

The police milled around, baffled by the lump of humanity before them. They tugged doubtfully at an arm or two, releasing shrieks and protests. They stood back and spoke into their radios. In the silence that had fallen since the traffic stopped a dunnock sang out sweet and true, suddenly. Heads of seated protesters turned to see where the song was coming from.

'All right. All right. If you don't clear this area immediately we will be arresting you for obstruction of the highway.'

'These traffic jams obstruct the highway! Every night at five o'clock!' someone shouted.

'Yeah, there's no room for our sound system!' yelled Kerry.

'I want to play football!' squeaked a little boy in face paint. His sisters laughed and they began to roll around on the road, repeating 'obstructing the highway, obstructing the highway...what does obstructing mean, Mum?'

'Getting in the way.' a woman with beaded braids and a patterned headscarf answered with a laugh.

'Mum, can I obstruct the highway to not go to school?'

Laughter.

'Er, we'll talk about that later.' the woman said, flushing and smiling.

'If you don't move immediately we will begin to make arrests. This is your final warning.' The police began to move with purpose.

Sarah and Martha clung together, there was a roar behind them. The seas of people parted to let through an electric milk float in full party regalia. Everyone jumped up to make room, and the drummers riding on top began to beat their djembes in a powerful rhythm, booming out over the town, mind altering. The party danced around the milk float, transported, police forgotten. The little boy pulled his football out of his mum's bag and was off, scoring a goal against the police car that was bogged in partygoers. Bam!

'Hey!' A couple of officers moved towards him.

'Hey, hey, lay off, he's a kid, he's a kid.' The crowd moved faster than anyone would have thought possible, shielding the boy. 'That was a goal fair and square. You can't send him off!'

Everybody laughed, Sarah sent a bottle of cider circulating round hand to hand. Martha looked around to see a fresh phalanx of protesters emerge from Woodbridge Road onto the main road. The police were caught in the middle, and it was their turn to feel vulnerable.

Sarah walked across and said to one of them:

'Cheer up. You're welcome to join the party. Have a drink, we won't tell anyone, honest.'

The constable stared ahead, wooden faced. A younger colleague next to him flashed a grin, then quickly wiped his face blank. Some of them tapped their fingers against their blue trouser legs. The beat was irresistible. The officer in charge was deep in conversation with Mel. Mel swung away and looked around the scene casually. She turned back.

'There's a lot more to come, yeah, we'll be here a while. I should relax if I were you. We're here to stay.'

The police sergeant muttered something Martha couldn't hear.

'Well, yeah but you can't arrest all of us. Why not just enjoy the party. Surely you don't want all these cars ruining the city? We might save a few accidents today'.

The sergeant ran a hand over his cap, put his hands on his hips, turned on the spot to take in the scene. He mumbled into his radio. There was a pause.

'Are you the organiser?' he asked Mel.
'No, we don't have leaders. I just spontaneously decided to come down here today to have a party and all these people turned up. Serendipity can be a beautiful thing, can't it?'
The sergeant looked disgruntled, and spoke privately to Mel, then turned and walked off back to his squad.
Mel jumped back up to her flower box.
'Attention everybody! The police have accepted that we are here and we aren't going. They're going to back off and allow the party to take place. Congratulations! We've reclaimed the streets!'
Huge cheer.

'There's only one way of life, and that's your own, your own, your own,
There's only one way of life, and that's your own, your own, your own,
That's your own..'

Mel was looking up at a lamp post.
'What's on your mind?' Martha asked.
'The cops'll be back in a few hours. They always let you have the first round, but they might wade in later on when there's less people here. Or they might leave it. You can never tell. But if we get some people up lamp posts they'll probably bugger off and leave us alone. I want to have a laugh and catch up with Sarah. Don't want to have to spend the whole day looking over my shoulder.'
'How about here?' There was a lamp post on the central Triangle opposite one on the pavement outside the Fighting Cocks.
'Yeah, that'd do. We can stretch a rope right across and people can have a dangle on it if it looks like we need them.' Mel mopped her face, let out a breath. 'Phew! God, I hate talking to the pigs.'

'Got any harness?' Martha was studying the lamp post measuringly.
'Yeah, a couple. You take one and I'll do the other. Get Kerry to chuck the rope up to us once we're up'. Mel looked round for Kerry and saw her still pedalling the sound system.
'Ok.' agreed Martha. She took the jingling harness and stepped quickly into it, looking over her shoulder. She buckled, twiddled and

turned expertly and, knotting a couple of bits of cord together, wrapped her prussik loops round the lamp post and shinned up.

'Bloody hell ! You didn't need to go that far up!' Mel was laughing from the other side of the road. She was about eight feet up, tying on the rope flung up to her.
Martha looked down, surprised. She had been looking with interest at the lens of the lamp, full of tiny spider webs.
'Oh, yeah, sorry. Coming down.'
She tied a short line to the top of the lamp post and used her figure eight, legs dangling as she slid down, to hang about ten feet up, waiting for the other end of the rope. She looked down. A hand was holding the rope end up to her. A hand with a bubble-gum tattoo on the wrist. A green and blue butterfly.

The green and blue butterfly. The bubble gum tattoo that she and Bridget used to fight over at first, then stick everywhere once they'd built up a collection. Martha stared, forgetting to take the rope.
'Here y'are then.' urged the woman at the foot of her lamp post. The tall, gum-chewing woman. The woman with the messy long dark curly hair and crooked incisor on the left hand side.
Martha stared on.
'Bridge?' She said it out loud without meaning to.
She jerked and bobbed lower, reaching for the proffered rope automatically, then prussiking up the post again to tie it firmly. She looked back down. The woman was staring up at her.
'Do I know you?' the woman asked finally.
'Er, I'm Martha.' admitted Martha.
'You're Martha? *You're* Martha? Up there? You're kidding me. Sorry, you looked a bit like someone I used to go to school with!'
'Bridge?' Martha said again, because it couldn't really be her and it was safe to do so.
'Yeah, I'm Bridge. Who are you?'
'I'm Martha.'
'Jeez.'

Martha slid rapidly down her abseil line, burning her fingers. 'You *are* Bridge.' she said.

110

She reached a finger out to the tattoo, but didn't touch it. She pushed her glasses up her nose.

'You always wanted the butterfly.'

Bridget stared, at a loss for words, a thing that did not happen often in the past.

'You can't be her. She's shit scared of heights.'

'I've been on the road protests. They taught me to climb.'

'Fuckin' hell! I can't believe it! Martha! Hey look Mick, it's Martha!'

'Oh yeah, I remember,' said a punk with a red mohican and a can of lager, 'Martha the Mouse.'

'Since when's that my name?' Martha asked, annoyed already and they'd only been talking for two minutes.

'Oh..Yeah, sorry, you know, we hadn't talked for like years and you know how it is..'

'Can't say I do.' Martha said icily. 'Anyway I have to finish this and get back to my friends.'

She stalked away to check the tension of the rope, gave up her harness to Sarah who was itching to try it out and make sure she hadn't forgotten her climbing skills, and headed over to Simon and a top up of cider.

'Friends? She has friends?' she heard Bridge ask herself in amazement.

'I thought you said she couldn't talk.' said the roostered punk critically. 'I remember she never said anything and went around with a kitten on her shoulder like a nut. Like Wurzel Gummidge or the Crow Man or something.'

Martha's ears burned as she recrossed the road to give Simon a swig of cider. Bridge. It's Bridge. She felt slightly faint, unreal.

'Mick. Do me a favour. Shut up.' she heard faintly. She was aware of being watched. She caught sight of herself in a shop window. A thin, straight haired girl in leggings under a short embroidered skirt and black Cure T-shirt, chatting and laughing with some tall dark guy who looked like a film star. She looked back at Simon in surprise. Do we really look like that? Simon laughed at this hat, she thought, pushing back the broad brim of the black felt with the homewoven

band. Bridge looked so different. But the same. Do I? Am I still the same?
'What did you say?' she asked Simon.
'Who's that?'
'Oh, it's this girl I went to school with.' she answered.
'Oh yeah?' Simon tried to sound offhand.
'Yeah.'

Kerry scampered up, out of breath as usual.
'Who's that?'
'We've already done that. It's an old school friend of Martha's.'
Simon pushed back his dripping hair and glugged on his cider bottle.
'What's her name?'
'Oh, uh - Bridget.' Martha said uneasily, turning away.
'That's Bridget?' Kerry was immediately interested.
'Yes.' said Martha tersely, and walked over to Simon again. 'Give us a swig.'
'Ok. I get it. Mind me own business. Come on, let's do some more dancing. The rope's good now. Don't let the kids climb it.'
Martha looked back into the distorting window reflection with its dimmed colours. She saw a shadowy Simon watching Mick, and turned away so as not to have to watch him drift towards the other side of the road with a bottle in his hand.

❊

I couldn't believe it was Mart hanging off that harness. But it was her cowering timorous beastie eyes all right. She may have got bolder, those hippies may have shown her the ropes and stuff, but she hadn't changed all that much. I'd have known her. I didn't need her to remind me how she always wanted the butterfly tat out of the bubble gum packet. We'd have arms like pirates after a long afternoon of bubble blowing under the willow.
But green and blue butterflies were rare. And a perfect tattoo transfer was rarer still. You had to stick it on and press it so carefully, too much pressure and the whole thing just crumpled. They were fragile, those butterflies. If you mucked it up, that was it

until you got another turn at the butterfly one. If you got another turn.

I made sure of mine. The minute I turned eighteen – well, I was seventeen really but don't tell Ted's Tattoos – I got the green and blue butterfly done, alighting on my wrist, mine, forever.

It's been harder than I thought writing all Mart's story. I keep remembering stuff I'd forgotten. And some things sort of look different after all this time. Even by Birmingham RTS the past had kind of – evolved – in my mind when I came to look back on it.

I was mad, so mad, seeing her again. I lost everything because of her, her and her 'I'm scared of everything.' Some of us don't have the luxury of being scared. Some of us have to be tough to survive. Little Miss Martha Mouse with her respectable family and their tidy garden and their tidy house – what I could see through the window and from Mart's descriptions – and her summer dresses that her mother made her. All right, they were all droopy on her, but catch my mum making me a dress when I could wear Mick's old jeans and Robert's old jumpers, Sean's old trainers and Joe's old T shirts that came down to my knees.

She'd never be able to understand – getting caught means getting walloped. And getting caught with those bits of good planking that my dad had been saving for ages at the back of the shed, the bits that made such a brilliant floor in the treehouse, meant getting walloped big time.

It was her fault. My dad was all right long's you didn't rile him too much. Keep your head down, use your loaf, run for it when you have to, have a few good hideouts, and you were Ok. You just had to know when one of his moods was about to rip through the house, like the Phantom jets that used to break the sound barrier over the village, huge, black triangles gliding silently past like shark's fins, but always with the following roar that ripped the sky apart.

But when you've got some wet drip hanging around who gets you caught red-handed...

Mick would never have dobbed me in. But Robert was a right bastard. Nearly sixteen and shaping up to be just like our dad. Even growling at our mum and slamming his plate back down if his dinner was a bit cold.

If she'd just moved it when I heard him coming. If I hadn't got down to help her up the yew. If she just got it, if she wasn't so dim, if she wasn't such a drip. We'd have still been in the village instead of bloody Acock's Green.

Acock's Green! Sounds more like an STD than what it was, a boring grey suburb of Birmingham. You don't get much choice when it's emergency housing.

I never saw the silly cow again before we left. Didn't bloody want to either.

If it wasn't for her I'd still be in the village.

Under the willow tree.

With Martha.

If it wasn't for Simon I might have never spoken to her again.

❄

8. Thawing.

'Why Simon?   It was me who got you two talking again.'   Kerry objected.   She put my manuscript aside and went back to scraping mud off her boots.

We sat in weak April sunshine outside the polytunnel.   A few pocked, grubby patches of snow still lay in the shade of the hedge.

'You know your whole poly leans gently to one side, like a jelly on a plate that's a bit slanted?'   Kerry cocked her head on one side as she looked at it.

'Yes I do know that actually.'   I replied with dignity.   'I had to put it up by myself and it was a windy day.'

'You put up a twenty-foot poly single-handed?   Why didn't you ask for some help?' asked Kerry, amazed.   She looked around the plot.   It was mostly still sheeted with black mulch mats but the ragged remains of winter crops still showed at the far side.

'I did.'   I said shortly.

'Anyway,'   said Kerry, caught between two argumentative stools, 'how come I don't get credit for sorting you and Martha out?   If it wasn't for me you'd have gone off without another word to her.'

'Simon was the one who got her to Birmingham.   And he was the one who talked Mick into getting me to, you know, apologise about all the – you know - rodent stuff.'   I was still ashamed of that Martha the Mouse crack, actually, looking back.   Because although we'd called her that for years and had a whole raft of cheese and cat jokes, it was me that started it, after we got exiled to Acocks not-a-bloody-blade-of-grass Green.

'And I thought it was my brilliant plan to entice you with all my best treehouse stories, after Mart let slip that you were massively into them.'   Kerry said.

I brightened up. I did love the treetop tales. Wish I'd been there, in a way.   But I'd have gone batshit crazy when a bunch of thickwits came to cut them down. It hurt, really hurt, writing the bits about that.

'Yeah,' I conceded, 'you were pretty cool that night. And – and the camping on Cannon Hill Park, that was a great idea.'

'Yes. *My* idea!' said Kerry. She threw her boots aside and came to sit next to me on the lumpy grass.

'Yeah, me and Mick were too pissed to ride our bikes and I was sick of kipping on his sofa anyway.'

'Camping in the rugged wilderness of Brum.' Kerry said. 'They say people never see their own town,' yawn, 'as a tourist destination.' She stretched out her legs.

'Yeah, the wild West Midlands.' I started to laugh. 'D'you remember when Simon heard that lynx snarl in the darkness and screamed like a little girl?'

Kerry was laughing too. 'Well, it was a bit tight of you to park us right in the bushes behind the nature centre and not tell anyone they were there.'

'It was funny though.' I reflected. 'I used to like going there. You never see British wild animals in zoos usually. I hate zoos, but still it was good to see stuff like wildcats and snowy owls that you never see anywhere else. And those red squirrels with their ear fur all done with crimpers.'

'Oh yeah, I remember. Spot the girl who used to hang out with Goths.' Kerry relaxed back on her elbows.

'I lit a good fire that night. No smoke.' I sat up, cross-legged, alert, looking into memory's distance.

'No smoke without fire. But you can have fire without smoke.' mused Kerry sleepily, drifting off as she lay in the afternoon sunshine.

It was all fire that evening, I remembered.

'*Pssst!*'
'*Yeah, I am.*' chuckled Mick.
'*Shush.*'

Giggles rippled through the cider-soaked group as they stumbled into the clearing deep in the bushes, thrashing about in the branches.

'I damn near pissed myself! You could have warned me!' came indignantly.

'It's the Lynx effect!'

'You bastard.' Simon complained. 'That's not funny.'

'Shush, Simon. C'me here, si'down, I put th' blanket down over here.'

Simon wobbled over and collapsed with a long loud breath on the old pink blanket.

'Over here, Mick. Quiet now. Ge' down there next to Simon.' Bridget ordered.

'Ooh, la la!'

'Si, I keep telling you, I'm not interested, mate.'

'Ah, you don't know what you're missing!'

Mick laughed. 'You don't give up, do you? Here, have - have a s'mosa. Sober you up a bit.'

'It's been a long time since a man's offered me a bite of his samosa.'

'What is he like? Where did you find him, Mart?'

'Oh, just hanging out, in my bedsit.'

'I was not hanging out! I've always kept myself decent an' proper, an' decent, furthermore...' protested Simon blurrily.

Mick was really hooting with laughter now.

Kerry was shaking with giggles as she pushed through the bushes clutching a demi-john in her arms.

'You're all noisy buggers!' Bridget complained.

'You're lucky Sarah couldn't stay. She'd be all Native American hippy chanting by now, with her hair full of pigeon feathers.' Kerry answered. 'Come on, here's a good place for the fire. Budge up, lads.'

Bridget stood alone, swaying only slightly from the Brynhelyn press. She looked around, listened keenly. Satisfied, she scouted around for dry twigs and had a small pyramid of them lit in seconds.

'Ok, gimme your bundles of sticks. And – Martha - pass us those bits of plank you found on the waste ground.'

Martha heaved the bundle off her shoulder and dropped the heavy wood at Bridget's feet.

'Ta.' said Bridget gruffly.

'She's bossy, isn't she?' Kerry said to Mick.

'Oh, yes.' he said, grinning. His mohican glowed fiery red as the flames grew.

'I just don't want us to get kicked out of the park, or nicked or something.' Bridget said defensively.

'We're all right. No one can hear us here. Or see the fire.' Kerry said calmly.

Bridget looked around, and seeing it was so, relaxed.

'So, tell us about the Mothership again.' she said to Kerry.

Later. The fire had burned low. Several caterpillar-like forms lay around the circle of embers. Mick and Kerry had gone from sitting up to wriggling into tatty ex-army sleeping bags and lounging on elbows, to slowly sliding to the horizontal. Martha roused and looked across at Simon. He was asleep on his back like a dead soldier, uncovered. She got up and covered him up with the rumpled pink blanket, and put his coat on top. Martha stumbled off into the dark to find somewhere to relieve herself.

As she picked her way carefully back through the dark, she jumped as Bridget was suddenly there.

'Oh.'

'Oh, it's you. Been for a piss?'

'Yes.'

'Me too.'

Instead of getting back into her sleeping bag Martha stood, aware that she was staring at Bridget.

'What?' Bridget asked grumpily.

'Just – it's weird to see you again.' said Martha.

'Bloody weird.' agreed Bridget. She looked uncertain. 'I'm going for a bit of a walk. The ground's hard, I'm aching.'

'Shall I come with you?'

'If you want.' Bridget's eyes were still on the ground.

There was no sound for a few minutes but the swish of their feet through the grass. Streetlights showed far away in a line to the park's northern boundary. An occasional single car sounded faint, the lonely sound of an early-hours return home. Beyond the bushes the sky glowed faintly orange over a dirty blue wash. Bridget strode on, Martha giving a little jump to keep up every now and then.

'So, it's been a long time.' Martha ventured.
'Yeah.' said Bridget curtly.
'I used to wonder where you'd gone. You just vanished. You - you didn't say goodbye or anything. You just went.'
Bridget stopped.

I remember the rage, smouldering, like dying embers. The night air was fresh and cooled my face. But the glow of fury was rising. It only needed one puff of air. One good puff.

'I really missed you. It was – a bit crap – on my own after that.' Martha persisted.
'Really?' Bridget's voice sounded taut.
'Yes. It was.' Martha said simply. 'I could never understand why you went without saying goodbye.'
Bridget reached flashpoint.
'Oh yes? Oh yes? Well it's a bit difficult when you're fucking unconscious isn't it?'
'What?' Martha stopped in shock.
Bridget strode on. 'Nothing, Just nothing. You're so dim. You were always so dim.'

Martha told me after, that she just stood there, perplexed, starting to feel a familiar sensation of guilt, a faint voice nagging furiously at her 'Look what you've done! Look what you've done! You stupid girl!' She said she could almost hear it, hear the voice screaming at her.

But I don't know what I've done, she thought angrily to the voice.

I haven't done anything. Anything to deserve this from my best friend.

119

She ran after Bridget.
'Hey! Hey – you! Who do you think you're talking to?'
Bridget stopped, swung round in fury.
'You! You bloody stupid little mousy mouse! 'Ooh I'm scared! Ooh hold my hand! Ooh protect me!'
Martha's mouth hung open.

Later I remembered her telling me about the bulldozer tracks she'd climbed on. The way she spotted the driver's intent just in time before he spun the top round and sliced the legs off everyone up there. She'd screamed 'Jump!' just in time. And inching up an eighty-foot line into the trees for the first time, white and shaking. The moment the bailiff cut the walkway and she fell, screaming, twelve feet until her safety line caught her. In the police cells, cold, frightened, defiantly drawing trees on the walls, wearing her pencil to a stub writing Earth First! as big as she could. Being dragged off by big ugly men in white helmets and yellow jackets, and dumped, bruised and skinned up, outside the cordon. I couldn't believe, didn't want to believe, that Mart had done all that. Her. The Mouse. I was sort of jealous, if you want to know. I never went out looking for trouble, because I'd invariably find some. What kind of nutter goes out and confronts the bastards? Keep your head down, that's my way. You've got to admire her guts though. Even if she is off her head.

Martha took a deep breath.
'What the fuck is your problem?' she asked, carefully pronouncing each word. She stood as tall as Bridget now.

God, I remember the flames of fury blazing. But underneath that was an unfamiliar, regretful sinking feeling. A feeling that got worse as I remembered that she never had known what had happened that night, after all.

'My problem? What the fuck is my problem?' Bridget began, but she was already losing momentum. 'I see they taught you to swear as well, after all this time.' she said nastily.

120

'No. I taught myself that.' said Martha coolly. 'So, what is your problem? You never answered.'
Bridget turned abruptly and started walking slowly back towards camp.
'Nothing.'
'Doesn't sound like nothing. So tell me, what happened?' Martha followed her. She had no difficulty keeping up this time.
'I don't want to talk about it.' Bridget mumbled. 'I blamed you. It wasn't your fault, Ok? I realise that now. It wasn't your fault.'
'Well that's comforting to know. What wasn't my fault?'
'I'm not telling you here. Over by the fence. Not where the others can hear.'

❄

I told her. About coming home after ten, hoping our dad had calmed down by then. About walking into the house and him sat there waiting for me, Robert grinning away in the background.

'Where've you been till this time? What's this about nicking my wood? I told you to keep out of my shed! You bloody disobedient little devil!'

'I – I didn't know you still wanted it. Honest! It was there for ages! I didn't – I didn't know...'

Bam. I didn't even see the first blow coming. I was too shocked, too terrified, to feel the second one that slammed me straight into the wall.

I was out, then dimly conscious, hearing Mum wailing, screaming, like a hurt animal, like nothing I'd ever heard before. There was blood on the threadbare carpet. A Lego brick under the settee. Mick crying. A shrieking, far away, a breath of cold air like the front door was open. Shrieking, shrieking, wailing, up and down, then I slipped back down into the dark.

❄

The two stood in front of the enclosure fence. Saying nothing. Bridget because she couldn't say any more, Martha because she didn't know what to say.

121

'Where – where do you live now?' she asked eventually.
'At Mick's at the moment. I had a room, but I couldn't keep it going. Nothing but bits of casual work. Factories, packing, warehouses. They never want you for more'n a few months.'
'I know about that!' Martha grimaced.
'There's no jobs anymore. It's shit.'
'It's shit.' Martha agreed. They began to move, back to the camp, chilled now. There was the thought of hot coffee if last night's embers would kindle. Martha yawned and stretched, grabbed the wire netting in front of them and peered through.
'What did-' she began.
'Pschiiitt!'

Both of them sprang back, together, screamed loud, as one.
'What the bloody hell? What's going on?' Simon called distantly.
They stood panting, clinging to each others' arms in terror. Martha looked. Wild green eyes, flattened ears, snarling mouth ready for another vicious hiss.
'Let's get out of here!'
'Agreed!'
'What was that? What are you doing? Have you got any coffee?' Simon demanded.
'Hush. It was the wildcats. Yeah, we've got coffee. Shush, and move over, let me get at the fire.' Bridget spoke more gently than Simon had yet heard her.
'Hah! So now you know, it's not funny!'
'No, Simon, it's not. It's not funny at all.' Martha answered absently. But there was still a faint, thoughtful half-smile on her face.
'Hey, Bridge.' said Mick.
'Huh?'
'Who rattled your cage? Get it?'
Heh. That was a good one.

❄

'So how come you were even friends when you argue so much?' Kerry was wide awake now. Too wide awake.
'I dunno.' I squirmed. 'Mart's my best friend.'

122

'You always say that, but you're so different. Martha used to be scared of everything. You're not scared of anything.'

Kerry could be a pain at times.

We were finishing digging over the long bed outside the poly, for the runner beans. I'd be tempting fate to put them in first week of May even in this unseasonably warm spring, but you can get away with a lot down South. Except being a Midlander and having a mouth sometimes bigger than your brain.

'You two were weird that RTS weekend. One minute hissing and spitting, next minute giggling and whispering in corners like a couple of kids.' Kerry was still trying to unravel the mystery of what she liked to call 'the least likely friendship between the two least alike people ever'.

'I hadn't seen Mart for like – years. Didn't even recognise her at first.' I was defensive. Kerry always asked such searching questions. Never afraid to lift up a rock and peer into the dark places of your soul. Back on Cannon Hill I'd watched the others dousing the fire and fitting the turfs back into the sward without even feeling the need to take over and worry about embers catching the grass or litter getting left behind. I liked to cover my tracks, like a cat. But that morning I'd been more than a little distracted.

'C'mon. We have to fold our tents and steal away before someone sees us. Get cracking.' said Kerry.

'We haven't got tents.'

'Martha, stop being logical, fold your metaphorical tent and move your ass.' said Simon. He already had two bedrolls strapped to him like a faithful mule.

Martha rolled up her sleeping bag and joined him. Bridget got up unsteadily and pushed a lot of empty demi-johns into her rucksack. Clinking gently, she followed the other two out of bushy seclusion into the white mist that was rolling off the boating lake.

'Which way's the gate?' Martha whispered to her.

'Over there – I think. It's a bit thick, isn't it?'

They walked on, swishing a trail through dewy grass until they reached the path.

'What time do they unlock the gates?' Kerry asked.

'You mean we're locked in?' said Martha nervously. 'How are we gonna get out?' she said, shivering in the damp morning air.
'Climb them.' Bridget said.
'Lurk in the bushes until the parkie's gone, then slip out.' That was Kerry.
'Find a hole in the wall?'
'Mick, you'd better not try to make one.'

❄

'It was a lovely morning, though.' I said reflectively. I watched the linnets as they tumbled about in the shelter belt.
'Yeah. Remember the greenhouse?' said Kerry. 'You had a bit of an epiphany in there, didn't you?' A linnet reached the top of a hazel and belted out a fast song ending in a drawn-out wheeze, then again. 'I dunno if I'd call it that.'

'What's that ahead?' asked Martha.
'Oh. Oh, I know where we are now. That must be the greenhouse over by the east gate.' Bridget speeded up. Clink clink. Clink clink clink.
'Shhh.'
'It's cold.' Simon shivered. He ran up and tried the door.
'It's open!' He slid the door back. Tropical air wafted gloriously out.
'Oh, nice!' he said. 'I'm in!'
Martha followed, her glasses instantly steaming up. She pulled them off impatiently and wiped them.
'We're gonna get caught.' said Bridget warningfully.
'Nah, look how thick the undergrowth is. We can lurk here quietly in the warm.' said Kerry. 'They can't see us from the gate and they'll think we came in early. They won't reckon they forgot to lock it and even if they do they'll keep quiet about it.'
Mick had already slipped past Simon and disappeared into the damp vegetation.
'Oh wow, look at this..' came faintly.

Bridget entered last, reluctantly. As she slid the door shut, she glanced warily behind. Nothing. She stood basking in the warmth,

looking around. Wet foliage, banana trees showing through the mist,
and further in, a tree with a twisty trunk and broad spears of leaves
in a variety of rich greens and browns.
'What's this one?' asked Mick.
'Theobroma cacao...' came Martha's voice, 'Chocolate.'
A chocolate tree! Bridget forgot her twitch about uniforms and
pushed her way eagerly through dripping ferns, luxuriating in the
warm humid air.

❋

Kerry's breathing slowed. She was asleep. I picked up my pen and
started scribbling in my notebook. I had to get the memories down
while they were at the surface of my mind.
Until that weekend of RTS I'd never been in the hothouse before.
Mick's Selly Oak bedsit put our stamping ground at the western end
of the park. The east corner, nearest Moseley, was less known.
Anyway, planty stuff reminded me of – Martha, kneeling painfully
on the gravel, not noticing the way it dug into her knees as she
examined a frond in the minute way she'd always had. I remember
how she stood up and reached for a broad green leaf above her head.
'*Musa acuminta* – if it's not an ornamental one.' she mumbled to
herself.
'What?' I looked closer at the broad shiny leaf with the channel
running down the centre.
'Banana tree – well, it's not a true tree, the trunk's really a
pseudostem made up of petioles formed into a sheath...'

Martha had always done this, I remembered. She'd go deep into
every plant and insect she found, examining, learning, until she
knew it down to the microscopic level. I half-expected her to whip
out a microscope on the spot and have the banana leaf - if it *was* a
leaf – sliced and diced and stained a weird pink by that dye they used
to use in the science lab at school.
She knew everything – about nature that is. But she also knew
nothing. When it came to actually interacting with other humans,
she was clueless. I'd always been fascinated by her science lectures,

but had trouble connecting them to real life. A bit like Martha. She only connected with real life now and again, by accident.

'Where's the bananas then?' I asked, practical as always.

'There's some green ones over there. Not ripe yet.'

'Pity.' said Mick, craning over my shoulder. My little brother was always hungry, even now, at six foot two. Perhaps it was needed to nourish his foot-high hair.

I looked around. The humid air was heavenly to breathe after the chilly mist outside. None of the plants were familiar. None of them spoke to me in my own language. They weren't the villagers I'd grown up with. Yellow labels on stalks held strings of Latin up to me in vain. Beautiful exotics, trailing creepers with handlike leaves, huge pink blooms, wildly-shaped cacti with woolly spines and the odd starry red flower amazed me, but I missed the bluebell, the campion, the hawthorn-blooming hedgerow.

Then there was the bright yellow forsythia that showed up so bravely against a watery blue March sky, and the flowering currant and guelder rose that took turns to adorn the willow walls of my den. Our den.

※

'Why's it shaped like that?' Martha had been silent for a long time, even by her standards.

'What?' Bridget spoke lazily as she lay on her back with a kitten on her chest, watching the flicker of sunlight through the shifting willow roof.

'This leaf.' She blew at a narrow spearblade of willow until it wafted over.

'Huh? It's shaped like that because it's a willow. Weeping willow. That's what shape a weeping willow is.'

'Yeah, but why long and thin?'

'I dunno. It just is. It's just like that. That's how they are.'

'Yeah, but why? There must be a reason.'

'Why anything? Why is the sky blue?' Bridget was impatient. Martha had been known to keep this up all afternoon.

'Oh, that's because of er, diffraction in the upper atmosphere bending the light, and the light gets split like in a rainbow, and blue gets scattered the most cos it has the shortest wavelength, only the light doesn't really bend. I didn't understand that bit.' Martha sat up, animated, her face alight.

'Reflection in the atmosphere?'
'No. Diffraction.'
'What's that when it's at home?'
'That's the bit I don't understand yet. But I will.' Martha came alive when she was thinking. Even her limp hair seemed to spring up a little. 'There's this book at the library and I can't take it out 'cos you have to be thirteen to get anything out of the adults section, but I've read most of it and it says how colours are made. There's all stuff about pigments as well.'
'Pig muck?'
'No, pigments. The coloured stuff that's in things. Like what paint's made of.'
'Pigments. Sounds more like pigmuck.' Bridget oinked. 'I yam an artist! Give me my palette of pigmuck and I will create a masterpiece...' She made realistic splattering noises amidst the grunting.

Martha was laughing.
'Slap it on the easel and I will show you my genius! You can smell eet as well as look at eet!'
Martha was rolling around. The kitten – the black one – had shot off in alarm, but had been halted by the willow leaf as it drifted to earth. She batted it fiercely.
'I don't even need a brush! I can just direct my bottom onto thee canvas!'
Martha was heaving with laughter. The trailing willows on her side were shaking.
'Shhh!' Bridget stopped suddenly. 'What was that?'

They listened keenly.
'Nothing. Phew. We better not make so much noise.'
'Yeah.' agreed Martha in a whisper.

'So, you've gotta wait til you're thirteen to get at the good books?'
'Yeah. It's stupid.'
'Just cos they're too stupid to read them they won't let us.'
'Yeah. They are stupid. What you got there?'
Bridget passed her book to Martha. The wind rustled the willow branches above them.
'Watership Down. Oh, it's a story. I prefer books that teach you things.'
'Richard Adams teaches you things. Things about rabbits. How they dig burrows and stuff. And he made up a language for them. Rabbits speak Lapine.' Bridget dug out another wine gum, then pushed two into her cheek to form a gum ball while flicking some over to Mart.
'That's Latin for rabbit. I'll have a look then. Oh, ta.' Martha picked up the wine gums and nibbled on one, neatly biting it in half.

'Wanna hear a word in Lapine?'
'Go on, then.'
'Bet you can't guess what hraka is.'
'Grass?'
'No, rabbit shit.' There was an intake of breath. *'I mean, rabbit crap.'*
'Rabbit poo?'
'Only little babbies say poo. Say it. Say rabbit shit.' Bridget prodded at the ceiling with one shabby trainer irritably.
'I don't want to. I'm not supposed to talk like that.' Martha was reverting to the tense, wooden state that the people who'd never heard her speak - which was everyone - were familiar with.

Bridget wisely left it. They'd been through this before and the afternoon was too perfect to spoil with the same old argument.
'When rabbits swear they just say 'hraka!' You could swear in Rabbit. No one'd know.'
Martha liked the sound of that. *'Hraka!'* she hissed fiercely, and looked guiltily around.
'You're all right! Even if anyone heard, how many people round here can talk Lapine?'
'The rabbits?' Martha suggested, with fake timidity. Bridget shot a look at her.

128

'Yeah, you should watch your language. There might be baby rabbits listening. Down the hole.'
'Right under our feet!' This time the laughter could be heard at the other end of the garden, but both girls had forgotten to care.

'Bridge! Where are you? What have you done with my bike pump?'
Bridget shot upright.
'Hraka! My bloody brother Robert heard us!'
'Hraka, let's get out of here.' agreed Martha.
They slipped silently under the willow wreaths and through a hole in the ragged hawthorn into the wood beyond, like a couple of stealthy young rabbits scenting a predator. They ran along the woodland path where the remains of bluebells showed purple and went to earth in a fern-hung hollow. Only the faintest of giggles hung on the air.

'Mart?' I said to her back as she stood with her head among banana leaves.
'What?'
'This here is a tree. I think you're talking a load of hraka.'

Mick was hungry. He pulled at my arm.
'Let's go, the gate'll be open and I want a bacon butty.'
'In a minute.' I was watching Mart. She was tracing the groove on the banana leaf with a finger.
'I know why it's that shape...' she said finally.
'It's that shape because it's a banana leaf. On a banana *tree.*' I said firmly.
'No. Watch.' She moved over to the centre of the greenhouse where there was a fishpool I hadn't noticed before. She pulled her mug out of her pocket and scooped up a full cup, then poured it slowly over the leaf.
'See? It's a drainage channel. It never stops raining in the tropics. The plants have guttering.'

‘More than our house has.’ said Mick. ‘That fell off ages ago, the rain just pours down the wall and in the windowframe’.
I watched as Martha poured another cupful over the leaf. She was right. The waxy surface shed water and funnelled a sparkling rivulet down the centre until a crystal chandelier formed at the tip. Rainbows flashed in the rising sun as light dawned.

❄

‘What else do you know about bananas?’ asked Mick as he bit into his bacon sandwich. Rowan had roused to our gentle tapping on the van window and slid back the side door. It had taken no time for us to pile in and direct Rowan back to the wasteground where we found the firewood the night before. There we lit the gas stove and fried up bacon and egg sandwiches all round, spreading out the old pink blanket to sprawl on the ground outside the van’s back door.

‘No bloody vegans here are there?’ Rowan had asked.
‘Nah. We’re all freegans here.’ said Kerry.
‘What’s that?’ Martha asked.
‘We’ll eat anything as long as it’s free.’
‘I think I saw some old cheese in that skip we passed on Salisbury Road.’
‘So funny, Simon.’ Kerry grimaced as she tackled a tough bit of bacon rind. ‘Now a skip round the back of the Coop would be a different story.’
‘Really? We could go take a look.’ Mick finished his sandwich and looked hungrily into the food bag which was starting to look very empty.
‘I thought you wanted to know about bananas.’ said Martha.
‘I do. Badly. But I’m still hungry. I could do with eating some.’
‘You don’t mind the banana equivalent radiation dose?’
‘The which?’
‘The banana equivalent dose is the amount of radiation in a banana.’
‘Whoah! They’re radioactive?’ Kerry didn’t sound convinced.
‘Yes. They’re high in potassium and everything with potassium contains radioisotopes of potassium 40. One banana contains 15 becquerels of radiation.’

Martha munched her sandwich while we chewed this over.

'But – hang on – the human body contains potassium doesn't it? Otherwise why eat bananas?' Kerry objected.

'Yes, loads of things contain natural radiation. They came up with the banana equivalent dose to help people not to panic about tiny doses of natural radiation.'

'Did it work?' I asked ironically. Mick was looking at his own finger, squinting as if he expected to see it glowing.

'So, how much is a lot of radiation?' asked Kerry.

'Well, after Chernobyl, they allowed reindeer meat to be eaten that had 1500 becquerels per kilogram. That's five times the normal limit.' Martha said.

'Fuck! Rudolf's nose must have been glowing.' said Simon.

'All the plants and animals were - fucked up. Red conifers, deformed butterflies, hedgehogs the size of a cottage loaf, all that.'

'You've been reading *The Star Chernobyl*, Mart?' said Kerry.

'Yeah. I didn't used to read anything but factual books until I discovered Richard Adams. He researched his natural history properly.'

'And that did it for you?' mocked Simon gently.

'That's right.' Martha sounded a bit puzzled. 'Well, all the stories and novels I could get out of the children's library were so childish...not many were really readable.' She threw her breadcrust out to a sparrow that was eyeing them hopefully.

'They were childish because it was – the *children's library*.' said Simon.

'Yes, but I wanted something challenging.' said Martha simply.

'Ok, so can we go and have a rummage in this skip? And find some non-radioactive food to eat?' Mick was getting restless.

'Ok, let's do it. You coming?' Kerry looked around the group.

'Yeah!' 'Bring a rucksack!' 'Who's good at climbing massive fences?'

I grabbed my rucksack and bounded after them.

It was Simon who – surprise – managed to scale the gate in the chainlink fence and open the skip.

'What have we got here?'

'Don't bring any meat.' Kerry warned.

'I thought you weren't vegans?'

'Yes, but I draw the line at skip meat. I don't want to end up in hospital.'

'Ok.' His head disappeared into the skip. 'Give us a hand.'

I got over the wall beside the fence with the help of a boost from Mick and lifted myself up to look inside the skip. There was a slight smell of sour milk but also lots of only faintly sticky cartons and packets. Egg noodles, mushrooms, eleven bags of pasta, some bread rolls that weren't too tough, five pizzas, some onions, a bag of red peppers...

'And this!' cried Simon triumphantly. He heaved it out. A wine box.

'There's another! The house red!' I leaned further in to take it from Simon who by this time had climbed inside.

'Look out!' shouted Mick. I froze with my head halfway into the skip.

'What?' I hissed back at him.

'Cop car.'

'Look normal!' I shot at him, and shut the lid on Simon before scurrying round the back of the skip to hide.

'Hey!' I heard his muffled voice say. 'It really stinks in here!'

'Shh! Pigs.' I whispered. I waited, heart thumping, wishing I could see, until Mick called quietly, 'All clear. You can come out.'

I wavered.

'It's Ok. They've gone past.' Mick insisted. 'Hurry up, I dunno how much longer I can look normal.' I stood up and lifted the lid to reveal Simon.

'God, that was disgusting.' he said crossly. I helped him out, trying not to breathe. He wasn't kidding. He definitely whiffed a bit.

We dragged our rucksack full of booty back to the fence and, both heaving together, got it over the wall. I couldn't help glancing each way before I dropped over the wall.

'Oh wow, we feast tonight!' said Kerry.

'Pity we can't get our old campsite back.' reflected Simon.

'You can all come to ours – if that's all right with you, Mick?' I said. I wanted to get under cover. There'd been enough scares for one morning.

'With two boxes of wine? And all that grub? You can live with me forever!'

'We'd better get our bikes.' I said.

'Bung them in the back of the van and we'll take you there. Where is it?' said Rowan.

'Selly Oak.' said Mick.

'That's a bit posh, isn't it?' said Rowan.

'Not the bit we live in.' I said. 'Ours is more like Smelly Oak.'

'Simon'll fit right in.' Martha said, daringly for her I thought.

'Hey!'

You know, I felt almost shy showing Martha and the others in to Mick's. Martha never came round to ours when we were back in the village, and I never went to hers – I didn't think Martha's mum would welcome one of the scruffy kids from the house with the bits of old car in the garden, the house where all the shouting went on. And Martha never asked me home. I suppose her mum was a snob. It wasn't her fault. But it hurt my feelings at the time. I knew that Mart and Simon were on the rock and roll as well as us and they only had some crummy bedsits back in Bristol, but everyone knows Bristol's posh. Not posh in bits like Birmingham, where you could live in Selly Oak and still be as poor as a church mouse without any cheese, as Mick used to say, but posh all over. It was the South. That's where all the money was. I thought then.

'Come in. Up the stairs.' Mick said. We filed in lugging rucksacks and bedrolls. I noticed afresh the sticky, wrinkled lino on the floor, the nicotine white walls with the fire regulation notices and curt notes from the landlord. 'No cycles to be stored in the hallway.' 'The use of paraffin and gas stoves in rooms is prohibited.' 'Maximum occupancy of rooms is 1. Sub tenants not permitted.'

We parked our bikes in the hall and tiptoed up the stairs. The timer ran out on the light on the first landing, and Mick felt around to push the button again. Click. We almost made it to the second floor before we were plunged into darkness again. Mick clicked on the penlight on his keyring to open the big padlock he'd put on our door after the first break-in.

'Come on in. Sorry about the mess.' Mick ushered everyone in and sat down on his bed. I wished I'd had time to fold up the sofa bed and clear away the breakfast bowls before we went to the party. Mick had been so impatient for the off.
'Hurry up. No one's going to see it. Let's not miss the start.'
I saw Martha's hands instinctively reach for the dishes, then stop. I grabbed some plates and put them on the drainer of the kitchen sink in the corner.
'Pass us them over.' I asked her. She handed dishes to me until the table and chairs were clear. Kerry sat at the table and started unpacking the food. Simon crashed on the old beanbag in the corner.

'I think I should warn you, Simon. My mate's dog's been sleeping on that.' said Mick.
Simon groaned and started brushing dog hair off his coat, then gave up and slumped again.
'Smells of dog.' he complained. 'I hate dogs.'
'Cats generally do.' said Martha.
I looked my question.
'Oh, Simon's basically a cat trapped in the body of a human. That's why he likes the upstairs room at home even though it's tiny.' she explained.
'All the fun of being up high, and all the security of being in a box.' Simon mumbled drowsily.
'Come on, old puss.' Mick nudged Simon with his foot. 'Up you get and let us at the fridge.'
'Mmm.' said Simon, and moved half an inch.
'Up you get! Chop chop!' I'd hardly known Simon anytime back then but I knew you had to be tough with cats or they'd walk all over you. Literally. He roused reluctantly and getting up dragged his dog

bed across the room a few feet before nestling back down in a miasma of dog smell.

'Is it safe to open this fridge?' Martha looked at me.
'Safe?'
'You should have seen what Mart kept in hers at home.' Simon mumbled. 'She made me tackle it. I was lucky not to be slain by toxic fungus.'
'There's nothing in there except Mick's trainers.'
'Eurgh, you're joking. I thought that lot at Brynhelyn were bad.'
Kerry came over with her arms full of skip food.
'I like 'em nice and cool,' said Mick cheerfully. 'nothing worse than hot sweaty trainers.'
'Except cold sweaty trainers.' Kerry screwed up her face as she picked up the laces with the tips of her fingers and and dangled the trainers onto the floor with the expression of a supermodel called on to deal with a dead mouse on the catwalk.

'Put the kettle on, Sis.' said Mick as he lay back on his bed, feet propped up on the mantelpiece over the tiny unused grate.
'Hang on a minute. Why have we got two men lounging around and three women doing all the housework?' Kerry straightened up from the fridge.
I didn't really mind all that much. Normally I wouldn't take any crap from boys but Mick had been working so hard the last few weeks on the loading job he got from the agency last time. Ten hours on shift at all hours playing Tetris with artics and he could barely straighten up when he got home. I used to have to take his boots off. He earned his weekend off. I hated not being able to bring any money into the household so I did all the clearing up and washed our clothes in the bath, treadling them with my feet like a French wine presser.

'Simon. Give us a hand.' said Martha. He groaned again but stood up, swaying, and went over to the sink to fill a kettle for hot water.
'I'll do that. You go down the road for some milk.' Martha took the dishmop from his hand.
'And Kitty shall have a saucerful.'

135

'All right, Mick.' said Simon. 'We've had enough of that one.' He passed his wet hands over his grubby face to freshen up a little.

'Catbath!' Everyone laughed. Simon scowled, but grabbed the front door key from Mick's outstretched hand and headed for the door. 'Back in a minute,' he mumbled. 'Do we need anything else?'

'Nah, we're good.' I went back to looking for mugs on the shelf made of the old bricks and planks that Mick had scrounged from the building site up the road. Three mugs between five. Martha pulled hers out of her pocket again and rinsed off the pond water as the kettle boiled.

Innumerable mugs of tea later, we fell silent, drowsing in the dusty sunbeams that made it through the yellowed net curtains and grimy window. I put my hands behind my head on my sagging sofa bed, kicking the quilt away for coolness. Kerry put her head down on the table, yawning, and drifted off. Mick fell asleep quickly and peacefully with his feet still propped on the mantelpiece. Martha was stretched out on the floor with her head on Simon's beanbag. I saw Simon watching the dancing dust motes for a few minutes more until his eyes closed, seconds before I slid into deep afternoon sleep.

❄

'How's the hangover?' Mart was the second to wake up. I'd watched her yawn and stretch as I raised my head from the pillow that was sliding from my low bed onto the floor.

'Gone. But I'm hungry.' She got unsteadily up, joggling Simon who moaned but didn't wake.

'Let's get some grub on shall we?' I said shyly. I still found myself taking furtive glances at her, trying to see the girl she'd been in the willowy, pale faced woman she'd turned into in a flash, it seemed to me. There was something missing.

'Yes.' She opened the door and I heard her feeling her way downstairs to the shared bathroom.

Simon was next to surface.

'Mmmm...yaw...ah..nn.' He rolled over, falling off the beanbag and looked up surprised, blinking on the floor.

'Morning Bagpuss.' I couldn't resist that one.

'Very funny.' he yawned. 'Where's Mart?' I heard his sudden anxiety.

'Gone down to the bog.' I answered. 'You can help us get the grub on when she comes back.'

'Ok.' he said absently.

Kerry woke up all over, all at once. She sat up, wide eyed, and immediately got up and stretched her arms above her head, then paced the small square of threadbare carpet in two strides, there and back, yawning.

We'd already started chopping onions and peppers and got the frying pan heating on the Baby Belling by the time Mart reappeared.

That was it. She didn't have her glasses stuck together with insulating tape anymore.

'You've been a long time. Did you fall down the bog?' Simon asked.

'No, it was the landlord. I heard him coming through the front door just as I was about to come out of the toilet and I had to hide in there for ages. He was after the rent from the guy downstairs.' said Martha. She dug her penknife out of her pocket and cut open a bag of pasta.

'He's not going to come up here is he?'

'Nah, we're all right. The rent's paid up to date and he never comes near us for anything else.'

'Landlord?' asked Mick sleepily.

'Yeah, he was after John downstairs. Hang on.' I waited, wooden spatula in air, listening. 'Yeah, there he goes. The front door just slammed. We'll hear his car in a minute.'

An engine started up then faded away down the road.

'Yeah, we're good. We always pay the rent first.'

'Pay the rent before you do anything else. Pay the rent before you eat or get your boots fixed. Pay the rent before you so much as fart.' Mick chanted.

'S'right. Then at least you've got somewhere to be broke in.' I agreed.

'Us too.' said Martha. 'Pay the rent, put some gas and electric on the meter, then starve in comfort.'

'Yeah, there's always ways to get food. Food's easy.' agreed Simon. 'Look at this weekend. You two were stony when we met you and now you're going Italian.'

'Yeah, good one. Let me get at that wine box.' Mick jumped up, staggered a bit, went over to the table and started gouging at the cardboard until he found the spout.

'Just tryin' to get the tap – to prolapse out...' he said between struggles, '...that's it!'

He balanced the box on the edge of the table and delicately pressed the button, filling one mug after another until we were all ready to raise a toast to skipping.

'Ladies and gennel'men – and Simon, who's a cat – I give you the back of the Coop! In these days of scorched earth capitalism and mass unemployment let's be grateful for the grand ol' British tradition of being so fuckin' rich you can afford to throw food away while people are on the streets. Long may the trickledown – keep tricklin' down!'

We cheered and chinked our glasses together. We had run out of cups so Mart's was an enamel camping mug and Simon's an elegant cut-glass marmalade jar.

'Nice jar.' Simon said, sticking out his pinky and grinning.

'Yeah, I've had it for years.' I told him. We were nearing the bottom of the first winebox, scraping up the last of our pasta sauce with skip bread rolls.

'Do you do this in Bristol?' I asked.

'Oh, yeah. We do regular runs, me and Michael, this guy who lives in the cellar. Mart hasn't met him yet. But while he was away in Ireland and Mart was off saving the trees, I couldn't get a hand with the stuff - Michael's got an old car, see. So, it was famine for a bit there. All I could get was what would fit on the back of the bike.' Simon threw his plate aside on the floor.

'What's it like job-wise down there?' I was curious about that. I still thought the streets were paved with gold down south, in those days.

'Well, there's more work, but the rents are so high that until we get a minimum wage we're running to stand still. And most of it's temporary – by the time you've done a few weeks, you haven't earned enough to save up enough to cover you for the three or four weeks it takes to get your benefit claim up and running again afterwards, or to tide you over til you get some more work. I went round and round with it until I got fed up of it. What's the point of working if you end up in debt?'

'It's the same here only with even less jobs.' I said, automatically picking up his plate and passing it to Kerry. 'That's why I'm staying with Mick. I don't have to sign on again and I can take any bits of work that come up, but in between we're both living on nothing. It's too hard to keep signing on and off. That loading job was quite well paid but it only lasted two weeks and then Mick had to get me some boots, my feet were out of the others, and he top-loaded the meters so we wouldn't run out of gas and electric, but there's been nothing from the agency for a month. I'm gonna have to sign on again next week but it'll take at least three weeks til I get any money. And I won't be able to earn anything. Officially. So you have to break the law to survive and you're worrying all the time about getting caught. I can help down the market now and again but God help me if some snooper dobs me in.'
'Yeah, been there.' said Simon. 'And Mart – well, you must've seen before - what she's like with strangers, they won't even give her a chance. She's getting better, but...'
'There's nothing wrong with me.' Martha said defensively. 'I can talk to people if I want. I just don't want to talk to those arseholes.' She kicked at the hole in the carpet angrily.

I wished Simon hadn't said that about Mart. She was so sensitive about the talking thing. When we were kids she wouldn't talk to anyone, except me. No one else even knew she could talk. At school she wouldn't even answer the register. The teacher got used to glancing up to see that she was there. They just accepted it. Didn't occur to the stupid bastards to do anything about it. What use is learning to read and write and ingesting whole libraries if you can't talk to anyone? But she always did well in tests and was so quiet and well behaved that they didn't see it as a problem. Correction – it wasn't causing *them* any problems and that's all they cared about. I watched Martha's fate being sealed back then. I saw the beginnings of her unemployability. Right there in the corner of the tiny village classroom.

'S'right.' I said, glancing at Martha. 'Who wants to work for those tossers anyway.'
'All they do is trash the Earth and kill people.' said Kerry. 'They can fuck off if they think I'm helping them. They can do their own dirty work.'
'It's all arms trade stuff in Bristol.' Simon explained. 'They employ half the city. They even have their own train station. I went past Abbots Grove once first thing, and I saw all the drones piling out to toddle off to work at the murder factory. You should have seen the graffiti on the station platform. All swastikas and NF.'

'I just wish I could work for meself.' said Mick. 'My brother Sean got a start with an electrician who he knew at school and he's learning how to wire up houses now. If he can get enough training he could set up on his own one day. That'd be good.'
'Yeah, that's why I'm learning IT.' said Simon. 'I want to be able to help set people's computers up – sort out their printers and fix software problems and that sort of thing.'
'You should see his room – it's like the Lone Gunmen's flat.' said Kerry, starting to laugh. 'Remember that episode when Scully goes round to see them cos Mulder's gone missing and Langly's talking to her, then suddenly Frohike comes out doing up his dressing gown and you realise – they actually live in that den of computers, like it's their natural habitat.'
'Oh, yeah, I remember.' Mick said. 'You're into your sci fi then?'
'Well...' she said reluctantly, but smiling with it.
'S'all right. Simon's officially the biggest nerd in the room.' he reassured her.
I laughed. Poor Simon was really getting a pasting this weekend. He took it all on the chin though. Nice guy. I was glad that Mart had found a friend.

'What time is it?' asked Martha suddenly.

'Er, seven-thirty. Why?' said Kerry.

'Oh – I thought – what are we gonna do next? We have to get home sometime.'

'You're welcome to stay the night.' said Mick. 'It'll be a bit of a squash but you're all right.'

'Thanks.' said Kerry. 'We might take you up on that. Rowan will be wanting to get back to camp by tomorrow. He said he has to get on the road by about midday if we don't go back tonight.'

They looked at each other.

'It's too late to go back tonight.' Martha frowned. I saw her glance at me uncertainly. 'It'd be good to stay til tomorrow – if it's Ok.'

'It'll be great.' I said, with more confidence than I felt. *What must she think of our family now? Maybe I shouldn't have told her. Not going to think about it. Thank God for those wildcats and Mick's feeble sense of humour.*

'Well, we've got our sleeping bags and enough booze to float a battleship.' said Kerry.

'All right then! Crack open the other wine box!' said Mick.

The three of them spread out their bedding and settled down, grinning shyly at each other.

'Where is Rowan? He chipped off pretty quick after he dropped us off.' said Simon.

'Oh, he's seeing his sister in Edgbaston. That's why he was good to drive up here.' said Kerry. 'He would have gone over there last night but he forgot to stay sober.'

'Oh yeah, that.' said Mick. 'Anyway Simon the cat, tell us something about these computers you work on.'

Simon brightened up. He got up and went over to the table to talk to Mick more easily. 'Well, I got my first computer down the market. First thing I did was open it up and put more memory in...' The murmured conversation continued, their heads close together.

I was soon bored. I went and sat next to Kerry on the floor. Oh damn, she was interrogating Martha.

'So, you haven't seen Martha since – when?' asked Kerry.

'Uh – since we were about eleven.' I said quickly.

'I was ten.' Martha supplied.
'How on earth did you recognise each other after all that time?' said Kerry.

I dunno about Martha, but I was relieved that that was Kerry's first question. She seemed to have a knack of making people squirm, that girl.
'Well, it was the tattoo. The butterfly.' Martha said.
Kerry glanced at me. 'D' you mind us talking about this?'
'Course not.' *This girl who was my only proper friend who I got violently wrenched away from years ago turns up magically grown up and I don't know who she is any more. And now I'm hanging out with her as if all the time in between never happened, just because I bump into her at a party where everyone was pissed up. That's not weird at all. Nah, it doesn't bother me. What do you think?*

'Can we see your tat?' Kerry said.
'Oh, yeah.' I said unwillingly. I pushed up my sleeve so they could see the green and blue butterfly on my wrist. Frankly, I'd rather have stood in front of them starkers. But you don't let people know that.
'But you never had that when you were eleven?' Simon objected from the other side of the room. *Blast. Didn't know he was listening. That means Mick is. Please, please keep your mouth shut, bruv.* 'I know Brum's a bit rough, but...'
'Yes, but we always used to do the bubble gum tats. You know, the Happy Tattoo gum. There was a stick-on tattoo in every pack.' I explained.
Everyone looked at Martha.

'Yeah, we used to be covered in them, and there was this one that Bridge always wanted...' she said.
'That *you* always wanted.' I corrected. *God, give me another drink, someone!*
'It was a green and blue butterfly. *That* green and blue butterfly.'
'May I?' Simon asked. He picked up my wrist and looked closely.
'So you're telling me that you two long lost friends, or enemies, or whatever you're supposed to be, found each other again because of a bubble gum tattoo?' Kerry said.

'Well – yeah. Who else would have that tat, and be in Birmingham, and be called Bridget, and look just like Bridge?' Martha said.

'Blimey.' Simon sat back, eyebrows working overtime.

'That is amazing.' said Kerry. 'What a story. It's like something out of a film.'

'I always wondered why you chose that one, Sis.' said Mick.

'Well, I didn't want it to wash off.' I muttered. I telegraphed him desperately with my eyes but he didn't take the hint, or more importantly give me a refill.

Simon noticed my discomposure. He was sensitive to that sort of thing, I was becoming aware. He sat looking thoughtful while the others chattered and I took the chance to fill my mug up again with skip wine.

'You know what you need to do,' he said eventually to Martha, 'you need to get a matching tat. Full circle. To celebrate finding your best friend again.'

'Who says she's my best friend?' said Martha to her scuffed army boots.

'Yeah, who says?' I chimed in, with a bit of a grin to cover Mart's confusion.

'You should have seen them at school.' Mick reflected. 'They were inseparable. We didn't get it. Mart never spoke in those days and...' He finally caught my eye. *Thank God! At last!*

'Anyway, they were good mates back then. Bridge was a bit on her own with all us brothers. Me and Sean were glad she'd found someone to hang out with.'

'I had other friends.' It was my turn to be defensive.

'Sure. But none like Mart. She was just like you.' Mick laughed and ducked, expecting me to chuck a shoe at him.

'Do you think?' I said, softly for me. I thought about that for a long time, all the time that Simon and Kerry were persuading Mart to go and get tattooed at Ted's the next day.

✸

God knows how much Mart had to drink last night, but she did it. As we climbed into the van she was sporting an arm wrapped in cling film, and she stunk of Germolene.

'Welcome to the club!' said Mick, displaying the red roses on his arm. 'I got mine to remind me of my favourite Pogues album'.

'Red Roses for Me?' said Rowan.

'Yeah.'

'Thought you were a punk?' said Simon, turning Mick's arm around rather awkwardly to see the roses better. It was a fine-drawn bit of work. Ted excelled himself that day.

'Yeah, well, I'm eclectic.' He grinned down at Simon, perched on the van floor.

'Are you sure about coming down to Bristol?' I asked him. 'You don't have to. I'll be all right. It's only to see what it's like.'

'No, I fancy having a look.' he said. 'There's not much going on at home after all.'

'Yeah, well I've been thinking.' I said. 'About working for yourself, and plants, and - maybe - I could set up doing people's gardens.'

'She knows loads about it.' said Martha. 'She used to know all the plants when – when we were in the village. And there's courses at the city farm, and – you can practice on our yard, Bridge.'

'Bristol's a good place for a gardening business.' said Simon excitedly. 'Loads of rich people with more money than time.'

'And more money than sense.' Martha added.

'Sounds like a winner to me!' said Mick.

I didn't answer. I was watching the motorway unroll before us. I'd never been this far south before.

'M5 South West'

I watched the sign flick past. Wondered what it'd be like. I didn't know then that I wouldn't see Birmingham again for three years.

❄

144

9. Freezing.

I was pleased with the way the plot was going. The poly was full of healthy seedlings champing to go out, the tomatoes were beginning to reach for the sky in there and the runner bean bed was ready, poles and all.

'Aren't you worried about frost?' As well as asking all the wrong questions Kerry was also inconveniently good at gardening.
'Nah. I'll wait a week before I put them in. They'll be Ok. Anyway, this isn't your Welsh back of beyond mountain. We're practically at sea level here.'
'Yes, there is that I suppose. We used to catch every bit of weather at Cerrig.'
'I noticed.'
'Didn't know you ever went there.'
'Once.'
'Must have been after I left.' said Kerry.
'Pretty much by definition.' I agreed.
'Oh. You mean...'
'Yes.'

It irritated me the way Kerry still wouldn't talk about what had happened to Martha after she'd left her at Cerrig-cwm. I know Mart made the decision in a hurry to go up there, she didn't hang about for long once we got to Bristol, and Kerry probably blamed herself for encouraging her, but she wasn't to know. None of us could have known. I thought about it all the time I was saying goodbye to Kerry, who'd put her cleaned boots back on, walked down the field to the yard and climbed into her van.

I thought about it as I climbed the worn stone steps to my room in the old farmhouse, and while I sat at my desk looking over the manuscript. Kerry went on the defensive whenever Cerrig-cwm was alluded to.
It's not as though anyone was blaming her – Mart had seemed so happy there, her vulnerabilities seeming to fade away in the glory of

a mountain summer lived almost completely outdoors. She was writing to me practically every week, her breathless style speaking of how thrilled she was to be living deep nature.

She was always such a romantic – but maybe romantics need to live a romantic life.

Me, I was well and truly down to earth. Literally. Since the moment I arrived in Bristol and moved in at Mart and Simon's I'd been more busy than ever in my life before. Hope galvanised me. The city was humming with community this and that, free courses on the city farm over in Bedminster where I learned the rudiments of soil conditioning, composting, propagation. I sucked the knowledge up so fast it was like I'd always known it and just had to be reminded.

Plants were everywhere – Bristol's such a green city. I used to learn my garden ornamentals just by walking down the street, going Viburnum, ilex, euonymus, geranium...I felt like some old monk chanting Latin. Simon took me to car boot sales where I sorted through rusty garden tools looking for some basics that still had some metal on them. I'd wished like hell I could afford to learn to drive, but Simon had assured me I didn't need to.

'I'm doing comp-fixing all over town on my bike.' he said.

'Yes, but you don't have to carry a load of spades on the back.' I pointed out.

'Kerry did a bit of gardening round here before she went to Brynhelyn. She says that the customers most often have all the tools you'll need. Most of them are old and did their gardens themselves before they got too creaky and decrepit to do the bending. They've usually got a shedful.'

'Oh, yes?'

That had made me thoughtful. To tell the truth, I knew that by then I had enough basics to get started. Hell, even if you can push a lawnmower and know a weed from an ornamental you can get some kind of gardening job, and I knew a lot more than that. I just didn't have the confidence to take the plunge at first.

'What if they think I'm no good and I get the sack?'

'Go down the road and get another job. This is Bristol. There's gold in them there yuppies. You'll get the hang of it. A lot of it's just finding the right customers for you.' he said.

Things looked up for Simon after that RTS weekend in Brum. He really perked up when he got home. He seemed to find a new confidence, and tentatively at first, putting postcards in shop windows, he developed quite a little business running around town fixing up sick computers for bewildered students faced with having to word-process all their work for the first time, older people baffled by the technology, broke gamers wanting him to speed up their old machines - he could always cannibalise one of his dead ones to give them more memory – and in between, coding, coding, coding. I'd hear him come down for coffee late at night, and wandering into the kitchen I'd say 'Hi' only to be met with the glazed look of a man whose mind is on a higher plane. I'd even begun to comprehend some of the secret language of computers that he absentmindedly spoke to me when he wasn't paying attention. I used to clean house for someone like that when I was a penniless teenager still at school, before I was a penniless adult. She was from Denmark, and would sometimes break into fluent Danish as I walked into the kitchen carrying my mop and bucket.
'Oh, sorry, I forgot you weren't my sister.' she'd explain, smiling, embarrassed. 'I've been talking with her on the phone every day this week to arrange her visit.'
So when Simon gabbled away in his heathen lingo of modems and usb sockets and megabytes I learned to pick out a word here and there, just as I had with Majken.

And, bit by bit, I was finding my own way out of the poverty trap. They say that work's the route out of poverty, this is bollocks, the route out of poverty is cash in hand work so you don't have to sign off, so that you can dream of the time when you can actually afford to sign off, which for me, was a magic moment about eighteen months in to my business.
It was a time fraught with peril, all the time worried about getting caught, but when I compared it to a lifetime in desperate poverty I didn't waste much time deciding what to do. Benefit rules exist to

147

criminalise people for being poor. Like that Enterprise Allowance they used to have. You had to have a grand in the bank before you could sign up to it. How the fuck did they think someone on the dole was going to get a thousand pounds? Sell a lot of smack? Maybe that was the business startup they had in mind. It was certainly a growth industry back then.

I can't get over the way they assume that everyone's got rich parents to support them til they get to where they can support themselves. Or a rich husband who can support you if there's only part time work to be had. Or a mythical past job that pays enough to amass vast savings to tide you over between jobs. What we need is – some sort of basic income that's there all the time, so you can take whatever job you want and you'll always have enough to subsist on no matter what. Surely this country's wealthy enough to do that? They're supporting all these people to be out of work, why can't they support us to be in work?
Because the government's full of stupid rich people. There's MPs who are female or black or gay or disabled or whatever, not enough, not many, but at least there's some - now. But there are none who are poor. And there's no way they'll ever ask us what we think, because everyone knows that poor people are stupid, that's why we're poor. It's the rich who're stupid. They wouldn't have lasted five minutes in St. Pauls or Sparkhill on a Giro.

But anyway, it'll never happen. The only people who had a guaranteed income round my way in Bristol were the Trustafarians. Seen them? They're still out there, rich kids playing at being poor. Mart was so taken in by them. On the protest camps you couldn't tell who anyone was or where they came from, she said. They were all covered in mud the same. But when it all ended, the class divide opened up again. And the dirtiest ones, with the most matted dreadlocks and out-there lifestyles, were usually the most privileged. Mart told me about that van ride home at the end of the Newbury bypass protest. It was like they all just dropped back into a nice safe little life, like everything they went through in the trees immediately started to fade, until one day it'd just be an adventure to tell over a dinner party when they're all thirty-five and got their own houses or something. Mart felt really low when she got back, Simon told me.

I knew that heartsink feeling, every time I met someone I used to go to school with back in Brum I'd get that feeling. I must have been one of the few sixth formers who wasn't from a posh home, didn't have a dad who could give them a start, or at least a mum who'd cheer them on while they applied for jobs, make their sandwiches, give them kisses when they set out for interviews instead of huge bollockings about wasting time on books and why aren't you earning yet, home consisting of the sofa I slept on because the house was too small and I couldn't share like my brothers. And Robert – Robert *'has to have a room to himself because he's working now. He's paying his way.'* And I was doing my homework on my knee after everyone else had gone to bed, and failing my 'A' levels – except English - and getting kicked out into a Sparkhill bedsit with mould on the walls and a drug dealer living upstairs.

There was Ann, and Helen, and Samira, all comfortably living with their folks with real rooms of their own, while they mucked about with voluntary work and part time stuff and jobs in the family shop until they'd get that break and I'd never see them again because I couldn't afford to hang out with them anymore. They'd be paying five, ten quid to go to a nightclub or gig, or going to London to a show, or to Glasta at £60 a pop. They had nice clothes and shoes instead of ex-army boots from Poland and charity shop shirts. They wore Levi's, not Stag jeans, the cheap black canvas jeans that we called Slag jeans cos they always split at the crotch after three months so that you had to keep patching them and being vigilant about how you sat so you didn't expose yourself. They weren't going to sit in the park drinking Wild Oak cider at £1.65 a bottle. Me and Mick called it Wild Soak. We'd sit on the swings in the kid's play park and swing and drink, and talk, and fall silent as we looked up at the first stars, the dusk falling all around us, blackbirds singing in the royal-blue dark tinged with orange sodium streetlights. We'd stay til it got too cold and dew started falling on the grass, then walk reluctantly home, back to the poverty and the problems.

❄

Anyways, as Simon would say, I took the plunge. I put up some postcards in a shop window in Picton Street and waited. A week passed. I put up more cards, getting more and more anxious as my Giro dwindled and Simon had to start feeding me. Michael had moved on by then and his car sold for scrap, so it was just as well Simon could afford to buy most of his food now. Mart was in Wales by that time and her room was free but I couldn't afford to take it on. The landlord wouldn't waste any time, he'd soon have a new tenant. He didn't know about me, drifting from Simon's floor to Mart's to the kitchen chair with a footstool and a quilt over me...three months I spent like that. Then, just when I had given up all hope, someone phoned on Simon's new mobile. I had to get him to field the calls, there was no landline in the house. I went out with the two numbers he'd collected to find a phone box that worked. The first one was smashed. The second one had the cash box ripped off. The third one was covered in puke – I kid you not. Carrot chunks everywhere. The fourth one was not there at all. On the fifth one I got as far as keying in a number when I became aware of wires tickling my ear. The receiver had been smashed. The next three were full up. The ninth, ah, the ninth one worked! I dived in there, paper in hand, and breathlessly introduced myself to my first customer. She already had someone, she told me in a voice so posh I almost needed subtitles. Damn. Last chance. I called the next one.

'Hi, I'm..er, I'm calling back. You said you needed a gardener.'
'Oh, yes, oh...get down Dizzy..sorry, it's my dog. Yes, I have quite a big garden and I'm not keeping up with it these days...I've been ill, all right Dizzy, there's a lawn and shrubs that need pruning and the path's a mess I'm afraid, good girl, there you are, I've never had a gardener before...what do you want to do?'
'Oh, er, I had better come and have a look, er, what's the address?' I asked, trying to sound professional.
'Forty-three Bishop Road, past the school with the pencils...you know, the posts, yes, is that nice, do you want another one, sorry it's Dizzy, she always wants treats when I'm on the phone. Oh, and I'm Deena. When can you come?'

150

'Erm..' I wanted to get there as soon as possible but didn't want to sound like I had nothing else on, like some kind of failed gardener. 'Uh, it's ten now, I could see you at eleven?'

'Ooh, that's fine. I'll be here. See you then. Come on, girl. Come on.'

'Yeah, see you then, thanks, goodbye!' I echoed. I was a bit dazed by Dizzy and Deena but it was dawning on me that I just might have my first job.

Really, I never looked back after that. All anxieties I might have had about gaining the customer's approval melted away when I first met Deena. She was trying to open the porch door while stepping into her trousers and missing, with her long tunic hanging down like a dress, getting two legs down one trouser, disappearing from view before rematerialising magically fully trousered, laughing, breathless, apologetic and asking if I wanted a cup of tea and cake before I'd even opened the garden gate. Good old Deena. And Dizzy, despite the name, was a calm, dignified collie cross with noble ears and a relaxed, slowly-waving fringy tail. She and Deena should have swapped names. Deena was endlessly dizzy, talking to me nonstop all the time I walked up and down assessing the garden and realising that I could handle it, all the time I was agreeing to the price she offered and fixing up a weekly slot, all the time we sat on the garden bench drinking tea and eating lopsided pineapple cake - it was supposed to be upside down cake but in Deena's hands, even that went awry.

Good old Deena – she gave me my start, and for all the bewildering and tiring afternoons trying to keep track of her verbal non sequiturs, lightening-flash word associations and rambling digressions, there were others when I was bone-weary from lugging tools on and off my bike and weeding in the rain on my least pleasant customer's least pleasant steep flower bed. Days when I just wanted to fall over and cry, until Deena, unfailingly sensing my exhaustion through her smokescreen chatter, would sit me down in her kitchen with more peculiar-shaped cake and endless mugs of tea. I'd protest feebly about how little work I'd achieved and she'd wave my guilt pangs away and offer me another chocolate biscuit.

151

By the time she'd told me about her son's career and her daughter's wayward lover and told all her colleagues at the homecare service where she worked about me, I had old mums' gardens coming out of my ears and had moved into Mart's old room on the ground floor. I had my own bed, my own garden shed full of decent tools, and was saving for a second-hand petrol mower that would give me the freedom of the posh gardens with vast lawns out of reach of any flex. I was making it.

It was shortly after meeting the bipolar whirlwind that was Deena that the first envelope with a Welsh postmark hit the mat. I looked at the envelope for quite a while wondering what 'Post Brenhinol Cymru' meant and trying to work out whose handwriting it was. Does everyone do that, I wondered later. Spend ages looking at a letter trying to work out who it's from instead of opening it and finding out. I ripped it open and found out. It was from Martha at Brynhelyn.
I put the kettle on and sat in the old armchair next to the cooker.

'Hi Bridge! Well, it's me. And I'm here. Brynhelyn is up a big hill, actually that's what Bryn means, it's Welsh for hill. Dunno what Helyn's Welsh for, oh, Kerry says it's the name of the stream that falls down the hillside here. We get our water from it. It's amazing here. We've got a treehouse in the pines and there's lots of people at the moment but they come and go. That's why it takes a while to get things done I suppose. The roof on the treehouse still has a lot of leaks to fix but it's sunny for now. We spend the days planning actions and collecting firewood, going skipping, fixing up the house and just looking at everything. Ash wants to go down the valley and start a farm. I see what Kerry meant about it being too dark to grow anything here. It's black at night. Like Mirkwood.
Yeah, I know, I've been catching up on all the kid's stuff that I never read before for a few years now. It's sort of relaxing. The men seem to do all the wood cutting and the women all the cooking. But you have to be strong to lug branches and cut them up on the saw horse, and I don't mind cooking. Every evening me and Kerry are the last to sit down once everyone's got a bowlful, but the fire's really blazing by then and we're so warm. Not like in my room in winter.

Hope you're not too cold. Anyway, us women can relax at night and just watch the flames. The men keep alert to keep the fire stoked up, and they're always talking and planning campaigns, going over what happened before and how to make it better next time. Sometimes they're so busy explaining the plan of action to a new guy, the fire gets low, and I jump up and put another couple of logs on. I don't mind. I'm learning so much about planning campaigns. At Newbury a lot of planning went on in the office and we just followed the leader once Will got a message through on the CB. It's different here.

Nothing much is happening at the moment. I kind of like the farm plan. I'm going down tomorrow to take a look at the site down the valley that Ash keeps talking about. It's a little side valley called Cerrig-cwm. That means 'stone valley' in Welsh. It's getting dark now, I had better light some candles and serve the stew out. First night I was here, I heard a tawny owl calling from a tree right above the camp. Then one answered from a bit away, then another, til the whole valley was alive with them. It was a still, warm night, and all the sound we could hear was owl calls in the dark.

Bye for now, hope you're Ok, love Martha'.

She sounded Ok. Must be nice to fall asleep to owl calls. Don't fancy Donga slop every night though. I made my coffee and climbed the stairs to show Simon.

After that, the letters came pretty regular once every ten days or so. Mart always used to say she was rubbish at writing but it didn't seem to stop her. Never knew she had so many words in her.

'Hi, it's me. Martha. You should see Cerrig-cwm. I'm living there now. The camp at Brynhelyn got a bit boring, just waiting around for something to happen. They reckon the quarry extension might not go ahead after all, which is brilliant, but people are drifting away. There's so many rumours, one day someone swears we're gonna get evicted before September, other times we think we could be here a long time. Anyway, as a result of that no one's really

working on the treehouse and it's been quite wet lately. I've moved out and made myself a little bender out of a bit of tarp I found.

When Ash asked who wanted to come and look at Cerrig-cwm, I said yes straight away. He didn't hear me at first, because he was busy trying to persuade Big Johnny and Larch to come. They're really seasoned activists, they've lived on site for ages. In the end I was the only one who joined him when he started down the hillside track. He looked surprised and asked what I wanted.

'To see Cerrig-cwm' I said.

'Oh. Go on then.' he said absently.

He was carrying a rucksack and an empty jerrycan. I had my rucksack with all my worldly wealth in. No one'd touch my stuff while I was away, but if someone was hungry they might eat a bit of my chocolate and replace it next time they went to the village. And one time I was away all night when I went to a party in Ystrad and next morning there was someone in my bed. With boots on. He'd come late at night and well, everyone has to have shelter don't they? So, if someone was going to crash in my bender I thought I'd rather they used their own bedding. I might not be back for a while and Kerry's mate Lorna hasn't had chance to go down the village yet so I only have a couple of choc bars left and I need them. Also I took out a couple of library books and I had to pay a fine when the other one went missing for two weeks after I left it by the fire one night. We share everything. Some people turn up with nothing, if we didn't share with them where would they be?

I asked Ash if I could help with anything and he gave me the jerrycan to carry. It was pretty awkward getting it down the hill and over the stile, but I didn't want him to think I couldn't pull my weight if we set up a new camp, and he did do the driving, up that hairy mountainside track. I thought we were going over the edge a few times.

My first glimpse of Cerrig was incredible. It's a hidden valley, just a bit of a dip in the ground originally but then someone dug a small quarry for house-building stone. The footpath winds around and enters a rocky gateway framed by the sides of the stone pit. It's magic. Once you're in, no one can see you unless they peer over the

trees and brush at the top of the cliff on the mountain side. Like Stig of the Dump's pit.
There's heaps of stone and small canyons between. A trickle of water coming down the wall, not enough for a water source. We kept looking and found a beautiful pocket spring falling into a bowl just outside the far end of the valley. Not too far to lug a jerrycan. Small willows everywhere, Salix alba I think.
There's a rough bit of field just up above, where Emrys said we could do some growing if we can give him a hand with the fences and give him a bit of veg now and again. Down the mountain there's some woodland and loads of hazel! I've been down there to cut some poles, so I'll write again when I've finished building my bender. Don't want many more nights under the stars, it looks like rain again.

love Martha.'

Wow, a whole field. I'd had a bit of success with some raised beds in the yard, but what couldn't I do with a bit of field, I remember thinking. Dream on. Things were going well for the first time in my life. I still couldn't get over the novelty of having money left over at the end of the week, plenty to eat, money to spend, occasional new clothes and - money to save.

As the year turned, Mart's letters became a high point. It was like a sort of hippy soap opera. Really livened up that first winter at Prospect Road.

'Kerry's here now. She's got a thing for Ash but she won't admit it. He is good looking though. The other day he was making himself a pair of leggings out of sheepskin and he was sitting there trying them for size. He looked like Robinson Crusoe with his long hair all loose. Kerry has got on with the field, she's cleared a lot of land and started sowing seeds. I'm on fencing and bird scaring duty. I suggested that we just stick Ash up there to frighten the birds away but Kerry didn't see the humour. She's got it bad.
As spring comes on the air's like wine, the brief showers of rain are accompanied by rainbows scattered all around the valley. One was

155

*upside down, like a smile in the sky. I've read about this, it's a
circumzenithal arc caused by sunlight hitting ice crystals in
cirrostratus cloud at about 46 degrees...it's really a piece of halo.
We probably had such a good view because we're up so high, it's
more than 1000 feet above sea level here, which makes Allt-y-Grug
officially a mountain.*

*I found some demijohns at a jumble in Ystrad and am going to make
some wine this summer, the mountain's covered in bilberries and
there's wild raspberries and overgrown damsons everywhere. The
bender's finished and cosy, Kerry's too, hers is lined with the old
Indian throw she had at Newbury. The red and yellow one she
managed to save from the wreckage. I try not to think about all that.
The little willow trees are such great playgrounds for the cats, Ash
has a couple and they love to race around running up and down
trees. Big Johnny used to say there was a big black cat in this valley
but I think he's smoking too much dope. Do you know anything
about cryptozoology? It's illogical, how could there be a big cat
living up here and no one's seen it? Big Johnny says, loads of
people have seen it, but I pointed out that most of them were stoned
at the time. He and Larch have been up a few times now. We should
rename the place Stoner's Valley, Kerry says. Not much work gets
done with them around.'*

Hippy blokes. Lazy buggers. Could have told her that. But she's not
used to blokes. She seemed to be having the time of her life. I was
getting more and more curious to see all the things she described.
But I had my first big jobs. One woman in Redland wanted me to do
her massive garden long term, every week, six hours a time. This
was the big league. I imagined myself living in a cottage at the
bottom of the garden in some English shire with the lord of the
manor giving me my orders, standing in the middle of the lawn with
me tugging my forelock and agreeing to everything while doing as I
like, cos I'm the gardener. And if anything doesn't turn out the way
they want, *'frost'* would be my permanent excuse. *'Frost'* and *'they
danged pigeons, sir'*. You could generally bank on the average rich
idiot knowing nothing about how anything worked. In those days it
was an article of faith with me that no one outside the labouring class

could put their own trousers on without the help of a diagram. Oh, I didn't mean any disrespect to Deena with that. That was a one-off.

I thought about starting to grow my fringe specially. And growing old as a fixture with supreme power over a vast kitchen garden and acres of shrubbery, a cantankerous wizened figure, like Ben Weatherstaff, with birds lighting all over me and a whiff of magic. Sometimes I awoke from my daydreams of being Head Gardener at Lady Muck's country spread to find myself standing stock still staring at nothing in a Bristol garden, the sound of a passing bus rousing me.

Don't get me wrong, I can't stand the gentry. But I don't see any other way I'm ever going to get to live and work in a place like that. And the gardener's a law unto herself. *'For where the old thick laurels grow, along the thin red wall...'* Apart from the imperialist bollocks, a poem that really understood gardens. Rudyard would have made a good anarchist - if he hadn't been such a conformist. Pity.
'Now Chil the kite brings home the night
That Mang the bat set free...'
Martha told me that there were rumours of red kites further up the valley.

'There's so many buzzards up here, Emrys's sheep are so manky they're always hanging around waiting for one of them to die. There's often a dead one on the hill. The lads are so flippant about it. How hard is it to dip them and feed them properly? I don't like Emrys, whenever he comes around he ignores me and talks to the men. Kerry says you're lucky he ignores you, I wish he'd ignore me. She's uneasy these days. Ash barely talks to her. Well he doesn't talk to me either but I'm used to that. I don't know much about anything really.

Kerry and me got hold of a double handed saw. It's great for cutting up big logs, and I thought, what if I could split the biggest ones until they were small enough to cut. There must be a way, get something into a split and lever them apart. Some sort of wedge. Like an

axeblade. The wine came out Ok, it's more or less ready but we're saving it for winter. We've got jars and jars – ruby and golden and pale - rowed in the back of my bender, where the blokes can't find them until it's time.
Kerry's making blackberry jam on the gas stove I used to pot up the surplus peppers back in July. I make frasers – practically wallpaper paste fried really – but they're good with some of my strawberry jam on. I got a knitting book out of the library and am going to make us all socks, hats and gloves this winter. Kerry says she's going to do rag rugs for the floor. Larch is drying his Purple Haze harvest. Ash spent three weeks building a solar dryer for dope plants. I couldn't get him to help with anything for a month. Me and Kerry carried all the poles for the tipi kitchen ourselves in the end. I'm tired. Be glad of the rest come December.

The woodpile's growing. Winter's coming, the ferns are brown and crisp and the sprays of heather are dry and crumbling. Swallows are long gone, and the pipistrelles don't flitter around our heads at night while we sit by the fire anymore. All holed up in the derelict barn, and the lesser horseshoes in the old mine workings. I love sitting by the fire at night, picking out splinters by candlelight, trying to turn a heel, Kerry with her rughook eyeing up our most colourful clothes, waiting for them to fall apart. The lads arguing about monkeywrenching and passing the spliff around.'

I frowned as I read the latest missive. These blokes weren't like the Newbury lot. What a bunch of bums and puffheads they sounded like. I hoped Mart and Kerry were Ok. This would be their second winter up there.

Wished I had time to make things and grow things to eat and drink. Most of the time I was dealing with bloody useless hardy perennials, but I tried to slip in a good word for the native plants, rebranding the prettier ones as wild flowers not weeds. I also wanted a cat. But the landlord wouldn't buy it.

Simon wanted to move out of Prospect Road too, sick of the damp – literally, he spent all last winter coughing. But though we were now rich by the standards of people who got their dinner out of skips, we

158

were still scraping by as far as getting a better house was concerned. If the gas didn't cost so much we could've got together the deposit on something better. Simon was still getting a bit of Housing Benefit and I was going to have to claim some as well over winter when the ground was frozen and the gardens were sleeping – there's only so many apple trees to prune and shrubs to relocate.

Back then Housing Benefit was the death-knell for getting a decent rental. The vast majority of landlords still have *NO DSS* on their adverts. That rules out everyone who can't work full time. Everyone whose health isn't a hundred per cent. Everyone with a kid once they get divorced, like Deena.

She told me once, breathlessly, about the nightmare she went through when she left her kids' dad after she got her diagnosis. He'd made her so much worse, calling her a nutter and threatening her, she'd got more and more anxious. She went through hell and high water before she got her house - after her son was old enough to work and landed a plum job with the local authority. Deena had helped him tooth and nail all through school and despite all the moves, the shelter, the six months lets that were reclaimed once Deena had spruced the place up, he flew through sixth form and aced his public health course at college. Three times Deena had a notice to quit after she'd done up some mouldy dump. The landlord would invariably rent it out to rich students at twice the price he'd been charging Deena. Three times she had to move the kids on a couple of months notice. But now with Richard working – she had a little palace, and a gardener. Me.

I was worried about Simon. He was still coughing. It had been four weeks.

❄

'How do you feel now?' Bridget was worried.
'Like death warmed up.' Simon said. He looked at her from glittery feverish eyes, hair wet with sweat. 'I didn't get a wink of sleep last night. Coughing my guts up all the time.' His shoulders shook with

another coughing fit. It went on and on, like rocks rolling down a hill.

'Ugh.' he said at length. He pulled his handkerchief away from his mouth. 'Oh God. Ugh..Oh...'

Bridget saw the blood and her heart froze.

'I'm calling the health centre.' she said, when she could overcome the suffocating feeling in her throat.

'You won't get any argument from me. Ough..couf..' Simon bent over his hanky again.

'Hello? Yes. Yes, four weeks. Has he lost weight? He's always been so skinny it's hard to tell.' Bridget thought about Simon's finely drawn cheekbones. Sharper than ever in recent weeks. 'Yes, I think he has. But...listen, I called because - because he's coughing up blood.' she finished, and waited in terror for the receptionist's reply.

'Oh, oh that's a relief. Yes, you can call us back on this number. Thanks. He'll get an appointment by the afternoon? Thanks. Thanks, g'bye.'

She clicked Simon's mobile phone off and pushed the aerial in hastily.

'They said not to worry, it sounds like a chest infection and they'll call you with an appointment within the next two hours'.

'Cheers. Oh God, I want to go back to bed, but I don't want to have to climb up those stairs again.'

'Use my room.' Bridget helped him up and led him to her room. He was soon tucked up and asleep, in a far tidier bed than he'd known in years. Bridget was left waiting for the phone to ring.

Oh God, I remember that morning. It went on for ever. Until it was time to help Simon on with his coat and lend him an arm down to the health centre. I didn't enjoy that half hour in the waiting room while he saw the doctor.

'They're sending me for a chest X-ray. They think I've got pneumonia, but they're checking for TB as well.'

'What?!'

160

'Yeah, apparently it's on the increase with rotten housing and people not getting a decent diet cos of all the unemployment.' He suppressed another cough, and went on, 'Thatcher's legacy. Victorian values, Victorian diseases. A traditional Christmas for us.'

'Bloody Dickensian!' Bridget burst out.

She phoned for a taxi to take them to the BRI. They rolled smoothly past the landmarks, all but lost in the cold November mist. The old squat on Ashley Road where Simon lived as a squeegee merchant. The traffic lights where he plied his trade. The dust shop. The boarded-up old carriageworks with MELT inexplicably graffitied across it, where Mart used to stick all her flyposters. The Sally Army shop that stood on the site of the old Demolition Diner – the squatters' paradise of 1992 vintage.

'I remember Wilbur asking for a G and T when we had that party.' Simon mused. 'Joe Mackay brought a barrel of home brew and there was Wilberforce hoping for something with an olive on a stick in it. At a squat party.'

'Was he really called Wilberforce? Or did he just talk posh?'

'We never found out his provenance.' Simon answered. A fit of coughing stopped his reminiscences. His breathing was fast and shallow, wheezing slightly.

'They're going to do tests too.' he added. 'For TB. And...HIV.' he said as lightly as he could.

Bridget was still, a cold feeling washing over her. 'Because your immunity's a bit low?' she ventured. 'But that could have been anything. The damp, all those months you didn't have any decent food...'

'Yeah, I told them all that. But you know what they're like. They still think it's a gay plague. Anyway, I've always been careful, on the rare occasion I've had any need to be. It won't be that.' he said comfortingly.

'Sure. It won't be that.' Bridget agreed, hiding the terror in her heart. 'Look at the state of our house. Mould everywhere. Slugs roaming the range like bison on the prairie. Walls dripping with damp. It's enough to make anyone ill.'

'Yeah, the doc says TB's on the increase for just that reason. He calls those council flats nearest the surgery 'the punishment block' because there's been so many cases from there. My chest hurts.'
'Don't talk any more.' Bridget advised him. Held his hand all the way to the BRI, through the long wait outside the Radiology department, in the cafe where they got an insanely extravagant round of coffees, all the way home in another taxi, until she saw him back into bed and ran down the chemist for his antibiotics.

She remembered what the doctor had said to her:
'If the results come back positive, everyone who's been living in close contact with Simon will have to have tests and chest X-rays too.'
That's me, she thought. Plus Michael, and...
Martha.

'Hi Bridge, it's me. How are you surviving over there in Bristol? Hope the house isn't too cold. How is Simon? Thank goodness it wasn't TB. Or – or any other bunch of initials, either. Hard to believe that you can still get that in this day and age. But I'm not surprised he went down with pneumonia living in that place. Any luck on the housing list? I remember Simon telling me that Wilbur was mad as a fish and had asthma and he still had to wait three years to get housed. That house is so fucking cold. Yeah, I'm getting good at this swearing thing aren't I? Remember when I wouldn't even say 'rabbit shit?'

I'm all right anyway, my burner keeps the place warm as toast. It's the warmest winter I've had for two years. Christmas in two weeks and I'll be breaking out the homebrew. I've made socks for Kerry and hats for each of the boys, and Kerry's made a load of cakes and there's all the fruit pies we stashed in Emrys's auntie's freezer. We haven't got a big enough hearth for a proper Yule log but we've piled up a whole range of big logs under the bender so I can reach under the tarp and grab one when evening comes. One of those babies will last all night. They are to a Yule log what Cadbury's mini-rolls are to a Swiss roll.'

162

I was starting to worry about Martha's safety living up there. I'm not paranoid about health but if she'd seen Simon, sweating and shivering in bed for that awful two weeks, me running back and forth with cool drinks and antibiotic tablets, she'd question whether halfway up a bloody mountain was the best place to live. Simon was still coughing and a bit breathless, but improving. He needed summer's warmth to get him really well again. We had to, had to get out of Prospect Road though. We couldn't go through another winter in this place. Back then, I didn't know what to do. I couldn't think of a solution. Wished we had a wood burner. All that skip wood out there would soon warm us up.

※

'What do you reckon, Si?' Mick was here on a flying visit while he helped Sean with a house wiring in Southville. 'Where you gonna go? You can't stay another winter in this dump, mate.' He shrugged deeper into his leather jacket and stood contemplatively, watching Simon's face keenly.
'I know.' Simon shivered. He was curled up in the old armchair next to the feeble radiator in the downstairs bedroom. Bridget was in the 'catbox' upstairs for the duration.
'I'm too hot now.' he objected, as Mick tucked a blanket round him solicitously.
'Tough. I'm not having you ill again. Ran my feet off looking after you.' Bridget said firmly, flashing a grin at Mick.
'Seriously, ol' puss. We can't have you dying in all directions of the cat flu or whatever. Where are you goin' to go for next year?'
'I dunno.' Simon frowned, then reached out for his orange juice and took a swallow to wash down a couple of huge white antibiotic capsules. 'I've had squats that were better than this place.'
'Squatting?' asked Mick. 'Never tried it.'
'It's an experience.' said Simon.

※

I never really understood what happened to Mart up there at Cerrig-cwm. Her letters became less frequent and more obsessive. Kerry never wrote, she left it to Mart to catch us up with all the news. So I never knew just why Kerry upped and went just after New Year like that. Didn't even find out about it til Mart finally wrote again.

'Hi Bridge. Hope you and Simon are doing Ok. I am, just about. Plenty of wood and food. But it's weird up here with nothing but these blokes. Ever since Kerry went -'

What? Bridget was surprised.

'- Ever since then, I've been on my own with them. They don't talk to me, they sit around all day arguing. Big Johnny's really surly these days. The Purple Haze ran out ages ago and Ash can't afford the petrol to go down to Swansea to score so they're all irritable all the time. Larch is Ok, he helps with bringing wood in and comes with me to push the bike when I go to the shops and load up the panniers. He says it's always the same when the dope runs short.
'Bang goes all the love and peace,' he says, 'and out comes the booze. It'll be better when spring comes and we get more visitors bearing stash.'

He's right. Big Johnny is on the cider every night now. He sits by the fire arguing with Ash about politics and doing nothing but bend his elbow. The camp is a mess, no one's done any recycling for weeks and I haven't had the energy with everything else there is to do. Big Johnny wants to pile it all up and set light to it. I knew there was no point in me saying anything as they wouldn't listen, but Larch objected, thank goodness.

'You're not burning all those plastic cider bottles next to where I live. I flamin' risked my life to stop road building for four years and I didn't do it to breathe fried fucking hydrocarbons because some lunchout can't get off his arse to take the rubbish and recyc. down to the village. Bag it up and get down there tomorrow.'
Big Johnny seemed to be ignoring him, but he didn't light the rubbish heap. He didn't bag up the bottles. He opened another can and sat there. Staring at the fire.
I miss Kerry. I want to go home. Wherever that is.'

164

I didn't like the sound of things. Why on earth would Kerry just split like that?
It wasn't like her.

'Hi Bridge. I dunno why Kerry left or where she's gone. It was just after New Year like I said. I think she had a argument with Johnny. She came out of the tipi, red faced, looking furious and - something else in her face, I don't know. I went up and asked her what was wrong. All she said was;
'I'm out of here. You want to get out too, quick.'
She practically ran to her bender and came out a few minutes later with her rucksack and bedroll.
'Look after Twinkle for me – I – I'll be back for her but I have to get out of here for a few days. Catch you soon.'
She was off down the mountain track before I could speak to her again.

I soon found out what she was so mad about.   When I went into my bender I saw that one of the three remaining demi-johns had gone. I went to the tipi and there was Johnny, tipping the last of the ruby elderberry wine into his mug. It was really hard to confront him. It's been months since I've bothered expressing an opinion about anything to anyone but Kerry or maybe Larch, when he's on his own. But I thought of all the work...picking the clusters of small tart elderberries, black and shiny as a woodmouse's eye, plucking the berries off and fermenting them in the brewing bucket for days with the bags of sugar Kerry and I carried up the mountain in a rucksack, filtering, racking off, sterilising demi-johns, fitting traps, and caring for the jars for months, shifting them round to keep them warm and bubbling. A labour of love. I thought about the Christmas evenings we spent swigging white gooseberry and rich red blackberry and the rabbit stew Ash made us.

'What the hell do you think you're doing?' I asked angrily.
Johnny stared at me insolently, then smiled a blackened smile, with gaps like fallen tombstones where his missing teeth should have been.

165

'You made it to drink, didn't you? For Christmas? Well it's Christmas. Or New Year, anyway. And I wanted to celebrate, like. You can have a glass with me.' He leered.

I took a step back, not because I was scared of him, but because his breath stank.

'You went into my home and took it without asking.' I said angrily.

'Keep yer hair on. What were you goin' to do, drink it all yerself? I needed a drink, that bitch friend of yours...' his voice trailed off into snarls of drunken anger.

I stood in angry frustration glaring at him, then stalked out. There was no point in talking to him in this condition. I always thought he was a jerk, but Ash sung his praises;

'He's a good activist, tough as nails, you should have seen him at Stanworth Valley, he held out the longest, it took three climbers to get him down, like.'

'Probably too pissed to know the eviction was going on.' I said furiously. 'Look what he's done! Kerry's gone!'

'Kerry made her own choice to come, and to go. People are free to do what they want in this community.'

'Johnny went in my bender and took my wine. How can we have a community without trust?'

'Yeah, well, see, Johnny's been having a rough time lately. It's only a drop of booze. You shouldn't be so hung up on material things.' A rough time sitting on his arse doing nothing? Ash was a blithering idiot. What did Kerry see in him?

'What'll it be next? People can't just take other people's stuff.'

'Lighten up. It's not the end of the world. You've got some left haven't you? There we are then, you were going to share it with him anyway.'

I couldn't believe him. I just walked away. What else could I do?

Kerry still isn't back. I think she's really gone. Twinkle misses her - she's sleeping on my bed but she gets up and wanders about in the night, meowing, sometimes.

It's not the same without Kerry. I wish I could see you and Simon.

Love Martha.'

166

Now I really was worried.

'I think I should go up there.' I told Simon. He looked sceptical.

'What'll you do up there with all the hippies and sheep and drugs? Mart buggered off up there. I told her not to. Now she's messed her life up again. She'll come back when she's had enough. I wish she'd grow up.' he growled, like the grumpy, off-colour cat he was.

I wasn't fooled. I knew he was scared of my leaving him alone.

'Mick'll look after you. He's in Bristol for another two weeks finishing the roof repairs on that other house in Southville, you know, the neighbour of the first place that wanted Sean to look at the wiring in his loft conversion. Mick can stay in the catbox. You know he likes nursing. I reckon he missed his calling.'

Simon watched me with eyes that failed to hide his dread.

'Make sure you come back!' he said nervously.

'I'll be back. With Mart as well.' I said firmly.

I was packing my rucksack with extra woollies when Simon handed me the grubby envelope with the Welsh postmark. Dosbarthwyd Gan - delivered by - troglodytes, judging by all the muddy fingerprints. I opened it with a feeling of doom.

'Hi Bridge. It's Mart. They've all gone. I woke up this morning late, because I had a bit of a cough and it kept me awake til two, and when I went to the spring to get water I noticed that Ash's place wasn't showing smoke, and he's usually up first. Johnny's crummy drunk's bender had the door flap hanging open and there was more rubbish than usual strewn around. When I got to the end of the quarry I called up to Larch in his bender just around the corner of the rock pile. I didn't expect an answer, he's been at his sister's over the New Year.

I got the water, struggling to carry half a can, and went back to base to make some tea. It was so cold and my chest hurt a bit so I got back into bed. When I woke at 1pm I was still tired and cold so I pulled out all the spare blankets from under the pallet bed and snuggled back down. The light faded and I lit the lamp.

I must have slept right through til morning, but when I woke up I found I couldn't get up. I went dizzy when I tried. I grabbed a spade from outside the door and used it to help me over to the gorse bushes. It was too far to the compost bog. I went back in and got back into bed. I felt light headed and didn't want any food, but nibbled some oatcakes just to keep myself going. I thought I heard someone outside and I shouted 'Ash!' 'Larch!' Sounded like the games of I-spy trees that we used to play on rainy afternoons when we hid at the back of your dad's shed.

I'd rather die than shout for help to Johnny, so I didn't. There was no answer anyway. And then I heard a 'Maa!' The sheep had come down. They only did that when it was really deserted. I was a bit scared now. Where was everyone?

'Larch! Ash!' For the first time I wondered why hippies had to give themselves pretentious new names. No answer, not even an ovine one.

I was too tired to work it out. Next time I woke up it was dark again. This evening or tomorrow morning? Could be all the way to tomorrow night for all I knew. Two weeks from solstice and dark at half past three. I ate some tangerine segments and stared at the bender wall, at the pink blanket tucked under the poles for insulation. I remember tucking Simon up in that blanket on Cannon Hill...ages ago...where was Simon? Why wasn't he here?

'You shouldn't have gone up there. I told you not to. Now you're dying of the cold like Scott of the Antarctic. Light the fire. I'm cold. Light the fire, Mart.'

I woke up. Light the fire. There was wood in the basket, and kindling in an old fish and chip box. I crawled out of bed, shuddering at the cold, and, grovelling in front of the burner, I built a pyramid of twigs and stuck a match in. It flared up, sap boiled out of the ends of the twig and smoked. Wood frozen. How many days have I been lying here? I shoved the fish and chip wrapper on. Went up like a firelighter. Thank God for greasy nourishment. I hastily stuck the bigger sticks on and soon had a tiny warm cone of heat. One big log at the side. Another leaning across it. Snap. Crackle. Pop. Like Rice Krispies. I chuckled, croakily, and wrapped the blanket around me.

168

I put the kettle on top of the burner. It would take forever to boil but at least I wouldn't have to sit up and sort out the gas stove. I dragged my nest of blankets over to the rag rug Kerry had put in front of the stove. Nestled down in reach of the wood basket. Drank some cold water while I waited for tea.
When I got it I stared into the flames. The wood was running low. Simon's right. I shouldn't be here. I want to go home.
I want to come home, Bridge.'

Shit. Double shit. Double shit with cream and sugar on top. Yeuch, that's disgusting. Oh hraka.
I pushed the letter into my pocket and practically ran out of the front door, yelling 'I'll be back! Keep well wrapped up! Mick'll be here after work! Five-thirty!'
I had to get the earlier bus. There was just time if I ran and ran and ran.
Panting, lungs aching, I staggered into Maudlin Street and into the coach station. Slumped down on the back seat, I watched the grey February day roll past the windows without really seeing it.
I was going to bring Martha home. Where she belonged.

The bus pulled into Swansea coach station, at the base of a strange building in brown and white layers, like a double decker sandwich. I was cold and cramped. The sight of the shopping centre made me hungry. Wholemeal and white. I staggered off the bus and looked around.
'Er - er.' Oh God I even sound like Mart now.
'Er, scuse me, which is the bus for Swansea valley? Yeah, up past Pontardawe. Oh, I dunno. It's near Y-strad gine...lace...this place here...Thanks.'
I blushed. I forgot I didn't know how to pronounce it.
The bus bumped off, on its long journey up the valley.

I wondered where to get off. The bus rose further and further up the misty valley. I felt like I was nearing the ends of the earth. Wondered what the hell was going to happen and where I was going to sleep tonight. As I neared Pontardawe I asked the other travellers if they knew a place called Cerrig-cwm. They all looked blank except a middle-aged woman wearing wellies, who carried a lot of shopping bags.

'Cerrig-cwm? That's on my nephew's farm. You looking for the hippies?' she enquired.

'Yeah, er, well sort of. I've come to see my friend Martha.'

'Not moving in up there are you?'

'N-no. No, not at all.'

'There we are then.' Where? Where are we? I wondered, until I realised it was just a Welsh verbal tic.

'I'll show you where to get off. You can walk up with me and I'll show you where the footpath is. Take you straight there.'

'Uh- thanks. Thanks a lot.'

Relief flooded me. As we got off the bus at the end of the world, I offered to help carry some bags. The farm woman gratefully offloaded some of them and we started the climb. I had black spots in front of my eyes long before we got halfway.

'From the city are you?'

'Yeah.'

'Not used to climbing hills, is it?'

I grinned at her but saved my breath for climbing. Just before I knew that any doctor would have said I was about to have a coronary we reached the fork in the path.

'This is you here. Say hello to Martha for me, there's tidy. I haven't seen her in a week.'

'Thanks. Yes, I will, ta.' I waved awkwardly as the farm woman's wellies stumped on untroubled by the forty-five degree slope.

I wandered lonely as a sheep along the faint, muddy track that wound in and out of frozen heather clumps and frost-blackened bracken.

'Where's this valley then?' I muttered to myself. I remembered Mart's description of the steep stone walls opening up and stumbled across the entrance to the quarry almost by accident. I walked in, feeling as if I was in a dream. The misty, damp stony hollow looked back at me, water dripping endlessly down the black cliffs that backed it. Apart from a couple of grouse that put up, calling 'Go back, go back' to me the place was deserted.

Go back. I couldn't do that. Not til I found Mart.

As I walked along the stony path I looked for signs of habitation. A rounded, snug shelter made of green canvas tarp stretched over branches was around the corner. The stovepipe poked cheerily out of the roof, with a little pointed hat on. Pixies obviously lived there. I called out.

'Er, hi, anyone in? Anyone at home? I'm looking for Martha. I'm her friend, 'Scuse me for coming in.'

I remembered that Mart said her bender was in a small hollow of its own near the end of the valley so I walked on. A derelict rough shelter flapped its door sadly as I passed. The entrance was littered with empy bottles. I hurried on past, shuddering.

There. A small neat bender hung with fluttering bunting. As I got closer I saw the butterflies on the fabric. Had to be. I called, and tapped nervously on the canvas.

'Mart? You there?'

I wondered what the score was, then decided that I hadn't done an eighty mile journey to dither outside a tent. I lifted the grey woollen blanket that covered the door. Peeped inside. A witches' cottage of herbs bunched hanging from the ceiling, colourful wraps lining the inside, a tiny stove made of a Mazola corn oil can by the looks of it and resting on, no way – a baking tray! A hearthstone made of a slab of the same grey stone that littered the quarry floor. Pots and dishes ranged neatly on the table that was an old door set on two beercrates. A faint smell of incense and garlic with a touch of rabbit stew and socks. A half-knitted bright red stocking cap and a large envelope lying on the bed, pushed between the pages of a copy of Ursula Le Guin's Wizard of Earthsea.

An envelope. Addressed to me.

❄

171

10. Darkness.

I was warm now I'd managed to find the matches and light the fire. Martha's gas stove still worked so I had the kettle on. The spring water in the jerry was still fresh luckily, as I didn't know the way to the spring and dusk was falling.

I wondered about the letter. But it had my address on and everything. Martha wasn't anywhere to be seen. I'd wandered all over calling her and been answered only by sheep. I unrolled my sleeping bag and slipped the letter out of the envelope. It was surprisingly bulky. I'd come all the way here. I couldn't find Mart. She was lost, and so was I, now. At the end of my wits, I picked up the bundle of papers and started reading.

'Hi Bridge. I feel a lot better now.'

Now she tells me. I shoved another log on the fire and poured out a mug of red wine to stick on top of the burner.

'My lungs are still making a noise like bagpipes but my fever's nearly gone and I can walk round the camp. I brought two big baskets of wood in so the bender's all toasty again. I'm hardly coughing at all after the first three days of being kept awake. I had some of my homemade violet and honey cough mixture and a sort of weird garlic decoction that I learned from Kerry last winter. Ash and Johnny still haven't come back but Larch was over yesterday and he says they've gone over to Neath to sell some Big Issues for a mate of theirs who's got bronchitis too. They'll be gone for a few days probably.
Kerry wrote, finally, but I didn't get the letter til this morning as it was at Emrys's auntie's house and the boys weren't around to fetch it over the mountain to me. She says they're planning to open a squat in Bristol. She didn't tell me the address, just that it might be a house on Sussex Place. She asked me to go on looking after Twinkle and she'll be back up to get her and the rest of her stuff in a couple more weeks.

'Mart, I think you should get out of there. That Johnny can't be trusted. He's been after me for weeks. It was bad enough that Emrys was always creeping round me but at least he didn't live nearby. I know they never bothered you, it was always me, but you never know. Come back with me when I come up. I shouldn't have left you there. I'm sorry. I was really upset, I didn't think until I was on the coach, and then it was too late.
I thought Lorna was on her way to Cerrig, I met her coming up, on my way down the mountain, and she did say she'd be coming over after Christmas. If you see her tell her she can have my bender if she wants to kip over. And hide the chocolate! You know what she's like. Got the permanent munchies. I'll see you soon. Give Twinkle a stroke for me. Love Kerry.'

Well, Lorna never came. But Johnny came back alone today. He was in a filthy mood, says Ash is a bastard. I'm guessing that Ash got sick of doing all the work while Johnny smoked himself into the Stone Age, as you'd say. Wish he was here so I could tell him to lighten up, it's only material things. I'm glad Larch is here, don't fancy being alone with Johnny now I know how dodgy he is. Maybe I should go with Kerry when she comes. Could I really go back to the city? It's so beautiful here. But too many jerks. Too much work. I don't know what to do. Twinkle is lying on my arm as I write. I won't be able to post this today, too busy sawing wood. Larch might be able to post it, he took the last one...'

'...Hi Bridge, never got to post the letter so the story continues...Lorna's here, but she's about as much company as a sack of potatoes – less even. She never stays the night, but comes up every day to get stoned with the lads and hang around the fire in the tipi all afternoon gossing about the village, who's taking what, who's pregnant and who's a bitch. So boring. She comes up with her leopard print jacket and bleached hair piled high and the first thing she says when she gets here is 'Where's Ash? I want some dope.'

This place is useless without Kerry. She was the only one doing anything real. The rest of them just want to get stoned all the time. It's really lonely. Kerry's supposed to be here soon but no word from

173

her. I think she's waiting til the weather's better to make the trip. It's been nothing but cold rain lately. I know I ought to take this down to the postbox but can't be bothered to move. I'm in my bender writing by the fire. At least it's warm and dry here, the bender poles are starting to crack in the heat a little even.

The odd slug wanders in and eats my books but I've got hardened to picking them up tweezed between two bits of kindling like a morsel in chopsticks and flicking them out. There was a mouse, but Twinkle nailed him and crunched him up. Firm but fair she is. God, I'm turning Welsh too. None of the others apart from Ash is Welsh but they've all picked up the accent. Drowsing in the fire's warmth, remembering the summer days on the mountain – maybe the last summer here...'

I drowsed too, stretched out on a lumpy rag rug, warmer than I'd been in months. I turned to the next sheet.

'...buzzards mewing, circling above my head, spiralling up, up on the thermals above the cliffs of the quarry. Two, three, then four, five, six of them. Two of them swinging figures of eight in the sky, courtship flight. I watch them until they're almost invisible specks in the sky, then lose them, eyes watering. Afternoons roaming over the heathery sides of Allt-Y-Grug, a sea of humming, buzzing purple, almost floating on the scent, surrounded by clouds of honeybees. A trip to the spring with the jerrycan in a wheelbarrow, walking heel to toe along the narrow sheep track to the waterfall that tinkles into the stone bowl below, frothed in harts-tongue fern, maidenhair, blueish lichens, and moss cushions, beautiful green crystalline architecture.

Skylarks ascending, lifting lifting into the blue, singing higher and higher until they drop with a peeow peeow peeow. I look up to the mountain top, craggy and brown with deep shadows where the July sun can't reach. Old workings. I see a dark shape below the nearest cliff – a cave mouth? Don't remember seeing that one before. It moves slightly. I freeze, seeing the body language for cat. Johnny's stories about big cats come back to me. It's just a shadow. It raises its head. It's no shadow.

The black shape perched on a rock taking the sun swung its head round on its long, graceful neck. I crouched behind a heather clump, getting a glimpse of it loping away down the mountain towards the lower path that I'd just come along. Vanished into the bracken. I ran back down the path, running towards a big cat – but it didn't look that big and I had to see – just in time to see it shoot across the path and disappear back into the sea of shoulder high bracken that tumbled sixty feet to the village below. A big black cat – about the size of a border collie or a bit bigger – square jaw, muscular body, a long tail with a rounded tip. Like a miniature Bagheera. Oh my God. Larch and the rest of them were right. Even Johnny. The Beast of Allt-Y-Grug was real.
I suppose you'll think I'm crazy now.'

Blimey O'Reilly's pants! A big cat! Dunno what scares me the most, the thought of Mart going off her trolley or the idea that I'm sleeping in a tent tonight with a leopard or something on the prowl. It can't be. Not really.

'For the rest of the week I found myself looking nervously over my shoulder, but the way the cat fled from me made me think that it wasn't much of a threat to us.'

That's all right then! Puts my mind right at rest.

'Later, Emrys complained that something had been at his sheep. Apart from warble fly that is. Being catted was a far more humane death. We all agreed not to say anything in the village. Some fool would come up and shoot it, or anything else that rustled in the bracken, like us for example.
On autumn evenings Ash would brew up the mushroom tea after he'd been foraging on the Sleeping Giant all day. He says, once you get your eye in they're all over the place. Remember Mick saying it'd be easier if magic mushrooms were nine feet tall and blue?'

Heh. He was funny that night.

'I wasn't sure at first, my head's already weird enough.

175

But all the 'shrooms seemed to do to the others is cause a lot of giggling followed by the silence of what could be peaceful reflection or, knowing this lot, complete catatonia. So I took a good swig.

At first it was a world of mushroom-flavoured air, the feel of them in my mouth, rubbery, long after I'd chewed a mouthful and drank the juice. Then, once I'd got used to the feeling that everything, including my own flesh, was made of mushroom and the smell had faded, everything just got bigger and brighter and somehow more meaningful. At first I laughed at anything, everything Larch said was hysterical, but then there was a sense of ascending, lifting lifting like the skylark.

Higher and higher until you reach a plateau when every sense is suddenly intense, but different, so that the grass around my feet as I wandered across the bowl of the quarry to get a drink of juice from the jug looked like a tiny forest of sprouting pines. I bent down and touched it. It was grass, whatever it looked like, dancing and twirling spirals like a '70s carpet. The scattering of small fragments of rock at the bottom of the old stone mounds was like the craziest paving ever, I spent what seemed like hours watching the pattern shift and change. But when I came to myself I was standing holding the jug of orange juice in one hand and a mug in the other and Larch still hadn't told me to hurry up and pass it over, so it can't have been that long. I drank a mugful of orange. Taste explosion, like a world of oranges, like munching your way through a grove of them in one bite.

Funny, the chocolate Lorna gave me tasted like candles. Guess it's mostly fat and not much chocolate at all. Off-putting or what?

I roamed about the quarry for an unknown time. Larch came up to me.

'It's like..' he said.

'What?' I asked, expecting something profound.

'It's like...Skaro.' he said at last.

'Skaro?'

'You know.'

Dr Who. I looked around. Oh God, Bridge, he was right. It just needed the barbed wire and ruined fortresses.

'I hope..I hope there's no Mutos wandering about.' I got out.
'Who are you calling a Muto?' said Larch.
We laughed and laughed for about ten years...

I sat back by the fire and dreamed, a world of ideas and imaginings flowing faster than thought through my head. Felt the interconnectedness of all things, sounds like what the Buddhists go on about, but it's true. I've always known it but I felt it - felt it, for a second, then lost it again. Up, up into the dim grey sky again on lark's wings, to the next plateau and the next.

Hard to describe what it was like up there, endless laughter and joy and the feeling of utter belonging, like the whole earth was part of me and I didn't know where my body ended and the mountain began. I walked to the spring, watched the water sparkle and was washed away with the cool, clear, peaty stream that tumbled down the mountain. I stood, breathing great breaths of fresh mountain air, felt it flow right through me and wash me away like my body was just more flow and knew that I was, I was part of everything, knitted in, just one small part like one of the stitches in my woolly hat. Unravelling and blowing away across the mountainside, and happy to go.

I know it's a load of old hippy cliché. But it happened just the same.

In the early hours I clicked back into my head to see that Orion had risen and was striding over black, heather-fringed cliffs to the east, sword swinging at his belt. My molecules reconnected and I found myself sitting by the fire, wrapped up in the old pink blanket, stiff with cold and inaction. I gathered up my remaining stray atoms, curled up under a pile of quilts in my bender and dropped into crowded and colourful dreams.

I saw the black cat again late in the year, a grey November afternoon. It darted away as I approached the spring and vanished into a desolation of chilly rocks above my head.
I don't know why I'm writing all this. I'll never post it. But it's good to get it down.'

177

January 15ᵗʰ·

Suppose I should put the date down as this letter's gone on so many days. Waiting for winter to end is getting weary. There was a warmth in the air today, a breath of damp earth, unseasonal and shortlived. Could it be climate change, happening already? Still raining most days. Found a slug overflowing an old matchbox this morning, gross. Why do they like eating cardboard so much?
I went outside with it, peaceful as I have been since overcoming that fever. It was a thin, blue day, watery sunshine breaking through rain, welcome. I almost skipped to the spring to fill my jerrycan and nearly bumped into Johnny coming back the other way. I jumped involuntarily.

'You don't have t'jump out yer skin at the sight of me' he said sourly.
'It's enough yer never talk to me any more.'
I felt awkward. And a bit sorry for him. He couldn't help being an alchy. Ash said he's had a hard time lately. I couldn't see it, but I felt kindly to everyone today, even smelly crusties like him.
'Well, I was ill for a while. Haven't got out of the bender much.' I said evasively.
'Oh yeah. Was bad myself for a few days.' he sniffed.

Yes, hungover to fuck and down with the DT's I expect, I thought, my charity faltering in the face of the reality of the dirty, hulking figure in front of me.
'I'll make yer a cuppa. Come and have a chat.' he grinned, or leered, his abandoned-graveyard smile giving me the chills.
I didn't know how to refuse, so cursing my stupid social ineptitude, I trailed after him with the empty jerry bumping against my leg.

In the kitchen tipi the kettle took forever to boil. Seeing Johnny drop a grubby teabag into each of two tannin-encrusted tin mugs, it couldn't take long enough for me, though I was itching to get away. He was just itching. He scratched, belched.
'Sos. Manners.' he said.
I mumbled something vague.

'Yeah. Been meanin' to say, er, sorry about that wine. I just needed a drink. I knew you'd gi' me some if I asked cos y'made loads to share and I just – should ha' waited to ask yer but I didn't know when ye'd be back. Sos, like.'

'Uh, that's Ok.' I said reluctantly.

'Yeah, it's been a bit tough lately. Been missing me girlfriend, like.'

'Oh, er, didn't know you had one.' I marvelled at how low some people would sink to be able to say they had a man.

'Ah don't, now.' he grinned. 'Tha's the whole point. Been really down, like. Miss my kid too.'

'You have a kid?' I tried to keep the incredulous out of my voice. He didn't seem to notice.

'Yeah, lil' boy. He's nine now. Chip off the ol' block.'

I stared and hoped for the boy's sake that that was a figure of speech. It was like imagining the results of binary fission of an amoeba with particularly low standards of personal hygiene.

He was encouraged by my silence to continue, not noticing that it stemmed from unmitigated horror.

'Yeah, game lad. E' nicked a swig of me cider when I went for a piss and he knocked it back like a good 'un. Staggered a bit though, threw his guts up before I had ter put 'im to bed. That's my boy. Won't be long 'fore he'll be havin' a drink with his old man.'

I couldn't speak.

'Yeah, and M'lissa, that's my girlfriend, says I shouldn't have let him get hold of it. Doesn't want him growing up like me, she says. So we had a right old ding dong about it.'

'You did?' The kettle was defying the laws of physics. Rewriting Boyle's Law. As the fire burned hotter and hotter underneath, the lid should have been jiggling, but it wasn't.

'Yeah. Hammer and tongs. You should have heard us. Anyway next day Melissa was complainin' that I 'it 'er.'

I went very still.

'I never 'it 'er. I shoved 'er cos she was shoutin' in my face. It's like she says I hit Kevin. I never. I only give 'im a slap cos he was whining. He shouldn't have been out of bed. She's so soft on 'im.'

'You hit him?' I said softly, tensing all over.
'Well y'gotta give 'em a smack now and again. Never teach 'em to behave, any other way. It's not like I 'it 'im hard. I don't believe in bein' cruel.'
'You hit your kid?' I said again, hard.
'Yeah, it's my duty as a dad. I take being a dad seriously. Spare the rod an' spoil the child. My lad's not spoiled. I've seen to it he ain't. He knows 'e'll get belted if he doesn't behave. He's a good boy. Doesn't run round screaming like some kids. Quiet as a mouse, 'e is.' He swigged the remains of a two litre cider bottle and belched again. 'Yeah. Quiet as a mouse.' he repeated.
I got up in a daze. My head was spinning like the fever had come back.

❄

'Quiet as a mouse. She's always quiet as a mouse.' The dinner lady was talking to my teacher. They thought I couldn't hear.
'House-mouse, house-mouse' teased my flat-mate at college.
'She never speaks. And her mother's such a mouse.' I was waiting at the counter of the village shop. The two gossiping women looked sideways at me. I pretended I couldn't hear them and they soon forgot that I was possessed of sentience and continued their psychoanalysis, shooting me quick, disapproving glances from time to time as if I was a piece of furniture that didn't match the curtains.

I looked at my mother that evening. She had mousy hair, a drawn face, twitchy movements like a frightened small mammal, restless.
'Eat up and get to bed.' she ordered. For the first time I heard the fear in her voice. It wasn't me she was angry at. It was him she was scared of. She wanted me out of the way in case I upset him.
Like the last time. I tripped over the stool that had been left in the middle of the floor. Jostled my dad's armchair. Heard the bellow of rage as he spilt his tea.
'Get that child out of my sight!' he raged to my mother who scuttled to do his bidding, cuffing me all the way up the stairs with a final almighty belt across my bottom that flew me across the room onto my bed.

'And stay there!' she yelled.

The bellowing didn't stop though. I heard the grumbling rage rise and fall, my mother's voice rise whining in self justification, sounding more like a child than an adult.
Smash. That was the tea mug. Bang. The footstool, scoring an own goal against the already marked kitchen door. I lay as tense as a board, wanting to put my head under the pillow, scared that if I couldn't hear what was going on then the worst would happen, like I could protect her by being vigilant. Like there was anything I could do.
Bang. Dunno what that was. Crash. Wailing, crying. What was he doing to her? Thud. Thud. The sound of an imploring voice.

I never knew what was going on, but it sounded awful. Next day she'd be tight-lipped and red eyed, but wouldn't betray anything of what she felt. Once there was a ring of red marks around her wrist, but with him it was mostly threat display, like an enraged primate. I never knew if one day he'd go too far and really hurt her. There was no way of knowing what'd set him off. He'd be quiescent for days, even jovial. Joking when I tripped over, my unrelenting tension making me clumsy, or when I stammered through a message from my mother.
'Mum says y'tea's ready.' Eyes on the ground. Submissive. Afraid to speak to him in case I got it wrong. The way you approach a dangerous wild animal.
Except that the big black cat never did me any harm. I never felt any threat from it – probably a female since it was quite small. She wasn't the dangerous animal on this mountain.'

❄

I felt uncomfortable. I wondered if I should be reading this. But it was addressed to me. She never told me. She never told me before.
I wondered why she was telling me now.
I thought how many times I'd envied her for her family.

I felt even more uncomfortable, despite the soft quilts and the warmth of my sleeping bag, the mug of wine I'd mulled on top of the burner, the heat of the crackling flames, Martha's absent hospitality.

'Johnny. For days, Lorna hadn't been around. Ash was away every morning to take the two buses to Neath. Larch was in and out, busy with some wood-turning work he'd landed. He was up at the farm most afternoons, borrowing their lathe for the bespoke chair legs he was making.
I kept to my side of the quarry, or went up the mountain to scythe bracken in readiness for another vegetable bed. Or down the mountain to get firewood. Or across the mountain to help Emrys's auntie. Until Larch got back in the evening and everything was normal again.

The tension was getting to me. I was like a bowstring when I went to bed at night, couldn't sleep, lying awake night after night with images of the past running through my head, no getting away from the memories I had buried deep.
Running down the garden, slipping through the forsythia into Bridge's willow cave. The joy I'd feel, speechlessly, when she was there, grinning her crooked grin, licking her arm to stick on another Happy Tattoo.

Bridge. Who was so brave. Who talked about her dad's tempers as if they were just another domestic problem that you called out the plumber for or something. Her network of secret paths and refuges all around the village made me feel safe. She wasn't scared of anything. What I most wanted, was to be like her. Strong, assured, resilient, indestructible. Fearless. She even had a penknife. Battered, with some blue pattern on the sides. But sharp and effective. She used to whittle us forks to eat stolen slices of pie, peel scrumped apples from Boston's orchard, carve a piece of white wood into a spiral just as decoration for the willow den...

The white shavings on the ground were reassuring. They meant that Larch was here. Safe, friendly Larch, passing a bowl of chicken and vegetable stew to me in an old teatowel. Whittling the evenings away.

'I've nearly finished the chair-legs.'

'Oh. Does that mean you'll be in camp tomorrow then?' I asked hopefully.

'Nah. Got to go down to Pontardawe. Griff's got a piece of old elm for the seats for me. Best thing for 'em. Cross-grained, see. Not easy to get hold of it these days.'

'Yeah, Dutch Elm and all that.' I agreed uncertainly.

A whole day avoiding Johnny. Not good.

Just then Ash appeared.

'Not going selling today?' asked Larch.

'No. Himself's back on the job now his chest's all right. Have to find something in the spring.' Ash said.

Ash here. Good. Well, not great, he's a bit of a twat, but still. Won't be alone with that creep.

I relaxed for the first time in days. Spring was coming. Everything was going back to normal. Johnny was talking about going back to Swansea to stay with his old mates. Good riddance.

I decided to spend the day spring cleaning my bender, although it was a bit early.

Only halfway through January. Still, it was another of those strangely warm days that felt like spring. I got busy pulling out all my bedding like a badger, making separate piles of rubbish, burnables, trash and treasure.

The demi-johns clinked as I pulled the last quilt out. I remembered Johnny glugging down the elderberry. Kerry's face as she stalked out of the tipi. Where was Kerry all this time?

I straightened up for a minute. Suddenly Twinkle dashed past and into the depths of the bender, ears flat.

'What's up with you, missy?'

Distant shouting. Tense all over. Larch? Yes, it was Larch!

Yelling his head off. At Johnny. Scrabble. Thud. Were they fighting? I ran up the nearest mound to watch. Yes. Johnny had just knocked Larch to the ground and was reaching for a rock.

'Drop it!'

I yelled louder than I'd ever yelled before.

Startled, Johnny looked up, dropping the stone.
'You're a fucking nutter! You can get out!' cried Larch as he scrambled to his feet and away. 'Get out of here! We're not putting up with you any more!'
'Yer can't kick me out!' Johnny roared. 'Yer not me landlord!' He grabbed a bottle and hurled it against the nearest stone pile.
Crash. Bang. Johnny stumped furiously back to his fetid nest, kicking trees as he went. Panic flooded me. I shivered on the spot. Wanted to run but couldn't. Dropped slowly to the ground, lay in the wet grass, trembling, huddling below Johnny's line of vision.

I lay there til I was stiff and cold. Lorna spoke from behind me.
'What you doin' there? Where's Ash?'
'It's Johnny. He - he went completely batshit.'
'Doesn't surprise me.' she sniffed. 'He's always in a barney. Where's Ash?' she repeated.
'Don't tell me. You want some dope.' I said.
She looked surprised at the sarcasm.
'What's wrong with that? There's fuck all else to do round here. You could do with some yourself. Come on, girl. Get stoned. Make the winter go with a swing.' She grabbed my hand and swung it. Surprised, my arm went with it, and despite myself my heart lifted. Ash strode up.
'Don't you reckon, Ash? We should get Mart stoned. She needs to chill.'
He grinned.
'Yeah, come on, I'll roll a spliff.
'Larch...'
'He's Ok. That Johnny is a fuckwit. I'll have a word with him. Time he fucked off, he's caused enough trouble.'
I gave up and followed them.
'Here' Ash passed me the expertly-constructed spliff.
I sucked on it, coughed, took the smoke back, held it until I was red eyed, puffed it out in a bonfire-scented cloud and found myself grinning a stoned grin at Ash. He wasn't so bad. Laid back, that's what he was. Johnny wasn't going to do anything with Ash here. I smiled merrily.
'Look at her face!' Lorna laughed at me.

Larch came up, wincing angrily as he sat down.
'That arsehole's bruised me right down my back.'
I jumped up, a bit wobbly, and said:
'I've got some comfrey ointment. I'll get it for you.'
'Ah, thanks.' he said, smiling up at me.
I felt warmer than I had in weeks. A warm glow all over me.
I came back to the fire and accepted another puff. And another.
After that, I sat and smoked with them in the afternoons. Included at last. One of the gang.

Jan. 19th I think.

Ash got us some dope. I owe him a tenner. Haven't finished tidying up the bender yet. Made my bed nice but the rest can wait til a sunny day. Wonder what Kerry's doing.
Lot of birds flying over the quarry. Was going to get my binoculars and look them up but Larch passed me the spliff just then so I forgot. The days are nice, easy, not getting much done but who cares. Feel relaxed. Life's chilled.

At night when the dope wears off I feel light headed, heart pounding, uneasy.
Jumping at every noise. A bit paranoid. That's the dope. Heh, Ash always said it makes some people paranoid a bit. Silly. Nothing there.
Rustle. Someone coming? Is that Johnny? Creeping up to my bender. Maybe he wants to get his own back. Not safe to get in conflict with a bloke like that. The stone in his hand.
'Drop it!'
Shouldn't shout at a bloke like that.
Rustle. Crack. Pitter.
The stone in his hand.
Drop it.
Sleep.'

God. Never knew Mart to get wrecked all the time. Wasn't really her thing. Catholic hangover and all that. Hope she'll be all right on it…

185

Jan. About the 23rd or something.

*'Wednesday. No, Thursday. Got up. Had a spliff. Ash gave me a bit
to take home last night. I keep my Rizlas in my pyjama pocket now
to keep them dry overnight. Ash keeps his in his socks hanging over
the fire. Chopped a bit of wood.*
*Stared at the paper for ages before deciding what to write. Should
post the letter to Bridge 'fore it's a whole book.*
*Where's my coffee? Know I left it in here. My books are all fallen
over. Has someone been in? Not that Johnny again. No booze in
here. All gone.*
*The coffee's by the fire in the tipi, I remember now. We ran out last
night. Stupid. No one's going to come in your bender, silly.*

***January. End of winter sometime. Not February yet. I don't think
so anyway.***

*Dark night. New Moon. Pitch black. Candle's burned down. Been
burning it at both ends, hah hah.*

*Crack. What was that. A twig underfoot. I think Johnny's out there.
I think he comes out at night and creeps around. Ash says he went
back to Swansea two days ago but I think he's come back in the
night. Don't be daft.*

Ssswish. Tap tap.
Twinkle. Coming in under the tarp. Batting the hanging toggle.
Go to sleep.
He's here!
A shape in the bender.
No, it's the blanket fallen off the ceiling.
Get up. Have some cocoa. Might as well roll a spliff now I'm up.
Comforting. Head expands. There.
*Lie back down in the dark. Rustle rustle. He's here again. Out there
somewhere. Be glad when day comes.*

Feb 2nd. Imbolc.

I know cos Larch brought a celebration bottle to the evening campfire.

Lorna and Ash were laughing about this horror film they saw. An old one. About that guy holed up in a hotel all winter and going crazy.

'All work and no play makes Jack a dull boy!' Lorna was laughing.

'Are you a dull boy Larch?'

'Huh?' Larch looked up vaguely from the spoon he was carving.

'Sorry if I'm not exciting enough for you.'

'Don't worry. Ash is exciting enough for both of us.'

'Here's Johnny! Here's Johnny!'

I looked round startled.

'Look at 'er! Not Johnny. Johnny. Y'know. Jack Nicholson. Remember when he comes through the door with the axe?'

'Here's Johnny! Here's Johnny! Are you scared Larch?'

'You think you're so funny.' he answered absently. 'Put the axe away Ash, you'll end up clobbering someone with it swinging it around like that.'

'He's not coming back is he?' I asked.

'Who? Jack Nicholson?' But Lorna's attention was distracted by the bottle heading her way. 'Mmm. Strawberry wine. Mad Dog. Mad Dog, get it?'

'Here's Johnny!' Laughter.

It's dark. Candle's guttering. Twinkle's right here on my bed.

Rustle. Pit. Pit. Pitter patter. The crack of stone and the rustle of water. The pittering of bits of debris off the willow trees. The clink of the axe against a stone.

He's here again.

Here's Johnny. Here's Johnny. Here's Johnny.

Fully awake, sweating, terrified, grabbing the headlamp. Click. Silent. Empty.

He's out there. Got to get up, quietly. Open the flap. Too terrified to shine the torch out there. Into his big mad face with the fallen tombstone teeth.

Shriek, and swing the flap open at the same time.

Nothing.

No. Someone's coming. Clunk clunk squelch slip curse.
Someone's coming. Shriek, and shriek again. Let it all out.
'What the fuck? What's happening?' Ash angrily, running up.
Larch's face in the torchlight.
'Steady. Steady. You're having a nightmare. S'all right now. Come
on. Ash, get her a drink.'
Larch crawled in and held me tight. I had stopped screaming by now.
'Steady on girl. It's just a nightmare. That lot shouldn't talk about
horror movies last thing. They know you're high strung-like. Ash,
get me that bottle of wine!'

Larch lit the candles and sat me up with a glass of wine in my hand.
'What was all that about then?' he said kindly.
'I heard him.'
'Who? Ash?'
'No. Johnny.'
'Johnny? He's gone.'
'I think he came back. I - I'm really scared of him'.
'This ain't right.' muttered Larch nervously.
'Look, you don't need to worry. He's gone now. He ain't coming
back. I know he's a creep but he can't hurt you. We won't let him.'
'I heard him creeping about.'
Larch looked even more uneasy.
'You don't want to go losing your marbles over a bloke like him.
Come on now. Drink up and get tucked up again.'
'Don't leave me alone!'
Larch looked bothered.
'You'll be Ok. We're right over there.'
'Don't leave me!'
'Bloody hell.' Larch muttered to himself.

'Has she lost it?' Lorna's voice carried across the clearing.
'Shut up, no, she's fine, it's you lot giving people nightmares with
your Shining rubbish. She'll be fine by tomorrow.'
'Look, I'll stay here until you go to sleep. Or – yeah, I'll kip here and
in the morning we'll see how you are.'

'All – all right.'

Early next morning, about seven, I woke to the dim beginnings of dawn. Larch had gone. I heard his voice faintly outside, talking to Ash.

'No, she's just a bit upset. It's that Johnny, he's got her all worked up. She's been frightened of him for weeks and never said anything. She'll be fine.'

'Larch?'

'Hello, hello.' he said with false cheeriness. 'How are you this morning? No more nightmares?'

'No. I'm all right. What were you saying to Ash?'

'Nothing, nothing, just saying you'll be all right after a bit of sleep.'

He was lying. He thinks I'm crazy. They both do. The heart pounding began again.

'You don't think I'm going off my head do you?'

'Course not! You had a nightmare. It's dark out here. Everyone's been het up over that dickhead but it's all right now.'

I was reassured. Got up, had my share of Coop scrambled eggs and home grown garlic. The chickens wouldn't lay again until at least six weeks past the solstice.

Ash offered me a morning puff. I looked at it.

'No, thanks.'

I heard him whisper something to Lorna that ended 'just as well.'

Did they think I was smoking too much? Did they think I wasn't sharing fairly? What if they threw me out like Johnny. Where would I sleep? What if they got angry with me?

'You Ok?' Ash asked.

'Yeah.'

I should have been more enthusiastic! I sounded sulky. What if they think I'm not grateful. I woke them all up last night. They're probably furious.

What if.
What if
What if.

189

I worried the day away and dawdled when it was time for bed. I sat up most of the night, burning candles, tense to every sound, fighting my confusion and paranoia.
I wished Kerry would get here.

Next morning I walked up to the kitchen. Ash looked into my face, obviously didn't like what he saw there and passed me a mug of coffee silently.
'Ta.' I said gruffly, just like Bridget.   So that's it! She was embarrassed!
'Er, I've been thinking.' he said.' Do you think you should go and see Kerry? You'll feel better with her around. Get over your nerves, like.'
'Yes. Yes I would like to see her. But I don't know where she is.'
'Oh, yeah. Have you got her number?'
'Yeah but I don't have a phone.'
'Go down the village?'
I thought about going down to the village. Realised that I was afraid to leave the camp's familiar boundaries.
'Will – will someone come with me?' I stammered.
'Oh, blimey.' He blew out his breath. 'I'll get Larch to go with you, Ok?'
He walked away.   Looked in at his bender. He and Lorna were talking but I couldn't hear, except … 'can't look after her. Yeah, yeah, I know...'
They can't look after me. They don't want me. I'm on my own. Got to get to Kerry.

I waited for four hours until Larch had time to walk me down to the village. I put my money in the call box and rang Kerry's number. No answer. I felt desperate. Larch walked me back home and I saw him consulting Ash again.
'Lorna? You've got a phone? Can you give Kerry a ring on this number and keep on til you get her? Ta.' said Ash.
I sat on my bed for the rest of the day and tried to be normal. The heart-pounding panics were not as bad today. They would go away. I'd be all right. I fell asleep, Twinkle curled next to me. I felt calm, peaceful.

190

Morning. Chilly dawn. I looked around at my home in that cold light of day. It was time to go. I thought I'd be sad but I didn't feel anything. That had to be a good sign.
I should have done this a long time ago. I know where I'm going, I know the way across the mountain. Just like I always planned when it all got too much. I just have to -'

❄

That was all there was. Oh crap. Oh crapola. It was too dark to do anything tonight. I wondered if Mart would come back this evening. I looked at my watch. Nine o'clock! I'd been reading for hours. What did she mean by that last line? Where has she gone? Oh Kerry where the hell are you?

Me, brave? Resilient? Flippin' indestructible?
I wish.
At least I still have the penknife though. I used it to pick out the cork from the wine bottle. Using the smaller of the two blades. Two blades, and forget-me-nots on the sides. My old battered knife, been kicking around as long as I have.
I fell asleep thinking about forget-me-nots, round and blue like children's eyes.
Forget me not.
Up there in the dark, it felt like Mart and me had been forgotten by everyone.

❄

I opened my eyes to a strange, low uneven ceiling. It was pink and woolly, crisscrossed with curved hazel poles and hung with all kinds of bits and bobs. A pair of socks, a cheap lighter set in an ornate twisted copper wire holder and dangling from a piece of cord, a billhook, its blade rammed behind a fork in the poles, baskets of onions, and a funny looking asymmetrical spider's web made of a thin willow twig tied in a loop and spun with blue embroidery silk. There was a flawed, lumpy quartz crystal tied in near the middle and coloured beads scattered around the web. Feathers dangled from the bottom – small, blue. Blue tit? No, jay. The thing or ornament or whatever it was twirled gently in the slight breeze from the partly open door – no, not door, there was no door, the flap of blanket that covered the arch of hazel that marked the doorway. Outside was a glimpse of grey sky, a fuzz of gorse, the caw of the odd passing crow.

And a sudden, weird, high pitched yipping sound. What the hell?
And again.
'Yip!'
What kind of animal was that? I crawled out of my sleeping bag hurriedly, last night coming back to me in a rush, along with a vague red wine headache and a mouth that tasted like stale wine gums, and not in a good way.

'Mart! You back?'
I poked my head out of the doorway.
'She's not here...' I tried to explain.
The two men in green army trousers and holed jumpers with tattered coats on top stopped and stared. They glanced at each other.
'Who's she?' said the one with the longish brown-blonde hair and patchwork leather jacket under a Barbour more ingrained than any Mart ever sported.
'Dunno. Better ask her.' grinned the tall one with dark curly hair and sawdust stuck to his blue fisherman's jersey under the long black waterproof coat he wore.

I stood up, wrapping my huge wollen cardigan more closely round the t-shirt and leggings I'd slept in and stepping out in thick socks onto the stone doorstep.
'I'm Mart's friend, from Bristol. I came to see her but she's not here. It got dark so I had to crash here. Hope you don't mind.'
'Nah, you're good, love. Just startled us a bit, like. We don't get many visitors this time of year. Er, when did you last see Martha?'
'Me? Oh, July I think.'
The blonde one looked at the dark one. It looked like his film-star blue eyes were the brightest thing about him.

'I thought she was goin' off to Kerry's, or something?' he said.
'She wrote to me last week. And she left a letter for me here. I don't think she knows where Kerry is.' I said.
'Shit.' I heard the dark one say quietly.
They looked at each other again.
'You're her friend, you must know where she is.' suggested the blonde one, as if wishing could make it so. Definitely a forty-watter. Good cheekbones though.
'No, I dunno, I came up to look for her. I think she's ill actually. She doesn't sound right, er, herself, really. When did you last see her?'
He looked away, scuffed his boot in the mud, looked at the tall one. Larch? Larch the carpenter?
'Come on, Ash. You seen her last. I've been up at the farm working the last two days.' said Larch.
Ash looked uncomfortable. He mumbled something.
'What? Ash, you'd better not have gone away and left her. It was your turn to keep an eye on her.' Larch's eyes widened, his voice rising.
'What d'you mean, keep an eye on her? She doesn't need a minder.' I joked, my turn to hope that wishing would make it true.

They exchanged a look that made my heart sink.
'Actually, her nerves have been bad, she's been kind of anxious lately. We've been looking out for her though,' he hurried on, 'giving her some grub and checking on her.'
'What's been going on? Why have people been upsetting Mart? And where is she now?' I asked slowly, anger rising.
Larch looked as if he wished he was far far away from here.
'There was this drunken twat used to live here.'
'Johnny.'
'Yeah, Johnny. He scared her, or something. She started having - nightmares, and being scared to be on her own. We were dead worried about her. Been trying to get hold of Kerry to take her home. Kerry's off in a squat somewhere.'
'Sussex Place.' I said coldly.
'Yeah, there.' he agreed, missing my tone completely.

193

'When did either of you last see her?' I buttoned up my cardigan and reached into the bender for my boots.

'Ash?'

'Er...'

'Ash! You twat! When did you see Mart last?' Larch glared at him.

'It was – yesterday, no, the day before. I saw her smoke anyway. She had her fire going first thing.' he said confusedly. 'I just got back from Clive's at Neath this morning.'

'You promised to stay here until I finished those chairs.' Larch said angrily. 'You know Mart gets on one if she's left on her own.'

'Yeah, but I needed the money. Clive was off sick again and asked me to work his pitch. He doesn't want to lose it by being away too long.'

'In other words, he had a hangover and you wanted to get stoned. Brilliant. Some community. Arsehole.' Larch turned on his heel and walked away.

Ash stared after him.

'It wasn't like that -' he said quietly. I wasn't listening.

'Hang on! Where could she have gone?' I demanded of Larch.

I ran after him, laces trailing.

'Sorry. Sorry.' he said. 'I just felt like punching that twat Ash. We've been trying to get hold of Kerry for days, to get her to come see Martha. Thank God you've come up.'

Typical blokes. Act the superhero all the time, order everybody about and make like they know everything and the minute there's a crisis they fall to bits and run about looking for a woman to take over.

'Has she got any friends round here? Where might she have gone?' I asked firmly, making a start.

Larch ran his hand through his hair.

'Well, she goes to help Emrys's auntie Glad. Emrys is the bloke that owns this place.

'I met her on the bus. She hadn't seen her.'

'There's no one else, really. Just Kerry. And she talked about you quite a bit.'

I stopped.

'She doesn't know where Kerry is. She can only have gone to ours. Hang on.'

I raced back to the bender, pulled on my jeans and warm shirt, threw my coat over my shoulders and ran back, pulling my phone out of my pocket.

'Good luck with getting a signal down here.' Larch grimaced. 'Come up to the farm and use Gladdie's landline.'

I ran back and quickly rolled up my sleeping bag. The fireplace was cold. I left the empty wine bottle there, with a candle stuck in it. Looked around at Martha's little round home one last time. Her books were all tumbled, and there were clothes scattered around. I shoved the letter and the Ursula Le Guin book into my rucksack at the last minute and ran after Larch who was already striding up the narrow stony valley.

'Hello? Hello, Simon?'

'It's me.'

'Mick! Where's Simon? Is he Ok?'

'Sure. He's cat-napping. Been moaning about you and Mart going off and leaving him. Hasn't put him off his Whiskas though. He's great.'

I grinned into the phone.

'Listen, Mick. Has Martha been there? Have you heard anything from her?'

'Mart? I thought you went up there to find her. No, haven't heard anything. She's not here.'

Oh crap. Where is she?

'Mick, I've got to go. Call me if you see her. The signal's rubbish though, you might not get through.'

'Ok Sis. When you coming back?'

'I'm leaving now. See you soon.'

The swish, swish of a plane led me to where Larch was slowly filling up the converted cowshed with wood shavings, turning it into something like a large hamster cage, I thought distractedly. I stood in the doorway, the dim room smelling pine-fresh. He looked up.

'Ah, it's you.' he said. He laid down his plane and smoothed the plank with his hand.

'Lovely. Satin.' he murmured.

'About Mart...' I began.

'Any news?' he asked quickly.

'No, well she hasn't been to mine - yet, but there's literally nowhere else she could go where she knows anyone she really trusts. She must be on the way to Bristol. Or – I mean, where else would she go?'

'Yeah, she'd go home. Or to Kerry, all right, she must have gone to look for her. To find her in that squat. In Bristol.' he agreed, a bit too eagerly.

'Is there a way over the mountain to get to Swansea?' I asked.

'Over the mountain? Well – there's sort of a short cut, but it's not the way I'd go. Past the spring and down through the woods, you can get to the bus stop that way, it cuts off a big corner but by the time you've slipped and slid all the way down, you don't save much. And there's -'

'There's what?' This guy was priceless when it came to making you read between the lines.

'There's – it doesn't matter.'

'I think it does. She said something about a way over the mountain.'

'Ok, it's nothing, there's a lot of cliffs further along, you have to watch out for them. We never go there after dark or when it's foggy. Too easy to get lost.' he said.

And Ash's last glimpse of her was on a dim grey winter morning more than two days ago. Jesus.

I made up my mind.

'Then you and Ash had better run along there and make good and sure she hasn't fallen or got hurt or lost or something.'

'I gotta finish these shelves for -'

'You've got to go and make sure that your friend hasn't got lost or hurt. She's ill, she's having a breakdown and she's missing. What do we do when someone that fragile is missing?' I said, hanging on to my temper by a thread.

'Er. Look for her? Check everywhere she might be, until we find her?'

'You've got it. Now. I'm going back to Bristol, she must be there somewhere. Call me tonight and report back. Here's my number -

no! Not on a bit of paper that you'll lose in five minutes. Here. Go and get Glad to put this in her phone pad.'

I grabbed his arm and scribbled my number firmly. He went like a lamb to the farmhouse door. He was back in seconds.
'Right. She's done it.' he said breathlessly.
'Good. Now you can go fetch Ash. And best crack on down that track before it gets dark. I'm off down to the bus stop, gotta get that afternoon coach. Ring me tonight!'
He was off, dragging his coat on and hurdling the barbed wire fence to the field where the path led to the stone pit. I turned to go back to the farmhouse, but looking up above the quarry cliffs saw Martha and Kerry's gardens. There was no time to lose, but. I could have a quick look, there might be a clue. She might be up there even. I could ring home from up there, the signal wouldn't be masked by stone walls. If only, if only I'd been able to afford the phone sooner, Mart would have my number by now. But it was so new, I was still picking cellophane off it.

The path up to the top field was clear enough, and well trodden. I set off.
I expected everything to be dead and brown this time of year, but they'd made little cloches out of scrap polythene and willow wands. There were hardy salads growing lush and green under there. Sad, dried runner bean vines still draped a wigwam of hazel. Old planks had been built into raised beds, full of ripe leeks, late carrots and kale. Herb bushes were bare and twiggy, except for a surprisingly well-grown rosemary bush. I walked over, glancing at my watch, crushed a sprig between my fingers. The scent, faded by winter but still potent, wafted out. Calming, cheering. I felt my mind clear. Below was a patch of late snowdrops, with their delicate green edging like the line on fine china. I snapped off a bit of rosemary and stuck it in my pocket. Rosemary is for remembrance.

Time to go.

❄

11. Cracking.

'Bridge? Bridge, did you find Martha?'

'Uh...'

'Did you find Mart?'

I roused. Where the hell was I this time? Why was my bed so slanted?

'Have you found Martha?' Simon repeated patiently.

Reluctantly, I opened my eyes.

My neck was at a very unusual angle. I lifted my head. I must have fallen asleep on the old armchair in the kitchen when I got in. God only knows what time of night. Old habits die hard. Missed the afternoon coach, of course. Tractors. Three hour wait for the next. Roadworks. I barely remembered the sleepy stagger home from Maudlin Street coach station last night.

 I struggled to sit up properly and face reality. Yeah. That place again. Had some pretty crap times there. It's Ok to visit but you wouldn't want to live there. Reality is for people who can't handle drugs. Drugs. Hippies. Martha!

'Martha.' I managed to utter, brilliantly.

'Yes, Martha. Your best mate, who you went all the way to darkest Wales to find. Where is she then?'

'I dunno. Hasn't she been here?'

'She has not. D – d'you think we should – y'know? Tell the cops?'

This was heresy. He must be really worried. Perhaps we should tell them...I must be really worried.

'No...no, did Larch ring last night?'

'Hippy bloke with a bad Welsh accent? Overtone of West Country? Yeah. He said 'Tell the dark-haired scary woman that we haven't found any sign of Martha and we think she must have left Wales. Let us know when you find her.' Message ends.'

'Scary woman? The cheeky fucker! They didn't have a brain cell between them! Stoned out of their brains all the time! I tell you...'

'Have we got time for this? Wait a bit, you can hate them later. Where can Mart be?'
'With Kerry.'
'Oh yes?'
'Yes. She's squatting on Sussex Place. But I don't know the address.'
'Spiritual home of HAB.'
'What?' It was way too early in the morning for initials.

'Housing Action Bristol. The squat group. In our heyday we had numbers 4, 5, 23, 62 and 31. We colonised the place.'
'Oh, I see. Well, let's get over there quick. She must be there.'
'Why must she?'
'Because she's nowhere else and I've run out of ideas that don't involve telling the pigs she's missing.'
'Oh. Ok. I get you. I'll call Joe Mac, he'll have the address.'
I jumped up with alacrity, staggered a bit on legs like sphagetti, and headed for the front door.

'Wait.'
'We haven't got time to wait.'
'You need shoes.'
I looked down. Damn, but he was right. I sat down again.
'Where are my boots?'
There they were, lying on their sides near the chair. And my rucksack and coat, flung aside as I got up. I pulled them on.
'Right, let's...'
'Let's sit you down to a cup of coffee and a bit of toast.'
'No time, we have to...'
'Have you seen your own face recently?'
'No, why?'
'If you had, you wouldn't need to ask.'
Simon pushed me back into my chair and handed me a mug of coffee, soon followed by a giant cheese toasty sandwich.
I was going to protest, but I was too hungry. And thirsty. And...well, to tell the truth, spent.

'Can I have some more coffee?'

'Here. Then we get on the road. Joe says it's no. 33.' Simon was pulling on an extra jumper – the blue one that Mick used to wear - and getting into his enormous work boots.

'Are you fit?'

'To go down Ashley Road? Yes. Just don't ask me to go to Abergavenny or Ulan Bator or anywhere.'

'It's further than Abergavenny. West Glamorgan.'

'Really. Shit.'

❊

Shit. We stood on the doorstep at number 33. We had knocked, we had pounded, I had been about to shout through the letterbox when Simon stopped me.

'Wait,' he said, 'If she is in there you'll scare her. It's a squat, remember?'

'Oh – Ok. But there's no one here.'

I looked up at the windows. Number 33 was a tall townhouse, part of one of those long terraces in pink and white and cream that look like Neapolitan ice cream. A narrow house with one lofty window in each of the three storeys. On the ground floor nearest us, a long-haired tabby looked out. I looked up. There was a black cat on the middle windowsill. And at the very top, a small black and white face peered down at us.

'Hi guys, what's happening? Hey, how did Twinkle get in there?' Kerry stopped in mid-greeting as she turned in at the gate and bounded cheerfully up the path towards us.

I had forgotten all about Twinkle. She'd grown quite a bit from the tiny ball of fur I met two years ago.

Kerry was different too, more serious, thinner in the face.

'Hi..we..we're trying to find Martha.'

'Mart? She's not here. Up the quarry, still. I've been over Easton helping at the squat cafe for the last two days.' she answered. 'But how did Twinkle get here?' She unlocked the door and ushered us in. Cracked quarry tiles, paint peeling off the banisters, it was just

200

like our house, but the woodwork was in better nick and the smell of damp was noticeably absent.

'I'm going straight up.' Kerry jumped up the stairs two at a time. We hurried after, explaining.

'...and I got there but there was no one there...Larch, looking for her on the mountain. Missing for two days, cracking up, the letter she wrote, the lads didn't have a clue, dead worried...'

'What?' The message had finally got through to Kerry.

'How long since anyone saw her?'

'Two days.'

'What's the big deal though?'

'She's...she's gone a bit...funny.   Cracking up. Scared, having nightmares.'

'Cracking? She's come to the right place, we cracked this place a couple of weeks ago.' Kerry laughed, then stopped.

'You serious? You really worried about her?'

She didn't wait for an answer but hurried up the last flight of stairs. Someone had wedged a matchstick into the push button automatic light switches to keep them on so we were spared the plunge into extravagant darkness usual in these places.

Kerry knocked at the door on the top landing. A voice said 'Hello?' uncertainly.

'It's Mart.' Simon said immediately.

I *knew* it was Mart. Twit. But I was scared to open the door. Scared of what I might see.

Kerry knocked again.

'Mart? It's Kerry. Can we come in?'

There was the sound of bounding feet. The door opened.

'Kerry! They said you'd be back but I thought you'd never come. I've fed Twinkle but she needs some cat litter. I think she's peed in a corner, it wasn't her fault, I'm sorry...'

'Where've you been, we've been looking everywhere -' I began.

'Shh.' said Simon. 'Hi Mart. Nice to see you again. You staying here or do you want to come home?'

201

Martha looked confused. Her face was very pale and she had dark circles under her eyes.

'I – I...is it Ok if I…' she began.

'Never mind. You stay put, we'll get you some bedding and stuff. Kerry. Tell Joe to get Hab to bring another mattress and some blankets and stuff. When did you last eat?' Simon watched Martha's expression keenly. If he asked too many questions at once, she'd blank out, her hands shaking.

'Fancy some grub?' he tried. 'I did Bridge cheese toasties this morning. Want one?'

'Yeah! Yeah I would!' Martha smiled. Progress.

'You go down and put the kettle on and sort out some grub.' Simon told me.

'But she's my best...what's been happening..?'

'Go!' I went.

❄

Simon came into the kitchen with its crumbling fibreboard floor, like a damp digestive biscuit.

'She's tucked up in bed, had something to eat. Kerry gave her a hit of valerian and she's out like a light. She'll sit with her for a bit then I'll take over when she gets tired. We're not leaving her alone just yet.' He stretched, yawned and sat down on a hard wooden chair wearily.

I looked up from the plastic deckchair I'd been in since the Hab lot came round with the mattress. My sole contribution apart from making toast and tea was helping lug it up to Martha's room.

'Shouldn't I -' I began.

'No, you shouldn't.' Simon yawned again.

'I haven't even had a chance to talk to her! She's my best -'

'And that's why she needs to recover a bit. Talk to someone who isn't so close. She can't answer all your questions yet.'

'Is she – is she Ok?'

'That's why it's best we see to her for now. You've been so upset about her, she'll start worrying about you and that's the last thing she needs. She's been taking care of everyone but herself. You heard her, worrying about the cat puddle.'

202

'Oh, has Twinkle got -'

'*Yes*. Stop worrying. As a matter of fact, you didn't look much better than Mart this morning. You've had too much on your plate lately.'
'Well, you were ill, and there was so much -'
'I know. Chill out. You can relax now. We'll take Mart to the doctor tomorrow -'
'What'll they say? What'll they do with her?'
'We don't know til they see her, but knowing the bloody NHS not much. I think her nerves are just exhausted. She's a nervous wreck but seems lucid enough. That's what I was worried about. She's only got the kind of confusion that comes of long term stress and anxiety, and no sleep. I think she'll be fine with rest, but it's going to take a while.'
'How long?'
'We're looking at three months, I'd say.'
'Three months!'

'Yeah, her nerves are exhausted. She needs a tonic, and peace and quiet, and no drugs or booze. Whatsoever.'
'D'you think the -'
'Do I think that tons of hash on top of her depleted nerves made her spin out into paranoia? Yeah, I do. Seen it before, a sort of dope psychosis.'
'She's not psychotic!'

I was terrified, thinking of Jack Nicholson, crazy people, McMurphy in One Flew Over the Cuckoo's Nest.
'Relax. It might interest you to know that depression is considered a psychosis. Don't be afraid of a word. She's never had this kind of episode before?'
'No. Not that I know of. She was really quiet as a kid, though. Never spoke to anyone but me. Scared of everyone.'
'Social anxiety. Selective mutism. Quite rare actually.'
'She's not some kind of mental case...'
'You think? Strictly speaking she should have had some help years ago by the sounds of things.'

I subsided. 'How did you find out all this stuff anyway?'
'Michael.'
'The drunk?'
'The drunk, as you call him, has a Masters degree in Social Psychology and a mental health nursing certificate.'
'Oh.'
'Yes. Oh.'

Simon sighed, rubbing his tired face.
'He taught me a lot, back when we were on our own, before Mart came, and while she was away at Newbury. And Leytonstone. And Wells. And Solsbury Hill – no, she only went there once. I was – kind of depressed at the time. Couldn't get any work. Hardly anything to eat. House freezing. Michael was a big help. He knew all about mental health stuff.'
'We're not mental! We're just poor!' I burst out.
Simon shrugged. 'He knew all about that too, how poverty and deprivation lead to mental breakdown. He used to campaign for Labour back in the '80s, and when they went all Tony Blair on us he got into social justice campaigns - for mental health services, stuff against the JSA, bloody benefit sanctions, all that.'

I never knew anyone was fighting our corner. All I knew was the endless struggle to survive. Mart's campaigns were all about trees. No, she did say something about a Claimant's Union once. I love trees, but people need to live too. Earth First? People are part of the Earth too. And – they're just as important. Even people like – Johnny.
I suppose Michael could've ended up a Johnny if he hadn't had an education, a decent family.
Wonder what Johnny's childhood was like? Don't go there.
That's what everyone says. Don't talk about the past. Keep quiet about it, it can't hurt anyone then.
But the past's already hurt people. Lots of people. Martha. Simon. Michael.
And – me. I suppose. But I'm pretty tough, really.

'You look about as tough as a newborn kitten. Do you want to get home to sleep?'

God, was he reading my mind?

'Yes. No. Yes, I want to go to sleep but I don't want to be left alone -'

'Don't blame you. There's some empty rooms here. Go and have a lie down and I'll get one of Joe Mac's minions to fetch some fish and chips later. Here. Have a blanket. There's a bunch of mattresses in the room opposite. Hab overdid it a bit but I think we'll be able to use them all somehow.'

I nodded, trailed off trailing my blanket, wandered through the first door I found, fell into a mattress on the floor and nodded off.

※

'But how did you know where to come?'

Martha picked at the fraying ribbon on the edge of her blue blanket nervously.

'Kerry.'

'But Larch and them never gave you a letter from her.'

'From the postwoman. Seen her by the bus stop.' she said sleepily

'Oh...that's why they didn't know what was going on! That, and they were born clueless.'

'Lorna..' Martha began, suddenly anxious again.

'Oh yeah, leopard skin girl - what about her?'

'Said she was goin' to see Melissa in Swansea.'

'Melissa? Oh, Johnny's girlfriend.'

'Yeah. I hope she...she – I hope she isn't going to go back to him. Kevin...'

'Don't worry. Lorna will take care of her.' I soothed, alarmed at how quickly Mart's thoughts spiralled back into blind panic.

'He hits Kevin. I've got to...'

'He's not near Kevin any more. Kevin is Ok. All you've got to do is rest and get well and not worry about other people. They'll be all right. Their friends are looking after them.'

'They couldn't look after me. I was on my own.' Tears were running down her face again. 'On my own. It was dark. I was so scared – it was like, it was like – Dad.'

I could hardly bear to watch, my heart wrung.

'I know. But you're not alone anymore. You're here with Kerry.'

'Kerry's at the squat.'

'Yes, the squat. We're all here and – and – we all – all love y'and want you to be all right.' I stumbled over that. I wasn't used to this sort of thing.

'Are we at the squat?'

God, she's disorientated. What shall I do? Don't panic, Simon said. Don't look as if you're worried. The doctor said she'll be fine once her system gets back in balance and the dope wears off. She hasn't even caught up the missed sleep yet. It's only been two days.

'Yes, here we are at Kerry's squat with me and Simon and Twinkle.'

'Twinkle? Is Twinkle all right? She needs some cat litter, she did a puddle. I'm sorry. I'll clean it up, I'm sorry, I didn't mean to let her...'

'Hey, chill. I cleaned it up ages ago. Twinkle's happy as Larry, we got her some chicken. She loves Simon now.'

'When I left, I just had to put her in her basket to carry her over the mountain. I didn't want them to see me go. I thought they'd try to persuade me not to. I thought, I'll just go over the mountain, slip down by the woody bit to the bus stop. They won't see me if I go that way. Always knew I'd have to go that way, when it was time to go...'

'Yes, that's right. You decided to go to find Kerry and you went over the mountain to the bus stop and came to Bristol and you had Kerry's letter for the address. And here you are!'

I felt like I was patronising her. I was talking to her like she was nine years old.

Maybe she was. That's how long she's been carrying this shit, this fear, this unceasing fear.

'Do you live here as well?'

❄

Good question. It was a damn sight warmer and Simon had already moved his stuff over to the topmost room opposite Mart's. Catbox II. Turns out Simon's technical skills run to hotwiring electric meters – shhh, don't tell the electricity board - and we had halogen heaters courtesy of the last Hab jumble sale glowing in each room, giving soft golden light as well as heat.

'Is it safe?' I asked doubtfully.
'Compared to dying of pneumonia in that cesspit, yes. But yeah, I've sorted out that bodge job they did when they first moved in. Don't worry, one of your Sean's mates used to work for the electric board and he didn't in any way tell me the safe way to do it. And I didn't take his advice and we're not having this conversation.'
I laughed. Simon was aces these days. I'm so glad I saved his life from cat flu, he came up trumps when Mart turned up all wobbly and gone in the head. Can't think of any more card game metaphors.
I considered Mart's question. Should I move in here? It might not last long but I couldn't stick paying to freeze at Prospect Road another minute. Insecure housing or freezing damp housing? Is that one of them there choices the middle classes are always banging on about?

I asked Simon:
'Did you pay this month's rent yet?'
'Nope.' he replied. 'Did you?'
'No, I meant to do it last week but forgot what with everything.'
'Guess we're quids in, then. Can you think of a single reason why we should show that git an ounce of consideration?'
I could not.
'Good, then we'll have a bit of cash to see us through winter. I'll call and cancel the utilities and Hab will help you bring your stuff over. There's a basement for your tools, it's safer than a shed.'
'What about when we get evicted?' I asked him.
'Hab will provide. We go down the road with a crowbar and crack another squat.'
I sat back, letting it sink in. Warm. Dry. Free. Insecure. Kind of exciting though.

Free. Free from that arsehole landlord and his cowboy electricians and overpriced mould farm.

I grinned suddenly.

'Go on then. Cancel the gas and stuff.'

❄

'Yes.' I said to Martha, my best friend and housemate. 'Yes, I do live here. You're home now, where you belong.'

Martha met my eyes for the first time. She smiled a faint, uncertain smile.

'I've just gotta get better. I'm gonna get better.'

'That's it. You've got it.'

'I'm hungry.'

I knew better than to leave her alone. I opened the door a crack and called:

'Mick! Little brother, find some food for Martha, cheers. Something hot.'

'Right you are Sis.' came faintly.

❄

'Bridge? Here's Martha's stuff.'

Kerry handed me a cardboard box.

'The pots and pans and blankets and stuff are downstairs. This is her books and personal stuff. I took down the tarp and stored it in the basement for her. Mine's in there too. She didn't have a lot of stuff. The gardening tools are with yours. Not sure which is mine and which Mart's, we can sort it out later. Main thing is all our gear is gone from Cerrig now.'

Gone. The round bender with the butterfly bunting was gone. The triangles of cloth trailing from the box in my arms were like the flags of a defeated tribe, wilted, sad and stripped of meaning.

'I gave her burner to Larch. His was cracked and he'll be up there for the rest of the winter at least.'

'Is he off somewhere then?'

208

'He talked about going on down to West Wales, something about a wood project in Carmarthenshire. Recycling old furniture and pallets and stuff.'

'Oh.'

'He was really relieved to hear that Mart's doing Ok, though.'

'Yeah? Well I suppose he did his best at the time.'

I was worn out from indignation and just glad that things were settling down. Spring was around the corner and we'd had an eviction notice. Our solicitor was certain he could get a stay of eviction due to Martha's illness though. Another two months maybe. 'I'd better give this lot to Mart then.' Hoping that the memories wouldn't upset her, but she'd been doing really well. Six weeks had made a difference, she was eating more, staying up more, even going for short walks with Simon round the park. They ventured as far as the city farm all the way down in St Werburghs at one point. No fun walking in this chill March wind though, she needed some spring sunshine. She came back with colour in her cheeks but the next day was white with tiredness after the exertion.

'Mart?' I knocked at her door. The door opened and she looked out, smiling her anxious smile.

'What?'

'Look, here's all your things. Your books and clothes and that weird spiderweb thing you made out of junk.'

'Oh, the dreamcatcher?'

'You're kidding me. How does this catch dreams?'

'Ah, well, see the bad dreams pass through the hole in the middle and the good dreams get caught in the web and absorbed into the crystal. Then the feathers conduct the good dreams down to you where you're sleeping.'

'I see. Far out. And this is cutting edge Native American technology is it?'

'Well...thing is they're only meant to work on dreams. No good if life really is turning into a nightmare.' she said quietly.

'I guess.' I decided that now wasn't the time to remind her that she was supposed to be a scientist.

Mart took out the blue dreamcatcher and hung it on the lightshade. It twirled in the draught from the door. All the doors were permanently open owing to the cat tribe that prowled the stairs and landings.

'How did we end up with all these cats? Not that I'm complaining. Just can't get over that first day when there was a cat in every window. Bit of a giveaway that someone had squatted the place.' I had had to walk slowly behind one on the way up the stairs. They don't hurry.
Martha sat down again on the edge of her bed.
'Twinkle came from Brynhelyn, she's Kerry's Welsh cat.. Those two girls in the middle flat brought Jadzia. She's the black one.'
'Jadzia?'
'Yeah. Star Trek fans. And the tabby is Michael's. Jeannie with the light tabby fur.'
'Michael's here? How come we haven't seen him?'
'He's been over to Ireland again. He always goes over winter to make sure his dad's all right. He'll be back in a couple of days.'
'Oh, Ok.'

I had never actually met Michael. He was a sort of shadowy figure. His drinking capacity was the stuff of legend. And Simon always referred to him as the station-master for some reason. I suppose he must have worked for GWR at some point. I was curious to meet him.
'How well do you know Michael?' I asked Martha.
'Not very. He moved out more or less as I was settling back in after Newbury. Only met him a couple of times as he was shifting his stuff. Very thin and quiet, always had a glass in his hand. Nicely spoken though, reminded me of one of my tutors at college. He has the back room in the basement, never been in there.'

I'd wondered where the other door led to, further down the corridor beyond the gloomy room we used as a store.
'Bit troll-like living down there. Isn't it dark?'
'No. It's more above ground at the back of the house, there's little windows. But he's pretty reclusive, hardly ever comes out even when he's here apparently.'

'Simon says he used to work in mental health.'
Martha looked away. She hadn't referred to her breakdown since she started getting better. Guess I'd be the same if I'd ended up that out of it. She went back to sifting through the box.
'Oh, my Wizard of Earthsea's not here. Oh damn...' Martha rummaged in vain.
I remembered.

'Oh, I've got it. Picked it up before I left your – your place in the quarry. Hang on, I'll get it for you.'
I hurried back up from my ground floor room with the tattered book.
'Here.'
'There was...I left something in it. I was writing something...'
Ah.
'Yeah, er, there was an envelope in it. A letter. Addressed to me.' I said awkwardly.
'A letter? I don't remember. I started a letter to you but then it turned into a sort of diary. I never posted it.' Mart was still looking through the pages of Earthsea as if she expected to find the papers there.
'Where is it? Is it in the box?' She started to rise.
'Er, no. Er, I thought it was for me. I've got it.'
'Oh. Can I have it?'
'Er, yeah.'

I ran back down the stairs and found the envelope after searching every pocket on my rucksack.
Martha tipped the folded sheets out of the envelope and looked at them.
'I can hardly remember writing this,' she murmured, 'so confused back then.'
I squirmed.
Martha was scanning the pages, frowning.
'God, I was on one when I wrote this. Good to have the memories though..'
'Er, there's a bit later on..' I began.
'What?'

211

'A bit about – that bloke, Johnny, that might upset you. You might want to wait a bit to read it all. Don't want to mess your head up again.' I suggested.

'Have you read it?' She looked wide-eyed at me.

'Er, well, yeah. It was addressed to me and I thought it was a letter. But some of it...'

Some of it. Was really personal. And it looked very much as if she hadn't intended anyone else to read it. Hell.

She flushed, slowly getting redder and redder. She looked at the envelope, saw my name and the Prospect Road address. Looked at me, then quickly down at the floor.

'Oh, I see, well you weren't to know...but I never thought – that anyone would read it.'

I was about to dissemble, to say that I hadn't read to the end, or that I couldn't remember what it said anyway. Just forget it. That's easier.

But I remembered how many times I'd given Mart a hard time for being scared of everything, not knowing that in reality she was only scared of one thing. Same thing I grew up in terror of. Both of us hiding under that tree. Both of us the same. Perhaps I always knew.

'Martha -' I began.

Her eyes were still on the floor, her head shaking slightly no, no. Her figure beginning to rock a little back and forth, just the way she had in the early weeks of her illness.

I plunged in, like the times as a kid plunging into a nettle patch to forge a pathway, or shoving my way under a thick hawthorn bush to find the secret cave beneath. Or pushing aside the branches of a forsythia bush to peer out at a crying girl. A girl who'd gone to hide at the bottom of the garden to cry. Like me.

'Mart. I saw what you said about your parents, pushing you around and fighting all the time. They were really bad. Just like my – my dad. You had a shit time. Just like me and Mick and Sean, and Joe. And - Robert, I suppose. You don't have to hide it from me. I know the score. You did well...you did well to keep going on your own. It must have been hard after. After we were gone.' I felt sick talking about it.

Martha rocked on. Back and forth. Back and forth. I wondered if I should get Simon.

'Simon -' I began to call.

'No. Don't get Simon in here. You're right. It was shit – after you went. I just kept out of the way. Kept studying. The teachers were really nice to me, when I went to secondary. Cos I always got A's on everything. I even starting talking to a few of the girls at school, when I was about fourteen. Then I went to stay with one of my teachers for 'O' levels and sixth form. Did really well, got into university to study biology. It was great til I finished and had to get a job.'

'And there were no fucking jobs.'

'And there were, like you say, no fucking jobs.'

'Not for us anyway.'

Martha sighed, and leaned back on her mattress. She stretched out her legs and put her arms behind her head.

'All we need is a roof of willow.' she said.

'That was poetry! Hey, you always said you couldn't write. But what you wrote about Cerrig – it was brilliant.'

'That's cos Cerrig was brilliant. I just put it on paper.'

'I saw your garden.'

'You did?' I could tell she was pleased about that.

'Yeah, it was impressive. You're a good gardener.'

Her face didn't change but she was smiling all over. Twinkle strolled in and climbed onto her stomach. She stroked her fur absently.

'You said you lived with your teacher.'

'Oh, yeah, that.' She closed up again. Hugged Twinkle, stroked her more intently, smoothing her cheeks, feathering her tail.

I dropped it. It meant so much that we'd managed to talk this much. Later, maybe.

Now I knew there'd be a later. I jumped up briskly.

'I'm gonna go down the shops for some decent grub and cook something up tonight. You want anything?'

'Nah, I don't need anything.'

'Ok, see you in a bit.'

I left, being sure to leave the door open a chink. For cats, and air, and calling distance. To keep the connection open, now we'd finally made it.

※

Simon was scrabbling for a foothold.
'Careful!' I hissed. The upturned galvanised bucket he was standing on was beginning to tip over.
'I'm all right.' came faintly.
'Can you see anything?' I asked.
'Yes. It's empty. No carpet, even.'
'Good. Come down now. The bucket's slipping.'
'Yeah. Don't want to kick the bucket.' he joked.

Martha appeared round the corner.
'Did you check the letterbox?' Simon looked down from his perch.
'Yes.' she said breathlessly. 'There's a huge mound of post on the hall floor.'
'Excellent.' Simon looked happy as he climbed down.
'But can you be sure no one's about to move in?' I asked.
'I've got a spy in All-Saints Housing Association.' he replied. 'A fifth-columnist.'
'Huh? You mean this belongs to a housing association? How come it's empty, then? Don't the words 'Housing Crisis' mean anything to them?'
'Don't think so.' Simon said seriously. 'Most of the houses we get are theirs or Bristol FirstSteps. Anyway, Petra works at All-Saints and she gives us all the intelligence on which houses are empty and which are about to be let. Dead useful. Last thing we want's a PIO.'
'How come she does that, won't she get in trouble? PIO?'
'Prospective Incoming Occupier. She's already been in far worse trouble and got out of it.' Simon said. 'She used to be one of us, squatted for four years before she got that job. And she hasn't forsaken us.'
'Cool.' I said.
'So, we're go on this one. Let's get back to the ranch and make a plan.'

214

I was nervous. I'd never cracked a squat before and was frankly terrified of the police grabbing us for breaking and entering.

'It's Ok,' Simon insisted. 'As long as you're sure the house is unoccupied and you don't get caught getting in, you sort the locks out and stick up a Section 6 and then you've got squatter's rights and they can't touch you without an eviction notice.'
'If only they'd given us longer.' The magistrates had granted us another six weeks on account of Martha's illness. Summer was coming on and I had my hands full with spring-rain weed-drenched gardens. But we had to get another squat. There were only three of those weeks left. Tension levels in the house were going up. The two middle-floor girls and Jadzia had already left for their sister's house, and Michael was wondering about going back to Ireland for good. He put in an appearance now and again at dinner times or turned up at random in the kitchen with a bag of food from his allotment or the skips that he and Simon still raided from time to time.

Michael was still very much a mystery to me. Tall, thin, bespectacled, with grey hair in a neat old fashioned style, he spoke like an Oxford don with the slightest brogue, but moved slowly, surrounded by a haze of wine fumes. His diction was only ever slightly slurred, and his manners perfect. How did a guy like him end up in a place like this? I wondered.
Simon said. 'You don't ask. You never ask people about their past in squats. If they want to tell you they will. If not, don't go there.'
So Michael continued to elude us, rarely coming out of his room where he seemed to spend a lot of time on handiwork. He would often emerge with a soldering iron or fretsaw in hand, to tend to one of his dozen demi-johns. Or tap off a jugful of elderberry or parsnip. He'd greet me with a shy smile but we'd never really had what could be called a conversation.
Simon set the kettle onto Mart's campstove and called for order. We sat around the kitchen. The window was open after a winter of fug and cooking fumes. I heard a blackbird trying out its tune at the top of the philadelphus at the end of the garden.

Wishing we could be here for the snow white glory of sweet blossoms. Wondering where we'd end up next.

'Are you listening Bridge?' said Simon bossily.

'Sure, Teacher.' I turned round hurriedly.

'Ok, so the best point of entry looks like those ropy sash windows on the ground floor.'

'But that's at the front of the house. We'll be seen. And...' broke in Martha anxiously.

'No worries. All-Saints will be sending round a team to inspect the windows prior to fitting a new frame..'

'Will they? Then shouldn't we try another house?' Martha asked innocently.

Simon smiled. 'No, this is it, you, Mart – have you got a black skirt? No?'

Of course she hasn't got a black skirt. She's a hippy, been living up trees and mountains for the last three years.

'And a white blouse...' Hah! Catch anything white staying that way for more than five minutes at Cerrig. It'd be a Spiller-special in about half an hour.

'Anyway you can get some clothes from Off the Streets tomorrow. Oh, yes, the community project had that charity shop that they offered us some gear from.

Simon was continuing, though I was distracted thinking about Mary Norton's little people, endlessly running from place to place trying to find a home.

It was true, there wasn't much accommodation in a kettle...but more than there'd be in a boot...

The kettle was boiling. I was startled back to reality.

'Mart, you'll dress up in your office disguise and we'll give you a clipboard to carry. I'll get into my blue boiler suit and scrounge a hard hat and hi-vis off Mick for the day.'

I was interested now. I poured out the tea and passed it round together with a bowl of broken biscuits. Weird things, green custard creams and other mutated seconds.

'We pose as an All-Saints inspection team and while I'm jemmying the window, Mart hides what I'm doing and the protective colouration makes us totally invisible to the neighbours.'
Wow. It's true. The minute someone sees a hi-vis they assume it's all official. Smart.
This I've got to see.
'As soon as I'm in, Mart shuts the window down again and goes to the front door. She does a bit of fumbling as if she had a key, I let her in secretly and we get the locks changed. Then we can bring in our gear after dark once I've got the Section Six up. Job done.'

It was impressive. And I was even more impressed when I saw how smoothly the operation went. We ran about the new house excitedly, clicking dead light switches and discovering random bits of left-behind furniture. Martha lit the camping gas lamp in the kitchen and put the stew she and Kerry had prepared earlier into the big cooking pot and onto the camp stove. Kerry was out in the street taking advantage of the cover of darkness to lift up the metal flap and turn the water on with a long key.

I was busy in the bedrooms, hanging the curtains. Which was tricky without curtain rails.
'What on earth are you doing?' Simon had appeared behind me as I banged away with Kerry's best hammer and a mouthful of tacks.
'Uh, just putting the curtains up.' I mumbled.
'Nailing them up?'
I spat out a couple of tacks. 'It's the only way.' I said defensively.
'Yeah, you do it, get on and nail some sense into them.' Simon was amused.
'Huh. I don't see you doing it.' I said grumpily.
'How will you draw them?' he asked.
'Just tie them in the middle with a bit of ribbon or something. It'll look a bit Little House on the Prairie but it'll do the job.'
He grinned 'Yeah, I guess so. Anyway. I came to tell you – Michael needs a hand with his stuff. Getting it up from the old basement.'
'Oh – Ok.' I put down the hammer and followed him.

Back at the old house, I climbed down the steps to the basement. Michael was there, greeting me shyly. He gestured towards the dark little corridor. I entered the back room for the first time.

'What do you want moving then?' I asked over my shoulder. Then I turned and saw it. The room was empty except for the trestles ranged round the walls. Laid out on them was a Hornby 00 railway network complete with stations, signal boxes, points and wooded hillsides. My mouth fell open as a small engine chittered past, drawing a long line of Pullman coaches in GWR chocolate and cream. I heard Simon laughing behind me.

'Told you, didn't I?' he said.

❄

By the time the stew was ready the house looked inhabited. Jeannie leapt up onto the windowsill on the ground floor and peered out into the dark street. Twinkle headed for the highest point – she had that in common with Simon – and sat aloft keeping a watchful eye on the city below.

The bowlful of hot stew acted like a sleeping draught. I rose, staggered off to my room with a sleepy goodnight, and sank gratefully into my mattress. God, but it was hard work lugging them down the road, one end balanced on a shopping trolley. Worth it though. I lay listening to the sleeping house for a few minutes until I drifted away.

❄

12. Settling.

Bridget drowsed in the July sun. Lying full length in the rough grass, her head pillowed on her arm, she looked sideways at a beetle running under and over through the grass stems. She watched as it disappeared under a tussock, sighed and rolled over onto her back. Sunlight dappled through the canopy of the gnarled apple tree, light shimmering and shifting with the breeze. A single tortoiseshell butterfly fluttered past. She watched it out of sight. The birds had fallen silent, busy with feeding young, the clamour of the breeding season over for another year. On the fence a row of sparrow fledglings gaped and fluttered their wings at their harassed mother, who rushed back and forth feeding them. The lone bluetit pair who'd raised a family in a hole in the rickety wooden shed had gone. So what was that? Tweep – tweep – tweep, loud and urgent. Alarm call. But whose? She sat up and looked around. A yellow bird, at the top of the skinny ash tree at the end of the garden, shouting its agitation, tail bobbing up and down with every call.

'Mart – Mart!' Bridge called. 'What's this? Looks like a wagtail but it's yellow.'
Martha looked up from her book, but didn't rouse from her restful, abandoned sprawl in the hammock they'd made from an old tennis net.
'Uh? - oh, grey wagtail.' she said absently, swinging the hammock slightly to feel it rock.
'But it's yellow.'
'Don't ask me, they just call it a grey wagtail, the yellow wagtail's different.'
'Wow...I've never seen one of these. They never had them in the Midlands. Only the pied ones. I thought they only lived near water.' Bridget was fascinated.
'You see them quite a lot in Bristol. The river's not that far but they'll go for any bit of water. Someone must have a garden pond round here.'
Martha sat up and took notice now that nature was the subject.

'What's she yelling about?' Bridget asked.

'Twinkle.' The little black and white cat was attempting stealth in plain sight along the fence, staring at the young sparrows.

'Why doesn't she shift her feathery ass, as Simon would say?'

'Looks like she's got young ones nearby. Must have had a second brood. She's trying to intimidate Twinkle into giving up.' said Martha.

'Wow, can a bird do that to a cat?' Bridget had never heard of the prey winning before.

'Yeah, I've seen swallows dive-bomb Twinks in the farmyard up at Cerrig. She swore off swallows after that, I can tell you.' Martha smiled, lost in the memory. 'They nested in the workshop every year. They'd be swooping in and out over Larch's head. You had to take care one didn't go smack into you as you came in the door. Glad had to leave the door open all summer for them.'

'Suppose they'll be off in another few weeks.' Bridge said. 'It's nearly August.'

'Yeah. And we've got to be off too.' Martha sighed.

✻

Yeah. Moving again. The second squat only lasted two months and I have to say that cracking another one wasn't as exciting the second time around. Simon got in through the bathroom window. He spotted the broken catch in his reccy as he lurked in yet another overgrown Sussex Place garden, and scrambled up the lean-to roof early one morning. He showed me how to change a lock this time, though I invented the marmalade method for getting the recess in the right place for the bolt to fit into. You spread the marmalade – or jam, anything sticky that shows up really - onto the end of the bolt and then turn the key until the bolt hits the doorjamb. Then you draw round the sticky oblong and it's just a matter of patiently chiseling out the wood. Yeah, marmalade's handy. You want to avoid the chunky stuff though.

June was a washout. Too many days spent cooped up watching the rain stream down the kitchen window, too many days having to cancel gardening jobs. I became restless, wondering how we'd get through winter.

The day we saw the wagtail came at the end of a week of halcyon days. July dawned bright and hot and we went straight out into the garden to celebrate.

The long garden still held the ghost of the elegant atmosphere it had once had. Tall trees at the back rustled and whispered in the wind, poplar, weeping willow, dancing fragrant philadelphus. Great clumps of rhododendron heavy with red and pink blooms that the spring rains pelted off far too soon, and a mock orange so big it had a trunk. The grass was long enough to lose a kitten in and even Twinkle's tail barely showed above the swaying seedheads.

I wished I could stay long enough to plant something. Martha was so much calmer she was like a different person, but she'd grown listless lately. She'd gone back into her childhood silence, spending whole afternoons frowning, staring into space for minutes at a time, then dropping her eyes back to her book.

She watched the wagtail until Twinkle took the hint and hopped off the fence full onto Mart's stomach.

'Ow! Twinkle!' She grinned, but Twinkle still got shoved over onto the blanket that covered the holes in the netting.

'Don't fall through the holes in the net, Twinkers.' I remarked.

'She won't. She sticks like Velcro.' Mart laughed, and stroked Twinkle's back.

'I wish – I wish we could plant something. It doesn't feel right, not growing food.' she said.

'No point, we won't be here to harvest it.' I lay back down, giving myself up with a sigh of contentment to the sun, the dappling shadows, the afternoon sleepiness that was heaven after a hard week's work.

'I know.'

'When do you think we'll find somewhere we can stay, like a proper home?' Mart persisted.

'Well, those Poles on Badminton Road have had their squat for three years. Pretty good.' I said.

'Yeah, but they'll still get evicted sooner or later. I mean our own place – somewhere we can stay.'

'Um, that would be – never, as far as I can see.'

I sat up. I wanted my own garden as much as Mart, but you had to be realistic.
'Choices are - crap landlord who can throw you out at a month's notice and never does any repairs. Squats that you get to keep for three months if you're lucky, but at least it's free. Council flat that you can only get after five years on the waiting list and then you can kiss goodbye to ever touching the earth or seeing the sun again.'
Mart had never brought up the subject of going back to Cerrig, thank goodness. I'd been dreading that, as I watched her chafe and pine in captivity. The dark terror of those last few days in the quarry had inoculated her against hippies for life. I hoped. Clueless bunch of wasters and stoners, I thought. Mart was worth a hundred of them.

And so was Kerry. But she hadn't let the worst of the tribe put her off running around fighting more Earth First! campaigns. The latest wheeze of the earth-trashers, she told me one evening over a jug of Michael's finest Blackberry Beaujolais, was translocation - digging up an entire chalk grassland and moving it to make way for a quarry extension. Ashton Court was supposed to be ours since Bristol City council bought it in 1959 - but Planet Peelers Inc. or whatever they were called had decided that digging a bloody great hole in the middle of it wouldn't detract from the public enjoyment. Enjoyment of that which was no longer there. The nothing was spreading, like in the Never-Ending Story. I wished I had more time to help out on the campaigns – Kerry had persuaded me to go along to some demos and help lug banners and stuff up to sites of actions – but I had to keep on top of the garden jobs. Martha was silent on the subject at the moment. I was glad, she was still in no shape to get into all that again.

'There must be another way.' she said. 'There's this project I've heard about...'
'Not some hippy commune I hope?' I was instantly alert.
'No, not exactly...more cooperative housing, run by and for the tenants. Non profit-making. Democratic decision making.'
'So are hippies involved? Is it some free for all ?'

'No, no, you have to apply to join and new tenants are picked carefully.'

'Who are these people?' I asked suspiciously.

'Well, some people Kerry knows from the Ashton Court campaign, some other squatters, Marianne from Off the Streets...'

'Oh, she's Ok. Mega-respectable, she's the manageress isn't she?' I was reassured, but my fur had not yet settled back down.

'Yeah, she always lets Hab hold their meetings there. Pretty cool.'

'Yeah, she is good like that.' I agreed. 'Might be Ok then.'

'You interested?' Martha asked.

'Me? Uh, what would I do with a bunch of communists -'

'Communards.'

'Whatever. I just wanna find a decent landlord, all this other stuff...I just want to get on with my job, and my life.'

I was restless now, sitting up leaning on my elbows. I didn't want to talk about this stuff on such a blissful day. I didn't want to think about it.

'Well, that's all any of us want. Except there's no such animal. So we have to fight all the time just to exist.'

'Whatever. I'm sick of it. I don't want to spend all my life yelling about the state of the world, marching in the streets -'

'You care about Ashton Court don't you? And the trees at Newbury?'

'Course I do. I just can't do anything about it. I'm just one tiny insignificant person who no one'll ever listen to.'

'Gandhi said..'

Oh here we go. Gandhi. Monbiot. Vaniegem. Jesus H. Christ. I'm always getting quoted some bloke.

'Ok, hit me. What did Gandhi say?'

'He said that everything you do is insignificant.'

'Great. That's what I just said.'

'No, I haven't finished. Then he said that it's still essential that you do it.'

'Why? If it won't change anything?'

'But it will. Just not immediately.'

Oh yeah. The liberal chant. 'What do we want? Gradual change! When do we want it? In due course!'

Heh. So funny.

'How long do we have to wait? I need a proper home now!'

'Come to the coop meeting next week.'

I sighed, long and long-suffering.

'I might. Where is it?'

'Off the Streets.'

God, that place is depressing. It's like the whole building was furnished from a jumble sale. Wait a minute, it was.

'I'll think about it.'

The wagtail wasn't wrong to give the alarm call. Bloody hippies, gearing up to mess Martha's life up again.

Why did I have a feeling of doom?

The tortoiseshell butterfly was back. It fluttered briefly around my head before settling on a straggly buddleia that grew out of a crack in the yard, clinging on to life in a scanty habitat.

❄

'It's dark!'

'Course it's dark. It's night.' Kerry led the way, barely visible.

Martha, beside me, was irritatingly calm. She often was in the face of actual danger, to my eternal mystification.

'Are you sure you know the way?' I asked Kerry.

'Memorised it.'

'I'm getting my torch out.' I fumbled in my pocket.

'No! Don't do that. We won't be able to see.' Martha objected.

'We could see if we had some light.' I pointed out, exasperated, fed up of stumbling around in the screen of holly bushes that lined the woodland path that we were only following by the soles of our feet, seemed like.

'You'll wreck your night vision.'

What? Is this some hippy garbage up there with eating nettles and planting by the moon?

'How can you see in this?'

'I just know exactly where I am. Kerry showed it me last week.'

Huh. Not sure I believe that.

Kerry had vanished somewhere in the blackness. A faint rustling was all we had to go on.

'Hurry up!' she called, dimly.

Martha slowed, and began to cast about among the yew saplings and holly bushes.

'Hah! See, you've lost us.' I wasn't sure why I'd be so pleased about this, mind. Leigh Woods was a big place and seemed even bigger after dark.

'Here we are.' She pointed to a small yew that looked just like the others around it as far as I could see, and plunged into the darkness of the woods.

'Hey! Gandalf says don't leave the path!' I hurried after her. We felt our way through what to me seemed total darkness. I heard Martha brushing branches away from our faces and the scrunch of old leaves underfoot. Suddenly I saw a twinkling of fire ahead. Great. Now we were going to be captured by elves. Again.

'Yip!' 'Yip yip!'

The coyote greeting of the Earth Firster. I suppose the sound did carry well deep in the woods, and at least you could be sure it was one of your own, I thought grudgingly.

We walked up to the fire burning in a large pit surrounded by logs. I looked around. Ancient yews looked back at me, or at least the faces in their bark did. Hidden deep in the yew grove, the camp was out of sight and sound of the nearest path, muffled by the dark swags of yew foliage. Martha was talking cheerfully to one of the women sitting round the fire. She sat down on the log next to her, still talking. Now she can talk, she never shuts up, I thought wonderingly.

'Any news?'

'Not much. Same old. We're gonna blockade the quarry entrance again next week. Are you coming?'

My head went up, scenting danger. Martha looked reflective.

'I suppose...' she began.

'Mart. Are you seriously volunteering for getting roughed up by the bloody police?' I asked quietly.

'Well, I might.' she said thoughtfully. 'It's only blockading the entrance. Plenty of chance to get away. Not like going on site. Maya, do you still have that banner we made last time?'

That was another thing about hippies. Even their given names were weird. They were never called Brenda or Phil. It was always Amelie or Poppy or Atreyu or something.

'No, we lost it when the first camp got evicted.'

'Damn. Have to make another in the squat.'

'You're not having my sheets, I've only got one left.' I thought it was time to stand up and be counted.

'Don't worry. Marianne can find us some old curtains in the shop.' That was Kerry.

'Good.' I reached into my rucksack and pulled out a bottle of Thatcher's cider. Such a shame it had that woman's name on it. Good stuff though. I took a swig and passed it on.

'Did'y' get CJA'd?' The other Ashton Courters were chatting.

'When?'

'When you got arrested for blocking the entrance the first time.'

'Nah, they're not using it much. Mainly 'cos it's such a ropy piece of legislation. The police don't like it. Not because they don't want an excuse to arrest us but because it was so hastily put together. Cases keep getting thrown out.'

'Yeah, I mean, aggravated trespass. What a load of bollocks. Trespass isn't a criminal offence, it's so weak.'

'Mmm. Remember at Newbury when we just had to keep on walking up and down the public footpath and they couldn't touch us as long as we kept moving?'

The talk went on, drifting down the years. Stanworth. Wells. Twyford Down.

'Those Dongas up Solsbury Hill...you know, they were the ones who nicked all our cooking pots.'

'Was that them? Blimey.'

Martha was smiling now - rather nervously, but she seemed to be enjoying being back with the movement. I was worried about her. This lot didn't seem to be big on taking care of each other. Always pushing for more and more risk-taking. Where we they when we we

226

stuck in that mouldy old dump? Why don't they ever do anything about poverty?

But. Martha did look happier than I'd seen her in weeks. Kerry was deep in some complex legal argument about squatting under the Criminal Justice Act. What an own goal that had turned out to be. All they'd achieved since bringing it out in 1994 was to unite various totally disparate campaigns under the anti CJA banner. So you had urban squatters and ravers and travellers and rural hunt sabs, all in the same boat, all joining forces to push back on the erosion of the right to protest, to travel, to hold a rave, to open a squat. Simon called it the Prevention of Fun Act.

'The only time they ever used the CJA on squatters in Bristol, All-Saints ended up with their office full of crusties with dogs on bits of blue string. The singing was terrible.' Kerry laughed.
'Sort - sort of wish I'd been there.' said Martha diffidently.
I smiled too. That was one of the few actions I made it to. It was funny. Dozens of dreadlocked and face painted folk pouring into All-Saints' office, knocking politely on the little glass window, the look of shock on the receptionist's face, the off key singing of protest songs, the dogs joining in, barking through the choruses.
I kind of liked the singing, awful though it was. Someone was always strumming a guitar or beating a bongo. A didg began to boom in the clearing.
Whuorl..whacka..whum..whum..whum..whum. Weird. Eerie. Echoing through the woods. Martha found a bongo and joined in.
Thump thumpa, thump thumpa.
I picked up a stick and began beating time on a nearby log. Thud thud thud.
Martha's high, thin, uncertain voice was raised in song. Mine too, after a few more swigs of cider. The men joined in, deep and harmonising, like dwarfs deep in their mountain home. The flames licked higher, real life slipped away. A jug of home-made wine went round, followed by the mushroom tea for those brave souls who didn't mind a little holiday from sanity.

A dog licked my sandalled foot and looked up at me. I got up for a wander, staggered over to the dark trees on the edge of the clearing. Just like my old treehouse tree, I thought longingly.

For once it didn't hurt to remember.

I peered up into the dark heights of the old yew. Easy to climb. That's one reason I chose it. I reached up, grabbed a branch.

'Where's Bridge?'

'Dunno.'

That's what I like to hear. You're well-hidden in the arms of a yew. I grinned and slid along my branch a little to see the fireplace. Flakes of reddish bark peeled off and fluttered to the ground. I frowned.

'What you doin' up there?'

I jumped so wildly I nearly fell out. Nearly another concussion there. It was one of the men, couldn't remember which one, they all looked the same to me. Beard, hair wraps, rainbow jumper. And they were all called Ben.

'Nothing.' I said. Like last time. I didn't want to remember. But my tree, my beautiful tree, the hours I spent lying on the wooden floor, swaying with the wind, hazel weave and old curtains shrouding me from view. Reading, swigging stolen lemonade smuggled from home in an old bottle. Eating scrumped apples and wine gums bought with weeding money, writing in my exercise book. Those stories! Wish I still had some of them. There was the one about the two girls who escaped from a dark dungeon, there'd been secret tunnels, magic trees, shipwrecked sailors and explorers lost in time. Lost, lost, like the past, like the two days I still couldn't remember that I spent in hospital having my head sorted out and my broken arm set. Gone, like my tiny bedroom in the shabby house in the village, my willow nest, my home. And Martha.

I wondered if anything remained of my yew-tree den. All those years ago, the wood must have rotted away. Even if the tree was still there. All my fierce anger and love welled up.

'You may drive a big machine, but I was born a big strong woman
And you just can't take these trees away without me fighting...

This old world's been walked by many people

Some died young and some still living
If you think you're gonna take these trees then
I'm not here to give 'em...'

I slid down the trunk and rejoined Martha. There was still some cider left. I joined in the singing, standing in the clearing, head high, above the flickering flames.

'I have walked on these hillsides since I first was my mother's daughter
And you just can't take these hills away without me fighting...'

I glanced at Martha. She had stopped singing and her eyes were looking far away.

❈

Martha yawned. She stood up, walked over to the cold firepit, scrabbled under the two big logs left half burned and crossed over.
'Any embers?' I asked lazily from the open door of the big tent. Dawn was dull and chilly in the yew grove.
'Yeah, a tiny one.'
'Get some pine twigs on it.' The nearest pines were well out of the clearing. I watched her as she stumbled across the forest floor, bending occasionally to pick up good bits of kindling. She came back with a handful of sticks and dead leaves, and snapped off some pine twigs full of resin in passing.
'Great.' I crawled out and took over, breathing on the tiny glow, feeding the small flame that burst forth with scraps and twigs. The fire began to crackle. We were making it. Martha hurried to fill the kettle from the jerrycan.
We were soon drinking coffee, listening to the crack and piff of the fire in the damp early morning. The rest of the camp snored like drunken goblins. Pixies really. Do pixies drink? Elves do, but it doesn't seem to go to their heads. They sing all the time anyway. An intoxicated elf is not a thing that Tolkien ever mentioned. Oh, except for the butler in the Elven-King's palace. And the lazy tosspots who

helped him. Could Tolkien really have made that mistake? Surely he…

Anyway. We'll never know.

Martha was silent. Just for a change.

'So, you goin' to that action?'

'Huh? Oh, yeah, for a bit.' she said briefly.

'Guess you want my artistic genius to help with the banner again?'

'Yeah.' she said absently.

'Y'know..' she began.

'No, what?' I said.

'Y'know...'

'No I don't. Not if you don't tell me.' I said, impatient.

She shot a look at me. I groaned inwardly. We hadn't talked about the letter that wasn't a letter since that cold March day back at No. 33.

'I mean – what do you want to say?' I began again, more diplomatically.

'It's just...well, they keep going on about mothers. Mother Earth, mother this, mother that. Like mothers are something wonderful. I don't get it.'

I thought about my mother. She hadn't been so bad. She'd tried, definitely. Look at the way she taught us stuff about nature. But all her yelling at us all day and leaving us to the tender mercies of our dad until..well, you know...that wasn't great. She had a lot to put up with though. All those boys wrecking the place. But she chose to have us – well, up to a point. The Pope sure had a lot to answer for there. He of course had no kids at all.

'I s'pose you've got a point.' I answered, after a pause. Martha looked relieved.

'I always feel like there's something wrong with me.'

'Nothing wrong with you.' I said gruffly. 'Something wrong with your family. *Both* our families.' I added hastily.

'I don't mind the 'Earth is our Mother' bit though.' she said. 'All right, it's pretty cheesy. But I feel like...well, I feel like it's true. The Earth's the only mother I ever had worth the name.'

I thought about that. About how the trees sheltered and protected us. About my network of hidden tunnels in the grass and paths through the guarding nettles. The barricade of hawthorn that enabled our getaways. And the totemic cats.

'I'm with you there.' I admitted reluctantly. It did make sense, cliché or no cliché. Glad Mick wasn't listening to this conversation though.

'You can rely on nature.' she persisted, 'It doesn't lie to you. It just is what it always is. You always know what the rules are, and they can't be broken. It goes on year after year the same. Life getting renewed over and over. Like this great complex machine. And there's so much of it. All for free. As long as you look after it, it looks after you.'

Well, Mart had definitely been spending too much time with hippies, that was for sure. But I could see what she meant, though I probably wouldn't have put it that way myself. Not in front of the lads, anyway.

I squatted and stuck another log on the fire.

'Yeah, it can't tell lies and it doesn't break the rules.' I agreed.

'How many people can say that?' Martha was frowning again, stirring the fire with a stick.

'None?'

'But people are part of nature too.'

'But the greenies don't seem that interested in people.' I pointed out, as tactfully as I could.

'You noticed that too?'

'They talk as if people were parachuted in from outer space. It's like the conservationists. They never account for the fact that people need to live in the landscape too. The countryside's not a museum.' I went on. That had bugged me for years, actually.

'Not even a natural history museum.' Martha agreed.

She still had something on her mind though.

'My mother -' she began.

'Oh, great. You've got coffee on.' The camp was stirring. One of the Bens had emerged.

Damn. Was getting somewhere then. Wait, he was off to the bushes for a leak. He stopped on the way back. Began to pick up firewood. That'd keep him busy for a spell.

I turned to Mart.

'About your mum..' I began.

'Oh. Yeah.' She had begun to close down again.

'No, really, you were saying how if we look after the Earth it'll look after us.' I said quickly.

'Yeah. Only – no-one's looking after the Earth, are they?'

I couldn't answer that. We were, of course, but who were we? No-one, that's who.

'Like - nobody looked after my mum. My dad bullied her non - stop. I was so scared, what he might do...what he'd do to her..' Martha's voice was rising.

'Steady. They'll hear you. My dad was a dickhead too. He never touched my mum though. Think he knew she'd kill him.'

'But he hit you.'

I squirmed. *I don't do thinking about that.* 'Yeah. And my brothers.'

'What, all the time?' Mart looked shocked.

'No. Well, not like that, anyway. We learned to keep him sweet. It was Ok most of the time. You just had to keep out of his way. My mum did help us sort of keep out from under his feet, she never told him half of what we did. Threatened to, mind.' *Change the subject now!*

Martha was thinking.

'But my mother, she didn't defend me from him at all. She blamed me for everything!' she said fiercely. 'Even when he drove her mad.'

Phew. I think.

'I remember, you said when I first met you. And I told you. My mum used to go mad on me too, all the time. Don't take it personally.' I soothed.

'You don't understand. She really did go mad. She was in and out of hospital for three years. Schizoid affective, they called it. Or bipolar, or schizophrenia. They never could make up their minds. I never lived with her again after that.'

I sat very still. Shocked, deep.

'Er, is that why...'

'Why I lived with my teachers? Yes. They were great.' she said.

'So you, er, went off to college after, and..'

'And got involved with the GERBill campaign and slowly got involved with the protest movement.'

'Gerbil?'

'The Great Education Reform Bill. When they did away with student grants. I was one of the last to get a full grant. Couldn't have gone without it.'

'You went native in the middle classes then?' I tried to joke her, ease the tension a bit.

'I did not! What else was there? My teachers were the only people who ever cared about me!'

'Apart from me.'

'And you.' She smiled, tiredly. I hurried to the fire, poured out another mug of coffee and handed it to her.

'Mart, you're doing well. You really are. You did brilliantly to get away from your family. And get through college, that was amazing. Look at me. I never even got my A levels. Just a thicko after all.' I said ruefully.

'You're not. I know what you can do. You can really write!' she shot back fiercely.

'Me? Write? Oh, yeah, all those daft stories, and...well I did used to write some poetry later. Laugh! Teenage stuff. You know. But writing?'

'You can. I know you can. You're the one who's going to write our story. I asked you ages ago. You promised you would.'

'I was eleven..' I said weakly.

'Doesn't matter. A promise is a promise.' Mart grinned up at me. 'One day you'll write it all. Our lives. The village. All of it. So we never forget. So people know what it was like for people like us.' She rubbed the butterfly tattoo on her wrist absently.

It was my turn to be unable to speak. After all these years.

The sun was rising, filtering down through the dark canopy. A white shimmer of misty light fell across the clearing. Martha looked like

233

an elf. Her pale face was captured in a timeless moment, lit by the morning sun as it shone down in beauty on the forest floor.

I sat down next to Martha. Held my wrist next to hers. The matching tattoos were bright, two butterflies settling to display themselves in a sunbeam, shining.

❄

The butterfly fluttered before my eyes. Martha was tugging at her boot, her wrist wavering in front of me.

'Hurry up.'

'I can't. I'm stuck.' came from above. She tugged fruitlessly, nearly knocking me off my perch on the stepladder.

'Here. Your bootlace is caught. Keep still.' I said impatiently. I unhooked her, and her freed leg disappeared rapidly upward. I reached up as far as I could and grabbed the sides of the skylight, kicking off from the top of the stepladder, walking up the wall as I heaved myself over the edge. Martha scrambled across the tiles to the party wall where it emerged from the roof, and sat on the warm coping stones. I followed, crossing the red pantiles on all fours. We sat in the sunshine, enjoying the breeze.

Martha looked across the terraced roofs speculatively.

'If we'd known it was this easy we could've come through the roof in the first place.' she remarked.

'What? You mean to crack the squat?' This was a bit inventive. I don't think even Simon's ever tried that.

Simon's head emerged from the skylight.

'Hey Simon, have you ever cracked a squat from above?'

'Above what?' he asked irritably as he wriggled his way out of the hatch and scuffled inelegantly across to us.

'Above. Through the roof.'

He looked thoughtful.

'Hey, that could work!' he said excitedly.

Not him as well, I groaned inwardly.

'You'd have to climb out of this one and scurry across the roofs to the empty. But how would you open the skylight?' said Martha.

'You'd have to be careful to keep track of which one was the empty, though.' he pointed out, and they were off, speculating, planning neck-breaking stunts that would get them nicked.

Across the roofs. No one would know you were up there, above their house. You could move from house to house. Like the Magician's Nephew. Polly and Digory had been able to explore the whole length of the street in the attics...the party walls in Victorian houses didn't go above the level of the attic floor. But they came unstuck when they came out in the wrong attic, though. But if they hadn't they'd never have got to Narnia and Digory would never have planted the apple tree that his grown-up self Professor Kirke used to build the magic wardrobe in the first place...

'Bridge!'

Huh? Where were they? Martha and Simon had disappeared – into Narnia? No, it was me who'd disappeared into Narnia. Back to earth, dammit. Where are they?

Simon shouted again. 'Bridge! It's starting!'

Oh yeah, the eclipse. The reason we came up here. The other two had scrambled right across the roof to the other party wall and were perched gazing southward over the city. Simon held up his bit of cardboard with a pinhole in it, trying to get a projection onto the grey coping. But the sky was clouded over. Will we even get to see the sun?

I scuttled hastily across to them.

'Budge up. Let me sit down.'

'Ok. Simon, shove up, puss.'

We watched. We waited. Simon fidgeted.

'Keep still! You're like a cat on a hot tin roof!'

'Meow!! Oh wow, it's starting!'

The thin cloud showed a bright smudge. We glanced at it carefully but couldn't see the disc.

'But look! It's getting darker!' Simon said.

Slowly, slowly, dusk was falling at noon. The bright, overcast day was fading to grey. Streetlights clicked on as we entered a pale twilight. It was even getting chillier. We looked at each other in awe.

'How dark will it get?'

'Not black dark. It's only partial from here. It's total in Cornwall.'

235

'It's cold.'

As the unnatural dusk deepened, a sweet whistle rose into the grey air. A blackbird singing from the squat garden. Another answered from further away – Mina Road park, sounded like. The twittering of birds rose over the sound of the traffic. Crows cawed, starlings began flying to their roosts, puzzled. The city dropped into an evening chill. Simon pulled his sleeves down to his wrists. Martha gazed in wonder at the darkening sky. I listened to the blackbird's song, waiting for the light to return.

❄

'Anyone there?' a prim voice called. Who could that be? Most of the squatters would've just yelled 'Si!'

I looked down the hatch. Marianne looked up at me.

'I followed your footprints.' she said.

I looked at the wall.

'Oh. Yeah. Whoops. Do you wanna come up?'

'This is far enough for me. I was happy to watch from the garden.' she said, smiling. Her plump, kindly face peered up at us. Sunlight was breaking through the clouds now that the eclipse was passing.

'Er, what can we do for you?' I asked awkwardly. I hadn't spoken much to Marianne, except when I dropped into Off the Streets to get some new clothes. She was usually behind a desk working on funding applications or organising the volunteers that milled around the kitchen on rainy days.

'It might be more what I can do for you.' she said.

I glanced at the other two, who were making their way across the roof, arguing about whose turn it was to make the tea.

'D' you mean me? Or Mart?'

'Well, both of you.' she said. Puzzled, I dropped my legs through the hole, scrabbling with my feet for the top rail of the stepladder, and quickly stepped down to the landing floor. Martha was not far behind.

'Shall we put the kettle on and I'll explain.' she suggested. We were soon thundering down the stairs to the distant kitchen.

236

Settled in the best chair with a cup of tea and a deformed bourbon cream, Marianne explained.

'My mother's had a stroke.' she said.

I stared. 'I-I'm sorry to hear that.'

'Don't worry. She's making a good recovery. But I've decided that she shouldn't be alone down there in Devon anymore. I'm going down to look after her.'

'Oh. What about your job?' She'd be missed at the project. She was the only one who could stop everyone arguing.

'Yes. it's a shame, but someone'll be found to fill my place. Meanwhile, there's my house left standing empty, and I'm looking for a good tenant. I think Martha would be perfect and I imagine you'd like to stay with her too?'

A house. Marianne's house. Wow. My mouth fell open. The emerged sun finally came out from behind the clouds and beamed down on us as we sat in the cluttered squat kitchen.

Her own house! I went there once for dinner not long after we started squatting. It was in a posh part of Bristol. St Barnabas. Up the hill. All the posher parts of Bristol were on high ground. To get away from the pollution caused by all the yuppy commuters using St Pauls as a car park.

I couldn't believe it. So this is what happens when you hang out with rich people.

We went straight round and looked at the two bedroomed house with the large untidy garden, big pond and small orchard. I said Yes before Martha had opened her mouth. She looked at me and nodded. It didn't take us long to pack. That's the great thing about squatting. You don't gather much moss.

We moved in by the end of the week. Autumn was coming.

❄

13. Earthbound.

'Which room do you want?'

Martha paused in lugging her mattress through the front door.
'Er, which do you want?'
'I don't mind. There's garden both sides. And no-one overlooking us, hardly.'
That was the beauty of the new house. It was set behind the other houses, in a patch of ground that used to be an orchard belonging to a big house, now long replaced by flats. Some of the handful of apple trees in the garden were very old, much older than the house.

'Can I go at the back?'
'Sure. But the room's smaller.'
'I don't mind. I feel safer in a small room.'
That was true. Mart had always been one for the concealed burrow.
'I'm going to miss Twinkle.'
'Yeah, me too.'
'Perhaps we can get a cat now.'
'Maybe.' I was wary of so much good fortune. Didn't want to trust life not to kick me in the teeth again. Not a good idea to add another timid creature to the crew just yet. Who knows if this would last?
But for now, just enjoy it. I wandered around the new house, marvelling. Clean, sound woodwork. Proper lino in the kitchen, a neat bathroom with no mould and a working shower! Cupboards with doors that weren't falling off. And radiators instead of dubious-looking gas fires or Hab makeshift plug-ins.

I never thought I'd have a place like this. I wandered out to the garden. Longish grass damp with dew soaked the ends of my jeans. The trees were loaded with russets. I picked a green one and munched as I looked around. Knelt to look into the pond. Green-brown depths, no sign of life apart from some water boatmen rowing along. See what spring brings. I pushed aside the duckweed and peered underneath. Was that a stickleback? There were some old logs scattered around the garden. We'd need to keep them if we hoped for any newts, they'd be hauled out on land ready for hibernation this time of year.

This was brilliant. I rose and went in to talk to Martha who was still industriously heaving boxes in from Marianne's estate car.

My phone rang from somewhere in the mess in front of me. I dug it out of my muddy jeans after pulling them from a bin bag.

'Hello? Oh, yeah Deena, I'll be there tomorrow, yes, sorry, we were moving house. Again? I know but this time's for keeps. Oh, thanks! I hope so. See you tomorrow.'

I hadn't put it in my pocket before it rang again.

'Hi, is that Bridget? I'll need you here in the morning, my lawn's got to be done before the weekend and the pruning needs finishing too...'

Oh balls. Ursula wasn't as easygoing as Deena. That was putting it mildly. I so needed extra time for the moving. But with her, your legs had to be falling off before she'd accept a postponement.

Trouble is, mine felt as thought they were.

'Does it hurt here? And here?'

Bloody quacks. Of course it hurts there. It hurts everywhere. Ow! Especially if you jab it like that. Just give me the painkillers, I have to get back to work.

I opened the van doors and stared moodily at the sack of compost, the ladder, the toolbag.

Ok so this is gonna hurt. No pain, no gain. I grabbed the compost first, heaved it to the edge, shoved it into the wheelbarrow. Balance the bag on top. No dropped kerb, so I have to twirl around and go at it backwards. Pity I didn't get that A level Physics. I was top of the class in the village school before my life got smashed up.

Ladder next. Tugging clumsily, getting it on my shoulder after a short comedy routine that belonged in Billy Smart's circus. All I need's a red nose.

Bang. Aahh! There's the red nose. Why do people leave crap all over the pavement?

If I hadn't tripped on that recycling box I wouldn't have banged my nose on the gatepost.

Later, I slumped under the shower, angling the jet of hot water onto the most tender part of my back. Scrubbed halfheartedly at the earth under my nails. What's the point? They'll be just as bad tomorrow.

I had my feet up on the sofa when Mart drifted in.

'Hi.'

'Hi. Want some dinner?'

'In a bit. I'm too tired right now. Wouldn't mind a beer though.'

'Ok.' Martha went to the kitchen to tap off a jug of home brew. It was a bit room temperature but she did so want to contribute something to the household and she never had any money. Her inability to make money was phenomenal.

Martha sat in the chair, the one we had in the squat that Simon found on the pavement. It was a luxurious plum-coloured velvet and we often wondered if the owner had really chucked it away or whether Simon had inadvertently walked by while they were spring cleaning. Least said.

She poured out a couple of glasses, drank some of hers and tapped the glass against the wooden arm of the chair.

Tap. Tap tap. Tap.

Morse code? Displacement activity?

'What gives?'

'I really want to get a polytunnel for the garden. But they're so expensive.'

'What would you grow in it?'

'Everything. Tomatoes, peppers. Seedlings for everything. It's ridiculous buying them and they're never any good on the windowsill.'

'Yeah.'

I'd love a poly. But I was so busy already.

'If I wasn't so snowed under with work I could think about stuff like that.'

'Could – could I give you a hand?'

I thought about that. Martha was so fragile. She was so skinny still. Wish I was. Honest toil may have given me muscles but too many exhausted fish and chip runs had given me a bit more weight than I wanted to carry around all day. All those years of pretending a bowl of Sanwa noodles was the same as a hot meal had given me an appreciation for my grub.

Martha didn't seem to have filled out even since the days of Reclaim the Streets. She was as waif-like as she was that day, all those years ago. With her pointed chin and wide anxious eyes she looked like a pixie or something.

She had made heroic efforts to hold down a job since we settled at Marianne's. The chemist shop, the library, odd cleaning jobs which she hated – she told me that her mother had her cleaning all the time at home and she'd done her share of drudging. Lately she'd sunk into her ancient silence, worn out with trying to understand the world of work and competition.

She frowned and tapped absently at the chair arm, withdrawn and silent. I could see in her face the way her anxious thoughts ran on, trying this or that way out of the trap, staring in her mind's eye into the world she couldn't join.

I was suddenly reminded of the day me and Mick and Sean put up the rope swing. Back in the village there was a bank that sloped steeply down to the river, just beyond the nettle maze that ended our garden. We used to slide down it on old fertilizer sacks that we found in the hedge, hurtling down the well-worn furrow in the middle to land in a prickly mulch of hawthorn leaves at the bottom. Tall trees surrounded the slope, hiding it from view. One hung over with a sturdy branch in just the right position. Sean shinned up the tree with me and Mick helping, standing in our linked hands to get a grip on the lowest branch. He used me as a foothold – Ouch! But then he was away, me massaging his trainer print out of my shoulder while he climbed higher.

'Right, chuck me the rope.' he called. We pushed it up as far as we could.

'I can't reach. Chuck it!' he ordered, sweeping his longish hair out of his eyes. I flung the end at him. It folded over and landed on my head.

'Bundle it up a bit first!' Sean called impatiently. That worked. The rough coil that I made gave the rope enough weight to be carried right up to where Sean was standing on the branch below and to the side of the anchor branch. He wrapped it round, clove-hitched it, pushed his slipping glasses up and wrapped and hitched some more until it was secure. Then he kicked off his foothold and swung-slid slowly down the rope, kicking his feet against the trunk now and again in the world's clumsiest abseil.

I grabbed the end and started tying a loop the minute he landed, scrambling for a foothold.

'Will I fit in there?' Sean asked.

'Yeah, I've made it extra big to fit your bum in.' I answered cheekily, and dodged a halfhearted smack round the head.

'Come on then. I get first go.'

'How come?'

'Cos I climbed the tree. Move over.' He stuck the loop over his head and shoulders and settled his bottom in the loop. Stood up straight, leaned back.

Off. Swinging up against the leafy roof of the hollow, laughing, cannoning back. I shuffled hastily out of his way, watching Sean as he swung back out into the void, fifteen, twenty feet up. Then it was my turn. I screwed myself up to lift onto my toes and hop off the slope, and swung gently out, barely making it back.

'You can go faster than that!' cried Sean, and gave me a shove as I swung towards him. I stifled a shriek as I flew through the air, thrilled by the rush of wind, intoxicated. Landed.

'My turn!'

'I want another go!'

'My turn first!' demanded little Mick.

As I handed him the rope and helped him get it on over his head, steadying him while he got into position, I realised that we were being watched. Martha was behind the screen of trees, staring wide-eyed at us as we swung against the sky.

'D'you want a go?' I called. She shook her head, mute. Her sandals scuffed in the leaf litter. She withdrew further behind the spiky trunks of young hawthorn, eyes on the ground. Afraid.

Earthbound.

❄

I remembered that day vividly as I watched Martha's frowning face. Remembered the way she'd hover uncertainly behind shelves in the shops while I persuaded her to go up the counter and ask about the job advertised in the window. The job in the library where she could barely make herself heard to the customers. The bar jobs where she'd last two days before the crowds sent her into a panic spiral. Worst of all, in meetings or any group of more than three people where no matter how much effort she made to speak up, they somehow never seemed to hear. I made a decision.

'Well, you're a good gardener, and I am swamped right now. Y'know what? I reckon you could.' I brightened up. This looked like a solution. There was only a minority of jobs that I could use another pair of hands on, but then Mart couldn't keep it up for long, she seemed to tire so easily ever since those dark days of winter in the squat. She might just work out as a casual assistant gardener though.

'There's a job I was offered up in Clifton. The garden's huge. I was going to turn it down, it's too much for me. But if you like, we can look at it tomorrow.'

I was excited. My back was frankly ecstatic at the thought of help.

'That would be great. D'you want your dinner now?' Martha jumped up and hurried out to the kitchen without waiting for an answer.

Next morning, I opened the shed door with a yawn. My tools were gone. I looked around and walked over to where Mart was just closing the back of the van. Looked inside. Everything on my list was packed with scientific neatness. There was even room for my dinner bag! That girl's a genius, in a nerdy kind of way.

She grinned at me.

'Ok, let's go!' We let rip with some old-school Julian Cope on the way up Redland Road. The day seemed to whizz past, chatting, laughing, being passed things instead of having to get down the ladder every time. But as ever, whenever the customer came out Mart shut down, shuffling behind me, eyes down. No matter how much confidence she had with the campaign folk she still couldn't look a Norm in the eye, she said.

'I don't understand them.' she tried to explain. 'They compete over everything. They believe that money's real. They squirt poison all over their gardens and then eat it. I don't understand them. They sing along with the adverts. Adverts just scare the hell out of me.'

I hated adverts too but I wasn't getting the actual phobia of them as such. Who cared, we were getting through more than twice as much work and the money was almost rolling in.

We put the poly up a month later, my back whimpering at the digging of the trench for the plastic, Mart shoving her sparrow-like weight in vain at the box of poles.

'Swap.' She took the spade from my hand and helped me out of the hole. I put my hand in the small of my back as I straightened up. Martha was already burrowing away like an industrious rabbit. I marvelled at her, using the smaller, sharper spade, the one that was like a toy in my larger hands. Perhaps I'd been underestimating her.

'Ok, we're ready for the cover.' I said triumphantly. The poles were up, the trench dug neatly all round except for the doorway. The cover once unpacked weighed a ton. I pulled at it impatiently.

'This is going to be a bit of a nightmare.' I remarked.

'No, you need to do it scientifically.' Martha answered. I sighed. I needed some strength behind this, not a physics lecture. I looked away. It was getting late. The dunnock that perched in the elder tree was beginning his usual evening concert. You could set your watch by him so it had to be six o'clock already. The blackcap serenaded the morning, singing his heart out from the top of Marianne's neglected plum tree round the back. And around noon the belling note of the local great tit rang out, echoed by his neighbour across the road. I sat down on the edge of the trench, transported by the singing of a tiny brown bird.

'Here, pull on this.' Martha nudged me with a handful of plastic.
'What?'
By George, she'd done it. All the time I'd been dreaming she'd run and got the step stool out of the kitchen, climbed up with one end of the strip of plastic and thrown it as far as she could over the structure. I grabbed the other end and pulled it over and down.
'Wait a minute, why's it so narrow?'
'It's folded in two. Wait, wait, you have to get the right side outside, the side with the sun protection.' Oh blimey, she's only gone and read the instructions. If I wasn't always so busy digging and lifting and slogging I'd have done it myself.
'Right, now we can unfold. Here we are.'
We tucked the sides into the trench and infilled, watching it tauten beautifully.
'What about the ends?' I grabbed a handful and started stuffing it unhandily into the end trench. It didn't want to go in. It wouldn't fit. I stood back, sighed.
Martha whisked past me and with great patience began to pleat the plastic neatly, starting at the middle and working out to the side, then repeating on the other half of the back wall.
'Pass the scissors.' She trimmed the ends and tucked them down in the trench.
I shovelled earth in with the toy spade. Neat as neat. Perfectly taut.
'Well done. What made you think of that?' I asked.
'Well, it's like dressmaking. Making pintucks to take in a waist. Transferable skill.'
'I didn't know you knew dressmaking.'
'Oh, I had to. If I wanted any dresses. They'd never have got finished if I hadn't helped. Mum used to cut them out and start pinning, then

she'd sort of wander off halfway. I had to do all the tacking. But once they were in one piece she'd do the machining.'

Those dresses. All made on the same pattern, all limp floral fabric. All a little clumsily put-together.
Martha was a good cook too. And much as she hated it, excelled at all housework.
I thought about how white and tired, how silent she'd be some days, slipping in through the forsythia tunnel.
'You must have done quite a bit of housework stuff, at home?' I ventured.
'I did everything.' she said bitterly. 'Cooking, cleaning, sewing, shopping. That's why I came in for so much flak. She was never satisfied. I was only a kid, I couldn't do it all perfectly the way she wanted. But it wasn't her fault. She was always ill, always tired.'
'Why didn't anyone else in the family help?' I said, appalled.
She considered. 'Well, there isn't anyone much. She has a sister up in Newcastle. Some cousins in Ebbw Vale. We never saw them. Anyway, she never let on. She didn't want anyone to know that she wasn't coping.'

She never let on. Sounds like it was a family trait.

'You never told me.' I tried not to make it sound like an accusation. She'd had more than enough of those in her life.
'She told me not to talk about what happened at home…
We can't have the neighbours knowing all our business.
..I wasn't allowed to bring friends home.'
We don't want people to see how we live.
'I was warned off not to play with any of the village kids, except the posher ones. And they didn't want to play with me.'
Keep away from those Dohertys, I don't want you picking up bad habits.
'And I didn't have any friends anyway, so it didn't matter...
Speak when you're spoken to! Be quiet! Sit down!
...she didn't want me so she sure as hell wasn't going to want any friends of mine.'
Get out of my sight!

'What did she think about me being friends with you? The dreaded Dohertys?' I joked.

'She never knew anything about it.' Martha said, with a hint of pride. 'That tunnel we made through the forsythia was brilliant. I took care not to even disturb the tops of the bushes. It really helped that no one did any gardening, apart from mowing the bits that showed.'

'She didn't have you slaving away at that too?' I was surprised.

'No, that would have involved getting dirty and tearing my clothes. And my dad sure as hell wasn't going to do it.'

'He should've had some boys.'

'Yeah, then they could've beat him up when they were big enough.' Martha sat up violently. The pleating was finished and we shovelled in the last of the earth.

We puzzled over piecing together the door, and together managed to wrap it in polythene and tape it round. Fitting it on was a challenge.

'Left – no, right a bit!'

'Up! I said up! Got it!'

We swung the newly hung door back and forth proudly.

'I'll get the chairs.' Martha brought in the stool and the plastic deckchair. We sat down in our poly, warming up already. I looked around.

'This is brilliant. Think what we can grow in here.'

'Everything.' Mart agreed. 'Just wish it was a bit bigger...'

'Oh, come on! This is great!' I protested. It was even starting to smell right. Damp earth, steamy humid air. Just needs a banana pseudostem or two.

'If I'd known, I'd have beat him up for you.' I said suddenly.

She looked at me. *Yeah, I know, you can take bravado only so far.* Involuntarily, a hand went up to touch my head. Martha glanced away, confirming that she'd noticed.

'He would have killed you.' she said. 'But – thanks.'

She smiled at me, trying to stretch out her legs on the stool that wobbled on the uneven ground.

'We can do anything. Anything at all.' she said, a finger reaching up to touch the drop of condensation already forming on the ceiling.

'There was an old Ikea shelf unit in the skip down the road. Make good racking if we cut it up.'
'Shall we?'
'Yeah!' We ran-staggered down the garden path, me grabbing the wheelbarrow on the way.
'Ow! My back still hurts!' But right now, I didn't care.

※

The tomatoes were nearly over. Martha was cutting down the remaining strings. We'd been hard at it, bottling and drying, bell peppers, chilli, crunching on cucumbers, picking and freezing beans. My skin glowed and even Mart's pale elvish face was looking rosier with a constant diet of fresh organic fruit and veg. There were strings of onions in the kitchen, baskets of garlic, boxes of apples.

'Wow, can't believe how much food we've grown in this little space.' I marvelled.
'Sometimes it's easier to grow more in a small space than in a big one. Less work. You make best use of every square foot.' Mart answered absently. 'At Cerrig-'
She stopped. She didn't seem to like thinking about Cerrig these days. She was so happy growing, picking, pruning, harvesting, preserving, cooking. Spending her whole life in the garden, brushing past herb bushes that released their scent into the air.

Now she was clipping lavender. Snip, snip.
'What's that for?'
'A lavender bag. Deena wants one to put in her linen cupboard.'
'Oh.' I was nowhere near so tired these days but the late September sun was making me magnificently lazy. I reached up and picked a russet from the ancient apple tree.
'They're still green.'
'I like 'em that way.' I answered, munching away.
'We could have pear trees, when we get our hands on some land.' Martha said.
I sat up, idling forgotten.

248

'That would be awesome.' We loved dreaming our farm. I had built chicken sheds, planted rows of potatoes, filled compost boxes in the imaginary cellar for mushroom growing, you name it. I was planning the fantasy orchard – plums for winemaking and a hedge of raspberries flourishing in the shade.

'A fishpond. And a huge poly. We could sell seedlings every spring.' That was Mart.

'Yeah, and water collection. A physic garden.' I said. Kerry was always looking for stuff for her herbal potions.

'Hiya peasants!'

Simon appeared round the hedge and bounded up the path to us.

'Hi yourself, you moggy. Where have you been all this time?'

'Helping Hab crack a squat.'

'Thought you were done with all that when you got your new flat.'

'Yeah, but they still need my brilliant cracking skills. There's a whole family needs somewhere to go tonight.'

'Wow. Did you get them somewhere?'

'Yeah, they're just moving their gear in, so I thought I'd come and see how you wurzels were doing.'

'Cheeky sod. We're making our living here. Sit down, help us peel these apples.'

'Honest toil?' Simon said in dismay.

'Yes. Do you good. No, the peel goes in the compost bucket. The apple goes in the pie. Remember that.'

'What are you going to do with all that?'

'Feed it to people. There's a load of them in the freezer already. No! don't take the peel off that thick. Here. Use a potato peeler. We'll feed you in return. Mart's doing a casserole.'

We peeled and chattered, Simon's computer customers were idiots, they were geniuses, they were intimidatingly smarter than him, they couldn't tell one end of a mouse from the other.

'You seen much of Mick lately?' Martha asked Simon.

He scowled. 'Not a lot.' he said.

'Why sad face? You two are the best of friends aren't you?' I asked, puzzled.

'Yeah. Friends.' he said.

I changed the subject. 'How's Kerry?'
'Oh, she's still fighting the good fight. Getting tired of squatting though. And I think Twinkle's getting sick of being an urban cat. She's on about college now.'
'What, Kerry?' I was surprised she of all people would even consider the confinement of academic life.
'No, Twinkle. Yes, Kerry. She's applied to Exeter University to do Ecology and Conservation.'
'Wow.' Martha said wistfully.'There used to be a Masters there I always wanted to do.'
This was a conversation I was firmly excluded from. I peeled on grimly.

'Can't see Kerry in a lecture hall though.'
'Yeah. Kerry, obeying rules. Being on time. Not arriving at college in a woolly hat covered in Earth First! badges and mud.'
Martha laughed. 'I can just see her turning up to lectures with her pockets full of kindling and Twinkle following at her heel like Dick Whittington's cat.'
They laughed. I moved on to scraping carrots.

'D'you ever think about going to university?' Martha asked me.
'Me? To do what? Mow their lawn?' I scoffed. 'Not interested.'
'You used get through all those books. Write all the time. Your stories were ace.' she persisted, most unwisely in my view.
I didn't answer. Remembered seeing the results in the paper back in Birmingham. Our school published a list of ex-pupils who'd finished degree courses, complete with smiling graduation photos.

Ann Francis, BA History, Manchester. Helen Tredshaw, BA Art and Design, Wolverhampton. Samira Desai, BA English Literature, Cambridge.
Bridget Doherty, MDQ - member of the dole queue.
Not that I cared.

I picked up another carrot. Started scraping. The declining autumn sun had gone in. My hands were wet and cold now, covered in tiny cracks ingrained with earth.

✳

I was pricking out spring cabbage when Kerry called to say she was in town for Easter holidays.

'Shall I come over?'

'Yes, that would be great.' I said. I pushed my phone back into my apron pocket and carried on levering seedlings out with the wrong end of a teaspoon. I was tucking them up carefully in pots when Kerry popped her head round the poly door.

'Hard at it?'

'Yeah.' I said. 'What have you been up to?'

'Just the usual. Studying. We've got a field trip up to Mid Wales next week. Stream surveys and bank vegetation quadrats.'

'Oh.' I thought about telling Kerry that I'd managed to grow an aubergine plant. But it didn't seem much of a big deal in comparison.

'Listen, is Mart here?'

Yeah. Don't want to waste time talking to the thicko gardener.

'She'll be back from Off The Streets in about an hour.'

'Ok, I can wait.'

'What's it about?'

'Oh, it's a plan for this summer. Have you ever been to an Offgrid festival?'

'Nah. Went to the Big Green once or twice. And me and Mick smuggled ourselves into Glasta once, and spent the whole weekend tripping our faces off on this cheap acid he bought off a traveller. What's Offgrid?'

'They have it every year near Cheddar. Part of the Sunrise festivals. Are you up for it this year?'

'I dunno. How much is it?'

'Free if you come with me. I'm doing a herbal medicine stall.'

'Oh yes?' That put a different complexion on it. 'Could you use some calendula?'

'*Could* I? How much have you got?'

I pointed wordlessly to the flowerbed that ran the length of the garden fence. Halfway along was an expanse of orange.

'They seem to practically flower all year round these days.'

'Climate change.' said Kerry.

Climate change. T-shirt weather in January. Spring blizzards. Frost so rare these days that Lord and Lady Muck might have questioned my stock excuse. Funny weather all the time. Drought followed by torrents of rain. You really notice it as a gardener. Last year Deena's apple tree flowered in November. And I've got used to December roses and June bugs in April.

'Can I pick some of these?' asked Kerry.
'Help yourself, Just leave enough to look at and for seed.' I gestured towards the patch of marigolds. Kerry didn't need telling twice. She was on her knees picking. I passed her a mushroom box.
'If I infuse them in oil then I can make up some ointment.'
'What's it good for?'
'Pretty much everything. Sore skin, infections, antifungal. Chapped lips and sore hands.'
'Can you do me some?' I looked at the ragged remains of my winter hands.
'Of course. Oh, have you got any wine left?'
'Gallons. What do you want?'
'Got any gooseberry?'
'Yeah, I'll get you a couple of bottles.'

We spent the next hour picking off marigold petals. Martha was thrilled about the Sunrise plan when she came in. Later we pulled our tent out of the cupboard to check for rips and count pegs. I was surprised how excited the thought of a trip made me. Something to look forward to. Earthbound, but looking forward to the strange excitement of the lengthening evenings, those eerie moments before dusk when I'd feel a silent mystery unfolding. The light returning. Summer is icumen in.

❄

14. Fierce Light at Sunrise.

I strolled along the grassy track, looking around. Martha scampered at my side, her green and blue skirt foaming around her knees.

'Look at that!' She'd found a hat stall.
'That'd suit you.' I said, pointing to a felt pixie hat with a foot-long point.
'Oh yeah, well this is yours.' she retorted, unhooking a broad brimmed Gandalf with a long misty silken scarf for a hatband. She dropped it onto my head and burst out laughing.
'Hey! I can't see!'
'You should see yourself. It's really you.' she said.

Kerry caught us up.
'Oh yes! I think you should wear it all the time.' she agreed.
I looked in the tiny mosaic-framed mirror on the stall. My long curly brown locks fell from under the brim, the streaks of grey showing at the temples now that I had loosened it from the eternal ponytail. My brown eyes looked back at me, more mournfully than I would have imagined. I looked like a sad Shetland pony in a silly hat.

'Looks bloody stupid.' I grunted, pulling at it.
'No! Leave it on! It makes you look wise!' Kerry pressed the hat more firmly onto my head. I looked again. Hmm. Maybe it did make me look a bit wise. Lord Muck would be intimidated into letting me grow what I liked in a hat like this. There was plenty of room for robins to perch on it, too.
'You are so getting this hat.' Martha declared. I looked at the price label.
'You're kidding me. I can't afford Trustafarian prices.' I said, regretfully taking it off and walking away. I walked on down the grassy marketplace, trying to look casual but secretly revelling in the medley of colourful fabrics, knitted earflapped Peruvian bonnets for llamas with cold ears, the shiny, the tinkly, the richly-embroidered. Dainty elvish mirrors and oh, the lovely earrings and bracelets.

Everything was so pretty, right down to the black price labels written in gold ink. Not that I was into that sort of thing. I stopped to covet a pair of silver and moss agate earrings. Like drops of greenish frozen ice. My head was enveloped suddenly.

'Here you are!'
'Whatcha?'
'We clubbed together. The hat is yours!'
Oh I say, that's a bit pricey. But - what a hat. That hat is so me. Mart was right. I made up my mind as we walked on and the smell of chocolate pancakes drifted into range.
'Well..er, thanks. Thanks. Anyone for pancakes?'
As I stood in line I straightened my new hat and preened discreetly, half-smiling. Hoping no one I knew could see me. Then sort of wishing they could.

❅

Dusk was falling. Strings of coloured lights popped quietly into existence, orange and green-lit smoke wafted over the site. There was a hubbub of voices and snatches of violin music, shouts, shrieks of up-late kids, running free all over the fields. The smell of pancakes mixed with curry and veggie burgers, fried onions scented the air, ankle bracelets jingled, accordions wheezed cheerfully as brightly dressed people strolled past with a trudge of boots strung with rainbow laces, the lighter step of sandals and the pad of dusty bare feet. Embroidered waistcoats, Paisley shirts, anarchist T shirts, pixie hats and Peruvian deerstalkers created a swirl of colour. As it got darker men strolled past with children on their shoulders and fairy lights round their necks, the kids waving lightsticks. The whole field smelt of dope and nag champa. I took a deep appreciative sniff. The moon was rising against a beautiful dark-blue sky. I caught sight of Mart's green-blue skirt in the crowd and ran after her.
'Where to now?'
'Chai?'
'What, no alcohol?' said Kerry.
'Chai with a shot of brandy?' suggested Martha.
'Wow, that ticks all the boxes. Come on, then.'

We set off across the darkling, sparkling field, following our noses until the spicy, chocolately, heady scent of brandy-laced chai wafted past. We followed our noses like the Bisto kids, stood in line, paid our 50p deposit for real china mugs and found cushions to sit on in the marquee. Lights twinkled on the colourful throws that were draped over the pale canvas. I absorbed the beauty silently. Could have done with some of this in my treehouse, it would've really made it. Not good for lying low, though. Just think, with a bit of a wood burner I could have solved all my problems by just moving into the treehouse. Yewtree Cottage – says what it is. I daydreamed on, half-listening to the couple sitting behind me who were talking about solar panels and Passivhaus design, watching the way Martha continually shoved her glasses up her nose as she talked animatedly to Kerry. Sean was always doing that, I thought. Heh, Wellington. Remember you're a Womble. What?

'Huh? Did you say something?' Martha was looking at me expectantly.
'Earth to Bridget... come in, Bridge.'
'She hasn't got her aerial up.' Kerry said cheekily.
'What?' I said again, irritably. Way to interrupt a perfectly good daydream with insults.
'I said, do you want to watch a film with us tomorrow?'
'What film?'
'The one we've been talking about for the last half hour while you were not on the Enterprise.'

Huh. Nerds.
'What's it about?' I asked, ignoring their cruel jibes.
'Er, it's about activism.' said Kerry.
'Well - *spiritual* activism, really.' added Mart, hesitating as she dropped the S-bomb.
'Come again?' I hope crystals aren't involved. Or robes and chanting.
'No, really, it's about what makes people become activists. Their beliefs and how they motivate them to do stuff to change the world.'

'Er, madness, boredom, frustration, lack of trees...I dunno, why did you two get into it?' I asked.

Kerry and Martha looked at each other.
'Er, I..' Mart began brilliantly.
'I – well..' added Kerry, with equal genius.
'Maybe you should watch it then. You might find out.'
'Let's just all go.' Mart said.
'All right then.'
Don't mind sitting in the cinema tent for a couple of hours, hippies are always so entertaining when they're being earnest. I always wondered how Mart got into all this digger diving stuff. Could be interesting.

It wasn't until much later, after the film was over, that it occurred to me that what I'd asked them was quite a personal question really. No wonder they didn't answer.

※

It was the angel that I remembered. Right at the beginning, protesting the 'dirty war'. The angel washing the Mexican flag with a bar of soap in a bowl. Like that Fairy green laundry soap that our mum made us wash our hands with in the kitchen. Fair took the skin off you.
The way she looked up when she heard the helicopter. Folded her hands to pray, closed her eyes tight, waiting for death. That didn't come. The way she peered sideways, then turned and looked up at the sky.

The first bit of the film was shocking. The footage of the very moment the journalist got shot, the film shaking as he staggered across the road and dropped his camera onto a bench and collapsed. The blood spots, the gunfire... oh God! At least Kerry and Mart only have to worry about getting arrested. No one's going to shoot them anytime soon.
Think about all the brutality of those bloody security guards at the tree evictions though...makes you wonder how they can stand it.

256

It was good. The Dalit activists in India. So many faces – Desmond Tutu. Oh, look - Alice Walker. Of course, she was up to her neck in the Civil Rights movement. I remember the first time I read Color Purple. An everyday tale of family life. Huh. Got that right.
And Bell Hooks explaining the title, the fierce light she saw one morning, in a flower, in a bird. What I saw in my yew tree. In the forsythia, yellow against the blue March sky. In the weeds, surging past the boring ornamentals, groundsel with flowers like little yellow and white shaving brushes, sow thistle growing a stem like a tree, given the chance. In a sunlit dandelion clock, trembling with the breeze. In a flower, in a bird. In the morning of our lives.

I glanced at Martha's face from time to time. She looked absorbed, but gave nothing away. Kerry was smiling a private joke kind of smile. I turned back. John Lewis, explaining how he walked the bridge at Selma only to stagger back bleeding, the march smashed to pieces by thuggish National Guards on horseback, clubs and whips flailing. What was he saying?
He said. We could not hate these men. We had been taught to love.

What?
How? How? How do you love someone who just broke your skull?
I didn't see the next few scenes, something about an urban garden in LA, something about the riots.
If anyone else had told me to love the bastard that breaks your bones I'd have told them to fuck right off. No messing.
But.

They did break his bones. They killed his friends. They treated him worse than an animal. Heh, funny how no one ever sees the irony in that. Why is it somehow Ok to treat animals horribly, to the point where we use it as a yardstick for cruelty to humans?

But. He didn't say, we shouldn't hate. We ought to love. He said we cannot hate, we have to love.
A distinction there. Could he, could he really return love for that much hate?

257

Could anyone?

I withdrew into myself to brood, or sulk, or think, or something.

Martha turned to me, bright eyed. She was about to whisper to me, but stopped when she saw my face.

Later, we didn't talk about what we'd seen.

❄

I wondered if they thought about it later, like I did.

I never asked.

❄

I tilted my hat to a jauntier angle as I strolled through the booths and tents. The geodesic caught my eye. Oh yes. It was all made of short lengths of hazel pole, fixed together into triangles and the triangles built up into a hemisphere. Brilliant. But how were they attached? Oh. Metal hooks and eyes, bolted together. Got to try that.

What's the use? Without access to land, we can't do any of this stuff. Maybe one day though. Maybe. One day.

Martha was very quiet the rest of the day. Even for her. Kerry was busy selling calendula cream and comfrey ointment and testing her garlic brew on unsuspecting members of the public.

'Bridge. You're wise.'

'Huh?' What was Kerry saying?

'Which of these seedlings is evening primrose?'

'Huh – oh, that one.' I pointed.

'Thanks.'

'Don't mensh.' The hat was working!

It was such a relaxing weekend. Kerry talked me into being pummelled by a Tui Na massage practitioner. Oh my goodness, the bliss of getting all the knots taken out of my back. I was well impressed. Tui Na – seemingly it's as old as acupuncture and Chinese herbal medicine but never caught on the way acupuncture did. Works on the acupressure points. Turns out there's a button on the soles of your feet that makes you relax down to comatose the instant it's pressed. I could feel the energy flowing back into

258

muscles I'd given up on. Came out of the tent feeling young again, like a kid, light and floaty, ready to scamper up the nearest tree.

Martha had been deep in conversation with some T-shirted people on a stall. Oh. They all had the same shirt. I floated like thistledown over to Mart.

'What's it all about then?' I asked.
'I'm joining the party.' she said. Or rather, announced. I could tell it meant something big to her.
'This lot? Party politics? Thought you didn't do that sort of thing.'
'Yeah, well I didn't. But people can't spend their lives getting arrested and shoved around by the police. We need some real influence. All the campaigns that worked were stopped in the planning stage. Legal challenges, planning appeals, that sort of thing. Once they start cutting trees down you've already lost. We saw that at Newbury. Direct action may make you feel better but it doesn't work.' she said bleakly.

'Oh, I don't know,' said Kerry beside her, 'it helps put the pressure on. It helps when they know they're going to have a load of resistance.'
'Yeah.' agreed Martha uncertainly. 'But ultimately we have to be on the councils, in the House of Commons, passing the laws we need.'
'It all helps.' Kerry conceded. 'All of it together. You just have to decide where you can contribute. The Party's Ok, it helps having someone on the council who's on your side.'

Martha turned her new badge round to look at the logo. She still seemed doubtful about her new status. She shoved an armful of leaflets into her pocket and sighed.
'Yeah. I hope. Nothing seems to work. But something's got to.'
'You gonna run for office?' I teased. As if Martha would ever put herself in the limelight.
'I might.' she said thoughtfully.
'You? Giving speeches? You'd have to talk to the press and everything.'
'I could do that.' she said defensively.

I looked at her. There was a stubborn light in her eye I hadn't seen before.

'Well, you could give it a go. Can't hurt to try.' I said, trying to joke awkwardly.

'Yeah, do it!' said Kerry with enthusiasm. She never could imagine that anyone'd fail at anything, ever. I have to hand it to the activists, they don't give up. They're brave.

Never thought of Mart as a brave person before, but when you think about it, she is. She's done it all on her own. College, going off to protests, living up the mountain. I looked at her with new eyes. Mart, a councillor. Or - an MP, even. She'd tell them. She'd really tell them!

Why not? Why the hell not?

That night as I turned over on my Karrimat trying to find a soft bit of ground, I thought about the film again. Wondered what had kept Mart going all these years. What internal clockwork drove her on, gave her the strength? I'd have packed it in years ago. Suppose I did, really. Just getting by, drudging away. Keeping out of trouble.

Not like Mart. She sees a wrong that needs righting and dives right in.

Wish I could be more like her, sometimes.

You know.

Fearless.

❄

'It's cold.'

'Yeah. Radiators are freezing again. They need flushing.'

'Call Marianne.'

Martha looked up at me from under her quilt. 'You're kidding. I've told her four times about the heating breaking down all the time.'

'Well, she'll do it. She's cool.'

'No, *we're* cool. We're bloody freezing. Though we'd put all that behind us.'

'I'll call her tomorrow. Remind her. It'll be fine.'

Martha looked sceptical.

260

I went into the kitchen to heat my leftover stew. Damn. Forgot the front rings don't work any more. Damn and damn. Waited ages and it didn't heat up. What a muffin. Better do the toast while I'm waiting. Talking of muffins.

'That grill doesn't work.' Martha said as she came in.

'Since when?'

'Since we have a crap landlord all over again.' Martha said bitterly.

'Nah, you can't put Marianne in the same league as that Prospect Road arsehole.' I objected.

'Why not?' Did she say she'd get the heating fixed?'

'Er, well she said that the boiler was pretty new so it should be Ok.' I said.

'She had it put in fifteen years ago! And what about the radiators?' Martha demanded.

'She said she'll see what she can do at the end of the month.' I said.

'That would be the month of October?'

'Yeah.'

'Didn't she go on holiday to Malaysia this year?' Martha said.

'Did she? Suppose that's why she's got no money...'

'Yeah. That'll be it.' Martha said acidly.

'Hang on.' I said suddenly. 'You can't have a go at Marianne. She's the reason we're not squatting anymore. She trusted us with her own house!'

'Yeah? And now she's taking money off us for a place that's falling down, while she swans off abroad.'

'Well, she's had a lot of expenses, what with her mum and that. And there's no work down there in Devon. She isn't getting the wage she did in Bristol.'

'Diddums.' said Martha.

'You know, you don't know how hard it is, earning money. We work and work and we're still juggling money to pay bills. We can't all afford the luxury of faffing about with politics all our lives. People need a decent holiday after that. You know?'

There was a deadly silence as my words hung in the air. I longed to take them back, soften them, but no chance. Martha was very still, her face white. She opened her mouth to say something, then shut it and quietly left the room. I heard the front door slam.

Well, it's true, I justified to myself. I know it's not her fault she can't get jobs but she shouldn't be having a go at Marianne. Marianne saved us. Mart just doesn't have a clue what it's like getting up day after day after day every day of your life to try to please other people.

I mean, she's had jobs. So she does know. And she'd take a job like a shot if she could. But.

Then I remembered all the days Martha had spent helping me with my garden jobs and my heart sank a bit further.

I spent the afternoon feeling like shit, wishing I hadn't said it. I went into the kitchen to make some dinner. Thirty minutes later I realised that the oven hadn't heated up. My piece of fish sat, half thawed and droopy, on the draining board.

'Bollocks!' Made a cheese sandwich and went into my room, turned the halogen heater on and sat on the floor in front of it, chewing angrily.

❄

I roused. It was dark apart from the glow of the halogen heater. I got up clumsily and shut the curtains. My watch said half twelve. Mart must be back by now. I went to look for her, checked the lounge and kitchen. Her door was open and the room dark. Her bed was neatly made.

'God, where is she?'

I shoved my feet into clogs and wandered out of the back door. She can't be in the garden. It's freezing. I walked round the back anyway. A shadow moved. Martha was sitting on a damp log under the old apple tree.

'God, you scared me! How long have you been there?'

Martha didn't answer.

'Come on in.'

No answer.

'Come on, Mart, stop being a dick - I mean, look, I'm sorry, I'm sorry I said that Ok, I was just angry.'

The dark lump that was Martha made no sign.

'Fine. Be like that. Stay outside. Freeze your arse off making some obscure point. I'm going to bed.'

I left the back door unlocked and lay awake for the next hour.

Damn.

There was a crackling sound coming from the window. I smelled smoke. God, was the place on fire?

I got up, wrapped in my quilt, and looked out. Martha was still sitting on the log, hunched over the small fire she'd kindled. She looked so lonely sitting there. As I watched I was the one who started to feel left out. There's something primeval about sitting round a fire.

Fine, I'm going to spend the night in the garden. Can't be any colder than this fucking house.

I sat down on the log and wrapped my quilt round me, throwing half over Martha. We just sat there like a couple of idiots, staring at the flames, until I woke to find Mart slumped against me. The fire was out. I hauled her up and into the house, steered her to her bed and heaved her in, lifting her feet up and undoing her shoes. She mumbled a bit in her sleep. I covered her up and stood at the door, watching. The room smelled of woodsmoke. I quietly closed the door and went to my own bed.

✳

I got up from my desk and stretched. It was cool in the old farmhouse, a refuge from the scorching midday heat outside. It was a new one to have to spend the middle of the day inside to keep out of the searing July sun. I stood and gazed out of the window at the overgrown field maples and hazels that encircled the farm. If it was possible, I'd say the trees were wilting. Never seen that before. I went back and looked at the last page I'd typed. Seemed to have come to a full stop.

Really, that's because that night under the apple tree was the beginning of the end – sort of. Everything changed after that. That was when we both agreed later that life stopped making sense. Looking for a home, rebuilding our friendship, surviving, gardening, was all just an extension of childhood really. Neither of us got to grips with being a grownup. Overrated, that's why.

But both of us were living in limbo, feeling like we weren't doing it right, like we were waiting for a life to turn up like our teachers had said. We'd get discovered, make money, our talents would get recognised somehow by the people that mattered. Not anyone we knew, obviously. It goes without saying that the likes of us didn't matter.

Waiting for real life to begin, like Kerry's did. Like Mick's, once Sean put him through his apprenticeship. He was a carpenter now, Sean paid for his training after the electrics business took off. Sean was so lucky, his helicopter arrived. His first boss Alan was impressed by his ability and agreed to sub him through an electricians' course. He was right, of course. Our Sean's a clever boy and no mistake. His glasses always made him look intelligent. Turns out he was. Sean worked the cost off afterwards, living in the old caravan in the orchard behind Bob's farm. This farm. Where Bob - that's Alan's uncle - offered me the landshare back then, after the wheels came off Mart's political career after the incident at conference.

❄

Suddenly Martha was popular. The phone never stopped ringing. 'Is Martha there? Can you tell her to call back about the agenda item?' About the meeting, the subcommittee, the policy document.
There were leaflets everywhere. Party members dropped in more often as winter drew down. Already they were anticipating the long haul to spring. And not just any spring - local elections were due next year. But Sunrise seemed a long way away.

'What's this?' I picked up a leaflet from the kitchen table. 'Basic Income?'
Miranda looked up from folding newsletters, her plump, knotted hands put down the papers.
'Ah, Basic Income Guarantee.' she began, 'One of the first policies we had, actually. It dates back to the time of the Earthpeace Party,

that grew out of the peace and environmental movements of the '70s.'

'What is Basic Income Guarantee? Without the history lesson?'

'Well, it's kind of counter-intuitive, a bit controversial...'

I waited impatiently.

'It symbolises land rights...that is, these days most people wouldn't know what to do with land rights -'

I would!

'- so instead the Party postulated a guaranteed basic income for all citizens.'

'Like the dole?'

'No, it's completely unconditional. Of course, the first thing most people say is that no one would go to work if they had a living on a plate, and...'

'I wouldn't! This is what we're always needed! It would totally spring the benefit trap! And make seasonal work easier to deal with.'

'...some people worry that it'd undermine wages.'

'Why? What really undermines wages is sheer desperation. When it's that or starve on the dole, people'll put up with anything.'

Miranda looked at me with mild surprise.

'That's not most people's first reaction.'

'I think most people would agree with me. Most people know what it's like to struggle to get by.'

'I don't know.' Miranda gave me an arch look. 'Bristol's a wealthy city. People here have aspirations. They worry about their taxes going to support people who aren't contributing anything.' She flicked her plum-coloured pashmina back across her shoulders.

'You mean like the Royal Family and the bloody landlords?' I joked, trying to lighten the mood.

She regarded me, her expression that emotional blank that the middle classes are so good at. I could tell that I'd crossed some invisible line, but God knew what. These people were so hard to read.

'Anyway, Basic Income Guarantee is hotly debated at every conference but it's still considered an essential foundation of our social policy.'

What social policy? I've read the manifesto, and they don't have one! I put on my best business manner, the one I used for the customers who lived on the hill.

'I think that's right. You've got to have a safety net for a decent society. And this one's much more flexible. People can say no to environmentally damaging jobs without worrying about how they'll survive.'

Miranda looked relieved. I was talking her language again.

'Yes, exactly. And – it's social justice. There'd be no more poverty and exclusion -'

You wish, remarked my inner Brummie.

'- Labour never went this far. No more benefit stigma -'

Hey!

'- everyone will have a living, and everyone will be able to work whatever hours they can on top without stoppages.'

My inner Brummie quit misbehaving and extended her grudging approval.

'Hey, you know – that's – that's a really good idea. You know, it's funny, I had an idea like that quite a while -'

'Yes, you wouldn't catch any of the Big Three coming up with anything like it.' she said smugly.

I gave up.

Martha and I were back on speaking terms, it hadn't taken long after I'd sneezed my way through an apology the next day and she'd coughed her acceptance. We were both laid up with impressive colds that week, and days spent shuffling round the house wheezing 'D'you wad sub garlic brew and Beechab's?' at each other and snuffling into wads of tissues over dinner, I felt pretty forgiven. Just to make sure, I tried to take an interest in her new Party work. It wasn't hard. They had some great ideas. I mean, all right, they were shatteringly middle-class. But, well, middle class types are cut out for politics. You don't see people like me and Mart in the Council House do you?

Still, making roads car-free, taking back space in the city for bikes and pedestrians and kids to play and where cats may safely cross can't be bad. Banning pesticides. Plastic recycling. It would be so great if they could pull it all off. They had only three members on the city council but were campaigning for five more, come May. I always forget that Hazelmead ward's got the posh areas like this thrown in with some of the poorest parts of the inner city. Don't think the Party was right keen on slumming it, though. I once heard the campaigns officer complaining about what happened when he canvassed the whole of a large council block in St Pauls when there was a local election down in Ashley ward, our old stomping ground.

'There was only one vote in the whole place. I'm not going back there this time.'
'But if you don't canvass they won't have the chance to know anything about the Party. They might not be familiar with the policies, you're only a small party.'
'If I lived there, I'd make it my business to inform myself. Anyway, it's too hard to get into the blocks.'
I was silent. Steph, who cut my hair, was usually Labour and so were most of her neighbours, but quite a few of them had taken Mart's election posters to put in their windows last time. Steph had been quite happy to let the Party canvassers into the block, and her sister was over in the next block, she'd let them in too. All they had to do was press the right buzzer. I tried to tell Paul.
'Look, people are concerned with economics over there, not with the state of the environment. There's a lot of - social issues. It's best Labour takes care of them. We'll get round to those areas once we've built up more support and got more seats on the council.' As far as he was concerned the matter was closed.
'They're concerned with economics because they haven't got enough money!'
'Money won't save us when climate change kicks in.' was all he said.
I wondered if he could hear himself. I sighed, and went out to tidy the poly for winter. By the time there were plants in here again, election day would be here.

❄

We waited outside the meeting hall in the bitter wind of November. Miranda was due to unlock the building, but she was late. I stamped my feet. Martha looked uneasy. A chattering group approached across the square under the bare sycamores that were outlined against a sodium-orange tinted sky.

'Ready?' one of them asked Martha warmly. I was surprised. Most of them ignored Mart or patronised her by turns.

'Yes.' she smiled back.

'Know what you're going to say? Don't forget, everyone has to answer the same questions.'

'Yeah, I'm ready.'

'Mart, are you -'

'Yeah, I'm running for nomination.'

Wow. She kept that quiet. When she asked me to come to the party hustings I never knew she'd be in them.

Oh wow. This was exciting.

'D'you really think you can do it?'

'I'm going to have a go.'

'Go for it!'

We filed in. There was a bench at the top of the room, with five chairs pulled up. The chair sat down the the centre and called for order. Two older men and a woman in a business suit rose and took the other seats, then Martha stood up shakily and walked up the centre aisle to take the last one. She looked a bit pale, but composed. Her Off the Streets cast-offs were a bit shabby, but neat and clean. That cardigan and the tunic top were nice and bright, and for once there were no holes in her jeans. She fiddled nervously with her pendant, a silver butterfly.

The chair was a dignified, dark-bearded man – a grown-up Ben – who introduced each of them.

'Now I'm sure you're all keen to ask questions of our nominees, one of whom we are determined to get onto the City Council for Hazelmead Ward. There are no shortage of burning environmental issues in Bristol – yes, I know, the old scrapyard down in Ashley has been known to catch fire from time to time. Then there's air

268

pollution – rates of childhood asthma are rising. Plastic recycling, pedestrian crossings, the 25 – Stay Alive campaign. We know that our party members can make the difference the planet needs in Hazelmead. So, who would like to ask our nominees the first question?'

Hands went up and the clamour began. Martha answered quietly but clearly, flicking her head back to stop herself staring down at the table, smiling and gaining in confidence as they were asked what experience they'd had.

'Well, I'm an environmental science graduate. I work as a part-time gardener.' She stopped, baulking, then began again.
'I was a full time eco-protestor for four years and I have experience of the poor state of Ashley's housing stock, similar to the worst housing in Hazelmead. I spent years trying to find better accomodation. I've been a squatter and have lived in a self sufficient rural community. I have seen firsthand the effects of years of Thatcherism and Blairite Labour on communities, the unemployment, mental illness and homelessness. I also volunteer at Off the Streets in Bishopston with a variety of social projects. I'm assisting the founding of a housing coop at the moment, and I grow food for myself and the community at home and down at the allotments.'

The audience looked at one another. If there was one thing the Party wanted it was someone who could relate to the poorer parts of Hazelmead. They were right out of their depth there. I could hearing murmers of approval, and 'we don't have enough female nominees, either..' was whispered somewhere behind me. God, it looks like Mart's really in with a chance here!

❉

Two weeks later, we were back sitting in rows in the church hall. The votes were about to be announced for the candidacy selection. The chair rose and called for silence.

269

'May I have your attention please, the votes are as follows:
Graham Bentley, St Mary's 126 votes.
Ben Eddington, St Aldred's, 178 votes.
Annelise Edwards, Mountfield, 204 votes…
So our new city council election candidate for Hazelmead ward next year is…
Martha Jones of St Barnabas, with 212 votes!'
He turned to Martha, white-faced on the podium:
'May I be the first to congratulate you?' He shook her hand.
Slowly at first, uncertainly, then with increasing enthusiasm, the audience began to applaud. The other nominees leaned over to shake hands with Martha one by one.

Behind me I heard a murmur:
'Controversial choice.'
'Yes, what just happened?'
I was about to whip round and give them a good hard Doherty state when I stopped myself. For once, Martha didn't need defending. The could press their sour grapes if they wanted. I turned back to the front to enjoy the most thrilling moment of my life.
I sat still waiting for her to come back to her seat, but it wasn't happening anytime soon. Everyone wanted to congratulate her, talk to her – five minutes ago they wouldn't give her the time of day. I allowed myself a tiny bitter thought that was soon lost in the flood of joy and relief. Mart was going to make it! My phone pinged.
Simon.

What's the verdict? :)
Did u know she was standing?
Of course, whats happening?
She won! She got it!
Wows let's meet after for a drink at the Star :))
Ok will tell mart when I get hold of her she's in demand
I locked my phone and walked forward to greet Mart. She came towards me, flushed with excitement and pride.
'Well done, you!' I gave her a hug.
'Thanks!'
'Have they finished grilling you, Simon wants to go out for a wet?'

'Yeah, oh I just have to speak to Miranda about the paperwork then I'll be with you.'

It was black dark by the time we carried Mart triumphantly down the road, singing, laughing, almost dropping her at the pelican crossing. She dropped her feet down to the ground and landed gracefully as we came rolling home.

❄

'I still can't believe it.' Martha had been saying that for days.
'I know. Talk about the minority getting the vote.'
'Huh.'
'Simon – Mart's really achieved something here. This is the beginning of better things.'
'Keep your hair on, Bridge, I was only joking.'
'I know, but...'
I'd just heard too many comments like that that weren't joking.

Mart didn't care, she was busy in her happy whirl. Winter didn't seem so grim and grey, thankfully the weather was mild enough that we could forget our heating woes slightly, the halogens were keeping us going. The mould on my bedroom wall was a pain though. I kept scrubbing it off and it kept growing back. The gutters were the problem, I scraped them out every winter but they were starting to drop off the roof.
I'd given up getting on to Marianne, she was ever more distant now, down there in Devon. She spent more time recounting her financial woes when I rang her than discussing when we'd get the house repairs. Still, it wasn't long til spring now and who knew what the future could bring if Martha could tip the election. They were only a few votes away from overtaking the Social Liberal Democratic Alliance, or whatever they were calling themselves these days, in Hazelmead. All right, there were several small parties standing in Bristol by now all calling themselves Earth this or Ecology that, but ours had the most supporters. If only everyone would agree not to split the vote. There was an air of excitement among the party members who milled around in our kitchen at all times of day. I

loved the way Mart's acceptance had turned their attitudes around. Nothing succeeds like success, eh? This year was gearing up to be the most exciting yet.

✻

15. Snowflakes.

Summer was over. It had been such a long, weird climate-changed year that getting a normal, bog-standard autumn was almost confusing. It was still much warmer than usual though. But the trees had been browning since August, and it was nearing the end of October now. The year with two winters. It seemed more like two years since last autumn what with the late March blizzards that left the farm cut-off and blanketed with snow. The cold spring that followed onto a parched, blazing midsummer had left me not knowing what to expect any more. The garden had spent months with soil bone-dry and iron-hard, crops kept alive by hand watering. I remembered the day late in July when it finally rained and a woodpigeon had squatted by a growing puddle in the lane, its open beak turned up ecstatically to the sky. You could almost hear the earth's sighs of relief.

Fruit still swelled, though rather dry and puny compared to other years. The thrushes and blackbirds still pecked and flurried on the great crabapple tree, and the goldcrest followed right on cue as the overripe fruits began to attract small flies. I hoped that the year didn't have anything else exceptional to throw at us. I walked up to the field where dozens of pumpkins glowed orange amidst brown, collapsed vines. A few giant, stringy runner beans still hung on the remains of the beanpoles. Rainbow chard glowed in the poly, next to mizuna and a late, spectacular purple and white flowering of the sweet potatoes I'd experimented with this year. A year for new things. The book was close to completion, but I still didn't have an ending. Because the catastrophe that had ended Mart's career had never been resolved.

It had been well over a year since we'd really made contact. She'd been her usual self by all accounts, struggling with housing management at the housing coop where she went to live after our house imploded on us. The disaster, when it came, had been so complete it was hard to know what to say afterwards. I tried not to blame Mart, I made that mistake once already, but I wondered, as always, why, why did this girl have to make her own life so hard? It was like, the minute she had something worth keeping, she threw it away. Sacrificed on the altar of her own inconvenient truths. I sighed. It was no good. I couldn't kid myself. If my friendship with Mart was so over, then why had I spent the last six months obsessively writing her story?

It had all begun with the newspaper that lit the fire back in March. But really, such a scrap of hope in a world of disappointments – who did I think I was fooling? Mart was born to lose. If only she'd learn to grasp what happiness she could and hang on tight. She could be out here, watching the fast dusk fall, waiting for the first light, dry snowflakes of winter to materialise out of the dark sky.

❄

And it had all started so well.
Mart had bustled into the lounge with her entire wardrobe over her arm.
'I don't know what to wear.'
'Never stopped you before.'
'I mean it.' That was true. She'd been working earnestly on her image this last couple of months. My scruffy friend with the jumble-sale cardigans and worn jeans was no more. She even had a smart black skirt and a green silk blouse to go with it for more formal meetings. Off The Streets had really come up trumps that day. With her serious, intelligent eyes and firm mouth she looked the part. Pity her self-esteem was so leaky.

'I'm so worried about the impression I'm going to make. What if I clam up or start babbling on?'
'You won't. You did great in the hustings, and the press briefing. Look, they chose you. Not one of those interchangeable Bens or mass-produced Emilys. You. Martha Jones. The weird one. Which means they *wanted* you, Martha Jones, the weird one. So get out there and rock it!'

Martha frowned when she should have laughed at my sparkling wit.

274

'But which of these trousers should I take, or should I take a dress?'
'A dress? Steady on, they may be intimidating in a conference setting but they're only glorified hippies y'know.'
'Not all of them. Some of them are sucessful, professional types. I shouldn't -'
'And so are you, now. You've got the silk blouse, it looks really swish. Just take the neatest, least weird casual stuff for everything else. Be easier to get people to take you seriously then.'
'All right.' Martha said, sounding fractionally more confident.
'Once more with feeling.'
'Ok.' Martha said again, and this time she smiled.

'What time's your coach to Birmingham?'
'Ten-thirty. I don't want to miss the opening speeches.'
'Where you staying? Didn't you say Edgbaston?'
'Yes, near the cricket ground.'
'Surely even you can manage something more up-market than the bushes behind the Nature Centre?'
Mart finally laughed.
'No, I – I'm staying with that woman from National Exec. She's an environmental consultant, they're loaded. I'll have to be on best behaviour, they're probably not used to associating with the dregs.'
'Mate, in three months' time you might just be Councillor Jones. In what universe does that make you a dreg? Go on, finish packing your bag and get some sleep. I've got apple trees to prune tomorrow so I'll make sure you're awake.'
And that, I thought, while loading more paper into the printer as cold autumn rain blew wildly against the windows, was the last we heard of Councillor Jones.

❄

Martha crouched in the warm darkness, heart pounding. Every muscle was tense, listening for the slightest sound. Was he coming back? Was she home yet? Not that she could be relied on for back-up. She heard his footsteps stumble down the hall. Her hand on the floor touched something soft. A slipper. She grabbed it and wedged it firmly under the door. Hammered it in tightly. Found the other one and did the same. *Softly she got to her feet, trembling but resolute. Listened intently. Down the hall a bolt went home. A thud, a grunt, tinkling water. She felt for the door handle and tested it silently. Ease down the handle. Don't let it click. Now pull. Tug harder. It was immobile, as good as locked. The flush came hard, sooner than Martha expected. She shivered against the wall. This was it. No, he was going to his room. Bump bump curse thud. Out again.*

'Martha?' *His cool, educated voice was blurred with drink.* 'Now where have you got to?' *He was trying to sound pleasant but Martha knew better than to trust that.*
She heard him mumble to himself as he bumped back down the stairs.

This was it! The only chance! Martha grabbed her things, laid out so neatly, and stuffed them into her rucksack. She slipped on her shoes and was about to put on her coat when she heard doors opening downstairs. Martha opened the bedroom window quietly and looked out into the black garden. She quickly tied her coat around her waist and put one leg out of the window. The tall, skinny ash tree that he'd talked about pruning before spring had branches that nearly touched the house. She held her breath as she slid one foot down to the nearest one. Eased herself out over the windowsill, nearly getting wedged on the rucksack. The branch bobbed up and down, terrifyingly. She gasped, clutched the trunk and was out. Her blouse snagged and she heard it rip. She pushed the window shut. That'd slow him down. He wouldn't guess right away which way she'd gone. Be too busy checking the many rooms of the large house on the edge of the park. She embraced the ash trunk and just hung on for a few seconds, calming her thudding heart. Then she slowly and carefully climbed down from branch to branch, slipping her rucksack off and dropping it into a shrub before stepping onto the lowest branch. She waited to see if he'd heard the slight impact of the rucksack on dripping bushes.
'Martha? You're not outside are you?'
His voice was suddenly louder. Martha froze in terror, clinging to the tree, stilling the slight rattle of bare twigs.

276

He was here! No, he was at the front. Sound carried well in the damp air, echoing off frozen pavements. Click. That was the front door. He'd have to go all through the house to check the back. No time! Now! Martha sat down on the lower branch, swung her legs off and dropped the last five feet onto crispy grass. She grabbed her bag and ran, careless of noise, down the garden path, even in her panic avoiding the grass which would leave her trail clear as a dawn rabbit's. She was behind the large shrubs at the bottom of the garden. The back door clicked, then shuddered as he struggled to get it open. Swollen with damp. Martha found the back fence and was over it in a flash, running across the lawn of the house behind, down the side path and onto the drive. The dark street was deserted. She looked about, slipped under the cavelike shadow of a frosted mock orange in the next garden along, and crouched, panting. The back door had thudded shut. He'd missed her. He wouldn't be in a hurry to get involved with wet vegetation, not in his socks. He'd be checking the bedroom next. Forcing the door. She kneeled up, dropping her rucksack and pulling her coat on. Then on with the rucksack and clumsily zipping up the coat. No hat in her pocket, or gloves. God, it was cold. Martha got up stiffly and peered out of her hiding place. There was someone coming. The click of solitary heels announced a woman, alone. Martha waited while she passed before crawling from her den like a hunted animal. She looked around wildly and set off down the road in the direction with least streetlighting.

The chill wind was taking the skin off Martha's face and sleety rain had found its way into the neck of her blouse, her shoes, her sleeves. Her hair was sleek and dripping. If I only had my hat, she thought. She tucked herself deeper into the bushes in the pitch black park. The sleet eased up a little, but when she looked out from under the swags of vegetation she saw why – it had been replaced by large soft feathery flakes of snow. Her hair was no longer dripping. It was freezing to her head.

'I'm gonna die of cold out here.' she mumbled. She thought about phoning someone. Who? At two in the morning? The

embarrassment, the explanations. Bridge couldn't do anything for her now. Another Party member? She shuddered at the thought of the exposure. But she was going to die of exposure if she didn't move. She stood up, snow slipping off her shoulders. Paced up and down the path next to the icebound lake with its thin coating of snow. So cold.

'They picked up their beds and walked.' she mumbled to herself. Whose joke was that?
'Martha, stop being logical, fold your metaphorical tent and move your ass.'
Simon. That night behind the Nature Centre. Wish Bridge was here with a box of matches. Wish I had that firewood again. The camp in the bushes. The early mist burning slowly off the lake. The lake! It lay locked in ice. The dark blue city sky was obscured by freezing fog. Fog that wouldn't lift til morning. The chilly morning after Reclaim the Streets.
Martha turned and strode, shivering, numb, towards the east end of the park. It was still there, but would the door be open?
She took hold of the metal handle and dropped it again hastily, grabbed it with her shrugged down sleeve and pulled. For a miracle, it slid open with a waft of steam. She slid in and stood gasping on damp gravel. Thin white beams came faintly, cutting through the mist from the streetlight on the pavement outside the park's boundary wall. Martha sagged onto the bench around the fishpool, emptied of fish for winter. Her hair was steaming. She shrugged off her soaking coat and rummaged in her rucksack to see what she had. The hat! She pulled it on. Found a chocolate bar in the side pocket. She let out a couple of involuntary sobs as she thawed out, her breath puffing in the chilly air. Then she wiped her face impatiently and ate the chocolate bar, and another she found in the top of the bag. She set to unpacking the rucksack properly and wrapped herself up in every shirt and scarf she had. Then she made a pad with her half-empty rucksack, there on the greened wooden bench, and curled up with her coat over her and her hat pulled down over her ears. Slowly the cave of warmth she'd made heated up enough to let her drift into fitful sleep.

❊

'Why in God's name didn't you call me?' I said angrily.

I heard the hesistation in Martha's voice before she answered.

'What were you going to do at that time of night from eighty miles away?' she said.

'I dunno. Called the cops, maybe.'

'And what would they have done?'

I didn't know what they would have done. They don't exactly have a great track record on dealing with stuff like this.

'I was too cold to think. Maybe I would've called them if I hadn't thought of the greenhouse. Thank God I didn't have to though.'

'Why didn't you call them from the house?' I demanded.

'You're kidding, right? He might have heard me. They might not have come, or they might have come too late. I had to run for it. Too bad it was freezing outside.'

'Yes, I suppose you did the right thing.'

'I got out, didn't I? And I don't know why you're shouting at me.'

I sat down tiredly. Mart's phone call at eight in the morning from Birmingham bus station had totally floored me. God knows what had been going on. It was Wales all over again.

'I'm sorry I shouted. What are you going to do now?'

'I'm coming home. Getting a new coach ticket.'

'Are you Ok? Is there anyone who can help you?'

'Like who?'

'Mick, maybe. He's not so far away.'

'I thought of that. His flatmate says he's gone up to Sheffield on a job.'

'I'll come up and meet you.'

'No. No, don't do that. It'll take too long. I want to go home.'

Home. That was a thought. A terrible one, but a thought.

'Could – could you call your mum, even?'

There was a silence that radiated meaning.

'Mart? I'm sorry, it was a stupid idea. I know you hardly ever see her.'

'Stupidest idea you've ever had.' she breathed, her fury barely controlled.

'I know, I know, but you still see her from time to time don't you? I'm not suggesting you go there, but you have seen her since you left home, haven't you?'

Mart suddenly sounded very tired.

'Yes, a few times. I even talked to her when I was at Newbury.'

'She came to Newbury?'

'No, you dolt! I phoned her. It was the dead of winter and there just wasn't anyone else I could think of. Everyone was calling home. The work was starting next day. I wanted her to know – that I was doing something that scared the hell out of me. I thought I was going to get hurt, or worse. I thought she'd respond for once. Even be - proud of me. But no. She just told me I was a loser, as usual.'

'God, that's awful. You don't need people like that.'

'Yeah, I worked that out some time ago.' Martha said sarcastically.

'I'm sorry. You were right. Stupidest idea I've ever had. Here, have you got enough money?'

There was a frantic rustling.

'...um, no, I don't think I've got enough, well, if I go without breakfast I have...I have to change my ticket, you see.'

'Which bus are you getting? I'll call the bus station and pay for it with my card.'

'Oh, good idea. Thanks.'

'If you call me at the cafe I'll pay for a proper slap-up breakfast too. You need warming up.'

'Er, thanks. Thanks.' Martha sounded gruff.

'No problem. Go and find out the bus times and text me. And get some hot food into you. And take care! Call me once you're on the bus, or if you have any more problems!'

'Ok.' She hesitated. 'She told me-'

'Yes?'

'She told me I wouldn't be able to change anything. She told me - to go home.' She rang off.

I was left reflecting on the irony.

❄

Martha entered the lounge and sat down wearily. Her hair was wet from the hot shower she'd spent an unheard-of ten minutes under, and with typical neatness she'd unpacked and hung up her things, dropped her wet, muddy clothes into the laundry basket and combed her hair before finally coming to rest.

'So...' I was reluctant to question her.

'You want to know what happened?' she said defensively.

'Well, yeah, you'd better tell me, or someone.'

'He was just – all over me.'

'How do you mean?'

'Like all over me! You know what all over me means don't you! Do I have to draw you a picture!' She took a deep breath.

'First, he seemed nice, attentive, getting me a drink, asking me about my work in Bristol. A bit creepy, you know, standing too close, putting his hand on my arm, being jovial, that sort of thing. I didn't think that much of it. But...later his wife popped back to the conference venue to get some papers she needed to go over for the next day. It was seven o'clock then. The minute she'd gone he got up and came and drew his chair near to mine. I felt really uncomfortable. I edged away, but he moved closer. I got up and walked across the room and sat on a sofa. Next thing I know he followed me, sat on the chair nearest to me. I was in the corner of the room. That made me really nervous. He kept asking me all about myself, quite deep questions like what made me join the Party, and what friends did I have. Did I have a partner involved with the Party? I moved as far away as I could, but he put his feet up on a footstool and blocked me into the corner...all I could think was - this isn't happening. He can't mean what I think he means...it was like that all evening, me edging away, him following, until there was nowhere else to go and he was pressed up against me on the sofa.'

He stretched his stockinged feet out on the footstool.
'Ahh! My feet are sore! All that walking around today. A lot of stairs in the university building.'

281

Martha mumbled something indistinct.

'I could do with a foot-rub. I used to have a friend who did fantastic ones, she was a lovely girl, used to run a Reflexology stall at the Green Gathering. Gwennie French. Did you ever meet her?'

Martha shook her head no.

'Lovely girl. Lovely. She taught me a thing or two. About foot massage that is!' He chuckled. Martha shuddered and pressed herself further away. He leaned in and put a hand on her arm.

'How are your feet? Would you like a foot rub?'

'No!' said Martha loudly.

'Steady, no need to shout! I'm not going to eat you!'

He moved his hand to her leg, gripped her knee.

Martha stood up suddenly, surged across the room, stepping unsteadily over the footstool, terrified of falling against him.

'What's up? Can I get you anything? A drink?'

'No..er, yes, a coffee, how about coffee?' Martha headed hastily towards to the lounge door, glanced about the hallway and darted into the kitchen. She edged towards the back door. There was a key in it. He was quick to follow, putting the kettle on, asking her how she liked her coffee.

'Do you like it sweet, or are you sweet enough?' he chuckled. He had manouevred himself between her and the back door. She sidled around the round table towards the door to the hallway. He strode across the kitchen floor, put down the coffee mugs on the table, freeing his hands.

'Not ready for bed so soon? Shall I bring you a nightcap? A tot of brandy in your coffee to keep the cold out?'

'No, thanks.' said Martha. She moved towards the door.

'Oh, well if you're going up I'm sure you wouldn't begrudge me a good night kiss.' Suddenly he grabbed her, pushing her against the wall, forcing his face down to hers. Martha turned stiffly away before his lips could make contact, squirmed out of his flailing grip and dodged out of the door.

She ran up the stairs and round the corner, into her room and shut the door. She turned out the light and listened, heart pounding. Stumbling footsteps sounded on the stairs. He was coming up.

'There's no need to run away. I was just being friendly. I must say I'm surprised. I would have expected to be treated with more – courtesy, as your host. Surely you don't think I'd hurt you?'
Martha stood rigid in the dark.
'Feminists...' he said under his breath, and something about *'...always such a fuss about nothing.'*
He knocked on the door. Martha held her breath.
'Martha? Are you in there? How about I bring you a nice hot drink in bed and we can talk. You've clearly got some issues, but I've a lot of experience with vulnerable people. I can be very comforting, you know...'
She didn't make a sound. Martha heard him tut and enter the bathroom. Then he went back downstairs. Checking to see if she'd slipped back into the lounge. She only had a few minutes. She had to move fast.

❄

'Oh my God! What a gigantic creep! God, no wonder you were scared. And nowhere to run to either. Where was his wife when all this was going on?'
'I dunno. She never came back. Maybe she stayed up at conference for the evening.'
'What was she doing, leaving you alone with that octopus?'
'I dunno. She married him. She probably thinks it's normal.'

'To be married to a cephalopod?'
Martha laughed at that. I was relieved to hear it.
'I'm the biologist. I should have thought of that one.'
'Thank God you got away. And that the greenhouse was open.'
'Yeah, you'd think they'd have put a lock on it by now.'
'Bloody lucky for you they hadn't.'

I asked Martha how the meeting for new candidates had gone, the one chaired by the members from the Association of Party Councillors.

'It was – good. It was hard to speak up. I was supposed to go to a workshop the next day. Saturday. Never lasted that long. I missed everything.'

Martha was suddenly angry.

'I missed the whole thing, as a time when I really needed to be there! All my work, totally obstructed, because of some creep!'

'What will you do now? Ask the local party to catch you up on what you missed?'

She stopped, looking thoughtful.

'What are you going to tell them about why you left early?'

She looked into the distance.

'I'm going to tell them the truth of course. What happened. Why I couldn't be there for the rest of conference.'

I dithered.

'How do you think they'll react?'

'Who cares? People need warning about stuff like this.'

Other women in the party. Yes. Other women who he might have to stay.

'Didn't the Party arrange the accommodation? You didn't know him before?'

'Yes, they have a scheme for matching local members to visiting ones..I didn't think about it. Because the party arranged it, it made it seem Ok. And it was a female member that I made the arrangement with. But really, I went into the home of a strange man. It's a mad policy, really, it's dangerous. It's lulling people into a false sense of security. I've got to tell them.'

'Yes, you have to.' I agreed. 'Make sure nothing like that happens to anyone else.'

Martha sighed.

'Yeah.'

❄

'We missed you at conference. I thought you were going to be there.'

Miranda sat down opposite Martha with her cup of coffee.

'I was. I had to leave early.' Martha looked at the plastic table as she stirred her coffee.

'Oh, what happened? Something come up?'

'You could say that. I had to run for it.'

'What on earth do you mean?' Miranda frowned at Martha. The cafe where the other party members were gathering after the meeting was filling up. Talking about this against a background of coffee machines and clattering cutlery was excruciating.

'I mean, I had to run for it. My host in the members accommodation was harassing me.'

'What do you mean, harassing? Are you sure? What did he do?' Miranda's lips pursed.

'He was all over me. Really creepy.'

'Oh, some men are just like that. Tactile. I'm sure he couldn't have meant any harm.'

'He meant harm all right. He was trying to touch me. He grabbed me. I had to get out quick.'

Miranda looked severe.

'When was this?'

'Friday night.'

'But Emma was there wasn't she?'

'No, she'd gone back to the venue.'

'He's a married man, I'm sure you must have mistaken his motives. Sure you're not flattering yourself a bit?' She gave a smile that reminded Martha of her primary school teacher.

Martha looked at Miranda incredulously. This was the woman who never missed a Gaia Women meeting. The same woman who'd protested the sexual abuse of women detained in Yarl's Wood. 'No mistake. He grabbed hold of me and was trying to kiss me against my will. I got away and ran for it.'

'You mean, in the middle of the night? You just left?'

Now Miranda looked positively disapproving. 'You can't just – you can't treat a host that way. He's a City Councillor.'

'I don't care if he's the Queen Mother! He was harassing me. It wasn't safe to stay in that house!'

Miranda gave her a long, appraising stare. There was a crash from the kitchen behind her.

'Martha, I'm really glad you came to me.'

Martha brightened. This sounded better.

'You can rely on me to be confidential. I won't tell anyone else we've had this conversation.'

Martha began to relax.

'Yes, no one need know that this – awkwardness happened. And I can give your apologies to Emma for running out on them, if you wish. But you might seriously rethink the responsibilities you're taking on if you're so easily upset. Public roles can be very demanding.'

Martha stared.

'Are you kidding me? National Exec need to know about this. Other women should be warned. He shouldn't be allowed to stay in the Party after this!'

Miranda's patronising smile hardened into a line.

'Are you aware of how seriously an accusation like that could affect an elected Councillor? Not to mention the Party's reputation? Look, I know you're keen to promote – equalities and so on, it's very commendable, but the process of change is slow, we have to be patient-'

Martha couldn't believe what she was hearing.

' - unfounded allegations like this can't just be thrown around. We have a Code of Conduct -'

'Yes! We do! And he smashed it to pieces!'

'Look, I accept that your reaction has been a bit extreme, but, well, we're all aware of your anxiety issues. Like I said, this incident needn't affect your standing in the Party. But you need to calm down.'

'I don't think I should talk about this any more.' Martha said firmly, staring at the older woman's lined face, her crow's feet. That was it. Miranda was another generation. She should have talked to one of the younger women first.

'Now that's sense. I'm sure once the emotions have calmed down a bit you'll be able to get it all into perspective.' Miranda looked relieved.

Martha couldn't even dignify this with an answer.

❇

'You shouldn't have talked to Miranda. She's behind the times in these things.'
Martha smiled. Annelise was an intelligent woman her own age. She'd understand, and give her some back-up.
'She said you were flattering yourself? God!'
'Yes. I don't think she believed me.'
'Well, I do. I believe you completely.'

Martha felt a great surge of relief.
'Do you want to make a complaint?'
'Well, I think I should.'
'Emily and I can dig out the right forms and email them to you. I should warn you, it's unlikely that anything will be done. Prepare yourself for that.'
'What? Why ever not?'
'You know how it is. Sexual harassment complaints hardly ever get upheld. It goes with the territory. Politics is still so patriarchal, you know. It's just seen as an occupational hazard.'
'But he could do it again. Might have been doing it for years.'
'Yes, and word'll get round on the grapevine. NST.'
'What?'
'Not safe in taxis. Women'll get the hint to keep away from him. But he's -'
'A City Councillor. I know.'
'And it's your word against his. But I'll help you with the paperwork for making a complaint.'
'But we're supposed to be different. We're supposed to be making politics more accessible for women. How can we be involved if we're not even safe?'
'It all takes time. All we can do is protest it. We can't change it overnight. It will all be confidential, at least. The rest of the party won't know a thing about it. The main thing is to keep this from harming *you*.'
Martha was silent.

❄

I went into the bathroom after Martha had left. There was a flash of green on the floor. I bent and picked it up. Martha's silk blouse for important meetings. The side-seam was ripped, and it was greened with bark. I looked at it for a long time, then quietly dropped it into the washing basket.

❄

'Wounded laptop? Give it here.'
Simon lifted the open laptop onto his knee and began clicking away.
'You've just got too much junk on here...I'll do a defrag and clear off some of these old downloads.'
'Thanks. I should spring clean it more often but I'm been so busy...'
Martha trailed off. She looked around the room. Simon's flat was a mass of disembowelled computers, screens, cables. The coffee table was covered with papers with dirty cereal bowls and coffee mugs used as paperweights. Memory sticks and CDs, Rizla packets and chocolate wrappers were scattered around. Frohike and Langly would be popping their heads round the door any minute.
'Right, that should do it. Should be a lot faster now.' Simon handed the laptop back and extracted two encrusted coffee mugs from the debris. 'Want a coffee?'
'Yeah, that's be great.' Martha said absently. 'But-'
'Yes, I know. Clean cups.' Simon laughed as he left the room.

Martha clicked into the Party member's website. She searched for the harassment procedure. Nothing. Complaints, Code of Conduct, minutes of last National Exec meeting. Still no harassment procedure. Hmm. But there must be any amount of equalities stuff in the manifesto. Women's rights galore. She started scrolling through the Social Policy pages. A bit about equal pay. Something about helping women's voices be heard in meetings. Nothing about sexual harassment. Legalising prostitution. Plenty about a woman's right to be used by men. Nothing about her right to be protected from them. Ok. Code of Conduct.

'1. Members should at all times ensure that their words or actions do not damage the Party's reputation.'

288

That was a good one.

'2. Members should treat their colleagues with courtesy and respect.'
Pretty clearcut, that.

3. Members elected to public office or otherwise representing the Party in public should ensure that their actions and expressed opinions are in line with Party policy. If expressing dissent it should be made clear that the individual's personal opinions do not reflect official policy.'

Reflect official policy. But the policy isn't there. There's nothing, nothing at all about sexual harassment in the manifesto. Surprising. Would have thought Gaia Women would have showered conference with motions on women's rights, starting with the right to safety.

I wonder if Annelise knows, Martha thought. That's it! They just haven't got the policies. As soon as my complaint gets in they'll realise the oversight and we can put some work in on this. That horrible incident might just do some good after all. She began to feel better. She checked the complaint form. All done, details filled in. She pressed Send to direct it to the CEO's inbox. A job well done. Simon came in with the coffee and Martha clinked her mug against his.
'Celebrating?' he asked.
'Yes! Made some serious progress. Change takes a long time, indeed. It hasn't been that bad a job, getting through this.' Martha said.

'So, what did they say?' I looked expectantly at Martha.
'Haven't read it yet. It's going to be a relief to get it done and dusted.' Martha clicked on her inbox.
'Here it is.

Formal Response to SH complaint dated 24th February. Dear Martha, The complaints committee consisting of the Party chair, chair of the Regional Committee and five other duly selected officers met to consider your complaint on 3rd March. On due consideration, the committee found that the complainant's accusation of sexual harassment by the defendant named in the complaint was invalid, as the defendant's behaviour did not constitute sexual harassment. We respect the complainant's right to bring this misunderstanding to our attention but should advise her that unfounded complaints of this nature can do serious harm to the Party's elected representatives and Party reputation as a whole, though we accept that you made this complaint in good faith. As a result of this incident the Party will be running a series of training days on recognising sexual harassment and bullying in the workplace. You would be very welcome to attend, and we would strongly advise this. The complaint has now been declared closed. With best regards, Rebecca Minchin, Regional Committee Chair.'

Martha and I stared at each other in disbelief.
'*What?*' she breathed.
'What – what does the law say about the definition of sexual harassment?' I asked hesitantly. 'Surely we're not still living in the Dark Ages on this?'
'No.' said Martha. 'I looked it up. It clearly states in the Equalities Act 2010 that any form of sexual behaviour from jokes to touching to assault constitutes harassment if the recipient makes it clear that they don't consent to it. And I made it damn clear that I didn't.'
'And what you described fits that exactly. No possible room for doubt. But they're saying it's not sexual harassment.' I said, slowly.
'How can they say that? Legally it's nonsense.' Martha cried.
'Yes. They probably don't know the law. Hard to believe they'd be that ignorant but once you set them straight it'll be Ok. They're really big on women's rights aren't they?'
'Well, I thought they were, but when I checked the manifesto there was hardly anything on women's rights there at all. I was surprised.'
'Well, they've always been a bit slow on getting social policies in place. Too busy saving the planet. Write back and quote them what you've just read to me.' I suggested.

290

'Yes, I'll do that right now.'
'And didn't you say they had no harassment procedure? Why not point them to a good example of one?'

'Good idea.' Martha sounded relieved. Bureaucrats. Can be a bit dim. But once the paperwork was in place they'd reconsider. I went back to scrubbing seed trays, feeling much more cheerful.

❄

Weeks passed. The first daffodils were opening in the flowerbed nearest the front door when Mart came trudging up the path, head bowed.

'You look happy. See, the daffodils are out.' I said cheerfully.
Martha looked unseeingly.
'What's up?'
Martha continued to stare right through the daffodil bed.
'Come on, don't go into stasis on me, like you nerds say.'
Martha looked up with an effort.
'Is it the Party again? Haven't they updated those policies you were talking about?'
'No.'
'I though you said Annelise was going to propose them as an interim decision until you can get them ratified next conference?'
'They said it wasn't a priority, with the election coming up.'
'That's a bollocks excuse. This is important.'
'Not to them, apparently. So I appealed.'
'And?'
'They say I've got no right of appeal unless I produce more evidence.'
'But they've got the law wrong.'
'I know. But they don't care.'
'This is crazy! What are you going to do?'
'Well, when I asked if I could meet with one of the committee members they said no.'
'What about Skype?'
'They said they didn't have time.'

291

'That's ridiculous!'

'So I pointed out that I was an anxiety sufferer and that all this conflict was making me ill, and that I needed to speak to someone face to face to facilitate communication.'

True. Mart had been so moodily silent lately. I'd find her sitting at the kitchen table at 1am, scrolling endlessly through Party procedures, going through the Constitution with a fine-tooth comb. I'd wake at 4pm and see the light still on in the kitchen. She wasn't sleeping at all.

'What did they say to that?'

'They said it was irrelevant to the case.'

'What about disability rights?'

'What about them?'

'So, what next?'

'Nothing.'

'Can't you complain about how they've handled the complaint?'

'I did. That's what I've been working on. I spent a fortnight going through the legislation, and they're well and truly on the wrong side of it. I sent the second complaint in three weeks ago.'

'And?'

'They never answered.'

'What? They ignored a formal complaint?'

'Yep.'

'Have you been in touch?'

'Yes. I've emailed the chair, the CEO, the head of the Regional Committee and the Equalities Secretary.'

'And?'

'No one's replying. They're just not answering my queries.'

'They're stonewalling you.'

Martha looked up at me. She was sitting on the scrapwood bench we'd knocked together outside the front door.

'Yeah..yeah that's what they're doing. Ignoring me until I go away.'

'But you're not going to. You're going to have more influence eventually - if you can only get onto the council. There's nothing more you can do right now. It totally sucks. It's disgusting. But at least you told them. They can't say it hasn't been brought to their

attention. Didn't you say Annelise has been working on the new harassment procedure and some conference motions?'
'Yes. But I can't stop thinking about it. About how I missed the whole conference because of him. About nearly having to sleep out under a bush in February!'

And about what could have happened, if you hadn't been alert, awake to the danger, brave enough to climb down that tree and get out, not caring what anyone thought. With your good blouse ripped to shreds, I reflected silently. She'd never mentioned it. It was still hanging at the back of her clothes rail after she'd washed it carefully by hand. She hadn't even been able to bring herself to sew it with her neat, tiny stitches as she would any other torn garment.

'There is something else I can do.' Martha said. She stood up, gazed at me seriously, and without another word walked into the house.
That night I saw the light under the kitchen door again. I didn't ask Mart what she was up to. I was too busy trying to get to sleep with the leak in the attic above my bedroom ceiling starting up again with the spring rains. Drip. Drip. Drip. Water on a floor. Drip. Drip. Drip. Water on a stone. Change takes a long time.

❄

The outer walls were black with mould where the gutters had pulled away from the roof. My bedroom had developed black flock wallpaper again. The cooker hadn't worked at all since January and we were using Martha's old camp stove on the kitchen table.
Martha's bedroom windowframe was so rotten she could push her finger through it. And the noise the boiler made was so alarming that sometimes we just had to turn it off. Thank goodness summer was coming. Marianne's last letter had promised;

'Work on the house will get done this summer, I'm determined!! I just need to get my finances a bit healthier after the holidays. I had to go to Portugal to see my daughter over Christmas, she needs me to help with her wedding plans. She's very anxiety-prone, she'll never cope without me. I don't want her having a breakdown over it.

You and Martha are angels for being so patient. See you next time I'm in Bristol. I'll make you my speciality soup!'

She hadn't been to Bristol since last April, when she'd looked doubtfully at the guttering and said brightly 'Oh, it's not as bad as I thought, it'll do another season.' and talked about the new conservatory she was having built. 'It's *so* draughty in the sunroom, and it's my mother's favourite room now she can't get out. It's essential that I get it done for her. She doesn't walk well at all now.' I made sympathetic noises as I gazed at her in frustration. You simply cannot counter an argument based on the welfare of an old mum.

Martha was all for getting in touch with the Council about it all.
'They'll come and inspect the place. She might get an order to do the works.'
I stopped in the act of prising my toast out of Simon's dodgy skip toaster.
'Do you think? It won't come to that, surely.'
'It might have to.' she said grimly.
I wasn't sure. I hated the thought of confrontation. Marianne might decide we were trouble. She might even give us notice. After all, she was a bit broke, sort of. And she did save us, back then.

It was all very well. Martha's confrontation with the Party had come to nothing, and she was still getting funny looks from the few colleagues who knew about the case. We just had to get her through to election day, if she won that seat she'd have an allowance – we could think about moving. Mart, a councillor! Having some influence on what happens in this filthy polluted city! And a bit of money at last after years of campaigning for the environmental movement for free. She'd done so much for them. Now it was all going to pay off. Not worth the trouble of fighting Marianne over the repairs, we'd be out of here soon. It would be nice to be able to leave on good terms.

Marianne had taken a chance on us, and we hadn't let her down. Not a single late rent payment in all the years. We'd decorated the house regularly, Mart balancing on my hedge-trimming platform with a serious look on her face, running up curtains on her old Singer that was, she told me, one of the few things she'd saved from home when her mother had gone into sheltered acommodation after her third stay in hospital. The garden was lush, between us we'd grown roses and marigolds and built raised beds. There was a luxuriant-fragranced jasmine creeper over the door, a productive herb garden, the pond was alive with newts and water beetles as a result of Mart's brilliant sieve on a stick wheeze for removing autumn leaves. We'd pruned the apple trees regularly and they were giving us bumper crops.

No, she couldn't say she'd been sorry to have us. But once Martha was on the city council, who knows where we might go? Party membership was soaring in the wake of the latest climate news, and everywhere we went in the ward we saw Party stickers and Gaia Now! posters on doors and windows. There was only a handful of votes between the Party and the incumbent who won last time, and after his recent blunders he wasn't in good odour with the electorate. The Party were tipped to have a real surge this time. Five or six seats were teetering on the brink of falling to Mart and the eco-crew. That would be something. That would really be something.

I hurried to the church hall door. Kicked off my workboots before I slipped in and found a seat at the back. Heads turned and I felt their stares. Was it my muddy corduroys? My kneepads? Or the leaves stuck in my holey gardening jumper?

Whatever. I wouldn't have made the meeting if I'd stopped to change after work. The last one before the election launch next week. I'd promised to help. Even Simon had agreed to lug some flyers home and do his flat block, and the rest of the road too. It takes a lot to get that cat out of his basket. Mart should feel honoured. I was even ready to have a go at canvassing, if they trained me a bit. Excitement fizzed in my stomach. I could just see Mart's head somewhere near the front in the aisle seat she still favoured. Crowds still made her uneasy but she'd come a long, long way.

'Welcome, everyone. Can I have your attention now. We have a bit of urgent business to attend to before getting onto the exciting stuff – the election launch. We can't officially start campaigning til the whistle goes, as you might say, but we're going to hit the ground running. Before that -' He paused, and looked hard at two members near the fire exit who were whispering, 'before that, as I say, we have some unfortunate urgent business to conduct. It's my sad duty to inform you that Martha Jones, who the Party originally chose to represent Hazelmead ward, will not be in a position to take up the nomination, and that in view of this-'

A dull murmur began in the hall, a laugh, a cry of indignation. The chair waited out the mutterings, then went on, 'in view of this, in line with our selection process, the candidate with the next largest number of votes is duly elected official party candidate for Hazelmead in Bristol's Council elections this May. Congratulations, Annelise Edwards. We're sure you'll do a good job for us. See me after the meeting to go over the nomination papers. Now I know you'll all have questions, but all I can say at this juncture is that this decision is an internal Party matter. Moving on -'

'What the hell's going on?' To my surprise it was my voice that rose over the chairman's wittering and the audience's prurient murmurings.
'I beg your pardon?'
'What's going on? You can't drop Mart just like that! She hasn't decided to stand down!'
'Excuse me, are you a member?'
I hesitated. 'No, but I'm a supporter. I've got a right to know why Martha Jones has been dropped without a word! She knows nothing about this!' I caught sight of Martha's blank face as she walked slowly and with dignity down the aisle towards the door. She didn't catch my eye as she went. Her eyes were fixed on the distant wall, her head high. I longed to get to her but I had to sort this numpty out first.

'For what reason have you done this to a loyal member? Martha's worked her backside off for you people!'

The chair looked as if he was about to burst.

'As I say, this is an internal Party matter, and as a non-member you don't have the right to question our decisions. These are confidential matters. Until the official nominations are submitted we reserve the right to put forward a different candidate. It's not set in stone.'

'But she doesn't even know why you've done this! This is the first she's heard of it!'

'I can assure you that the Party has followed all proper procedures. Now, we have business to get on with and if you don't mind we don't want to waste any more time. You've had your say, but now other matters need our attention.'

'How can you do this? How can you..'

The chair stood up, his face tight with repressed hate.

'If you don't take your seat and keep the peace we will have to ask you to leave.' he said icily, though I could see a cheek twitching.

'You don't have to ask! I'm out of here!'

I stalked out, tripping over the centipede-footed Party, blushing furiously as I went. Lacking the poise of Martha. Nearly walking out in my socks.

Where was she? I went outside. There. Sitting on the low wall around the park, under the budding sycamores.

'Mart!' She turned a blank face to me. I sat down next to her.

'What -' I began. Then it was my turn to lose my composure. I opened my mouth to be angry, but all that came out was a hopeless sob. I just couldn't help it. I cried my face off like some stupid kid as Martha held me awkwardly, sitting on the cold wall.

❄

'What in the hell have they done?'

'I got the email the morning after the meeting. They didn't want to give me the chance to protest. They wanted to present the local party with a fait accompli.'

'But what have they done?'

'I'm suspended pending investigation.'

'What the hell for? For complaining?'

'I assume it's because I went on the members forum and let the other members know what had happened.'

'You assume? What did they actually say?'

'Nothing much, actually. They just said I was suspended *'for my recent actions.''*

'But there are laws protecting whistleblowers, aren't there?'

'In theory. But it looks like not in practice – like a lot of things.' she added bitterly.

I stood up and walked about the kitchen. I was glad Mart'd stood up for herself and helped protect other women - but – God, the timing was terrible!

'Couldn't you have, you know, waited til after the election?'

'How could I? How could I go out there and represent the Party knowing what I know? And there's another conference in the autumn. People will be asked to take strangers into their homes. It could all happen again to someone else. I can't just let it go!'

'But the policies, the motion to conference...'

'Won't make any difference. It didn't stop them ignoring my formal complaint the second time did it? They'll just do what they want. There was a total shitstorm on the forum. People were calling for the accommodation scheme to be scrapped.'

'Well, that's something.'

'You think? Not for the safety of women. No, to prevent male members from being accused falsely by us hysterical women with our imaginary complaints!'

'Some people must have agreed with you, didn't they?'

'God, yes there were several. Even some on the Regional Committee and the Executive. But it looks like they didn't put their vote where their mouth is, doesn't it?'

'Wait. Do you know who complained about you? They must have sent you full details of the complaint against you.'

Martha blinked. 'No. I just got this scorcher from headquarters saying I was suspended. The local chair got his message days before apparently, so Annelise told me later.'

'That turncoat bitch! I wonder how long she's had her eye on your nomination?'

298

'I-I dunno. Annelise is a good member. She does a lot for road traffic reduction. It's not her fault this happened.'
'You reckon? They're all in it together! The local party officials never wanted you to stand in the first place! You walked right into it!'

'It's not my fault!' Martha screamed. 'Do you think I wanted any of this? How could I keep quiet when there could've been a rape committed at any minute? Anyone could walk into some stranger's house with this scheme going on. It's a predator's charter. Someone could invite a – paedo into their home, even!'
'That's a bit extreme.'
'All right, all right! I agree. Not likely to happen. That's a worst-case scenario. But sexual harassment is as common as chips. He's probably been groping women members for years, or worse. And people don't report it. They stand by and let other women come to harm because they haven't got the guts to complain! It might cost them their precious careers!'
Martha's chest was heaving. Hyperventilating. I sat her down and soothed her into calm, made her some valerian tea. Sitting there in the herbal aroma of used socks, I swigged some myself for once as I surveyed the wreckage.
But the trouble was, Mart was right. They'd shot the messenger. She'd lost before the polling stations even opened.
I scowled at the kettle, perched on the camp stove.

May was a quiet month. Not one Party member darkened our doors. Mart was discarded like yesterday's recycling.
Annelise Edwards was elected by a landslide to represent Hazelmead ward, along with four other members. The Party now had a total of seven city councillors.
The day after the elections I found the green blouse, neatly repaired, lying on top of the other things in the donations box Mart had asked me to take to Off the Streets.

Really, that's it. There isn't much more to tell. We sat up late at night arguing about strategies to get Mart reinstated, but to tell the truth she seemed to have stopped caring. Simon tried to cheer her up, but she just sat and stared. She stopped working at Off The Streets. Stopped reading the politics news. Spent increasing amounts of time in the garden, studying insects. She'd spend a whole afternoon watching hoverflies as summer came on.

And I never knew what to say to her these days either. The disaster was so complete, there was nothing left to say. For the crime of being female, Mart had lost her precious career.

❄

16. Becksgate.

Well, I say it was the end of the story, but like I said, the story didn't *have* an end. I wandered about the farmhouse, thinking. Thought about it while I was putting the poly to bed for the winter. Pondered as I bottled up the leftover peppers. And still had no answer. Perhaps I'd never finish it. Perhaps it had been an idle vanity, to think I could really write a novel, write Mart's story. Who'd want to read about a couple of nobodies anyway. Who never did anything special. Who always got stitched up by life. I wondered what Mart'd say to that. She always wanted me to write our story, but she'd change her mind if she saw what it looked like written down. I didn't even have a working title, apart from 'Martha's Story.' Not very original. I wondered if I'd ever show it to her.

I flicked through the chapters. See, a story about an activist only works if she ever wins any of her campaigns. But the Earth was still getting trashed. Another generation of protestors had taken over. It was all about landowners anyway. People like us had no say at all.

But I still dreamt of my little farm, the imaginary wildlife pond, the imaginary flower meadow, me and Mart scything grass in July, laying hedges in autumn sunshine, kneeling in the imaginary fifty-foot poly transplanting tomatoes. Hanging around on Bob's place, getting stiffed for half of everything I earned in my veg box scheme, weeding rich ladies' gardens - I'd never earn enough for my own plot doing that. Still, it was something to be out here. Thank goodness for Sean, turning up in the nick of time when we had to leave the bungalow, thanks to Mart's precious bloody principles. No, I was behind her all the way with the Party stuff, she was dead right to do what she did. Only the timing, God, couldn't she have just waited a bit?

Oh yeah, that was the next thing. We had to go to the council about the house, it was just too damn cold in winter. Neither of us could face another season there. Marianne got this long list of urgent repairs that she was obliged to do, two weeks after the official's inpection of the leaky roof, the crumbling gutters, lack of heating, dangerous cooker, unflushed radiators...Ok it was turning into a pigsty, but I'm sure if we'd waited another few months Marianne would have got to it.

No, I'm not sure. I'm sure she wouldn't. I'm sure she was just like all the rest of those mealy mouthed do-gooders in Bristol who made the average Tory bastard look like an honest businessman in comparison.

Yes, you guessed it, a week after Marianne got the works order from the Council she gave us notice. After all those years we should have had security of tenure, but wouldn't you know it, turns out one of the bits of paper the bitch shoved under our homeless noses back in the old squatting days was a waiver allowing her to give notice in order to sell the house. And of course, once we were out she didn't sell up, but let it to her son rent free on condition he fixed it up.

It wasn't Mart's fault we lost our home. Hell, she succeeded. The repairs got done. For someone, somewhere, not us. But Christ, just once, can't she win a battle that doesn't result in her losing in the same breath?

Just once?

I put the manuscript down. I didn't have any answers, and I was as far from an ending as ever.

My phone rang. I found it after a search under a pile of Terry Pratchett paperbacks and wine gum packets.

'Hello?'

'Hi. It's me.'

Which of the many me's might that be?

'It's Kerry.' Doesn't sound like Kerry. Where's the breezy note of optimism?

'Oh, hi Kerry. How are you doing?'

'N-not so good. Can I come over ?'

'I thought you were in Devon, up to your neck in badgers?'

'I am – well, I'm in Bristol right now. But I'd really like to see you..'

Her voice trailed off.

God, not another one.

'What's up?'

'Nothing, I could just do with cheering up.'
'Ok, come on over when you're ready, I haven't got much on at this time of year.'
I put the phone down and commenced worrying.

❄

Later that afternoon I picked up my darning needle. I might as well thread chilli peppers on a string while I worried. Tiff soon spotted the moving end of the cotton, and pounced and batted the ends. I grabbed the chilli string hastily.
'Mate, you do not want to bite that!' Might cure her of nibbling everything...no, that would be a grievous scene.
'Put it down before it bites you back!'

Tiff looked innocently up at me. No one would ever believe that little white face could be responsible for the rabbit slaughter of spring, the vole massacre of summer or the dead stoat I'd found behind my chair. She was nearly two years old now, the ball of fluff I'd been handed the first spring I spent here had grown to a sleek, fine-whiskered hunter. I wasn't sure about getting a kitten at first but then I'd found the mouse nest in the pan cupboard, the rat highway next to the bins outside and the small edge-nibbled holes in the kitchen skirtingboard. And then I met Tiff, smallest and most inquisitive member of the neighbour cat's early litter. A snowflake cat – born in late March to a wide-eyed young tabby who hatched her out in a barn down the lane. I picked Tiff up and held her for a minute. She sure made a lonely winter bearable. I pushed my face into her warm fur.
'Hello! Oh...' I turned. Kerry had appeared around the open front door. Her smile faded at the sight of me standing there with my nose buried in Tiff's fur.
'Hi...just got here?'
'Y-yeah.' Kerry was not her usual cheery self.
'How was the journey? Oh, this is my new cat, Tiff. How's yours?'
'She's..Twinkle is...she – died. Last week. She's gone.' Kerry said, sorrowfully. She looked at the floor, avoiding my eyes, but especially Tiff's.

303

Twinkle. She can't be. Twinks always seemed like she'd go on for ever, but I suppose last time I saw her, in spring, she was getting to be a delicately frail old lady. Oh Twinks.

'No way. I remember her from...' Martha's stories of Cerrig-cwm. The old squatting days. Kerry's van. Twinkle sitting on Kerry's shoulder in every photo she had taken at college in Exeter. Twinkle. Twinkers. Twinks.

I didn't know what to say.

Kerry dabbed at her face and began to explain.

'She was really old...but she still loved her grub, and she used to enjoy wandering round site on sunny days. She used to spend a lot of time in the van by the stove but now and then she'd go for a wander and come back with a mouse. Everybody loved her.'

Yes. We did. Twinks. Cat of ages. The squat's totem animal.

'She started to get really thin a few weeks ago. Thinner and thinner. She didn't eat much, or move hardly. In the end she was just so sad-looking. The vet said her heart was giving out.'

Twink's heart? Never! She was a cat with the heart of a lion, or possibly a tiger! I remembered the many times Twinkers had climbed imperceptibly onto my knee when times were hard and we'd had another eviction notice. Suddenly she'd just be there, a warm ball of black and white fur, just when you needed her most. Like the grey cat I used to have in the village...under the willow. Twinkle reminded me of her, although she didn't look the same.

'And..and last week the vet said it was time for her to...'

'Go to the big sunny meadow in the sky?' I asked, sparing Kerry the need to say it.

'*Yes!*' Kerry sat down, trying not to sniff. 'I'm sorry, I don't know why I'm being such a wuss....but we had her such a long time. We went through so much together.'

'We sure did.' I agreed. 'Listen, I'll get you a cuppa. How about Bridge's special Merry Midwinter Cocoa with a shot of brandy?'

'It-it's not winter yet. But sounds nice.' Kerry looked up.

'Ok, two Merry Midwinters coming up! Anyway it's Halloween tonight. Near enough.' I went into the kitchen and got the kettle on.

When I came back with smouldering drinks Kerry was sifting through a handful of photographs.
'These are..oh, thanks.' She took a warming swig. 'God, that's lovely! These are some really old photos I dug out. Pre-digital. Look, there's Martha.'
I looked. Martha in her purple corduroy dungarees looking like Rod, Jane and Freddie out of Rainbow. Thin and ill-looking in the squat shortly after she fled Wales, cuddling Twinkle, her eyes far away. Mart in the mountains, with a wide grin and Twinkle on her shoulder against a backdrop of purple summer heather and blue, blue sky. Twinkle on Larch's workbench chasing wood shavings. On the roof of a bender. Hopping from Lorna's knee to Ash's, by the fire. God they look stoned. You can see the spliff in Ash's hand!

Twinkle on Simon's knee, cat to cat, identical high cheekbones and amber-brown eyes. A cat silhouette on top of a computer as he typed furiously on one of his one-page sci fi stories, the top of his desk a sort of computer scrapyard.
Then a lot of strangers. Kerry's college friends. Twinkle lounging on the back shelf of Kerry's van surrounded by badger leaflets and paraphenalia, lying cuddled up to a soft toy badger.

The last few photos were ones Kerry fished out of her phone. An elder Twinks high in the branches of the apple tree on a visit to the bungalow, frosted whiskers gazing down at the pond with interest. A faded campaign poster was visible in the window. Next - an accidental photo of what looked like Mart's foot in battered sandals next to the old willow basket that lay half-collapsed at the foot of the tree. Twinkle in my arms playing with the scarf from my Gandalf hat, the day we got home from Sunrise. And a sleepy old black and white cat lounging on the bed in a patch of dusty sunshine in the back of Kerry's van. Last April, here on Bob's farm. The last time I saw her.

'What about burying her? What did you do?'

'That's why I wanted to come over. I decided – well, Twinkle was special. I - I asked the vet to get her cremated. I've got the ashes. In the van, in a little pot. I wanted to scatter them somewhere in proper nature, not just some site where I'm here today and gone tomorrow. Simon hasn't got a garden and everyone else is in shared houses. So I brought her remainders here to the farm. Hope you don't mind.'

Wow. A cat funeral.

'Ok, how about somewhere in the wood? We can do it whenever you're ready.'
'Ok.' Kerry looked a lot happier after two mugs of Midwinter Glow, which was the improved blend with two shots of brandy in it. She giggled herself off balance talking about all the silly things the kitten Twinkle had done, the same as the stuff Tiff had done, that all kittens do, but uniquely Twinks all the same.

It was getting chilly. Time to light the fire.
'D'you want this bit of newspaper?'
I turned and pounced.
'Be careful! I'm saving that!'
'Oh, I thought you left it here to light the fire with.'
'God, no, I never use newspaper to light a fire. Doesn't burn hot enough. I'd have thought you'd know that, you old hippy.'
'I do.' said Kerry. 'It's just that it was here so I thought you were going to use it.'
'Nah, I use fine pine twigs or else split some kindling. Get it started with a bit of shredded cardboard.'
'What did you save it for then?'
'What, this? Have you seen it? It's amazing! It's what got me started with all the book-writing crap in the first place.' I was suddenly very self-conscious.
'Really? I just thought you got bored cooped up in the snow last spring.'
'I did. Here, let me smooth it out.' I flattened the wrinkled page of newsprint. The headline was a bit scuffed but could still be read.

Party chair defends stance on harassment row

'A party activist who alleged that she was sexually harassed during a national conference said that she was suspended without cause after blowing the whistle on what she felt was an inadequate and unsafe reaction to a harassment complaint...the member in question was not suspended pending investigation...all complaints dismissed...ignorance of equalities law...row at national level...a spokesman said that the party took all complaints of sexual harassment very seriously...'

'I haven't seen this, is this really about Mart? This explains - ' She broke off.

'Yeah, it is. That's them. She got it into the *Sentinel*, God knows how. How did she do it?'

'Well, there's been a lot of publicity about stuff like this lately, hasn't there?   Must have helped.' Kerry held the clipping up to the light, squinting to read the print.

'I suppose. They were asking for stories like that. But I never thought Mart's would get published. They haven't named her, look. They've done a really good job. That's exactly how it was. As soon as I saw this – well...that was what got me started on the book, actually. It was so unfair what happened to Mart. I suppose I just wanted to tell the whole story.'

'Was that it? And you wrote – how much? Last I saw you'd done about eight chapters.'

'I've done sixteen now. Nearly finished. Of course it's not a final draft. But I don't have an ending. I mean, Mart got stitched up. The End. Not very good, is it?'

'Have you heard from her lately?'

'No, why?'

'Cos I think she may have some news for you.'

'Oh, what?'

'She can tell you herself.'

'Some hope. Haven't seen her for a couple of years. She hasn't even met Tiff.'

'Well, you're in for a surprise.' Kerry smiled enigmatically.

'What? Tell me!'

'Then it won't be a surprise. Anyway, Simon can tell you more.'

'Simon?'

'He asked if he could come to the kitty-wake, as he called it. Twinkle's send-off. Shall I give him a call? He would have come with me but he had a customer.'

'Oh, Ok. Dunno where I'll put you all though.'

'There's the van, and we can light the kitchen fire can't we?'

'Yeah. I suppose. Tiff leaves her dead mice in there, mind.'

'We can put Simon in there then. He won't mind. Be a nice snack for him if he gets hungry in the night.'

'Heh.'

We got to work.

❄

'Bridge? Sis? You there?' Mick called outside the window. I looked out. Sean's van puttered in the yard. I waved and yelled.

'Come on up!'

I jumped into my clogs and ran down the steps.

'Hi! You've got Simon? You can park over there, Bob'll moan if you leave it out the front. Is this Sean's new van? Looks worse than the old one!'

Simon looked around.

'It's different without the snow. Whatever happened to those jackdaws?'

'Oh, yeah, Bob put a hat on the chimney pot to stop them nesting in there.'

'Pity. They gave the place a certain Gothic splendour.'

He scampered up the steps dragging his tattered rucksack behind him.

'Kerry! Sorry about your sad feline bereavement!' They were hugging before he got through the door. 'Hope I haven't missed the interment.'

'No, we're going to scatter her ashes tomorrow. Send her back to the earth. And we're gonna spend the evening drinking Twinkle's health.'
'She hasn't got any health. She's *deid*.'
'I know, but that's just what you say. Come on in. Where can we put Mick?'
'He brought a fancy folding bed. He's just lugging it in now.'

Chattering, excited, we bustled about making up nests on the floor, unfolding the camp bed, lighting the kitchen stove, mixing up more Midwinter Glows that were more like full scale conflagrations.

❄

I watched Mick and Simon's silhouettes in the firelight. The brandy was all gone and we were onto red wine mulled on top of the stove. Simon's spiky hair was as unruly as ever. He hadn't changed, beyond a little silver at the temples, and his breathless delivery was still the same, too. I couldn't get used to the flattening of Mick's hair though. Ever since he started receding a bit he'd grown his hair into a sort of old punk's ponytail, shaved at the sides and sticking out at the back. He still had a few earrings in his left ear and his rose tattoo showed briefly when he pulled off his leather jacket.
I barely remembered my butterfly tat. Only in summer, when I went into short sleeves for the first time and it would startle me. I could scarcely remember being the person who'd had it done all those years ago. The outlines had thickened a little, but the colours were as clear and pure as the day it was inked. Good work. I wondered how Mart's had lasted.

'and Mart -'
What? What was that Simon said?
'Yes, she went to Becksgate, I know, I know, they said she was suspended, but the membership secretary wasn't told about it -'
'She went to Becksgate? I heard she had a showdown but...' That was Kerry. I thought it was time I paid attention.
'What're you talking about?' They all turned and looked at me.
'Didn't you know?'

'Know what?'

'Mart confronted the Party. She checked the membership records and the membership secretary had no record of her suspension. No one knew a thing about it. It was just the Party heads acting on their own.'

'Shit! No way! Didn't they send her an official complaint?'

'Never. She never got it. To this day she doesn't know exactly what she's been accused of.'

Holy crap. That is so bent.

'So what happened? She met with them?'

'Only because she made them. Simon can tell you, he was there, it was so cool -'

Simon? A small voice said sadly that once upon a time Mart would've chosen me to go with her.

'Go on, Si,' said Mick, 'tell us the tale.'

'You've heard the saga twice already.'

'Bridge hasn't. Go on, I love this story.'

'Ok.'

❄

Two muffled-up figures got down from the train in Becksgate station. Pale sunlight came through the mist as they shoved through the barrier with their rucksacks and scuffled through the wet leaves littering the station approach.

'Where to next, then?'

'Straight to the venue, I guess. No reason to wait. We can't book into the hostel til after 2pm anyway.'

Simon slipped his half empty rucksack onto his shoulders. Martha heaved her bulkier one up on her back.

'What've you got in there?'

'You'll see.' She grinned up at him.

'Come prepared?'

'You betcha.'

They walked on, stopping to check the town centre map on the board at the end of the narrow lane that led to the station, comparing it with a folded printout from Google maps that Mart pulled from her pocket.

She hesitated, then pointed. A large building with broad steps leading up was barely visible through the light fog at the far end of the road.

'Is that it?'

'I think so.' They walked on. Martha's heart beat faster as she recognised the familiar colours of the Party banners, the logo fluttering in the damp autumn wind.

She stopped.

'You ready?' asked Simon.

'Yeah.' she said.

'You sound sure.'

'I'm sure. Come on.'

They stood to the side of the conference centre, eyeing the simple entrance as if it was the door to a demon-guarded labyrinth. A blackbird chacked urgently from one of the bare plane trees lining the pavement. They saw his throat move, but the alarm call was mostly drowned out by traffic noise. He flew away, leaving the dripping branch bobbing.

'How you gonna get in?' Simon looked doubtful, scuffing his boot on the pavement and darting a glance over his shoulder.

'The easiest way. Just walk straight in like we've got the right to be there. Which we have. Come on.'

Martha strode forward and began climbing the steps. Simon glanced from left to right nervously and followed. Through the glass doors they could see a line of people queuing to register. Martha hesitated only fractionally before pushing at the double door and walking in, head held stiffly.

'What shall we do?'

'Queue here. Get our tickets. Stroll on in. Keep your hat on.'

Simon fidgeted on the spot as they waited. Martha was as cool as the autumn morning outside. She stood impassively. Turned her head away casually as Annelise passed, dimly visible at the back of the lobby as she headed down a corridor into the depths of the building.

311

Mart stared hard at a handwritten sign saying 'Main Conference Hall.'

'Hello, welcome to conference. Are you a member?' The young woman on the desk smiled nervously at Martha.

'Yes.' Martha said.

'Booked or pay on the door?'

'Paying now.' Martha said.

'All right, if you can write your name and local party on the lanyard...while I just check your membership status – that's fine, you're fully paid up - here are your voting cards and a copy of the Agenda for the weekend. Enjoy your conference!'

'Thanks, I will.' answered Martha, and coolly strolled into the centre of the lobby.

'Hello and welcome to Becksgate! Are you a member?'

'Visitor ticket, please.'

Simon was soon processed. He caught up to Mart.

'Which way?' he panted.

'Follow me.' Martha said.

She headed down the dark corridor, following the arrow to the main hall.

They descended the auditorium steps.

'Here?' whispered Simon, pointing to an aisle seat with another free space next to it.

'No. In there.'

Martha gained the middle seats of the middle row and sat down.

'Will you be Ok here? Bit claustrophobic.' Simon whispered.

'It's Ok. Harder to get us out from here.' Simon shivered.

Martha rummaged in her bag, tugging out a corner of her homemade banner.

'What have you got?'

'Everything I need. We don't have much time before I'm spotted. I think I saw Miranda over there. I got a sort of dirty look from her.'

They turned and craned their necks. Miranda stood at the top of the stairs at the rear of the hall, gazing straight at them, it seemed like. They turned to face front hastily.

'What you gonna do when they see you?'

'All under control.'

Miranda was descending the steps now. She stood at the front right of the stage, waiting to announce the leader's speech. Martha looked back once, smiled, and turned to face front again.
'Scrunch down a bit! She'll see you!' Simon was dithering.
'Let her.' Martha sat up straight and pulled off her eclipsing woolly hat.
The crowd rose with a storm of clapping. The party leader entered. Miranda stepped forward and took the microphone.
'Hello, and welcome to our forty-fifth annual Autumn Conference! It's good to see you all !'
'Yes. It is, isn't it.' Martha murmured, smiling quietly. No one had taken the seats either side of her and Simon. The hall was sparsely-filled this early in conference.
'We're proud to welcome our leader, Emily Champion, who will now give the opening address.'
They watched as Emily walked forward. There was another storm of clapping. Miranda walked towards her front row seat to sit down, then stopped, staring into the crowd. Martha smiled serenely. Miranda's face hardened. She turned and strode quickly offstage via the side door Emily Champion had come in by.
'Uh-oh! It's on!' whispered Simon.
'Yeah, think so.' said Martha nervously. She sat up straighter than ever and tried to listen to the opening speech.

There was a murmuring, a door squeaked open behind them. Someone was squeezing down the row towards them. They kept their eyes rigidly front.
'Martha er – Jones. Are you Martha Jones?'
Martha turned.
'Yes, that's me.'
'I'm afraid I must ask you to leave.'
'Why is that, then?'
'Er, I believe you know that.' the thin youth said nervously, twiddling his lanyard.
'I can assure you I can't think of any reason why I shouldn't be here.' Martha said politely.

'I haven't come to argue with you, but you must vacate the hall now please.'
'No thanks, I'm here for conference.'
The scrawny minion dithered, then retreated saying.
'I'll just go and consult my superiors...but you shouldn't be here...'

Simon and Martha looked at each other.
'What are you going to do? They're going to chuck us out!' he whispered.
Heads turned irritably on the row in front.
'All is well.' Martha said, more placidly than she felt. Skinnymalink was back.
'Er, er, I have a message from the Party Heads, they've said that you are not authorised to be here as you have been expelled from the party. You'll have to leave the venue immediately.'
Martha held up her voting card and smiled at him. He looked horrified. He struggled back out of the row.
'It's turning into a comedy sketch.'
'Shh, don't make me laugh!' Martha implored, shoulders beginning to shake.
Skimbleshanks reappeared.
'I've been authorised to inform you that if you don't leave immediately we'll have to remove you.' He puffed out his non-existent chest and waited, like a schoolboy chess player who'd just got the king in check for the first time.
Martha looked at him.
'And how will you achieve that?' she said kindly.
'Er – er, we'll call security?'
Martha continued to gaze at him with a faint air of gentle puzzlement.

'Are you embroidering this story Simon?'
'A bit. Ssh.'
'What did she say next?'
'I'm telling you. Shut up.'

'Let me bring you up to speed.' said Martha. 'Party heads haven't produced a scrap of documentation around this alleged expulsion.

314

I've never even been cited a reason for it. The membership secretary knows nothing about the affair and I'm still listed as a member. The grievance procedure has been totally ignored in my case, and the Party has continued to accept my subscription money. Plus, incredibly, I've had numerous requests for donations and help over the last two years. I don't know in what universe the party chairs can declare me no longer a member, but it's not this one. Now, I have come equipped to stage a protest if you try to remove me. My only demand is the right to meet with party heads in person to discuss the matter. If you look behind you-' more heads in front and behind were doing just that, as Emily's speech faltered on stage - 'you'll see numerous TV cameras whose job it is to cover the opening of conference. Perhaps the party officials might wish to reconsider their position.' She sat back comfortably in her seat. Simon was trembling, half with nerves and half with suppressed laughter.

Lanky scurried hastily away, looking dashed.

'I think that's checkmate.' Simon murmured.

'It's not over til you capture the Queen.' Martha grinned at Simon, her eyes shining in the auditorium spotlights.

'So what happened then?'

'Mart stuck to her guns. She showed me her banner after. She never had to use it. She said she was going to run up on stage and unfurl it.'

'Blimey!'

'Yeah, never pick a fight with a seasoned activist. They sort of know how to run a campaign.'

'Yeah! She has done this before. Comes to something when you're fighting your own side.'

'Obviously they're not *on* our side, then. Not sure they're even on their own side.'

'Guess not. What happened next?'

'Well, they crumbled, and agreed to meet Mart and me. We finally got to meet the *new* Regional Committee chair. Frances Dillon. She looked at us as though we were a couple of computer viruses.'

'Slugs in her lettuce.'

'Wasps at her picnic.' put in Mick. He poured some more red wine into the pan on top of the burner.

'Go on.'

'Yeah, she looked at us like we were giving her indigestion -'

'Let's hope you did -'

'Yeah, and came out with a load of flannel about how her predecessor, Rebecca Thing, Minchin, hadn't briefed her about the case and she knew nothing about any of it. She *'wasn't familiar'* with the relevant procedures and *'couldn't comment'* on what former officers had done. She ended by saying that Mart should have gone through the proper channels -'

'She did! But, don't tell me, the head of the Party knows nothing about that?'

'Good guess. So she was forced to agree that *'the Party hasn't always used best practice.''*

'Let me guess. *'Mistakes have been made.''*

'Right. *'But we can't dwell on the past.''*

'God forbid.'

'By the end, she was shaking Mart by the hand, making all sorts of promises about how the case would be looked at again in view of what Mart had told her.'

'Result!'

'You'd think. The minute we got home Mart wrote to them for confirmation.'

'Let me guess. They blew her off again.'

'You got it. They've told her she's under a five year ban, but *still* haven't told her what she's supposed to have done, or refunded her subscription.'

'What a bunch of twats.'

'Quite. Then it all went quiet.'

'But - the article in the *Sentinel* -'

'Ah yes. That.' Simon smiled.

'What did they say when they saw that?'

'I believe their scream was particularly high-pitched.' Simon laughed.

'So what's going on now then?'

'I think Mart's the one to bring you up to date.'

316

'Mart? Haven't seen her in ages.' I sighed, and accepted another mug of wine from Mick.

'Yeah, I heard. Not to worry.' Simon jumped up and refilled his mug from the pan.

'Cheer up. Here's to us.' He clinked his mug against mine.

'Here's to Twinkle!' cried Kerry. We all stood for a solemn toast, to cats past, present and future. Tiff twined herself round my legs as I raised my glass.

'To Twinkle!'

There was a thud. And another. Kerry ran to open the door. It was Martha, red-nosed and shivering on the doorstep, dripping with fogdew.

❄

17. Blind Justice.

Martha grinned at me. I just stared.

'Can I put my bike away?'

'You came on your bike over the Severn Bridge?' Kerry was amazed.

'Yeah. It's electric.'

'Cool.' said Mick eagerly. 'Can I have a look?'

'Yeah, you can help me put it away. Where shall I park it, Bridge?'

I stopped staring.

'Uh, oh in the shed. Here, I'll show you.'

'Can I have a go?' begged Mick.

'In daylight.' Mart pried the bike out of his hands and pushed it into the shed.

'Come and get a drink.' I said, trying to catch up with events.

'What's everybody doing here?'

'Kitty-wake. Um, I'm afraid Twinkle's no more. She's an ex-cat.'

Martha's hand went to her mouth. 'Twinkle? Oh no. I wish I'd seen her again. Haven't seen her for ages. Oh, my little Twinkle. Where did you bury her?'

'We're going to scatter her ashes in the morning. It's nearly dark now. I can't believe you crossed the bridge at this time of year. It's freezing up there.'

'I know. I had to stop and put my extra coat on in the middle.'

'How did you know the way?' I asked.

'Simon told me, when he came in spring.' Martha said.

'Everyone seems to know what's going on around here except me.' I moaned.

'We don't have a clue. We didn't know about the *Sentinel.*' said Kerry.

'I did.' said Simon. 'I was just telling you before Mart so politely interrupted.'

'But you never told me about Becksgate.'

'Mart thought you wouldn't want to hear any more about it, being as it was all still a dismal failure despite our heroic venture.' said Simon.

'I supppose. But I wish I'd known.'

'We wanted to wait til there was some concrete good news. We knew -' Kerry stopped.

Knew that Mart's supposed best friend might just be a tiny bit of a jerk about the whole subject. That I, Bridget Doherty, Mart's oldest friend, hadn't spoken to her for two years, using the distance between us as an excuse for the distance between us. But we'd been separated by far more than two miles of freezing, turbulent muddy water.

'So what gives? Mart, how the hell did you get the *Sentinel* to cover your story?' I said.

Mart settled next to Simon on a cushion on the floor. She accepted a mug of mulled wine from Mick with relief.

'It was after all those high profile cases that there's been recently about harassment cover-ups. They were actively requesting stories from people, so I just emailed them straight off. It took weeks of negotiation but they finally published it. Thought it would never appear but it did.'

'Yeah, page 43. They really pushed the boat out.' I remarked sourly.

'True. But it was at the top of the political news online, and it stayed visible for months. Soon after, Frances Dillon was hastily replaced by yet another Regional Committee chair, Emily St Clair, and she emailed me *very* rapidly with all kinds of olive branches. They reinstated my membership, which they'd transmuted from suspension to expulsion by some mysterious and invisible means -'

'Yes!' I shouted.

'-but kept me under suspension. So I asked for a copy of the so-called complaint about me, and -'

'Guess what? They couldn't produce it. Because there never bloody was one, and RegCom got a bit coy about putting anything in writing for some reason.' I yelled.

'Right. So I pointed out that they couldn't keep me under suspension indefinitely without producing a complaint.'

'Which they ignored, praying you'd go away or die or emigrate or something.'

'Correct. It's like you're psychic.'

'So I got a solicitor on board.'

'You didn't! Why didn't you do that before?'

'Because they kept me messing about thinking it'd all get sorted out and we wouldn't have to have a load of bad publicity for the Party. It was the Earth I was thinking of.' Martha said.

'Yeah, the ultimate guilt trip!' You cannot argue with people who are *'saving the Earth, man'* unless you're some kind of ecocidal fascist.

'Exactly. They strung me along until the statute of limitation ran out-'

'Again, please?'

'There's a limit on how long you have to bring legal action, in this case a year, but as soon as they reinstated me the whole case came live again and I found Shania Dass to take the case pro bono.'

'Wow! What's she like?'

'I dunno. I never met her. The whole thing was done by phone and email. It was an internet marathon.'

'So what's happening? You taking them to court?'

'That's what I've come to tell you about.'

Martha looked around at us all. Kerry was pulling another bottle of wine out of her rucksack. Mick was shoving some logs on the fire. Simon was lying full length on the hearthrug with his hands behind his head. I was just sitting there, waiting.

'Shania was in touch this morning. They settled out of court. They so did not want the publicity especially right in the middle of all the other cases in the papers.'

'So what happened?' Simon sat bolt upright and gazed at Martha. Kerry stopped in the act of upending the bottle into the pan and sat down on the arm of the sofa. Mick slammed the door of the stove and looked up expectantly.

'They've been forced to reinstate my full membership as if nothing ever happened. They've wiped the suspension and expulsion off my record. They've confirmed that the members' accommodation scheme will never be revived. They've agreed to pay compensation and legal costs. And there's going to be a major enquiry into this and - all the other similar cases that it turns out they've been suppressing. For years. Some independent investigator's going to look into it all. Oh, and Emily Champion's instigating an official working party on sexual harassment in Westminster.'

There was a silence, then -

'Whoah!' The shout went up from everyone in the room.

'Give us your mug.' cried Mick. 'Fill 'er up to the brim!' He sloshed a generous dose of wine into Mart's mug and passed it over.

'I can't believe it!' I handed my mug over to Mick hastily. This called for another drink. A lot of drinks.

Kerry was on her knees on the floor, hugging Martha again and again.

'So are we going to conference next spring then? We might meet Skimbleshanks again. I liked him.' That was Simon.

'Yeah, he was a good comic turn.' Martha agreed, laughing as Kerry rolled her over onto the floor, still hugging and cheering. 'Hey! Don't spill my drink!'

Mick was striding round the room singing 'Victory! Victoorrreeee!' and waving his mug. He grabbed Simon and gave him a big smacker on both cheeks that definitely lingered longer than even victory joy required.

Simon blushed as he hugged him back, and I couldn't help noticing that for once he had no witty comeback. They sat back down on the rug, arms about each other, faces glowing. Kerry and I exchanged questioning glances, then looked away again. Looks like there were more stories than Martha's to be told tonight.

Martha picked herself up, pushing Kerry off. She sat up on the floor, leaning against the sofa, her mug held loosely in her hands, and smiled and smiled as if she'd never stop. I saw a peace in her face that I'd never seen there before, as she looked around at her friends, cavorting around her. Because it had finally happened for Mart. She was triumphant.

❄

'So, how much did they give you then?'

'Not including the legal fees that went back to Legal Help via Shania, £6000.' Martha said.

I gazed at her.

'But – I mean we'd have to save up a load more, but that would -'

'Way ahead of you. It would make a real start on us getting our bit of land.' said Martha.

'You still into it?'

'Are you kidding me? It's what I've been waiting for since I left Wales. Since I left the village, actually.' she added quietly.

'The pond.'

'The meadow. And the polytunnel.' she said.

'All the vegetable beds.' I put in.

'And the fruit trees!'

'Yeah. D-d'you reckon we can do it? We'd need to save a load more money.'

'Bridge, after today, I reckon we can do anything.' said Martha. 'But have you got any good moneymaking ideas? We could work on them together.'

'Well, there's this writing project I've been working on,' I said delicately, 'but I dunno – you might not like the idea.'

'What is it? Can I read it?'

'It's – well, it's what you said you wanted me to do.'

Martha was waiting, hope flushing her face.

'You've never -'

'Yeah. I did it, sort of. I wrote a story – about you, and all of us, and everything we did. I dunno if you'll like it...' I trailed off.

'Like it? I'm gonna *love* it! I was going to say, maybe now we could start on it, and you've already done it!'

'Well, yeah, just the first draft. And I'm not sure about the ending – at least, I wasn't.'

'Well, we can never be sure about endings, can we...we never know what's going to happen next.'

'I suppose not.'

'I realised that, along the way...after you left the village, then at Newbury, when I had to leave Wales, when – when the Party threw me out and the house went tits-up. I'm sorry about that.'

'It wasn't your fault. It wasn't your fault that Marianne stopped doing maintenance on her house the minute she moved out.'

'Yeah, I realised that – nothing's ever over. There's always another chapter. Always a consequence that you can't see, somewhere down the line. All you can do is do your best with whatever sort of falls in your way. You can't know what will happen next. Saved me from the worse depression, quite a few times, realising that.' she said in a low voice, glancing at the others.

'I suppose. When you think nothing good's ever going to happen again, and then it does. But we spend all that time worrying about how some shit's going to go down, and we never know what's going to happen next. Good or bad.'

'I know one thing. We're getting our land as soon as you get the book finished.' Martha said.

'But – I've never written anything that big before. The odds against getting it published are astronomical.' I objected.

'What did I just say? Anyway, I've got a contact at the *Sentinel* who might just get us a review.'

I sat back. That was a thought and a half.

'No doomsaying. I don't want to hear how we'll never do it. Let's have a look at this manuscript, then.'

'We're blind drunk.' I pointed out. 'Can we do it in the morning?'

'Good point. Blind drunk, celebrating blind justice.'

'How do you mean?'

'My solicitor. Didn't I tell you? She was blind.'

❋

I opened my eyes to Martha, standing by the window in the grey dawn, looking out.

The manuscript lay on the coffee table, open to the last pages.

'Have you read it all?' I croaked.

'Yeah. I've been awake a few hours.' Martha crossed the room and sat on her sleeping bag, unrolled before the fire.

'Are those two awake yet?'

'No, they're spark out still.' Gentle drunken-goblin snores came from the kitchen.

'When did they -'

'Get together? I dunno exactly. I sort of sensed there was something going on between them for a while though.' said Martha.

'For how long of a while? Last I remember they weren't getting on that well.' I was surprised.

'Since we left Marianne's. Yeah, they did do a fair bit of bickering along the way. And then Mick was down in Bristol for three months doing this big house, and he stayed at Simon's. I think it all came to a head then. I mean, they've always been sort of inseparable.'

'Didn't even realise he was gay. He never said anything. You know my brother better than I do.' I said sadly.

'Not really. He didn't get to grips with it himself for ages from what I can make out, but Simon – well, I think his gaydar worked it out a while ago.' Martha said.

'Yeah, he's always had a thing for Mick. Right from the moment they met, come to think of it. But I always thought it was just a bit of a joke between them. Mick always laughed it off.' I said.

'Yeah, I think last night's the first time he's acknowledged how he feels in front of anyone else.' Martha agreed. 'But they seem made for each other, when you think about it.'

'Yeah, they do.' I said thoughtfully. 'A good match, really.'

'Did I hear my name?' Mick pushed the kitchen door open. 'God, I feel like there's a load of smelly hippies camping in my head. What were you saying?'

'Um, nothing...'

'You talking about me and Si?'

'Er..'

'Twinkle may be gone, but I've still got an ol' cat.' He grinned shyly, and went back into the kitchen to make a lot of racket with kettle, mugs and running taps.

'That's it. That's all we're getting.' Martha laughed. 'Anyway, the book...'

'What did you think?' I said uncomfortably.

Martha looked at me, serious suddenly.

'I think – you make me look like a twit most of the time...'

'I'm sorry! I think I come over too cynical!'

'I'm not complaining. Most of the time I was a twit. So naive. A total mooncalf.'

'You weren't -' I began.

'I think you've done a great job. I've been sitting here laughing and crying all morning. I lit the fire at about five o'clock but it's burned out again, look.'

'We better light it again.'

'Mick! Job for you!' Martha yelled. I was startled.

'Since when do you shout?'

'Since...when.' she said happily. A van door slammed outside. Kerry's footsteps rang on the stone steps.

'What's all the racket? I've got some wood here.' she said, dumping the basket on the floor.

'Just a racket.' I said, yawning and stretching. I threw the covers off.

'Stay right there. We'll do everything.' Mart said.

Whoah. A morning cuppa without even getting out of bed. Kerry was shovelling ashes out of the stove. Mick bustled in with a tray, followed by a coffee pot.

Mart watched me, glancing at the others from time to time.

'What do you reckon?' she said.

'I reckon they can make breakfast without burning the house down.' I said grudgingly.

'No, I mean about the end of the story.'

'Sounds good to me. If we can really get the book published, and get our farm...'

'We have to. We just have to. This is all we've got. It's all we are, or ever have been.' said Martha, thunping the folder containing the manuscript.

'Mart..'

'I know. I'm a total and utter hippy.'

'Well, yeah.'

I picked up the old folder and flipped through the pages.

'What's this?' Martha had written something firmly across the still-blank title page.

'Oh, that. It was what they called me and anyone else who stood up for women's rights on Facebook. They called us snowflakes.'

It was the title I'd been waiting for.

❄

'I feel like the New Year's begun already.' said Mick.

'It has. The Celtic New Year starts on Samhain.' said Martha.

'Oh yeah. I forgot.'

'Everyone finished their tea? Is it time, Kerry? You ready?' I asked.

'Yes.' said Kerry. She picked up the small green cardboard tube.

'Is she really in there?' Simon asked interestedly. 'She didn't boil down to much did she?'

'*Simon!* You insensitive arsehole!'

'Sorry, Bridge'

'I was joking. But pull yourself together. This is a solemn occasion.'

'Ok.'

We walked across the yard and into the small wood. Kerry stopped under a yew sapling. The ground was hard and chilly-looking. Kerry opened the tube and hesitated.

'What should I say?'

'Whatever you think.'

Kerry scattered the few handfuls of ashes on the cold bare ground. Little eddies of wind swirled the pale dust over the earth.

'So long Twinkle. You were a good cat. Thanks - thanks for being with us.'

'Bye Twinkle. Goodbye, Twinks. Ta-ra, ol' puss.'

Martha didn't say anything, but watched the white flakes dance in the wind before settling into the leaf-litter to begin the slow journey back to new life, as a flower, a bird, a leaf, a tree.

We turned and went inside, to kindle a new year from the embers of the last.

✳

'So where do you think we'll end up?'

I was restless, dreaming of our own land. For the first time I could think about it without a door slamming in my head, denying my imagination.

'Could be anywhere. We just have to find somewhere that feels like home.'

Home. Really home.

'Martha?'

'What?'

'What do you reckon? Did we really change anything? Change the world, with any of it?'

'Well, we changed our world. That's something, isn't it?'

I considered her for a long time.

'Y'know what, Mart? I reckon you're right.' I said. I got up to put the kettle back on the stove.

✳

Epilogue: Words Have Power.

I'd barely finished hastily stacking the wood, and was pulling the tarp over the pile when the first snowflakes began to tumble out of the sky, turning Tiff into an instant snow leopard. We hurried inside. I pushed the aged oak door shut against the blizzard and laid a fire with wood that was only slightly damp.

It sputtered and popped, then began a warm crackle as we settled in for the evening.

I opened my notebook and began to write.

Outside, the lane was quickly being blotted out, the world transformed, by the quiet, relentless fall of snowflakes.

❄❄❄